The Angel And The Cuckoo

The Angel And The Cuckoo

Gerald Kersh

With an introduction by Paul Duncan

LONDON BOOKS CLASSICS

LONDON BOOKS
PO Box 52849
London SW11 1SE
www.london-books.co.uk

First published 1967
This edition published by London Books Ltd 2011

A catalogue record for this book
is available from the British Library

ISBN 978-0-9568155-0-7

Printed and bound in Great Britain by
Antony Rowe, Chippenham, Wiltshire

Typeset by Octavo Smith Ltd in Plantin 9.3/11.15
www.octavosmith.com

INTRODUCTION

Background: I was born 50 years ago. My life has been like a kind of chain reaction, and it's still going on. And the doctors tell me I have another 25 years of it to cope with. I've been in danger a good deal of the time. A familiarity with personal suffering has bred in me such a contempt for it that I desire to have nothing more to do with it. This applies also to death. When I was a child I decided that the most wonderful thing to happen to a boy was to write a story and see it in print. I swore a horrible oath that I would be famous and rich by the time I was 30 by means of writing stories and getting them printed. I missed my leadline by only two years, but all that I got I gave away, or frittered away . . . Now I want little and have less. My ambition is to write a novel which I can read over with pleasure and know what it's made of. I am, at present, engaged in writing a novel. When this is done, I shall write another. – Gerald Kersh, from Author Questionnaire for *The Angel And The Cuckoo*

On October 9, 1963, around 5.30 or 6.00am, Gerald Kersh rose as usual and began the first rough sculpturing of a new novel commissioned by Heinemann, tentatively titled *Poor Tom Henceforth*, which he hoped and believed would be a major work. More than that, he *needed* it to be a success in America. For the previous ten years, each of his books had been blocked or sidestepped, or simply rejected, by American publishers.

The Implacable Hunter, his brilliant novel about a Roman soldier pursuing his best friend St Paul on orders to execute him, had been published in Britain to some acclaim but had been rejected in the US by Doubleday, Lippincott, Mackay and McGraw-Hill, with several citing religious reasons. He switched tack and planned a series of light-hearted murder mysteries starring female reporter Little Snowdrop, the first of which was *A Long Cool Day In Hell* – published in the UK, and rejected in America – but it died a death, and so did the series.

Such was the regularity of these occurrences that Kersh and his wife Flossie suspected a wider conspiracy against them, as Kersh outlined in a letter: 'There is a new sort of editor, with powers of rejection only. Accepting is done by a kind of central committee or something. Things aren't the way they used to be. Huge mechanisms of management are set up for the express purpose of passing the buck. Thus, everybody in a group of editors may individually agree that such and such a story is superb, and that every one of them may asseverate that you are the greatest living storyteller, and yet the story will come back as "corny", "reactionary", "drivel". In other words, the author is on what they call a shitlist or a secret drop-dead list.'

Although born in London, Kersh had left for America in 1954 where he was already established as an author. Apart from a couple of paperback collections of his short stories, the last book to be published there was *Fowlers End* in 1957. 'You know me. I can write a story as well as any VS Pritchett, yet I have been surviving by writing little bits for the minor magazines and sometimes covering prizefights, at which point the visiting English sports writers eyed me with a mixture of curiosity and loathing as a species of Lord Haw Haw inexplicably unhung.'

In the 1950s, the heyday of the American magazine, Kersh's fiction and non-fiction had appeared regularly in *Esquire*, *Playboy* and the *Saturday Evening Post*, but by the early 1960s the markets had dried up for him and he was forced to look to *Dude*, *Cavalier* and *Escapade* for sustenance and the *Saturday Review* for his soul. 'Since I derive a certain enjoyment from it, I'm pretty good at covering most forms of what [Alan] Ross used to call "lowlife": prizefights, dog fights, executions, jam sessions, orgies, booze-ups, whorehouses, etc., etc. I usually manage to get a certain zing into what I write. I may also be counted on in matters pertaining to men's fashions, female beauty, physical culture, medical matters, objects d'art, furs, clothes, oriental rugs, tobacco and wine.'

Haunted by incredible tax duties, which meant that he received mere pennies from the high sales he made in the UK, Kersh and his wife were unable to afford New York City rents. Each move thrust them further from the centre of the publishing industry, losing vital contact with it. 'At present we inhabit an allegedly haunted house in the Shawangunk Mountains, or perhaps haunt a hitherto uninhabited house up there.' But Kersh remained sanguine. 'My wants are few. "A bowl of rice", as Bill Saroyan said to me, ordering the special Chinese dinner for eight at Abilene Sue's, there being only three of us at the table. "A bowl of rice and a friendship."'

His biggest blow came when *The Dabchick* was rejected. 'It's first title was *Storm Over Yandro*. The book was either much liked or much disliked by whoever read it. The late WJ Brown, a powerful politician in England, having read the first half, secretly denounced me to Scotland Yard for obscenity. The Commissioner called in, as a kind of judge on the matter, Sir JC Squire, notoriously my deadly enemy. But he, on this matter, said that far from being an immoral writer, I was a highly moral one. But nobody would touch the novel. I revised it and retitled it *The Dabchick*.'

The novel revolves around a woman who holds two men in the palm of her hand as they pursue her. Even Kersh's mainstay Heinemann rejected it. 'I can't imagine what seems to have inspired certain readers with something like pure horror, even in its modified version. Elizabeth Otis was utterly shaken by it and, inadvisably, she being my agent at that time, put about the totally untrue tale that Yandro was a portrait of my ex-wife. I never knew a work of fiction that had a more irritant effect on readers in general. Yet there were those who were smitten with admiration for it.'

Kersh's second wife Lee Kersh – she still used his surname after their acrimonious divorce – was a powerful, charismatic woman who, in the 1930s, threw revolutionary leaflets about the Houses of Parliament and fought in the Spanish Civil War dressed as a man. She had such sway over the media of London – socialist or otherwise – that Kersh believed she had used it to forever smear his name there. 'On the one hand I'm an anti-Semitic, fascist reactionary, and on the other a Red Jew communist. I'm incidentally smeared as a McCarthyite, a vulgar East European Jewish banker, a tormented pervert, an ex-patriot, a sadistic bully, a coward, a plagiarist, a masochist and a parasite. Oh yeah, and a coprophile.'

Kersh was convinced that her influence extended to America, where she held court in New York social, socialist and literary circles. 'Socialist boys are most distinctly in control. There is something in the atmosphere, something horrible. I have not been forgiven, and I never will, for the statement I made to the press when I became an American citizen, to the effect that I think that this is going to be the last stronghold to the free individual. Crazy as it may sound, it wouldn't surprise me if I turned out to be right . . .'

So it was under these circumstances, real or imagined, that on October 9, 1963, somewhere between 5.30 and 6.00am, Gerald Kersh woke and began the first draft of *Poor Tom Henceforth.*

* * *

What is the purpose of writing the book? The one and only purpose that should motivate any writer of a work of fiction – to amuse the reader whether he be high brow or low brow. Give him pleasure. Take him out of himself. Any novel written for any other purpose is not a novel but a varnished tract, sermon, news item or manifesto. I write because I love to tell people stories. That is all I'm fit for. In a word, the purpose of this book is to entertain the world at large. I don't do any violence to my conscience, which is private. – Gerald Kersh

Over a year later, during November 1964, Kersh delivered the first eleven chapters to Heinemann – just under half of the final novel. 'I have yet to come up with a title for it. I was thinking of calling it *Mad Apple Of Sodom*, but was afraid this may sound a bit too spectacular. For the sake of calling it something, I refer to it as *Poor Tom Henceforth* since he, the malevolent clown, the dabbler in all the arts and philosophies, the harebrained amoralist, plays a vital role in the story. But all the characters are necessary because they are connected by enmeshed events. Another title which occurred to me was *The Dance Of The Three Gray Sisters*. Again, I rather like *The Wind And The Rain*.' 'The Wind And The Rain' – a lyric sung by Feste, the Fool, in Shakespeare's *Twelfth Night* – never made it on to the book cover, but Kersh eventually made use of it for the title of his last short story, 'Hey Ho, The Wind And The Rain', published posthumously.

The novel is composed of several complex structures of time and character interaction, creating something akin to a prose version of those Russian Dolls that contain multiples within them; a character reminisces about another, then this second character takes over to recount stories in differing times and places, at which time a third character . . . Disconcerting at first, seemingly stream of consciousness, it eventually plays like a jazz piece, revealing its true structure after several chapters.

There are three love stories, all connected by Steve Zobrany, proprietor of The Angel And The Cuckoo, a café in a courtyard hidden beyond a doorway at one end of Carnaby Street. Beginning early one morning in 1937 – no doubt somewhere in the region of 5.30 to 6.00am – the good-natured and respectable Hungarian gentleman Zobrany reflects on how he purchased the café unseen in 1911 through the agency of his 'friend' Gèza Cseh. Cynical Cseh wrongs all he comes into contact with and profits financially from them whereas Zobrany trusts and believes in everybody. Thus Cseh's machinations garner him passage to pastures new, but Zobrany, cast away in Masham Court, finds Alma, the love of his life, and best friend John Howgego, proprietor of The Good Intention public house (nicknamed 'The Road To Hell' by locals). So who has profited most from the transaction?

Thomas Hardy – the young assistant to German artist Fritsch – takes it upon himself to make a sign for Zobrany's café. We follow his journey from Poland Street in Soho to Oxford Street to research cuckoos, then to sheds in Blackfriars where he talks Santini into giving him a plaster bird, then down the Farringdon Road, talking a dealer out of a cherub from a Flemish sideboard and, finally, after twenty-four hours of intense work, presenting Zobrany with the sign back in Carnaby Street (from a certain angle the sign is obscene and so becomes a landmark).

There is a simple inexplicable pleasure in following the journey on a map, or in actuality if you have the means. There are several such journeys in the book, and similar tracings of London and its suburbs can be found in other of Kersh's novels, including *Night And The City* (1938), *Prelude To A Certain Midnight* (1947), *The Song Of The Flea* (1948) and *Fowlers End* (1957). To the modern reader, these are travelogues to a lost history.

It is not a new idea. Émile Zola marked the passage of huge carts carrying fruit and veg to Les Halles in *Le Ventre De Paris* (1873), Guy de Maupassant charted Georges Duroy's opening walk through the nightlife of Paris in *Bel Ami* (1885), whilst John Dos Passos painted prose poems of New York citizens in *Manhattan Transfer* (1925). Contemporary authors such as Paul Auster, Ian McEwan and Don DeLillo know that exploring the urban landscape at eye-level can give a more accurate psychology of a place. But does man or the place itself determine the psychology?

In Britain, Peter Ackroyd, Iain Sinclair, Alan Moore and JG Ballard point to London's concrete jungle being a place of menace, murder and corruption, in some instances because it works against nature's own occult powers. Ley lines and suchlike. Guy Debord's 1955 definition of psychogeography points to the 'specific effects of the geographical environment, consciously organized or not, on the emotions and behaviour of individuals'. Kersh is having none of it. He finds the urban sprawl and decay a natural place and is careful to show that the corruption emanates from, and is passed between, the inhabitants. It's as if he is saying that the environment cannot be used as a scapegoat for the ills of society in general and the individual in particular. A man is responsible for his own actions.

This journey also highlights Thomas Hardy's facility with the spoken word and his ability to persuade others. Ironically for somebody so adept at the spoken word, at the end of the journey, Thomas Hardy, who hates his name ('Nobody has ever got to the end of a book by Thomas Hardy!') accidentally becomes 'Tom Henceforth' thanks to Zobrany mishearing him. Tom's persuasive voice, his questionable morals and his change of identity are echoed 250 pages later in a surprising pay-off, which I'm not about to spoil here. It's the sort of thing that's easy to miss, and the book is full of such elaborate patterning. In many ways Kersh is his own worst enemy because his writing is so entertaining, layered as it is with humour, plot and killer dialogue, that it masks the craft, construction and thought that goes into his work.

As Cseh and Henceforth take over the story, we follow their escapades, triumphs and defeats as Cseh becomes powerful Hollywood film producer Gabriel Chess and falls for Erabella Moon, and

Henceforth frequents the world of crooks, conmen, artists, writers and other forms of lowlife after falling for Lady Patricia d'Ordinay.

The story bounces between characters, between times, between locations (Brighton, Manchester, Sussex), but always we return to Zobrany and Soho.

It is not surprising to know that Kersh made copious chronological notes to keep track of it all, before sending a 558-page manuscript to Heinemann on March 27, 1965. Story analyses and anonymous critiques were made, resulting in many rewrites and the correcting of errata, so that by September 15 the beast had been tamed. 'With Flossie's help, I've just broken the ban. My new novel will be published by McGraw-Hill and Heinemann simultaneously. It's my first novel to be out in America for 10 years. As an indication of what I've had to put up with, I feel somewhat as I felt 33 years ago when I first got into print, kind of dully queer.'

* * *

> **What research was involved in writing this book? Give details if you think they are interesting:** The details are so interesting that they would fill several volumes. Everything I have even seen or felt has been research to me. I'm cursed with that kind of mind. Everything is astoundingly interesting to me. – Gerald Kersh

As the author of eighteen previous novels and hundreds of short stories, many translated into most European languages, Kersh had developed a stock company of characters and types. Much in the way that John Ford, Ingmar Bergman or Pedro Almodóvar cast the same actors to play their screen personas (sometimes against type to keep the mix interesting), so Kersh cast his novels with variations from previous works. In this respect, *The Angel And The Cuckoo* can be considered a summation of his life's work, since it features a number of these characters. The reason for their fecundity in *this* novel may lie in the discovery that during the planning and writing of it, Kersh was told that he had throat cancer.

On June 2, 1965, he wrote: 'I am just out of the Presbyterian Hospital, having had cancer of the throat. They removed my larynx, which had two malignancies on it, thereby saving my life and preserving me (barring accidents) for some time to come. If anyone asks you, tell them from me that it's extremely horrible. I am totally dumb, of course – don't even breathe through nose or mouth, but through a metal pipe let into my trachea. I must learn what they call "oesophageal speech" – i.e., a form of belching in the shape of words. A nice turn-up for the Old Raconteur: but I'll survive. What haunts me at the moment is a dread that a wasp might get into my breathing pipe.'

For most of his writing life Kersh had dictated at high speed, but now he found it necessary to type. 'I had to brush away the tears and begin with nothing.' He learnt to speak again, and typically the first words he uttered were four-letter ones.

'Twenty years ago I'd certainly have died, because it was then inoperable and 100% fatal. There are minor inconveniences conditional on continuing to live – one is dumb as a post, and has no sense of smell or taste for instance; and if one forgetfully jumps into water, one drowns almost instantly. I feel fine, and am told I look a lot younger: in fact the doctors consider me to be a phenomenon, and keep dragging me into town to show me off to people who, having lost their larynxes, have given up hope – the dopes. For the dread of what they call on Broadway "Grand Casino" (they are afraid even to say the word "cancer") hangs over people like a shadow. I talk to 'em in a loud, duck-like quack, saying, "Cheer up, you bastards – d'you want to live for ever? Cancer, schmancer – you should worry, so long you got your health and strength! If you can belch you can talk," and so forth.'

Before the operation, throughout the period of investigation and diagnosis of his cancer, it is not hard to imagine Kersh, in quiet moments and not performing for others, reliving and reimagining his past life in Soho and the people he knew and loved there. Kersh's father Hyman, a master tailor who died in 1929 when Kersh was just eighteen, is the basis for Mark Leonoff, a dignified old man of integrity and character in Kersh's first novel *Jews Without Jehovah* (1934). Hyman had known for two years that he had kidney stones but kept it from his family and died in tremendous pain. It is fair to say that Kersh wrote variations of him in most of the London novels – Colonel Bulba in *Men Are So Ardent* (1936), Ali The Terrible Turk in *Night And The City*, Zobrany here – and in each we watch the old man suffer, sometimes unto death, yet retain his dignity.

The pushy small man who, in true Horatio Alger fashion, rises from rags to riches on a little bit of luck and common sense but mostly on nerve is film producer Gèza Cseh/Gabriel Chess here, but has also been hunchbacked Solomon Schwartz in *The Thousand Deaths Of Mr Small* (1950), cinema manager Sam Yudenow in *Fowlers End* and film producer Walter Chinchilla in *An Ape, A Dog And A Serpent* (1945).

The troubled artist who cannot create anything worthwhile – Tom Henceforth here – has many brothers in Kersh's work, from author John Leonoff in *Jews Without Jehovah* to sculptor Adam in *Night And The City* and writer John Pym in *The Song Of The Flea*. Obviously an autobiographical figure, each of them is placed in 1930s London before Kersh became a bestselling author.

And then we have the most chilling character in the novel. The omnipotent criminal mastermind Perp is based on a real-life acquaintance of Kersh who provided the background materials of cons, robberies, blackmails and murders that were encapsulated in the Karmesin short stories.

In letters, Kersh refers to a man named 'Carfax' who told Kersh about a robbery he planned and executed at the Strand branch of Lloyd's bank in which five men simultaneously cashed five large cheques at a great horseshoe-shaped counter and walked out. The trick only worked because of the split-second timing of the transactions. This was the basis of the first Karmesin story. A later story, 'The Conscience Of Karmesin', concerns the robbery of the crown jewels from the Tower of London, which Carfax planned. According to Kersh: '[Carfax] had his technicians examine all the electric wiring leading into the jewel room of the Tower of London, and then rehearsed the robbery in all but its ultimate details over a period of two years. So he stole the crown jewels, or was about to do so, when purely sentimental considerations made him call the job off.

'King George VI you know had a very bad stutter. His wife, Queen Elizabeth, secretly held his hand when he had to make a speech, giving it an affectionate little squeeze when she sensed a stutter coming along. Now when King George VI and Queen Elizabeth visited New York he was told of a night school up in Harlem for people who stammered. He was very interested in it. Flossie and I had a servant named Kitty Hinton, a negress, a sort of female Jeeves, a copper-coloured Admiral Crichton, very beautiful what is more, but a stutterer. Being the brightest girl in the class, she was told that she would be required to make a speech to a foreign visitor and give him a little bouquet of flowers. On the appointed evening a little fellow of no great distinction turned up and told them of his lifelong battle against his vocal impediment and how he had, with his wife's help, got the better of it. Applause. Our Kitty comes forward with a bunch of flowers, loses her nerve at the last moment and stutters like a light machine gun. The visitor held her hand, told her to look at him, and to her amazement she got through the whole speech without pause or error. Later she learned that this quiet little gentleman was the King of England, who would come uptown unescorted, without a single bodyguard, to talk incognito to the likes of Kitty. I wrote this story, but it was never published "for fear it might offend minority sensibilities".

'One night, meeting Carfax in a hotel in Northiam, between Kent and Sussex, I happened to tell him this anecdote. It brought tears to his eyes. As a child he had been a stutterer and had continued to be one until cured at the age of fourteen by being beaten almost to death and thrown into the Thames below Limehouse in the dead of winter.

I little knew that my idle chatter saved the Crown and the Orb and the Sceptre too, among other things. For Carfax, as he told me later, at once went out and cancelled the Tower job. Two of his men went on with it, against his orders. What happened to them nobody knows – we'll find out when the sea gives up its dead no doubt. They pulled the robbery though. Carfax sent the loot back untouched, he swears. That sort of thing doesn't get into the papers of course.'

Kersh presented Karmesin as a loser – a master criminal does not cadge cigarettes and steal sugar lumps from the bowl – but here makes amends to Carfax by writing a story wherein everything Perp says and does exudes menace. It is the power of Perp's brain, his grasp of psychology, that is his real strength, since he seems able to exert pressure on the weak points of one's own nature. He does not need to blackmail Tom Henceforth, when under certain conditions Tom will want to do the same thing of his own accord. In this sense, Perp is of the same genus as Harry Fabian, faux-American ponce of *Night And The City*, whose actions precipitate the corruption of others. But Harry is not in the same league as Perp . . .

But don't think that such characters are empty repetitions or rehashes of previous books. If anything, this novel represents a deepening of Kersh's understanding of his archetypes. For example, Cseh/Chess could simply be the villain of the piece, but gradually we see that he is as much a victim of his unquenchable passions as the people around him.

Not only does Kersh cram all his characters into the book – there are at least 100 speaking parts – he also manages to crowbar references to his short stories, creating a sort of meta-fiction of his works. Blink and you'll miss references to 'Bone For Debunkers', 'Crooked Bone', 'The Mystery Of The Bottle' (the award-winning tale in which we find out the story behind Ambrose Bierce's disappearance) and others . . .

The novel is resplendent in cultural and historical references, somehow dovetailed into the lives of the characters, which gives the piece a pleasing cohesion and reality. The epic ballad that prefaces the book – the whole thing fabricated by Kersh, of course – tells the story of Martha Tabram's death at the hands of Jack The Ripper, an event still fresh in the collective mind of Edwardian Soho. In fact, it has never been proved that Martha was killed by the Ripper, although some believe that she may have been an early kill.

Just after World War One Perp steals El Greco's masterpiece *The Agony In The Garden Of Gethsemane* from a wealthy man, sells it back, and the painting is then donated to the National Gallery; in reality, the National Gallery acquired it in 1919. Bosch, Brueghel and Félicien Rops are also name-checked.

To illustrate a lost love, Kersh references Gilliat's terrific labours in Victor Hugo's *Toilers Of The Sea*. *Don Quixote*, Arnold Bennett and Shakespeare (Kersh's constant reference) also get a mention.

Although many of the streets remain, most of the place names are long-gone or forgotten. Not so The Fitzroy Tavern, which lent its name to the artistic quarter Fitzrovia; it remains standing proud to this day. Later home to writers and artists such as George Orwell, Dylan Thomas, Augustus John and Francis Bacon, Kersh places the Fitzroy at the centre of artistic London where the clients mention Jacob Epstein, Henri Gaudier-Brzeska, Sherwood Anderson, Ernest Hemingway, André Gide and Marcel Proust, to name but six. This is Tom Henceforth's watering hole of choice, and it's also a place that Kersh frequented.

All this, and it's as funny as hell. 'Have finished a new novel which McGraw-Hill consider the greatest comic masterpiece of the century. I'll be surprised and hurt if it doesn't go over big.' In the end, McGraw-Hill did not take *The Angel And The Cuckoo*, but New American Library did, publishing it on May 28, 1966. Kersh asked for copies to be sent to his friends and admirers – Henry Miller, William Saroyan, Al Capp, Ellery Queen, JB Priestley, Jane Fonda, John Steinbeck – and waited for the reviews. They did not come. Although recommended by the industry press and to libraries, the public at large did not get to hear about the novel because of internal disputes at NAL. Two years later, total US hardback sales were a meagre 2,554. This from an author who had reputedly sold over one million hardback copies of *Night And The City* 20 years earlier.

December 13, 1966: 'I went to be checked by my doctor and found I had got myself some more cancer – back of the tongue, which same tongue having split down the middle causes discomfort – which, after a kind of horror-movie nightmare of treatment, seems to have been cured. I suppose the disease in the long run really is worse than the cure they gave me, but I can't imagine how it can be. I was subjected to a thing called a Linear Accelerator, which not only hurts like hell, but creates such depression that people they try it out on have to be prevented from knocking themselves off out of sheer misery – and the suicidal stage is the cheerful part of it. But I set all the other guinea pigs at the Presbyterian Hospital such an example of sparkling cheerfulness under duress – croaking dirty jokes without a larynx, by oesophageal speech and generally larking about – that they presented me with a gift of Scotch as a testimonial. One sufferer, an undertaker, offered to embalm and bury me free in case I died – no small thing to offer in America.'

Heinemann published *The Angel And The Cuckoo* on February 19,

1967 with modest critical acclaim – Felicia Lamb, *Sunday Telegraph*: 'Long but enjoyable ramble through bohemian, pre-war London'; Claire Tomalin, *Observer*: 'With thunderous Niagara-like charm anecdote crashes on anecdote' – and equally modest sales. Acclimatised to Kersh after more than thirty years reviewing over thirty books, critics had become inured to his charms and blind to his quality. It's a situation that's unlikely to change. Some of his contemporaries, such as Angus Wilson and John Lodwick (sadly, another forgotten author), were reviewed and analysed in a far more literary fashion than Kersh, so there are no substantial literary sources for academia to draw upon for Kersh's contemporary reassessment, and perhaps reassignment, into the literary canon. And it doesn't help that the books are hugely amusing. Let's face it, comedy is not taken seriously. Yet the comedy in *The Angel And The Cuckoo* is not placed there for the simple enjoyment of the reader. It is used to distract from and dissipate the pain and suffering and embarrassment of the central characters. Reading an account of Tom Henceforth's hilarious first love affair, which we believe to be true, we then discover that it is a farcical retelling by Tom to cover up his failure to woo the maiden. It is a strategy taken from Kersh's own life, to transform distress and despair into laughter and amusement. It is his strategy to keep a pitiless universe at bay.

After completing his last novel, *Brock*, Kersh passed away on Tuesday, November 5, 1968, riddled with cancer, leaving Flossie alone to handle their many debts. A couple of months later Flossie wrote of him: 'Gerald was the quintessential artist-born. It does make sense that his kin, those of us closest to him, even physical pain – all were secondary. That is, early in life Gerald made his choice, or was chosen, it's the same. He was dedicated, vowed, given over. An extreme example is, of course, that five years of throat malignancy could be fended off, held at bay, because of a yet greater struggle. And that is, Gerald's tearing out of his own innards, apart from delightful short stories, two beautiful novels.'

Brock is fun and has a fascinating backstory, but if truth be told *The Angel And The Cuckoo* is the last masterpiece of Gerald Kersh.

Paul Duncan

What do you consider the distinguishing or important aspects of this book? It is amusing. It is readable. It is rereadable. It represents money well-spent by whoever buys it. – Gerald Kersh

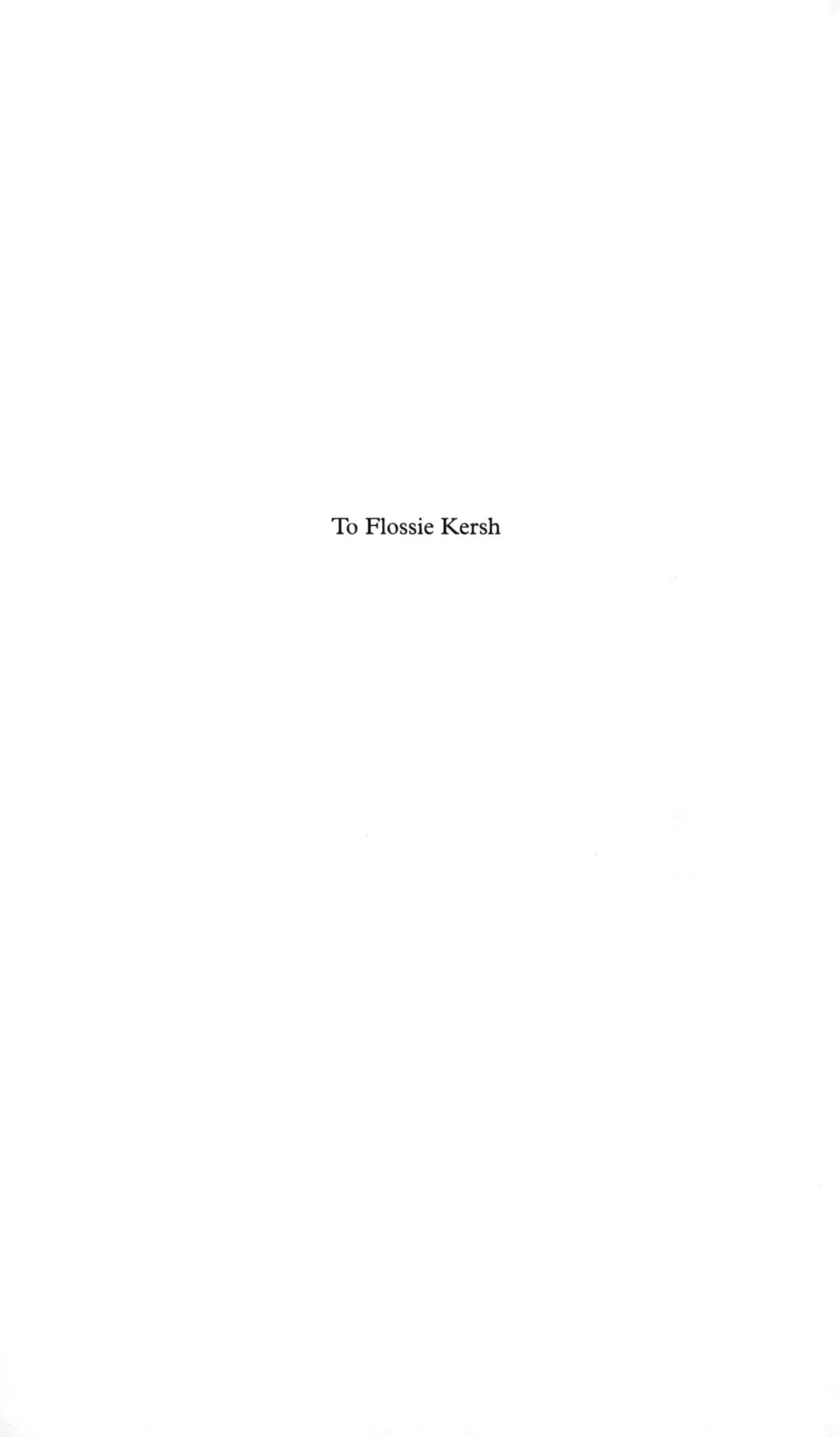

To Flossie Kersh

POPPY'S BALLAD OF MARTY TABRAM

There lived a girl in London Town
Whose name was Marty Tabram,
And at the height of her renown
She charged as high as half a crown.
Now she sleeps in the Bosom of Abram.

She walked the streets Whitechapel Way
When I was just a nipper,
Her life was carefree, blithe and gay
– She played by night and slept by day –
Till she met with Jack the Ripper.

He was a surgeon in disguise,
The greatest in the nation,
And highly thought of down at Guy's
For his bedside manner and nice blue eyes;
But he took to dissipation.

'You are the fairest of the fair,'
Says Jack while they was wooing.
'Pray walk with me to Mitre Square,
The railings are much softer there.'
She went. 'Twas her undoing.

'Pray let me savour your sweet charms,
You're nice as pie,' says he –
And soothed her ladylike alarms;
But the muscles of his brawny arms
Was strong as Lipton's tea!

She smiled at him so mild and meek,
But he biffed her on the boko,
And she let out sitch a horrid shriek
That those what heard it turned as weak
And cold as workhouse cocoa!

He bent her down acrost his knee
So hard it made her back sore,
And turned his cuffs back bold and free
With a tiddly-om-pom-pom, one-two-three!
And he cut orf her legs with a hacksaw.

'Twas awful what she underwent,
For with his hands so bony,
To her dismay and wonderment
He tore out her innards and fundament
Like so much macaroni.

Oh if he'd had it all his way
No more would have been heard of her,
He squashed her like a brewer's dray
With a right-fol-lol tiddy-bom-di-ay –
The dirty rotten murderer!

Half orf his head with gin and beer
He cracked her skull and croaked her,
And strewed her giblets far and near
And cut her frert from ear to ear,
Spat in her eye and choked her!

And, desperate as was that strife –
She was game as the Duke o'York's crew –
That dirty rotter had her life
With a twenty-bladed pocket knife
Like they sell complete with a corkscrew

And a handy little buttonhook
And a thing for opening tins with,
So it fairly gave you the sick to look,
For some parts he left, but others he took,
Including the Parts a gal sins with.

Legs never was spread in love so sweet
As those of that poor sinner is –
They found one of her feet
Down in Leadenhall Street,
And the other foot in the Minories,

And her kidneys the Blackfriars Bridge beneath,
With her stomach all wrinkled and sour,
And her thirty-two teeth
All over Blackheath,
And her brisket and tripes in the Tower.

Just like they tell you in Sunday School,
That's what you get for trolloping.
She wouldn't learn, the silly fool,
That as a pretty general rule
The wages of sin is a walloping.

Is your head to keep your bonnet on,
Or is it what you thinks with?
Her mummy warned her, years agone,
'That's sacred, what you sit upon,
And not to play tiddley winks with –

'You've only got one maidenhead,
So never lose your britches;
A girl is better wed than dead,
So save it for your bridal bed
No matter how it itches!'

Alas, she never understood,
But kep to her vile habits.
She would repent then if she could
When her sacred founts of motherhood
He skins like two dead rabbits!

She was not all bad, although far from good,
Oh ye Bible-bashing frumps!
She simply done the best she could,
And her ivory bowls of womanhood
Was smooth as babies' mumps.

She was pure as she could afford to be.
Oh ye of the Upper Classes!
She was as human as you or me,
So take your vain morality
And stick it on your looking-glasses!

PART ONE

ONE

There are certain dank, limp and melancholy mornings when – all the days of his life seeming to have sunk into a formless lump like cold tea-leaves from which goodness and badness and even the last tang of bitterness have been stewed out – Steve Zobrany almost forgets that he is supposed to be an Unforgettable Character. He even finds it difficult to recognize himself as one of God's creatures with a soul of his own. It is as if somewhere between two sleeps Zobrany has slipped into some dark dimension and is trapped in an ugly and unnatural symbiosis.

Now for example: is this Zobrany's house, or is this house Zobrany? How much of his essential self has gone into keeping brick on brick, board nailed to rafter and plaster stuck to lath, merely to maintain the sordid old edifice's identity as Zobrany's place? Really, it is as if the house with its perforated and patched gastric economy of cisterns and water pipes, its flatulent complex of gas fittings, its high-strung old-fashioned nerves of teased-out and frazzled electric wiring and its coddled but costive drains were his body, and Zobrany nothing but its melancholy and reflective ghost.

'I don't live here,' he thinks, 'I only haunt the house.'

Let him fly away at dawn with a hollow moan! All anybody recognized as Zobrany (and who ever knew the inwardness of the man?) will still be here, impregnating every pore of this deplorably porous place. For he has become one with the building. It will continue to smell of Zobrany as a fowl-house always stinks of chickens or a sty of swine. Scrape, scour, paint an inch thick, do what you will – an effluvium persists, pervasive and inescapable, be it ever so faint. 'Chickens?' you ask, sniffing. 'Pigs?'

When he is gone, it will be like this with Zobrany.

So he thinks and so he fears, when the fog is down and the day is ahead and he has a little attack of the miseries . . . Convert his café into a perfumery and his home upstairs into dinky apartments with American plumbing – knock out a wall here, put in a wall there – do what you will; one day somebody will twitch a nostril and say, 'I don't know; in this house there is a certain odour of Hungarians with dimpled chins. There is a twang of frustration and a perceptible niff of disenchantment and lost endeavour. I notice a pong of heartache . . . Is there a dead Hope under the floorboards?'

Such would be the legacy to Posterity of the servant of God, Steve Zobrany, to be written off as one who got watery melancholy on unrequited love for his fellow men! So Zobrany feels as the Angel writes and vanishes, and he is caught in the clutch of another day.

He puts one massive leg out of bed; whereupon his wife, who has been sleeping without seeming to breathe, makes a noise like a baby that has swallowed a tin whistle. At this signal Zobrany quietly carries his clothes to the bathroom where – as it sometimes happens on mornings like this – he looks with animosity and scorn at what he sees in the mirror, and can find no image appropriate to the distaste with which the sight of himself inspires him.

He picks up a corner of his face between the tips of a disdainful thumb and a fastidious forefinger, much as he might pick up somebody else's used handkerchief; lets it go, and thinks, *I wasn't at all a bad-looking fellow once upon a time, was I? And where has it all gone? Where? Into money? I am poor. Into fame? Oh, certainly I am well-known. As a fool. Then not into wisdom. Into pleasure, then? No, certainly not. Into being my own master, even? Oh, bah! – every loafer with the price of a cup of coffee and an arse to wear out my chairs with is my lord and master. What then? For a living? I am alive, granted. A living dog is better than a dead lion. Dogs also die, and I am a dying dog. The rats in my cellar live. Worms respond to stimuli. Ah me!*

But having put in his four upper front teeth which taste pleasantly of thyme and glycerine, Zobrany feels better. His face, which has appeared to him wearily flabby in ribbed layers and pallid in several shades of unwholesome pallor – slovenly as one of those empty bottles covered with stratified drippings which they use for candlesticks in bohemian cafés – takes on a firmness. It is possible, now, for Zobrany to look leniently at the lines of his jaw and to deal gently but firmly with his moustache which he twists into position with a certain concentrated ruthlessness, fixing it with black pomade. As he turns this notable moustache his back grows straighter, his neck longer and his muscles assume tone – he might be tuning himself like a stringed instrument, by means of ebony pegs.

This makes him feel better, but not well enough. Zobrany, at this hour of the morning, is remorselessly hard on himself – somewhat as a time-blasted sergeant-major has a tendency to be contemptuous of a sloppy parade of sleep-sodden recruits. Looking at his face he says, 'Oh, you horrible man! What are you supposed to *be*, you slack-jawed coffee-jockey?' It is of no use to remind himself that about thirty years ago, in 1906 or thereabout, his was a face and a figure for which high-born ladies might have sighed. This is 1937; and under the yellow electric light his image in the grey glass mocks him.

Zobrany hastens to lather his face and shave, enjoying the slap of the razor against the strop and the ringing note of the broad hollow-ground blade as it sings against the bristles of his beard. Then, having mortified his face in cold water and dealt it certain stinging blows with a handful of lavender water, and melded the pomade into his moustache, and got his countenance into alignment, and touched his cheeks with talcum powder, he slaps the back of his head; dismisses himself with an admonition, tying the cord of his dressing gown very tight, and turns scornfully away from himself.

Then he forgives himself; looks back at the mirror with a stern softening of expression, as if to say to his reflection in the glass, *I am a father to you*; and now his kind and humorous face is set in a look of grave benevolence.

Before tiptoeing downstairs for his morning coffee he goes to have a look at his wife, who is quietly sleeping. At forty-odd Alma Zobrany is, if anything, more alluring than she was at twenty: the cream of the girl has come to the surface and set; in obedience to the current fashion her dark red hair is unrestrained and bursts out in furious luxuriance. Her silk nightdress is blue-green and grey to match her eyes, and even in sleep she has a quizzical, half-smiling look with a dimple on one side of her mouth and the eyebrow on that side raised in a parody of surprise. At any moment (you might think) she will open an eye and invite tremendous intimacies.

You might think so. Nowadays Zobrany is by no means sure that he can at a moment's notice consummate an impulse (having so much on his mind) and he knows that if he wakes up Alma for mere dalliance he might as well sew himself in a sack with a corpse.

And still it cheers him to think that there is scarcely a man in London who would not give his eyeteeth for Zobrany's legal privileges. There is a libidinous delight in the thought: that if every man who looked at Alma in the past week had done what came into his mind, and cuckolds wore horns, Zobrany would be antlered like a Tyrolean hunting lodge.

He smiles at the idea. Exquisitely sentient and feminine though she unquestionably is, and a woman in a million, Alma Zobrany is a kind of Marvel of Nature – something like a termitary, entire of itself, having a coolly throbbing, plasma-pampered, plump electrified maggot for a heart; human only by far-fetched analogy. Steve Zobrany is passionately proud of his wife. Any other woman with her looks would have known that she was not so created without good reason; that beauty has its function as surely as function has its beauty; and she would have gone off the rails – made romances, scandals, heartaches – had neurasthenic crises, turning herself inside out fumbling after physical fulfilment with the desperation of a late traveller feeling for a lost ticket. Vanity is the mother of prurience; Zobrany has frequently encountered and pitied women who went about trying, as they said, 'to experience *feeling*', and whom the world called Nymphomaniacs as if they were perpetually in heat instead of being so to speak chronically in cold!

. . . All the same, he thinks, looking at Alma, here is a touch of the sacrilege that is Waste. Because a peach looks so pretty to peel and smells too good to eat, does one let it rot in the dish? . . .

Some women, conscious of their sexual indifference, go to extraordinary lengths to make their husbands happy in the false belief that they are giving pleasure to their wives. And why not? Zobrany asks himself. Some women who do not care what they eat put themselves to great toil and inconvenience in order that they may become good cooks, for their husbands' sakes.

But Alma is not 'some women'. She can be placed in no category. By no means what you would call a selfish woman, she somehow contrives to live by herself and for herself, almost in spite of herself. She is neither stubborn nor self-willed – she is simply spiritually and physically incapable of doing anything that displeases her. And nothing displeases her less than being in a state not recognizably unpleasant to her. In anyone else, such a state of being – or not being – might have the appearance of idiocy. But Alma isn't anyone else, and she is anything but an idiot; she is not even silly. She is an alien form of life in the shape of a sleepily voluptuous creamy woman with dark red hair . . . and so on, and so forth. *Enough!* Zobrany tells himself, looking away and leaving the bedroom.

Massive as he is, Zobrany can move quick and quiet as a fish in deep water. He has even acquired a knack of sneezing soundlessly at this hour of the morning – does it, somehow, with his eyebrows – when the effluvium of the house takes him by the nose on his way downstairs.

Much as he looks forward to his morning coffee, this first daily descent to the kitchen is always somewhat repugnant to Steve Zobrany. Mr and Mrs Sordic will be there, and the sight of this couple in the peculiar light by which the place is illuminated before the sun is up is something he has never managed to harden himself to.

A reluctant dribble of glaucous dawn with all the goodness sucked out of it seeps through an iron frame of glass prisms set flush with the pavement above – a most insipid filtrate of sooty daylight, adulterated by the incandescence of the gaslight which still burns in the street-lamp in the court. It hits a lime-washed wall which absorbs such virtue as it has left, and what remains of it leaks into the kitchen to coexist rather than mingle with the glow of the electric bulbs. Appropriately lighted by this disheartening subterranean radiance, Zobrany will find the Sordics.

Steve Zobrany is known far and wide as a reasonable man and a good-natured man. But neither Christian charity nor profane philosophy can ameliorate his bitter feelings for Mr and Mrs Sordic. He says, 'I am sorry; they set my teeth on edge. As the saying goes, there is a black cat between us. I can't help it – it is something stronger than Zobrany. You remember that song: "I Don't Know Why I Love You Like I Do"? So it is with me and the Sordics. I don't know why, I just *don't*. Shakespeare has a word for it: "Some that are mad when they behold a cat," et cetera . . . One man is repelled – and believe me, disgust is stronger than fear – by juicy things with thin, crispy shells that crunch when stepped on in the dark. Another man hates squids, earwigs or knives scratching plates. With me, it happens to be the Sordics. There is nothing personal about it. Compliment for compliment – they can't stand me, either.'

Ask him why, this being the case, he continues to keep the Sordics, Zobrany will reply, 'I don't know. They were here when I came, when I took possession of the property twenty-six years ago, in 1911. It was a case of hate at first sight.'

'But my dear Mr Zobrany, aren't you the master here?'

'Undoubtedly, sir.'

'Then go up to the Sordics like a man, give them a month's wages, and say, "Pack up and get out!" Just like that.'

Then the urbane Zobrany will reply, 'If I have done so once I have done so a hundred times. They refuse to go.'

'Refuse to pay them, then.'

'I have already done so. It makes no difference. It seems the Sordics are some kind of curse laid upon me. Some men have strawberry birthmarks, some have the rickets; others have six toes on each foot. I have the Sordics . . .'

It took even a dispassionate observer some time to get over his first pang of distaste on seeing Mr Sordic. To begin with, he *had* two heads – or almost, for his was a double-crowned skull shaped like an unbaked cottage-loaf. He *had* an epiphytic nose of indescribable shape, covered with ginger hairs, and so pockmarked and porous that he seemed to have a double cluster of pale nostrils. He was perversely hairy in the wrong places. Having neither brows nor lashes to shade his sore little sunken eyes, his face and scalp were glabrous; but his heavily flapped succulent red ears were overgrown in such a manner that one felt he uses them to trap insects; and that these insects he digested in secret. His mouth was pink and faintly glistening. Perhaps you have tried, idly, to flatten a plumber's rubber suction cup? Press in the middle and the comers spring open; press down the corners and it pouts at the centre; it doesn't want to close. Rimmed with white bristles, such was Mr Sordic's mouth. He had no chin; only a pleated red neck which sprang out of a ruff of grey hair at the collar line.

Sordic's wife was damply grey-and-white like an oxidized potato and, having no bones, appeared to move like a caterpillar by a system of stretchings and contractions. Zobrany sometimes had bad dreams about

Mrs Sordic's lips, which resembled mottled pork sausages of different weights and shapes: the upper, heavy and short, had squashed the lower lip flat, and a large fleshy mole at one corner suggested that it had burst its casing . . .

'But all this is nothing, nothing at all!' Zobrany would sometimes say. 'Nobody knows better than I that in this life one must give a little and take a little. If one is not to live alone, one must make allowances. One cannot help one's looks, we hear. This is true, to only a certain extent. The Sordics *can* help their looks. They look as they do because they are wicked, and want to spite me. Why? For the simple reason that I have never done them any harm – that is why they want to hurt my sensibilities. They are Mr and Mrs Smerdyakov, straight out of Dostoyevsky – they are horrible, horrible!

'Listen,' Zobrany would go on. 'I love the English language. I am very particular about the proper pronunciation of the English language – or any language. Language separates Man from the beasts that perish, and to mutilate it is a crime against Society. Now the Sordics always wait until I am within hearing distance before they talk out loud, and then they do so only to aggravate me. Sordic has no teeth; perhaps he can't help whistling his sibilants. But is it absolutely necessary deliberately to make a noise like an aviary whenever I am nearby? Besides, Sordic knows the difference between *P* and *V*. Then what right has he to go off like a piccolo out of tune saying to me such things as: "The pfsalad drefssing is too pfsweet – fut in a little more pinegar, a little more pinegar fut," eh? . . . And then again his letters, his atrocious letters. He writes to the police accusing me of dreadful crimes; and to rub salt in the wound he comes to me hissing like a fried snake, to correct his spelling! . . . "Mr Pfzobrany, how many hisses are there in *Pfrape*?" He means Rape.'

Then, more likely than not, Zobrany would exercise his stomach with an inward laugh, and say, 'No, really! Look at it whichever way God sends it, I have a Chamber of Horrors – a Wax Museum – eh?'

It is a fact that about twice a month for the past fifteen years or so, the Sordics have laid information against Steve Zobrany as having committed most of the more sensational crimes they read about in the Sunday newspapers: FATHER OF SIX SLAYS PARAMOUR WITH CUTLASS; and PROWLER RAPES, STRANGLES 9-YEAR-OLD; and PAISLEY MYSTERY: GIRL'S LEGS FOUND IN A SUITCASE. The police must make a routine check, of course. So it is by no means unusual that a man in plainclothes from Great Marlborough Street looks in of a morning to say, 'Ha, Mr Zobrany' – consulting a list – 'you didn't by any chance leave a dead baby in a brown paper bag 'round Hampstead way last Friday?'

'No sir, I did not. Will you take a cup of coffee?'

'Don't mind if I do, thanks . . . Didn't happen to rape the postmistress at Lower Woking around three o'clock last Sunday afternoon, and steal two pounds' worth of stamps and sixteen shillings in cash? . . . I thought not. I've got you down here for murdering your wife with a humane killer and cutting her head off with a sickle near Bedford. How *is* your good lady, by the bye?' The policeman gives Zobrany a keen look.

'In one piece and blooming, I thank you. Try a hot buttered croissant.'

Zobrany's manners are so elegant that the man from Great Marlborough Street lapses into French, and says, '*Merci* very much . . . I've got to look you up – you know that, sir. Rubber mackintoshes and cutting girls' back hair off around Richmond way? No. Setting fire to haystacks and unnatural offence against a sheep – not your line, I imagine?'

'Certainly not!' says Zobrany. Then he starts to shake with laughter. 'No, really! With a sheep! No, but I mean to say – a sheep!'

'Mr Zobrany, why don't you get rid of them pair o' nuts?'

'I don't know. Perhaps once they get it into their heads that I am amused, they will give it up as a bad job.'

'Taking 'em long enough, sir.'

'Ah, but Sordic is a Croat, and the Croats are a stubborn people,' says Zobrany.

'Well, it could be that his papers aren't in order and we could deport him somewhere,' the detective says.

The sweet-natured Zobrany replies, 'Oh no, no – after all, it is a dreadful thing to be homeless. Let them be, let them be.' He adds, in that half-coaxing, half-apologetic, half-reasonable tone peculiar to Hungarians, 'In any case, where the devil could you deport them *to*, Sergeant?'

'Wherever they come from.'

'Ah, but where's that? Croatia? They might as well come from the moon. The map has changed, my dear sir, the world has altered. Croatia – there is no such place. Like Slovenia, Herzegovina, Serbia, Montenegro and a hundred other places, it is generically Yugoslavia. Geography is not what it was when you and I were boys, Inspector. But England still is England, and here one does not say, "Go away, Sordic," and throw the pest into the sea – although it would not be a bad idea, at that . . .'

'He's one of your people, isn't he?' the policeman asks.

Zobrany's eyebrows go up and open like umbrellas, and his eyes flash. 'I beg your pardon. I said Sordic was a Croat. I am a Magyar.'

'Sorry, sir; anyway we've got you down as an Italian.'

'Now look here,' says Zobrany, pouring more coffee and offering more croissants, 'If you have me down as Italian, you must stand corrected. I was born near Budapest, in what was in those days the

Austro-Hungarian Empire. My political views were unacceptable to Franz Josef, the Emperor –'

'– The Italians were our friends, last war,' says the plainclothes man.

'No doubt. But in 1911 I came to England, and am now a naturalized subject of His Majesty King George the Sixth. I swore my oath to his father, King George the Fifth. I am proud to call myself British by nationality. I served in the cavalry, sir – the Third Heavy Dragoons.' Steve Zobrany does not feel himself called upon to explain that he was employed in the Officers' Mess at Dogworth for exactly seven weeks. 'I also served, as best I could,' he says, turning half his moustache tenderly around a forefinger, while his fine eyes fill with tears as he sees again the great yellow mahogany table and the candles burning steadily in their sconces, and hears over the tumultuous beating of his proud heart the authoritative but friendly voice of the tired little bearded King of England saying, *That was a very good pie.*

Zobrany, at this point, feels that enough has been said. 'Apropos of anything you may wish to investigate: I have literally a thousand alibis for any hour or minute of the day, since I seldom have time to step out of this café. Without me, it would go to the dogs in two hours.'

'I know, Mr Zobrany. It's just routine,' the detective says. 'If I was you I'd get rid of them Sordics.'

'Sir, there is only one human being on earth more stubborn than a Croat, and that is a Magyar,' says Zobrany.

At the door the man from Great Marlborough pauses to ask, 'In your opinion, whose side will Italy be on in the next war?'

'On Hitler's side,' says Zobrany.

'Well, that's only fair. We had Italy last time.'

. . . Smiling again as he thinks of this, Zobrany pauses on the landing below his bedroom to adjust a little tuft of cotton wool which he has stuck to a spot at the point of his chin where he cut himself shaving. To face a harmless fact – he likes to meet the housemaid Poppy, who is also a waitress, as she comes out of her room on her way downstairs. The sight of her does him good. The sound of her clears his head and the smell of her points up his general tone.

The French Romantics, he thinks, are full of ethereal guttersnipes who look like camellias, gardenias, lilies-of-the-valley, and such watery plants – as if there were anything wonderful about looking delicate and smelling sickly, having been born bloodless and bred sunless in a slum! How much more remarkable is young Poppy, of whom it may truthfully be said that she has seen no green leaf beyond the squares and the London parks, and was nurtured on bread-and-dripping, prayers, threats and promises of damnation, soot, castigation, stale buns, nit-combs, cocoa and carbolic – and grew up a flamboyant!

It delights the tender and susceptible Zobrany to look at her superb white arms and legs, and her breasts which seem so firm that (as the peasants used to say) you might crack walnuts on them. Zobrany feels that there must be good blood in this girl – that delicately flaring nose, those sculptured lips and dainty ears, and the lines of that firm jaw never were thumbed out of the watery loins of any common guttersnipe. He likes the generous breadth of her untroubled, unastonishable forehead, and the complete aplomb of her round black eyes – not to denigrate the serenity of Alma's. A dash of Spanish, perhaps; which might imply a trace of African? Zobrany does not know or care. Certainly, her teeth, which are powerful and perfect – so that it gives Zobrany a purely aesthetic pleasure to see her laugh – which she does frequently, with or without provocation – are no slum teeth. Neither is her voice, which is resonant and clear, anything like a slavey's voice trained to a half-snarl and a half-whimper.

From some blessed ancestor she has inherited a gift of laughter wholesome and clean. Yes, Zobrany thinks, clean is the word for Poppy, the untidiest housemaid that ever kicked dust under a rug, the slovenliest waitress that ever put her thumb in a plate. Somehow, a peculiarly personal sweetness is inherent in the girl – she transcends grime; or at least bypasses it. There is something aristocratic in the way Poppy can step over a fallen broom; breeding in her manner of picking up a fallen dishrag on her toe and flipping it out of her range of vision. As certain women are so made that they make the most preposterous dresses elegant, so on Poppy's shoulder spaghetti appears to be the product of painstaking design and breathless calculation. If she combs her black hair, well and good; if she does not comb her hair, so much the better. No apron can stay level on her animated belly; but on Poppy crooked aprons look curiously dressy, rakish, suggestive of the Steen-kirk or the Belcher handkerchief, and none the worse for a splash of mustard and ketchup.

It is remarkable, considering his pride and joy in the nobility of the English language, that Zobrany even likes the way Poppy talks. Perhaps some parallel may be drawn between this exception, which he makes in Poppy's case alone, and the fact that although he has a dainty nose and is given to the free use of Old English Lavender, he finds her redolence oddly attractive. And hers is a jungle away from the ivory armpit in the advertisements. It seems that just as Poppy has some mysterious glandular distillery which gets only what is attractive out of her odorous secretions, so her voice has a quality which refines crudities and filters impurities in her speech and intonation – in which she is Low Cockney, no image being too pungent for her, nor any word too coarse.

But ah, ah, blood will tell! Zobrany thinks; although God knows what blood he means. She has a voice like a set of tuning forks, as he sometimes remarks – searchingly vibrant. She likes to use it, too, although at this early hour she is mindful of Mrs Zobrany's need for sleep and keeps it down to an undertone. Where she picked up her repertoire of bloodthirsty, mock-pathetic gutter ballads nobody knows. 'It would not surprise me if she made them up herself as she went along,' Zobrany says. He likes to imagine that there is some great talent locked up somewhere inside Poppy, awaiting only the proper combination of stimuli to let it loose. Love? A searing passion? . . . *If I were twenty years younger . . .*

Only he isn't twenty years younger, and never will be twenty years younger; is almost inclined, this morning, to believe that he has never been twenty years younger – and is unlikely to get to be twenty years older.

Now, in a melodious whisper, she is singing 'Jack The Ripper' – one of those ballads nobody knows the beginning or the end of, or even how many verses it is supposed to have.

'. . . Oh if 'e'd 'ad it all 'is way
No more would 'ave been 'eard of 'er,
'E squashed 'er like a brewer's dray
With a right-fol-lol tiddy-bom-di-ay –
The dirty rotten murderer!

'Arf orf 'is 'ead wiv gin and beer
'E cracked 'er skull and croaked 'er.
And strewed 'er giblets far and near,
And cut 'er frert from ear to ear,
Spat in 'er eye and choked 'er . . .'

'Good morning, Poppy,' says Zobrany, suppressing a desire to give her a friendly squeeze.

Poppy sees the tuft of cotton wool on his jaw, and says, 'Father Christmas.'

With dignity, Zobrany pulls the cotton away, and then she says, 'Wipe your nose; your chin's bleeding,' and stifles a laugh.

And exactly what this is supposed to mean, or what there is humorous about it, Zobrany does not know. If Poppy says it and laughs, it must be funny. *Wipe your nose; your chin's bleeding!* 'No, really,' Zobrany murmurs, following her down to the kitchen. Ahead of him she bursts in on the Sordics. They are feeding. Sordic is applying his plumber's suction cup to a noisy and obdurate cup of coffee. His wife, like some monstrous schoolgirl writing a secret note, has her head down and her left arm curved about a plate; she is doing something nasty to an egg, with a sharp fork.

'Good morning,' says Zobrany. The man replies with a noise such as a child makes with a drinking straw in the dregs of a pop bottle; Mrs Sordic says nothing, but applies a swab of white bread to the hidden thing on her plate, lifts it dripping orange and devours it.

Poppy says, sweetly, 'Dracula's Bride. Don't be surprised if one of these days you wake up with a sharp stake up your –'

'– Poppy!' says Zobrany sternly, stopping her.

'– Through your 'eart, I meant to say.'

Then, as Mr Sordic starts a supersonic whistling, Zobrany snatches up his private coffeepot and escapes upstairs to the café.

TWO

Everything in life was so long ago! Zobrany thinks, feeling pleasantly philosophical after his first cup of coffee and a hot croissant, lighting a long, strong Egyptian cigarette – a Dimitrinos 'Dragoon' which, with its potent tang, virile bulk and luxurious gold tip, satisfies not only his appetite for hearty flavours, but becomes him as an accessory to his massive and somewhat outmoded elegance. Pouring himself another cup of coffee he watches young Poppy as she advances resolutely against last night's dust and ashes, blithely singing her unending ballad of blood and woe and holding her broom at the high port like a soldier going into battle with fixed bayonet. It is uplifting, to see her going after the litter – point, parry, butt stroke and kill – as if this is the hour she has lived for, and doesn't mind dying for, and ought to get a medal for.

There is, in fact, something of No Man's Land about the café at this hour – a battlefield atmosphere of smashed shards and tattered rags of daylight, congealed puddles of spilt coffee, and stained butts scattered in such numbers that the cigarettes of which they are the remains might have been fired out of a machine gun rather than puffed in peace and quiet. Over everything hangs a stale, pungent memory of smoke and wasted breath. An efficiently conducted café should be swept and mopped the night before, as Zobrany knows very well. But servants want watching, and a man must sleep.

Poppy sings:

''E bent 'er down acrost 'is knee
So 'ard it made 'er back sore,
And turned 'is cuffs back bold and free
With a tiddly-om-pom-pom, one-two-three!
And 'e cut 'orf 'er legs wiv a 'acksaw.

She smiled at 'im so mild and meek
But 'e biffed 'er on the boko,
And she let out such a 'orrid shriek
That them what 'eard it turned as weak
And cold as work'ouse cocoa.

But the muscles of 'is brawny arms
Was strong as Lipton's tea –'

Zobrany asks, 'Poppy, where on earth do you get hold of these songs?'
'Why, don't you like it?' she says. 'It's a moral song, it teaches girls a lesson . . .

'Is your 'ead to keep your bonnet on,
Or is it what you thinks wiv?
'Er mummy warned 'er, years agone –
"That's sacred, what you sit upon,
And not to play tiddley winks wiv" –

'That's a moral, ain't it?

'And, desperate as was that strife –
She was game as the Duke o' York's crew –
That dirty rotter 'ad 'er life
With a twenty-bladed pocket knife
What they sell complete with a corkscrew . . .'

'No, upon my word!' cries Zobrany. 'Corkscrew!'
'Those are the words . . .

'And a 'andy little buttonhook
And a thing for opening tins wiv,
So it fairly gave you the sick to look,
For some parts 'e left, but others 'e took,
Including the Parts a gel sins wiv –

'I think it's a pretty song. Like "Sally In Our Alley", but with twiddly bits. I can sing something higher-class, if you like. There's "The Catsmeat Seller Of The Isle of Dogs", and there's "The Wages Of Gin Is Breath", and there's "The Corpse Finder Of Limehouse Pool":

'Oh, many are the drownded wenches
I 'ave found the bodies of
But they was violets to the stenches
When Maggie took 'er bodice off . . .'

'Oh, sing your "Jack the Ripper", then,' says Zobrany.
Happy to oblige, Poppy goes on:

'Legs never was spread in love so sweet
As those of that poor sinner is –
They found one of 'er feet

Down in Leadenhall Street
And the other foot in the Minories,

And 'er kidneys the Blackfriars Bridge beneath
With 'er stomach all wrinkled and sour,
And 'er thirty-two teeth
All over Blackheath
And 'er brisket and tripes in the Tower . . .'

'Be quiet now,' says Zobrany. 'I am thinking. You have a pretty voice, my dear; why devote it to such nasty songs?' He chuckles. 'No, really – brisket and tripes in the Tower! No, I mean!'

'She was not all bad, although far from good,
Oh ye Bible-bashing frumps!
She simply done the best she could,
And 'er ivory bowls of womanhood
Was smooth as babies' mumps.

She was pure as she could afford to be,
Oh ye of the Upper Classes!
She was as human as you or me,
So take your vain morality
And stick it on your looking-glasses . . .'

'– Poppy, once and for all: enough!' Zobrany says, with severity. 'It is a point of discipline. You have a sweet voice, but . . .' Laughter overcomes him. 'No, babies' mumps!'

He looks at Poppy, Poppy looks at him; unable to keep a straight face he turns aside, spluttering coffee. 'Sweep the place,' he orders, composing himself; and goes to the front door to take his first breath of what passes for fresh air in Masham Court. As usual he looks up at his beloved sign, thrice repainted since Baxter the blacksmith fitted it to its iron bracket twenty-five years ago, fixing the bracket to the wall with spikes strong enough to moor a battleship. The cherub's hair is gilded, now, with the finest French gold leaf, and so is the plate holding the 'roast cuckoo'. That devil of a Tom Henceforth was right – sightseers really did come to Masham Court and bring their friends to look at the boy with the birds; but not for any reason that wayward young man could possibly have foreseen.

It happened that when the street lamp was lit, the cherub cast a monstrously priapic shadow. Strangers thought, at first, that Zobrany was operating a rendezvous for homosexuals. A policeman of the old school – they aren't like that now, as everybody knows – tried to screw hush money out of him, darkly threatening official action. Zobrany said, 'Move the lamp-post, then. There my little angel stands, and there he shall remain. No, really, is a man to pay tax on his shadow? Is this Russia? Is this Austria?' And he consulted one of his customers, a briefless young barrister, who made him a speech full of out-of-the-way knowledge and cogent argument, blasting the prurience of the public mind. 'To the impure all things are libidinous,' said this young lawyer. 'Take the portrait of the sailor on the Players cigarette packet. Apply a shiny knife blade to the mouth, just under the moustache, and the picture and its reflection will combine to produce something female, anatomically accurate, and legally indecent. In Westerham, in Kent, there stands a statue of General Wolfe which, looked at from a certain angle, appears to depict him in the act of self-abuse. At Southend-on-Sea, the statue of Queen Victoria – if you follow the direction of her outstretched hand – points straight into the doorway of the gentlemen's lavatory. In Philadelphia, the statue of William Penn appears to be urinating into the Cathedral of Saint Patrick. The Boy of Brussels has been flagrantly relieving himself in public for hundreds of years . . . I wish you'd demand to be prosecuted – I could make my name on a case like this.'

But it came to nothing.

One boat-race night, a party of Oxford scholars tried to kidnap the cherub; and then Zobrany fought a bloody battle on his own doorstep, assisted (to his amazement) by the gruesome Sordics armed with saucepans. And through it all, although the uproar could be heard three streets away, Alma sat by the till, meditatively working at a piece of embroidery.

It was almost as bad when a group of medical students in a fund-raising drive for one of the hospitals, all wearing white coats and surgical masks and carrying stethoscopes, carried Zobrany off bodily in a basket saying he was Dracula, and they wanted him for dissection.

'It is illegal for you to assassinate me before you are qualified,' Zobrany said; and that got into the evening papers, this being in the Silly Season.

. . . There were still die-hards who called Zobrany Count Dracula, although the incident took place as long ago as 1913, not long after Bram Stoker's death. Zobrany had said to the reporter, 'I am not a vampire – although to tell you the truth, I often eat raw meat in the form of steak tartare . . .'

Steak Dracula, the gossip-writer's headline said: the paragraph made it clear that *steak* was a play on *stake;* and so Zobrany renamed this harmless and nourishing form of ground beef.

Moral? It's an ill wind that blows nobody any good; or, as Zobrany puts it, 'Good seeds are carried in the droppings of wild birds . . . and

I can tell you, they hatch out pretty wild at University College. In the Great Raid of 1934, I captured a hostage' – he might be an American frontiersman talking of Apaches – 'thank God they had exhausted their ammunition, packets of soot and of flour, and Masham Court received only the last wave of the assault.

'In that attack I lost my collar and one sleeve of my coat, but I caught a ringleader, forced a parley, and won the day' – Zobrany's frown as he says this conveys an impression that he had burnt his captive's feet with matches and twisted a knotted cord about his forehead until his eyes fell out; in fact, he had apologized for turning the young man upside-down while carrying him under one arm, and soothed him with *baba au rhum* and coffee – 'he was then a medical student in his first year, and his name is Ody, and he has since become my very dear friend – almost like, if not a son, at least a favourite nephew. And a solid customer. That sign has brought me all kinds of luck . . .'

It really is extraordinary, Zobrany thinks, *how redolent the unlikeliest spot can be of pleasing associations and amusing memories!* The sign is still there. The little parcels of bread and leftover meat which he puts out on the doorstep for the beggars are all gone. Whatever the hour, Zobrany never forgets to leave some offering of food for the outcasts of the night, whom he remembers with a curious mixture of pity and dread, somewhat as country folk in wild places still regard gnomes, pixies, elves and underground people in general.

At dawn, thousands of times in the past twenty-five years, Steve Zobrany, blinking at his café in the early light, has felt bewilderment and shock like a sleepwalker abruptly awakened. What is a man like himself doing here? Looking at the mouldings on the shadowy ceiling he mutters, 'Is this where I am? Why, why?'

It is mere apostrophe. Nobody knows the whys and the wherefores of the matter better than Zobrany . . .

Many years before, when he was a romantic exile in Rome, Zobrany – then, as always, the best and easiest of men – had a friend whom he loved and admired above all men. This was one Gèza Cseh; an executive, a man of affairs, a rare combination of dreamer and man of action. Skinny as an alley cat and with lank black hair, lean-jawed and remorseless in his deadly lidless stare, compressed of lip and trembling with ambition too intense for expression, Cseh reminded everybody of the youthful Napoleon. And just as the cadet Bonaparte's schoolmates made fun of him, the other Hungarian exiles in Rome mocked little Gèza. They derided the way he panted when he talked and supplemented articulation with a whole Punch-and-Judy show of squeaks and a veritable *Kurlemurlehuff* of gestures and winks and nervous grimaces. They made a joke of him imitating the noise of an express train:

Gèza-Gèza-Gèza-Gèza – Cseh-Cseh-Cseh-Cseh! – while some whistled and others rattled glasses.

For although he always had a stock of flashy and audacious schemes in hand, anybody with an ounce of sense could see that the most plausible and moderate of his projects had (as the saying goes) holes in it big enough to throw a cat through.

Zobrany, for practical purposes, appears to have had considerably less than this proverbial ounce of sense. As his kind will, he compelled himself to believe in Gèza Cseh, if only for the reason that his faith in the little maniac conferred upon him the wild and dangerous dignity of a champion of lost causes, a backer of rank outsiders, a plunger on single numbers. But that was not the only reason. Zobrany felt somehow morally bound to stand by Cseh as later he stood by Henceforth, because popular opinion and common sense were dead against him . . . and also because he was such an exceedingly *little* fellow . . . Zobrany found himself saying to himself, 'Well, well; the smaller a man is, the larger he must talk. What the devil, a man must live; and the weaker he is, the more fuss he must make about it. Kick yourself, Zobrany! Don't blame Cseh . . .'

In 1899, an unfrocked waiter named Rasp, degraded on account of advanced years and flat feet to the position of lavatory attendant at the Hotel Politi in Vienna, looking for a disciple, happened upon the undergrown fourteen-year-old Hungarian busboy, Gèza Cseh. Rasp was full of tales of high life in the great hotels, but his contemporaries treated him with undisguised disrespect – they would interrupt his anecdotes with irreverent pantomime; wiping imaginary toilet seats, pulling imaginary chains, holding out hands for imaginary tips, closing their nostrils between finger and thumb and saying *Pfui!* But the boy listened, spellbound, while the old man talked, sounding like some bizarre Court Circular. '. . . Colonel von Diesel slapped the Baron von Osten in the face for peeing over his waistcoat, and they would have fought with pistols, only the Graf von Dusenberg arbitrated by explaining that the same thing had happened to him when in a hurry on account of his getting caught in the tapes of his abdominal support; the victim in the Graf's case being Major von Stoss . . . Fräulein Blum, of the Ladies' Room, told me this evening Captain von Festerburg gave her fifty krone to let him sit where the actress Lili Lux had sat while it was still warm, for just five minutes . . . I heard the Vicomte de la Tour say to General von Killinger, "It is *not* an argument for socialism, that after eating sauerkraut a gentleman's excrement smells the same as a peasant's. It is an argument for mortality, and therefore not a political but a theological point. Besides, a gentleman rarely eats sauerkraut . . ."'

Rasp could run on in this vein for hours. But, enchanting as young Gèza Cseh found such society gossip, he was more interested in the old man's general observations on Greatness. '. . . We cannot all be emperors, ministers, diplomats, prima donnas, archdukes, field marshals. There are plenty of kings, and what not, all over Europe. Ah, but how many great cooks are there? Everybody obeys the Kaiser. But the Kaiser himself bows down before his cook. The manager of the Grand Hotel himself falls on his knees before the chef de cuisine Angelini! A great chef can do no wrong. Listen: the Prince of Wales is a great gourmet. He is very fussy about his pancakes. One day the great Pierre, serving a pancake with burnt curaçao, accidentally sets the whole damned thing alight. Does he beg His Royal Highness's pardon? No. He says, "Eat it up and like it, sire – that's a crêpe suzette." And the Prince kisses him on both cheeks and gives him a medal.

'Remember, what the eye doesn't see the heart doesn't grieve for. Many is the time I have spat in a great man's ragoût if he displeased me. However, as I was saying, we cannot all be cooks. Ah, but listen, who else in the world does everybody defer to? A chief of police? Perhaps. A magnate? Perhaps. A *maître d'hôtel*! Do you hear me? A *maître d'hôtel*! After the chef, the maître-dee. He walks like a lord, lives like a prince, is treated like a diplomat and bribed like a politician. That's what you should study to be, my boy; a *maître d'hôtel.*

'Watch Monsieur Umberto at the Politi, while you have the chance; study every movement he makes, every wink of his eye. It is like dancing, only more difficult. Now there is a way to be a master of men – there's a way to live! Politi himself began as a *Wasserkellner,* learnt languages, became a *maître d'hôtel,* and now is his own *hôtelier* and a multi-millionaire whom kings are proud to shake hands with. Now listen. I will tell you a story about how Politi threw the Prince of Bulgaria out of his grill room for criticizing the Tournedos Rossini . . .'

And old Rasp took the boy in hand; taught him how to walk and carry himself. 'I want to see you with such a manner that if an escaped tiger came roaring into your restaurant you would only have to give him a cold look and he would slink out with his tail between his legs and go instead to a sausage shop. Or, if you deigned to receive that tiger, he would sit where you put him, and he would be ashamed to call for meat but would lap up a sole with mushrooms if you recommended it – such is the power of the *maître d'hôtel*! . . . But you must grow, boy, grow! You are too little, you must eat and eat and get big, tall!'

Then: 'What is to be must be, Gèza. So you are small. Then be small. When all is said and done, now that I come to think of it, I have never seen a really tall *hôtelier* – it's brains that count.'

And: 'Christ Almighty, child! You overplay, you overdo, you pick up all Monsieur Umberto's worst points. A restaurant is not a battlefield, damn it all; a customer is not a defeated enemy; a menu is not an ultimatum; a bill is not an armistice! You must not conduct yourself as if there was a famine in Vienna and you owned the last fried cat . . . Perhaps the restaurant business is not for you, after all. Perhaps we should put you into business. What is to become of you when I'm gone? Five years, now, I have been teaching you all I know, and you have been kicked out of seven different restaurants and are still a busboy! You play cards all night and never save a penny.'

And then one night Gèza Cseh, coming home to the room they shared, saw the old man sitting with his chin on his hands and his elbows on the tin cash box in which he kept his savings, his face like wet linen.

'What, home so soon, Papa Rasp?'

'Yes, I have got the sack.' Rasp tried to put a cheerful countenance on the matter; he even managed to get a note of triumph out of his cracked voice. 'Herr Politi himself dismissed me, as a matter of fact. He said, "My dear Rasp, you have for thirty-five years been one of my most valued assistants, but youth must be served and you are a little too old. The toilets will not be the same without you, but what can I do, my dear Rasp? But as a token of my appreciation of your loyal and efficient services I am seeing to it that you do not want in your old age. I have arranged for you an annuity of twenty-eight krone a month."'

'For what? For birdseed?' sneered Cseh.

'So I decided to leave Vienna and go to live with my nephew, who has an elegant little inn not far from Salzburg. He has often written saying, "Dearest Uncle Friedrich, you don't know how we need you, to receive the nobility and gentry who constantly patronize my little establishment on their way to and from Mozart's birthplace. Only the other day Prince Porfiry of Russia demanded Shashlik de Veau Grousinsky, and I didn't know what to say. Do come . . ." So I'll go at last and help the young people out.' This was a polite fiction: Rasp's nephew was a foul-mouthed drunkard married to a slatterny milkmaid with a goitre who had been debauched in a turnip field and got with child by her own grandfather; and his 'elegant little inn' was a reeking pothouse patronized by tipsy carters; and they had always regarded old Rasp with aversion, while he could not think of them without a qualm of disgust. He went on, 'So I was counting up what money I had put by. Seventy-five years old, and sixty-five of those years working like a fool; and all I could put aside for my old age was four thousand krone. That works out – you like working things out – at' – he did mental arithmetic, but the sum was too long for him – 'say, fifteen hundred insults a year for sixty-five years, four thousand krone for the lot; how much per insult? Still, I have eaten and drunk and slept in a bed, and had one or two good times. Gèza.'

'Yes?'

'If you needed money badly you ought to have asked me for it and not taken it out of my box.'

'I don't know what you're talking about. I never took a groschen of yours. All right, I borrowed five hundred krone. I had to get new trousers. I didn't like to ask. Why, if I thought you . . . If I imagined that every time I turned my back you went and counted every . . . Damn it all, if I'd meant to rob you, why, Jesus Christ! A thief would have . . .'

'Ssh! I was going to give you some money, anyway, before I left. It was foolish to keep it in a box, anyway; if you hadn't taken it, somebody else might have. It is just as you say, just as you say. Here, Gèza, take this thousand krone.'

Young Cseh shook his head. 'No. I'll pay you back the five hundred.'

'Take, take,' said Rasp. 'Where I am going I shall be fed on the fat of the land and want for nothing.' He thought, *I'll add a few krone every month to Politi's twenty-eight* – as *long as they know I have money coming in they'll keep me alive, unless Willy kicks me to death when blind drunk.* 'Kiss me goodbye, Gèza, and don't bear me any hard feelings just because you took a little money from me.'

Cseh took the money sullenly, with an air of affront, and crammed it into his pocket, and went out slamming the door. Old Rasp went to his nephew's place near Salzburg, where he lived in unendurable misery for another fifteen years. (There is nothing like unhappiness to ensure long life; go to bed praying that you may never wake up, and wake up hoping that you may never see the sun set, and you will live ninety years and greet Death saying, 'Better late than never.')

Cseh went to Rome, and thence, at Zobrany's expense, to London.

Now at that time continental restaurateurs and *hôteliers*, if they had made themselves any sort of reputation, could make money in London. As Cseh said, 'Look at Ritz! Look at Romano! Look at Gatti! Look at Kettner! Damnation, I know London like the back of my hand – all the money in the world is there – the city of London rules the earth! I speak English. I know the restaurant business' – he had been a busboy at the Albergo Inghilterra – 'I have contacts, plans, connections. What is Rome? Rome! I spit on Rome!' He spat.

Zobrany said, 'I am learning English, Gèza; but my politics are Classical Republican, and so I had thought of New York, Chicago, San Francisco –'

'– Oh enough, enough! Believe me, believe me, Zobrany *bacsi*, America is overcrowded, overdone, played-out, *gastado*, used up, *kaput*, *ausgespielt*, *foutu,* dead and done with, finished! Who goes to America? Peasants – shit-heel Bohemians, ragged-arse Polaks, Jews with whiskers, Irish scabs, Armenians, Romanians. God strike me blind – Syrians, Italian bricklayers, grape-pickers, nose-pickers, trencher-scrapers, arse-lickers! *No!* Now listen to me, Istvan – upon the grave of my mother, I swear to you that I will not rest until I have conquered England!' Tight-faced, white-knuckled, little Cseh swore an untranslatable, irrevocable, unprintable oath. 'I want those fat juicy golden English pounds! I shall get them and finance a Republican magazine. I'll fill a tub with slippery gold sovereigns and wallow in it with *Engländerinnen* basted with Benedictine and with apples in their mouths! *Nach* London, Zobrany, *nach* London!'

'America –' Zobrany began.

'– What is a dollar? *One-fifth* of an English pound –'

'– Calm, Gèza, calm! You are a poet, not a financier. A dollar is a fifth of a pound? So what then? A shilling is a fourth of a dollar –'

'– I do not think in small change. Enough!'

'Ah, now you're offended,' said Zobrany – born sucker – smiling in his conciliatory way. 'Let us hear your plan, Gèza . . .'

In the end he sent Cseh to London to spy out the territory they were to storm and sack. There was silence for a month. Then came a long letter in Cseh's Napoleonic handwriting, enclosing a kind of chart drawn after the manner of the ancient cartographers who decorated their oceans with whales and mermaids and galleons; for among other things, Cseh fancied himself to be an artist. (Could it have been the artist in him that most attracted Zobrany?) He had mapped a land drenched in the exotic, and musical with resonant names – Great Marlborough Street, Golden Square, Carnaby Street, The Quadrant, Regent Street. Where the ancient explorers might have put ivory, apes and peacocks, Cseh had illuminated his points of interest with men in silk hats, women in diamond tiaras, coaches and coronets. At the bottom, a compass with a smiling face in the middle indicated that this Eldorado was at the cornucopial West End of the city of London.

Ah, what a share-pusher was lost in Gèza Cseh! His letter, or prospectus, explained that he had managed, through the good offices of an estate agent whom he had got drunk, to find the one place in London which had been overlooked by the fools who had spent fortunes establishing such restaurants as the Criterion, the Café Royal and so forth. This place was going begging. Having its own courtyard, it was in a manner of speaking a *palazzo,* and it was at once aloof yet conspicuous; marvellously central and peripheral; at the same time accessible yet exclusive. It was named after the great lady who succeeded the Duchess of Marlborough as Queen Anne's confidante and companion. Masham Court! 'Say it aloud!' Cseh wrote.

Zobrany said it aloud. Little Gèza was right – it did sound good. He read on.

Cseh said he always had known that he was something of a man of destiny. Instinct had guided him – instinct illuminated by one of his lightning flashes of forked insight and intuitive foresight. There was a restaurant in Masham Court. As Cseh arrived in London on a foggy dawn 'like the fire and smoke of Austerlitz', the proprietor of this restaurant had died of a heart attack. With the breath of high bidders hot on his neck, Cseh had attacked the widow before her tears were dry, and secured not only this desirable property, but a lease on the house next door, so that they could establish not only an exclusive restaurant, but, if they chose, a small hotel.

Cseh felt bound to say that he had not procured a freehold. Freeholds in this neighbourhood were not for sale. But he had got a leasehold of ninety years. 'This should give us time enough to make sufficient to retire on,' he wrote. 'But time is of the essence. All you need to do is sign the enclosed document empowering me to act for you in this matter, and return it to me at the Langham Hotel, together with a banker's draft for one thousand pounds. Pack quickly, come forthwith (having wound up your affairs in Rome) and . . .'

. . . Even to this day, remembering with what haste he rushed out to send that draft for a thousand pounds, Zobrany blushes all over and itches from head to foot with shame. No faith like a fool's faith in a blind bet! But a thousand pounds was a great deal of money in 1911. Much or little, it represented half of all Zobrany had, after he realized his assets in Rome and came to London.

Tearful with eucalyptus which he was sniffing for a streaming head cold, half suffocated with soot and sulphur, and aching with the dreadful melancholy that strikes sensitive spirits when they find themselves alone and among strangers, Zobrany came at last into Victoria Station. (And even after a quarter of a century he has a womanish sentimental feeling for potted plants, which he tends to overfeed to death in cosseting them: he thinks he knows what it is to be uprooted.) But self-pity, like self-reproach, is retroactive. 'Thank God for that, or where would all of us be?' he says.

. . . There was always Gèza Cseh. Zobrany took a cab to the Langham Hotel – 'Where all the *Ar*merican millionaires stop,' as the cabby said, in recognition of the address. Nothing but the best was good enough for young Gèza now, Zobrany thought, with a fond smile. But at the Langham Hotel he was told at the reception desk, 'The Baron Cseh left the day before yesterday.'

He said, 'Gèza Cseh? From Rome? A gentleman somewhat under middle height, and rather pale?'

'Yes sir, the Baron Cseh,' the receptionist said. And, 'No, sir, the Baron did not leave a forwarding address.'

'*Baron* Cseh?'

'The Baron Gèza Cseh, sir.'

'Aie-aie-aie!' cried Zobrany. 'Can you please direct me to Masham Court?' He added, 'It is near Piccadilly.'

The receptionist called the hall porter, and the hall porter called a cab driver, who locked Zobrany up in one of those evil-smelling four-wheelers called 'growlers', and said, 'Yes sir, Masham Court it is, sir – right away, sir' – thrashing a ghastly travesty of life into an apocalyptic horse. 'By the way, guv, where *is* Masham Court?'

Zobrany tried to explain, in his untried academic English, with references to Cseh's chart. The cabby took him to a brothel in Panton Street. This proving to be the wrong address, Zobrany tried to explain that Masham Court was where people with diamonds were, and so the driver took him into Hatton Garden; and after that, in pursuit of silks and satins, to St Paul's Churchyard. At last, by way of all the devious and rain-washed winding roads of the twilight, they came back to Oxford Circus, where the cabby suggested to Zobrany that there was nothing like a quartern of hot rum for a runny sniffle.

Accordingly, they stopped at a bar, where the driver asked everybody, 'Where's Masham Court?'

Somebody said, ''E means Mitcham.' Somebody else said, 'No, 'e means Balham.' A third man said, 'Shut up, 'e means 'Ampton Court.' And at length a very old man said, 'Why, the poor gentleman means Pudden Bag Alley.' At this everybody knew exactly where Masham Court was, and the company in general was relieved. Zobrany ordered drinks all round, for he was relieved, too.

'But why, if you please, Pudden Bag?' he asked.

Some derelict shorthand writer who hung about the police courts by day and ran strange errands by night explained, 'The bag, sir, cooks boil puddings in, sir, has a way in but no way out except the entrance.'

'A cul-de-sac?' Zobrany asked.

'Quite right, sir. A blind alley, as it were. The name of Masham Court is not remembered, but if you had asked for Pudden Bag Alley, or The Road To Hell, these people would have understood you in a moment.'

'To Hell? But why The Road To Hell?'

'Because that's the name of the pub on the corner,' said five men, chiming in each to each in a fugal way.

'Then it must be a very bad place?' Zobrany asked.

'No, not a bit on it,' he was told. 'A very nice place.'

'Then why Road To Hell?'

The shorthand writer said, 'Because its proper name, sir, is The Good Intention. The tiles in the passageway are printed *Good Intention;* and as the saying goes, "The road to hell is paved with good intentions."'

Zobrany consulted his notebook. 'Is there, if you please, a restaurant there called Beau Séjour?'

The old man said, 'You must mean Greasy Kitty's?'

'Better known as Dropsy Kate's?' another man asked.

The shorthand writer said, 'The gentleman means Dropsy Kate's. She took the coffee shop over from Old Mother Cancan. I think she died . . . Are you a doctor, sir?'

'No,' said Zobrany. 'Why?'

'Nobody in a whole suit of clothes goes to Dropsy Kate's but a doctor, a lawyer, a copper or a priest. You having a velvet collar to your overcoat . . . if you ain't a doctor, though, you might want one round there if you don't watch out.'

The barman said to the cabby, 'The gentleman looks white, like. Take him to jolly old Hell, if that's where he wants.'

Back in the cab, Zobrany was thankful for the eucalyptus and even for the cold he had caught: they camouflaged the shameful fact that he burst into tears; from which he took care to protect his moustache with a silk handkerchief . . .

THREE

Since Masham Court was there, at the other end of Carnaby Street, people loyal to the neighbourhood argued that it was there for a purpose, and assumed that it had some reason for existing. Similarly, in ancient times, churchmen disputed the matter of Adam's navel with the artists. Not being born of woman, Adam had no umbilical cord; having no umbilical cord, why should he have a navel? Would the artist accuse God of superfluity? On the other hand, the painters protested, the human abdomen looks unfinished without a belly button, although it is good for nothing but to collect dust.

Masham Court was there because it was there – an architectural blind gut, if you like; a contractor's oversight, a bricklayer's miscalculation, a glossed-over redundancy. It had not been a mews, since no stables had ever been there that anybody knew of – the entrance was too low and narrow to let a horse through, let alone a coach. It was nobody's right-of-way. In diagram it would have looked rather like a small pair of bellows with a long bent nozzle. The nozzle was the entry to the Court, which was arched. A cobbled pavement led in about fifteen yards to a pear-shaped cobbled yard, at the widest part of which stood five narrow houses, all stuck together – five distinct houses of five different heights crowned with remarkable chimneys; earthenware chimneys in graduated clusters like foul pan-pipes, chimneys like hammerhead sharks, tin chimneys like skyrockets tipped with cones, slatted spinning chimneys which screamed like seagulls, forked chimneys, chimneys locked lip-to-lip like lovebirds, 'smoke-proof' corkscrew chimneys interlaced and one chimney which went out and down and up again like the leg of a dead dog.

The brickwork and stucco there had a quality which would have put you in mind of those novelties advertised as Serpents' Eggs: you touch a grey pill with a lighted match and with a splutter it swells, oozing a great leprous worm of ashes which looks solid but falls to dust at a touch. And by some quirk of air currents Masham Court really did seem to act in the manner of the bellows its shape suggested – or rather, perhaps, like a choked air conditioner for the immediate neighbourhood. It sucked foul air in, retained most of the cruder elements and sighed the rest back, half-filtered. The bracketed gas lamps at the two ends of the passage and the lamp-post where the houses huddled cast no more light than an electric fan makes coolness in a sealed room. They merely buzzed, stirring up the shadows.

When Zobrany at last dismissed his cab at the corner, he wanted something to put heart into him, and so he went to the public house known as The Road To Hell – The Good Intention. *Let it be like something drawn by Gustave Doré!* he thought, desperately. *Let me go the whole hog, and be damned!* He was sick and tired, and dreaded the moment when he must confront his doom and face it down.

So he thrust open the frosted glass door of the saloon bar, and strode in – and stopped, amazed.

The saloon of The Road To Hell was furnished in massive and sombre magnificence. The fixtures were of old mahogany, elaborately carved and adorned with brass. Bevelled mirrors intricately engraved with scrollwork at the edges hung in great gilt frames. The gleaming bar was buttressed by groups of brazen fauns with copper grapes in their mouths, and the spittoons reminded Zobrany of the story of one of the Counts Esterhazy: in a box at the Opera in Paris he kept blowing his nose between his fingers, onto the carpet; an attendant respectfully brought him a superb mahogany cuspidor; the Count said, 'I warn you, if you don't take that thing away I am likely to spit in it.'

A cheerful fire was blazing in a brass-trimmed grate, where a round copper kettle bright as a witch ball was whistling under its breath. The landlord, a burly old man with stern blue eyes, bulldog-jawed and broken-nosed, sedate in white sidewhiskers and looking wonderfully warm in a long red waistcoat, came forward and said, 'Good evening to you, sir. And what is your pleasure?'

Zobrany said, 'Frankly, I am cold and tired and without courage. Allow me to sit by your fire, and bring me what you please.'

'Take off your topcoat, sir, and let me hang it up for you, and I'll bring you a good glass of brandy-and-water, hot, with a lump of sugar in it . . . From foreign parts, I fancy?'

'This is my first visit to your charming city, my friend, and I am lost. Lost!' said Zobrany. 'Will you do me the honour of joining me in a glass?'

'I thank you very kindly, sir, and I rather think I will,' the landlord said. 'Allow me to make you welcome. If you'd care to take your boots off and dry your feet, I can get you a clean pair of warm slippers.'

'You are too kind.'

'Not a bit . . . I'll bet you a second glass I can tell you where you come from. I flatter myself I can always guess. Austria-Hungary? Am I right?'

'You have excellent powers of observation, sir. I am.'

'Oh, there's quite a few Hungarians hereabouts, don't you see – not gentlemen like yourself, but tailors and jewellers mostly. Although there is a customer of mine who's a baron. The rank is but the guinea's stamp;

the man's the gold for all that. A good spender, the Baron, but not born to the salt as they say – which I can see you are.'

'A baron, you say, and Hungarian?'

'Well, he's on a visit from Rome, sir – or was. Every day he had his bottle of champagne and his plate of sweet biscuits –'

'– Champagne and sweet biscuits! Is he, by chance, a very little nervous person who makes with his hands as if he is getting rid of dusty cobwebs, and speaks as if he is afraid he will fall down dead before he has finished what he has to say?'

'That's well put! He is, sir, he is.'

'Then do I guess rightly if I say that his name is Cseh?' Zobrany asked.

'You do, sir. The Baron Cseh.' Their glasses being empty, the landlord refilled them.

'So he is now a nobleman?' said Zobrany.

'Yes, that's right. Do you know him?'

'I think I do. I thought I did. I hope –' Zobrany took a sip of his hot brandy-and-water. 'What was his business here, if I may ask?'

'Oh, he was looking after some business for an old family servant of his – what you might call a dependant.'

'Isteném!'

'Pardon?'

'It is a general kind of expression. His servant, upon my soul! Cseh!'

'Why, you're quite pale,' the landlord said. 'Drink up and have some more. I'll stand drinks, if you'll allow – or even if you don't allow, because I don't take "no" for an answer, you see. As I was saying, the Baron bought the lease on a bit of property in Masham Court, here. It was going for five hundred pound. If he'd had patience I could have got it for the Baron for four hundred at the outside. It isn't in the best condition, and on a repairing lease; and between you and me, the Court has had a pretty bad reputation this past two hundred years or more. But the Baron was in a hurry to leave. He said, "Fifty or a hundred pounds is nothing to me. As for the place – to the fellow I am giving it to, it will be a palace." He said, "I tried to discourage him. I wanted to set him up with half a dozen pigs and a cow and four acres of land. But no, the poor fellow must come to London. The lower classes are tyrannical and stubborn," he says, "especially when they think they have a claim on you." So he settled before he left for America.'

'And for which part of America, may I ask?'

'Bless your heart, sir, I hope I'm not one to ask personal questions of the gentry. He didn't say.'

Zobrany asked, 'As a matter of curiosity, does this Baron Cseh – he should have added a *de*; de Cseh would sound better – does he owe you money, by any chance?'

'Only a trifle,' said the landlord. 'He came in to change a hundred-pound note. I didn't have that much about me, so I accommodated him with a fiver. He'll post it on to me. He said he would.'

'May you and I and those we love live to see that day,' said Zobrany, solemnly drinking. 'But this is all my fault. On my head be it. I have no doubt that he said if he did not post the money, you were to ask his servant, who would be given instructions to pay – something of that sort?'

'Why, how in the world did you guess? He said it would be attended to by a party of the name of Zobrany, the new tenant of that load of trouble over in the Yard.'

Zobrany said, 'I know that man.'

The landlord said, 'By the Baron's account, a clumsy-built person who looks at you like a spaniel dog that's just made a mess on the mat. Whiskers like a kudu's horns and a voice like a cherimoya – whatever they may be.'

'No, is that what he said?'

'Those are his words, sir; though what kind of animal a kudu is, or what a cherimoya sounds like, I haven't the faintest idea.'

Now for all his wretchedness Zobrany had to laugh. The brandy was beginning to work, and the most noticeable effect of alcohol on Zobrany was that it slightly exaggerated the outlines of life, making them comical. It was an embarrassment to him that the graver the situation, the harder he had to struggle to fight back laughter. With a couple of drinks taken, he stopped fighting and let himself go. Slapping his knees with his big hands he cried, 'No – a kudu!'

And then he threw back his head and let out such a guffaw that the landlord had to laugh with him, saying, 'Well, by God, sir, I like a man who can see the lighter side of things! But I don't quite catch the point of the joke. Or does kudu mean something funny in Hungarian, perhaps?'

'The joke is me. I am Zobrany. I am the joke.' Then, taking out Cseh's map, he told the whole story, and said, 'As surely as I live I shall have this put in a frame and look at it every day of my life!' After that he took out his purse and put down five pounds in gold, saying. 'Cseh was right. A fool is always a rascal's servant. I *am* Cseh's servant, therefore. Allow me –'

'– Damned if I take your money, sir! If he fooled you, he took me in, too, don't you see . . . And he's not a baron, after all?' The landlord sighed.

'If he is a baron, then I am a graf, a count. He is a busboy; he is not even a waiter; he fills water glasses and sets out hot rolls.' Zobrany then said, 'Kudu!' and laughed again.

'Count,' said the landlord – for come what might, he was not going to be done out of his title – 'Count, my name's John Howgego, and I like you. Shake hands . . . You don't want to go and look at that property by gaslight. We'll make an evening of it, and you shall walk across after breakfast tomorrow; for here, by jingo, you shall eat your supper and spend the night. You are a gentleman, and I shall be happy and proud to call you my friend.'

'Thank you, I shall be proud of your friendship, Mr Howgego.'

At supper – poached salmon with shrimp sauce and a bottle of still champagne, roast saddle of mutton and a bottle of old claret; a bit of cheese, a bite of dessert and a bottle of port – Zobrany asked, 'What is it that is so awful about this unfortunate restaurant, the Beau Séjour?'

'Count,' said Howgego, 'let us not spoil a pleasant evening. Change the subject.'

'This is superb wine, Mr Howgego.'

'I keep a good cellar for self and friends, my dear Count.'

'I have never eaten better mutton, my dear Mr Howgego . . . I am strong enough to hear the worst, I think. Come, let us make light of it. Let us be happy!'

'Your health, Count. Let's talk about kudus. I always thought a kudu was a kind of bird.'

'No, that is a dodo. But now that I come to think of it, a cherimoya is a Spanish fruit. It is also the name of a sort of squeaky bagpipe,' said Zobrany.

'I thought it might mean something like Jeremiah.'

'Ah, he was a melancholy prophet! . . . Touching the matter of which –'

'– Tomorrow,' said the landlord, 'tomorrow we'll be sober.'

'After all, my dear Howgego, the premises are a concern of mine,' said Zobrany, in an insinuating voice. 'No, really, eh?'

'Your Beau Séjour belongs to the morning after. This is the night before. Eat, drink and be merry. Tomorrow you're in for it,' said Howgego. 'Count – I drink to your better acquaintance . . .' The old man was intransigent.

'*A la vôtre*, dear Howgego . . .' Zobrany's voice was wavering, and his words trod on each others' heels. 'But I am a Magyar, and there is nobody in the world more obstinate than a Magyar.'

Howgego pressed his broken nose flat against his broad face and said, 'Do you see this conk? Do you observe my snitch? Tom Sayers' knuckles have been here, and Jem Mace's likewise. I'll out-obstinate anybody in London and Westminster, and I'm old enough to be your father. Come, try some old cherry brandy for your digestion . . .'

In London, as in all great cities, prowl certain ageless outcasts who live in and out of the garbage pails and refuse bins which they pick over stealthily in the deadest part of the night. Sometimes they trundle discarded baby carriages with two wheels of two different sizes and four different shapes, in which they keep sacks crammed with the devil knows what. The clothes they wear are rags the very beggars have thrown away as being too contemptible even to inspire pity.

These prowlers are of indeterminate sex. Some, with wispy beards, may be women; others, beardless, were born and baptized as male. The anarchy of despair sports the uniform of a sort of graveyard suffrage. Having come to this, you wear a gruesome bark of stratified and fragmentary jackets, jerseys, wadded newspapers, overcoats under waistcoats and sacking over all; the whole kept together with strings, tapes and even nails or wooden pegs. You don't beg; you scrape the streets for the beggars' leavings, between midnight and daybreak. For all we know, you have your pride, and will not be seen; but just before dawn you may be found at the doorways of the rag-and bone shops, carrying bags of empty bottles, horsehair out of abandoned mattresses, scraps of waste fabric from the dressmakers' shops, fragments of brass. Having a few pence you buy methylated spirits and get cacodemoniacally drunk – with impunity, since no policeman will touch you for fear of isolation, fumigation and ridicule.

You are at liberty . . .

. . . Zobrany, looking wildly out of the window of the bedroom in which he passed his first night in London, having awakened out of a vinous sleep, saw what seemed to be a bundle of rags with five legs and two heads crawling over the cobbles below. Shuddering, he found his trousers, took out a few pieces of small change and threw them down. As the coins struck the stones the creature split and became a scavenger and his wife: the fifth leg was a stick spiked with a nail.

Is this a good omen? Zobrany asked himself, making a Sign against the Evil Eye – although he was a rationalist and a freethinker, as he thought. (It is rational to make the Sign against the Evil Eye – two fingers extended like Horns represent the Horns of the Dilemma; one says, in symbol, *Dilemma, I, too, have horns – go elsewhere!*) But he was depressed at the breakfast table – kidneys, bacon, eggs, a Yorkshire ham, a round of boiled beef, muffins, a cottage loaf, tea, coffee, a cold roast grouse, a jug of bitter beer and a smoked haddock seethed in milk

– and whenever he managed to draw a deep breath he felt like a strong man in a sideshow who is getting tired of the business but must break a steel chain by expanding his chest every so often. 'Take a glass of sloe gin,' said Howgego. 'Do, now!'

Zobrany's moustache was then in its glory, and so was he in 1911 – silky and springy – as he gave it a twirl and a flourish, and shot his cuffs, and sipped his glass of sloe gin (which was attributed with encouraging qualities in the good old days) and lit a cigarette.

'By George, I wonder at your spirit, and I like you for your temper!' cried Howgego, in his archaic way. 'Wait a bit and I'll come with you.'

'No, my kind friend, no,' said Zobrany. 'Nothing is lost, nothing at all, whatever happens.'

'You'll come back, though?' Howgego asked.

'Of course.'

'I'll stand by, you know?'

'Indeed.'

Then Zobrany dashed across Masham Court and plunged right at the Beau Séjour without looking to either side of him. He stopped short as he caught a whiff of burnt fat. Zobrany, a man whom it was hard to put out of temper, was angry. Such a stench in the neighbourhood of a restaurant infuriated him – it was the stink of a conglomeration of several deadly sins; of Sloth above all – and it acted upon Zobrany somewhat as the reek of Fear acts upon a good dog. His neck prickled. There was palpable evil, there was a blasphemy of Waste in that burnt fat. Zobrany reasoned: *Miners wash their hands, ploughboys scrape their boots, sewer men sluice their legs, whores rinse what they have to offer – then who dares to let a restaurant smell like an* auto-da-fé *and an act of expiation?*

Already this place was sending Zobrany a challenge in terms impossible for him to ignore – spitting in his face and defying him to run away. He stood four-square and defied the building with his eye. He knew now why those two garbage-pickers had filled him with such a melancholy presentiment. It was his doom to undress the Beau Séjour rag by putrid rag; to strip her to her scabby skin and scrub away the patina of two hundred years of ingrained grease and filth; to attack her with brushes and swabs in every hole and crack.

And, as surely as if the walls had become transparent, he saw the insides of that house; every room with its layered petrifications of paint upon paint, and its strata and substrata of cheap wallpaper pasted slapdash over rotting wallpaper to form an unholy combination of cardboards which kept the plaster from coming down like so much spoilt pastry – and the house after the plaster, for all he knew. Yes, he would have to scrape right down to bone and cartilage, if he stayed.

If? Zobrany asked himself. *What do you mean, 'If'?*

If he had been a man to analyse his feelings, Zobrany might have found at the back of his mind – strangely enough – more of grief for the loss of his friend, crazy little Gèza Cseh, than any other sense of loss. So he found himself thinking, *Aie-aie-aie! – Poor fellow, why did he have to run away? A fool and a stranger in this huge, misty, terrible city, somebody made a fool of him. Poor Little Napoleon – he mustn't be in the wrong. He would rather Steve Zobrany thought of him as a swindler than let me think of him as having made a fool of himself. Oh dear me!*

And these thoughts made Zobrany feel better.

The window of that deplorable restaurant would be described as 'quaint' nowadays; but in 1911 it was nothing but old-fashioned in a poverty-stricken way. Shopkeepers had such windows because they could afford nothing better. It was a frame of mean little oblong panes of greenish glass, all distortion and bubbles. The woodwork was of that all-absorbing, melancholy tint known to house painters as 'light red' – the cheapest of all colours, the hue of squalor and of lost endeavour.

Art has its diatheses as well as pathology. If a man's face turns green he is likely to lose his breakfast; if his face grows blue he is likely to lose his life; but if the paintwork of his shop turns light red, with blisters, it is more than likely that he is about to lose hope. Light red is made by pouring the rusty heel taps of tins of paint left over from more lucrative jobs into a rusty can, and thinning the whole with turpentine. The result is invariably of the hue of mud, blood and soot. You have only to look at such a colour to see a sad tableau:

A drunken, hopeless jobbing painter and paperhanger, unemployable on account of a palsy caused by premature senility and too much heavy ale swallowed to dull the pangs of lead poisoning, haggles by lamplight with a haggard housewife worn out by childbearing, who does all the talking while her husband, wearing a waistcoat but no jacket, a watch chain without a watch, and a celluloid collar without a tie, stands in the shadows sucking a drowned rat of a moustache . . . Now, mum, a nice shade of blue? . . . Oh no, no, blue shows the dirt, and comes too dear . . . Well, a sweet shade of red, then? . . . Oh no, no, red's flashy, and comes too high . . . Well, what about a charming shade of green, then . . . Oh no, no, no, green stands for Envy, and anyway they can't run to it . . . Well, why not leave it to the painter? When he says he'll do a belching good hicupping job – by burp ('Oops, manners!') what he says he stands by. But how about half a quid on account? . . . Oh, all right, all right, seven-and-six it is – let's have the three tosheroons, then . . . In a frightful aura of ale, linseed oil, turpentine and the sweat of ages the shuddering painter reels, retching, to the nearest pub, while the shopkeeper and his wife stand in the doorway twittering. Who knows? Smartened up, the shop might sell to a blind widow as a Going Concern.

And it always comes out Light Red.

Zobrany pondered this Study in Colic.

By a kind of hopeless and whorish window dressing, somebody had made a silly effort to hint that the gastronome might find fresh and juicy viands in the Beau Séjour. There was a plated cruet stand and a metal pot of wax roses; a section of a log painted to look like a Stilton cheese, flanked by half a dozen plaster cutlets tinted with the dregs of that sad light red, and two crockery tomatoes on a papier-mâché platter; a mitred napkin, a setting of real knives and forks, two candle-sticks, a dish of oyster shells with a wax lemon, an empty magnum of champagne, a fishing rod and creel and a print of a jolly old cardinal with a napkin at his throat smiling voluptuously. This window wore a négligé of pink net tied with red ribbon. The glass door was similarly curtained.

The woman who owns this place is a foul slut . . . This was Zobrany's thought as he opened the door and went into the Beau Séjour.

The world will end before he forgets the long, low, fetid room in which he found himself. There were tables with cast-iron frames and marble tops, such as used to be favoured by the keepers of poor men's eating houses because they were too heavy to steal, required no cloths, showed no dirt, and might be wiped with the corner of an apron. The woman inside had also a smeared look, and an air of having just made herself presentable by brushing dirt out of sight under her skirts. *This,* Zobrany thought, *is Madame Nollekens.* He regarded her with a certain awe, she was so vast and looked so old. It was not that she carried with her any of the stigmata of a lived-out life. Simply, as one might say of an oil painting found in an attic: the subject matter was neither here nor there, the work was so-so; but the antiquity was unquestionable. *It would not be enough simply to give her a wash,* Zobrany thought, *she must be scraped, restored . . .*

'Good morning, Madame. My name is Zobrany,' he said.

'I don't know what you're talking about.'

'If this document is in order,' said Zobrany, producing it. 'I think I am titularly proprietor here.'

'I can do you a cup of tea if you'll wait five minutes, if that's what you want.'

A foul vision came into Zobrany's mind: of this dirty-watery woman kept on the premises to *do* cups of tea. He said, 'Excuse me. Are you Mrs Nollekens?'

The woman shouted, '*Alma!*' and then said, 'I ain't Mrs Nollekens. She'll be down in a couple o' minutes. I'm doing the dishes. She's doing 'er 'air. I can do you a cup of tea if you like – or a coffee, if that'll do you.'

'Thank you. I will wait if I may.'

'Do.'

Then Alma Nollekens came in by a side door.

As Zobrany said a little later, when he was sufficiently master of himself to make sense – or at least, to be half articulate – 'Life is full of surprises. This was as you read in the Arabian Nights: a poor fisherman opens a carp and finds in its bowels a pearl. A hungry widow kills her last hen to make soup for her dying child, and finds in its gizzard an emerald. A forlorn Arab kisses his horse farewell – and . . . it does not lay a golden egg, but something happens.' Zobrany was in a state of high exaltation. 'A miner, giving up hope, digs a grave for himself, intending to lie down in it and blow his brains out; but he strikes a vein of gold.'

'Fancy that, now,' said John Howgego.

'It is like a true story I heard. In New York City there was a person who pretended to sell a solid gold sixteen-jewel watch wrapped up in a hundred-dollar-bill, for only twenty-five cents. This was supposed to be an Introductory Offer to advertise his watches. Only, you understand, he did not sell real watches and hundred-dollar-bills for twenty-five cents – he showed his prospective customers a genuine watch and a genuine bill, but this valuable package was attached to a piece of india rubber, so that at a touch it flew up the salesman's sleeve and a spurious package took its place. Now a simple country lad offered his last coin in exchange for one of these packages, and at the critical moment the rubber band broke and the lad received the genuine package. The salesman did not dare to protest for fear of the incorruptible police of New York, whose vengeance is swift and terrible. The country boy started a railway with the money and was kind to the poor. The cream of the story is, that his own twenty-five-cent piece was counterfeit!'

'Go on, go on,' said Howgego.

'In Budapest, out of the subsoil in the ear of a nun sworn to lifelong abstention from washing, there grew a white lily. Then –'

'– Candidly, Count, I don't know what in thunder you're talking about. You're feverish, that's about the size of it. What you want is a quartern of warm ginger brandy with a teaspoonful of cayenne pepper in it – put your feet in mustard-and-water as hot as you can bear it – lie down with a hot-water bottle and sweat it out. In the morning, a dose of salts, and later a good breakfast and a glass of cherry brandy – though, after the salts have worked, some favour a cold roast pigeon and a bottle of port to settle the inside.'

'But is it possible, my dear friend, that you have lived in this neighbourhood so long without noticing the beauty and charm of Mrs Nollekens?'

'What, young Alma Nollekens? You're joking, Count,' said old Howgego. 'What *you* want is a glass of old brown sherry and a bite of lunch –'

'– Why should I be joking? What is the matter with the lady? What do you know of her?'

'Keep cool, Count, keep cool. I don't know anything I could say against her. Only I'm surprised at a gentleman like you – a gentleman that's seen life abroad, and all that – getting excited about old Nollekens's relict. You're such a cheerful kind of man –'

'– The lady is not a relict. I am not cheerful, I am a very serious kind of man. But even if I were – what of it? Is the lady in question uncheerful?'

'I don't know,' said Howgego. 'What's cheerful? A state of mind. Is laughing cheerful? Not necessarily – I hate a man that laughs too much. What I like about you is, when you laugh you really mean it. My grandfather was one of the cheerfulest men I ever knew, but the only time he was ever known to laugh was up North when His Majesty King George the Fourth was opening an Exhibition and his arse got stuck in the seat of a patent water closet. Laughing is touch-and-go. It can catch you on the solemnest occasion, sir.'

'True. A mayor gets up to make a speech and his trousers fall down. But we were speaking of this lady, Mr Howgego.'

'Well, she grins a lot, I'm told –'

'– Excuse me. It is a sweet formation of the lips. The Divine Sculptor's chisel stopped at a certain point. God said, *Enough – this is it!* Believe me, He knows when to stop. *Paf! – Right on the dimple! Perfection is good enough for Me,* said God. *And how do you like that, Michelangelo? How do you like that, Titian, Botticelli?* And all the great masters who are in Paradise because God has forgiven them their sins for the sake of their art, shouted *Wow!* Even Rembrandt and Rubens – who knew this type of beauty very well indeed – slapped God on the back and jumped for joy. Then –'

'– All right, all right, all right! . . . You just now referred to God. You'll be a Roman, I suppose? Those Nollekenses were rank Methodists.'

'What is that to me?'

'You believe in the Trinity, I dare say?'

'No, no, quite the reverse,' said Zobrany.

'What *is* the reverse of a Trinity, as a matter of curiosity? Sort of Minus Three? You've been in Rome – what's your opinion of the Pope?'

'This is no time for theology, dear Howgego. Go on with what you were saying.'

'Well, the only time Alma Nollekens was known to laugh out loud was at the deathbed of her husband,' said Howgego.

'What of it? I laugh whenever I hear the low note of a bassoon – I don't know why. Laughing is sometimes a way of crying.'

'Very likely, but it got her the name of being heartless. There's a time and a place for everything. I'm repeating only what people said in the neighbourhood, mind you. It was like this: Old Nollekens was a miserable, hypocritical, white-faced ranting Methodist. Live and let live, though, I always say.'

'Just so. "I hate every word you say, but I will defend to the death your right to say it" – Voltaire. And as the Russians say, "Some love the Pope, others the Pope's wife." So?'

'Well, old Nollekens was one of these here licensed fornicators. You know: "Lips that touch liquor shall never touch mine," and all that sort of thing. But they dash from chapel to bed in a shower of fly-buttons and sing, "*Up, up, up – higher, higher, higher*" to the tune of the springs. That was old Nollekens's kind –'

'– Pig!' said Zobrany.

'To look at him, you'd think there wasn't a teaspoonful of juice left in him, but he buried four wives, the dirty old dog. Nearly got himself into trouble once for slipping it acrost a sixty-year-old pew-opener when she was bending down to pick up a hymnbook, although some said she led him on, she being another of 'em. And I shouldn't be surprised, because the women are worse than the men at that kind of game when they get saved; and Nollekens liked 'em fresh and new-laid. Catch 'em young, treat 'em rough, and tell 'em nothing – that was *his* password.'

'Porco! Dreckschwein!'

'But pray? The bugger could pray the hind leg off a donkey. However, young Alma was the daughter of a decent sort of Belgian widow woman, an embroideress. I mean an embroideress who actually embroidered – not one of *those.*'

'One of those what?'

'Why, every morning they have 'em up for soliciting if they can't afford to slip the copper half a crown. Name? So-and-so. Profession? Embroideress. By the same token, your sneak-thief is always either a Journalist or a Salesman. Well, the widow's name was Meeus, and she died a matter of a year ago leaving Alma all alone, age eighteen, and a debt of three months' rent. Old Nollekens was sixty-seven at the time, but he ups with a slimy smile and marries young Alma presumably in lieu of rent.'

'Filthy *salaud*!'

'Yes, my dear Count, it was a trifle off-colour, especially when he started bashing everybody over the head with the Bible, about how

King David revived himself for the Lord's work in his old age by means of nude girls . . . They're like that, you know. There was one of 'em near here had up for incestuous relations with his daughter and two granddaughters – and *he* quoted the example of Lot, chapter and verse, and called the beak a blasphemous sodomite, what's more. They Bibled *him*! So, to cut a long story short, two days after the wedding old Nollekens was taken ill with a stoppage, or a strangulation, or something, and since he wouldn't go to hospital he was laid up at home. Well now; it seems that John Wesley, or somebody, feeling his end approaching, said to his friends, "See how a Christian can die", and piped up "Nearer My God To Thee"; after which he snuffed it with a sweet smile on his venerable chops.

'So the time came when old Nollekens felt it was all up with him. He got himself propped up with some plump pillows, and said, "See how a Christian can die", and called for "Hark The Herald Angels Sing".'

Here, Howgego became suffocated with laughter, and had to revive himself with a glass of brandy. Zobrany asked, 'What happened?'

'A miracle happened. All of a sudden, an old cuckoo clock that hadn't worked for two years, went off. *Cuckoo – cuckoo* twelve times. That was when Alma burst out laughing.'

Zobrany said, 'No, I mean to say – Cuckoo, cuckoo!' and slapped his knees in delight. 'You were there and you didn't laugh?'

'I held it back, I held it back. I covered my face with my handkerchief and pretended to sob. But when, after the clock had finished cuckooing and the bird sort of collapsed, and Nollekens let a kind of almost human-sounding high-pitched fart and passed away, I had to rush downstairs and across the Court or I don't know what I might have done . . . It was the expression on his face, if you understand what I mean.'

'And for this the lady is heartless?' Zobrany asked, laughing.

'Did *I* say so? It was what the others said – they must have been made of stone, not to laugh. And I can tell you, even now, if I feel low-spirited, all you have to do is say to me, "Hark The Herald Angels Sing – Cuckoo", and it cheers me up at once . . . Now seriously, Count, what are you going to do about that there property?'

'I must clean it before I can even see it, my dear Howgego. The situation is very far from hopeless. I redecorate, of course. I renovate. I put the kitchen in the basement and make of the two ground-floor rooms one large room to accommodate eighteen small tables and a coffee bar. My decor will be something quietly picturesque. A background, for there will be pictures in due course, photographs of distinguished customers, works by aspiring artists. An artistic enterprise, good conversation, dominoes. My menu, cosmopolitan. I can provide tasteful lunches and dinners quite cheap, and give good value.'

'You'll get the riffraff, at first, you know.'

'Howgego, riffraff goes to the riffraffery. Do you get the riffraff? No. Friend, a café is no better than its proprietor.'

'You never said a truer word,' said Howgego, 'but it wants experience.'

'As luck would have it, I was cast into the restaurant business at a tender age. Experience I had, in Budapest, Vienna and Rome.'

'The carriage trade, most likely,' said Howgego. 'You'll get a pretty rough lot around Masham Court, you know.'

'Oh, I can deal with rough people if I must. I have found that the best way is to pick them up, put them outside, turn their faces in another direction and push.'

'I don't doubt it,' said Howgego, looking at Zobrany's powerful torso. 'What's your weight?'

'In pounds? About two hundred or so, I think . . . I think poor little Cseh understood me better than I understood myself, and was really doing me a great service when he trapped me into coming here!'

Howgego looked at him closely. 'You've got what the fighters used to call *bottom,* Count – you can take your punishment and make an advantage of it, and I honour you for it! You're game, sir, you're game, and I love you for it! . . . But what you propose', said Howgego, 'takes money.'

'I have a thousand pounds, almost.'

'No more?'

'No more.'

'And you were going to put down a fiver out of your capital to pay that dishwasher's debts, was you?'

'What has that to do with the matter?' Zobrany said. 'I cannot see an honest man lose by my foolishness. The liability was mine, sir.'

Howgego said slowly, 'I like a man that accepts a liability. Now look here. You'll want a sight more than a thousand pound if you're to start off with clean feet, as they say. I've been a sporting man in my day, and I live by my feelings; I know a game-plucked one when I see him. I'd lend you as much as you wanted, only I promised my father I'd never lend money.'

'Your father was perfectly right,' said Zobrany.

'I promised my father I'd never back another man's bill, or I'd back yours at any bank in the country. Only I never go back on my word.'

'Your father was wise and you are quite right.'

'But count on me, old fellow, for whatever you need,' said Howgego.

'Howgego,' said Zobrany, 'I will not be a party to your breaking your promise to your father. Do I make myself clear?'

'No, you don't,' said Howgego brusquely. 'And you could hurt my feelings if you weren't careful, Count. Did I say I'd lend you money or back your bill? I've always kept my word. But I don't remember promising my father, or anybody else, that I wouldn't chuck my money down the drain if such was my fancy. I say, you can count on me for whatever you want. I'm a Briton; I said it, and I meant it – and talking of sediment, I've decanted a magnum of sound old port, and we'll drink to ourselves on that.'

Zobrany groped for words. 'But . . . but what you say is not businesslike, nor reasonable. You know me one day only. Does one trust someone one has known less than twenty-four hours?'

'Certainly. Trust on first sight or never at all, if it comes to trusting.'

'Like love?'

'Oh, blow that!'

Zobrany expostulated, 'No, but I mean, you should be more prudent. You trusted Cseh. He cheated you, eh? I trusted Cseh and – the poor little vain fellow let himself be cheated as my representative . . .'

Smiling, Howgego said, 'You can't bring yourself to admit that the little man is nothing but a common thief – can you, now?'

Zobrany said, 'Dear Howgego, look here. What if I *am* reluctant to admit this? "The sea is wide, the boat is small – God have pity on us all," as the Portuguese say. Just now you mentioned a matter of five pounds I put down for little Gèza Cseh. Legally, I was not bound; morally, I was obliged. We will say, if you like, that Cseh was a trickster. Yes, but if Cseh's behaviour was dishonest, remember that mine was foolish. Mr Howgego, in business it is better to trust a thief than a fool.'

'Oh – cuckoo!' Howgego filled two glasses. 'Count, I've been a licensed victualler for fifty years, mind that. I've been right in my time, and I've been wrong. But one thing I've learnt, and that's how to know a man when I see one. So; you're set upon this here café of yours, are you?'

'Yes, I am.'

'You mean to clean house, turn the place upside down and inside out and make a going concern of it, don't you?'

'Such, Howgego, is my firm intention.'

'All right. I know your sort, Count. I know bottom when I see it. For all your friendly ways, you're stubborn.'

'My dear Howgego, stubbornness is in the nature of the true Magyar.'

'And did I mention,' said Howgego, touching his nose, 'that Sayers' fists have been on this smeller?' He put this forward as an argument. 'Hark The Herald Angels Sing –'

'– *Cuckoo!*' said Zobrany, laughing and shedding tears at the same time.

And burly Jack Howgego, grinning to the hinges of his jaws and looking like a boiled bulldog over his old tawny port, found pleasure in seeing the big stranger sparkle and ferment; although he knew that the yeast in this fresh effervescence was Alma Nollekens who, he feared, was not in Zobrany's class.

FOUR

Scratch a reactionary, find a revolutionary – there is no innovator more enthusiastic than a conservative tickled in the right spot. Howgego's heart had been touched. Thirty-six hours earlier, he would have given you nine good reasons why the Nollekens's property was not worth touching with a barge pole, and might have quarrelled with you if you had an apologetic word to say for it.

Now it was Zobrany who had to say, 'Howgego, not so fast!'

Suddenly, the old publican saw Masham Court in a new light. When he seemed to go mad with glory and began to plan gilt bow windows and crimson plush settles, secret entrances and private little damask dining rooms with naughty silk sofas, it was Zobrany, the outlander, who cried, 'Little by little, my dear fellow, not all at once! Rome was not built in a day –'

'– This isn't Rome.'

'Howgego – everything to its place and moment. Would you try to comfort a crying baby with a cigar? I plan peace and comfort, solid, for my time. Do you understand me?'

'Damned if I do.'

'I will put it another way, dear friend. *My* place must be first and foremost my *own* place. I dare not therefore bite off more than I can chew. Fifty years from now, let it be said, "In Zobrany's there was peace and quiet, and a good time." This shall be my monument and my reward: given a happy evening, somebody must say, "I am reminded of Zobrany's in 1911." You are right: this is not Rome. Rome is a rubbish heap. Zobrany's *shall* be built in a day . . . but small and secure . . .'

Howgego turned this over in his mind, and asked, 'Are you sure you're sober, Count?'

'I am intoxicated, but not drunk, my dear Howgego,' said Zobrany, 'and my English is not fluid . . .' He patted Howgego's cheek. 'But you are right about the bay trees; we must have two little bay trees in green tubs. And a sign – you are right there again – we must have a fine sign to put outside our place.'

Howgego said, 'Hark The Herald Angels Sing –'

'– *Cuckoo*!'

They clinked glasses and giggled.

'Wait till you see my cellar book – Count, you shall have a wine list fit for a monarch! . . . What shall we call the place?' Howgego asked.

'The Cuckoo? That's vulgar. The Angel? That's the name of a pub in Islington.'

'At The Sign Of The Angel And Cuckoo?' Zobrany suggested.

'It don't signify – whatever you call a place, here in London people are bound to call it something else. The Black Swan becomes The Mucky Duck,' said Howgego, 'The Infanta Of Castile becomes The Elephant And Castle; The Bacchanals becomes The Bag O' Nails; The God Encompasseth Us becomes The Goat And Compasses. I've made a study of it. But if it's a sign we want, I know the man to make it for an honest price. Only I'm afraid he's a bit of an artist, if you know what I mean.'

'My dear Howgego, I love artists of all sorts. And a friend of yours is a friend of mine.'

'There's this to be said – he lost his arm fighting the French in '70.'

'Never mind. In Art there is a spiritual brotherhood. The artist says, "The World is my country, Humanity is my people and Beauty is my religion." Let us go to him at once!'

'He lives shabby, with a woman out of wedlock –'

'– *Vie de Bohème, vie de Bohème* – Art is its own morality.'

'He's had his misfortunes. You see, he was a patriot –'

'– He loved his country. He is an artist; therefore he loves. Let him be a German if he likes –'

'– And he's only got one arm; he lost the other one.'

'Let him have no arms, dear Howgego. If you like him, he is the artist for us,' said Zobrany, mellow with wine, love and friendship.

And old Howgego, who would normally have questioned the mental competence of anybody who ordered a sign before he had a shop to hang it out of, got his billycock hat and his gold-topped bamboo, and said, 'Come on, come on, what are we waiting for?' He left a man whom he introduced with a certain irony as his manager in charge of the house, saying to Zobrany, 'This is Lovely Joe Shelduck, The Pride Of Kent, who has fought five champions.'

'And won, no doubt?' said Zobrany, looking at Lovely Joe – a grotesque, a grisly pastiche of an old pugilist with an obliterated profile and a herringbone-stitched seam for a mouth, who blinked under cicatrized eyebrows.

'Never in his life. He's cost me a matter of two thousand pounds . . . But you meant well, didn't you, Lovely? And then you woke up.' Howgego chuckled. 'He's better than a pair of bull mastiffs to guard the house, though; and, being human, he don't require affection. *He* can't be hurt. But I thought he was going to turn out to be another Nonpareil, once upon a time. Eh, Lovely?'

Lovely Joe Shelduck nodded.

'He'll let you knock him down, for a shilling,' Howgego said.

But the old fighter had his pride. He muttered, 'If the genelman's a friend on a friend, the genelman can knock me down on the house.' And offered his jaw.

'He's got a good heart,' said Howgego affectionately.

So Zobrany and Howgego walked to Poland Street, in Soho, where the one-armed sign-painter Fritsch had his studio in a basement. Here were littered petrified splayed brushes and pots of inspissated paint, hopeless ends of wood and impossible cuttings of cardboard. The artist was watery and fat, limp and disheartened; but he smoked shag in a red clay pipe and wore a velveteen beret. With something like the titter of a boon companion who demonstrates an innocent-looking picture which, folded over, makes pornography, Howgego whispered, 'They aren't married, Count.' The object of his attention was a tall thin woman in a sackcloth apron. She, surprised, put her hand to her mouth and said, 'Oh my,' and disappeared.

Fritsch's basement was an easy place to disappear in, for it was dark except for such light as trembled on the yellow tips of five fingers of flame at a gas bracket. The place stank of coal tar and turpentine, glue and socks, beer and tobacco and burnt bloaters, mice and femininity slightly gone off under flannelette; and above all hung the miasma of a swamped drain. But Fritsch was toying with a kaleidoscope. As Howgego and Zobrany came in he said, in a ponderous tone, 'So, this machine produces Design from the Haphazard and from Asymmetry, Symmetry. From Chaos, Cosmos. Ach, here is something of God!'

From somewhere in the shadows a light, sneering voice said, 'Mirrors, mirrors, mirrors, you bloody fool! God is a mirror, Infinity is two mirrors. So you make God in your own image, Fritsch. Ha-ha! Infinity – shit! Beads and mirrors, you one-armed idiot! Fritsch, like a gnome of many-coloured arse, blinks at the radiance of Eternity. Get out, you twot!'

Howgego said to Zobrany, 'That's young Hardy, Fritsch's apprentice.'

And now there came lurching into the wavering light a tall thin boy with the crumpled, malevolent face of a mountebank. His mouth was triangular and clownish, and there was wanton caricature in the exaggerated weariness of his demeanour; a look of putty and buckram about his nose and forehead; satire in the bagginess of his trousers and scorn in the absurd abbreviation of his flannel jacket. Zobrany said to himself: *Aie-aie! When a boy of seventeen makes such a travesty of himself, proper pride has gone underground and Malice is showing its teeth!*

Fritsch shrugged. Howgego took out a five-shilling piece and handed it to the boy, saying, 'Get us a bottle of Old Tom and an ounce of red shag.'

Young Hardy made a foot and darted out. Howgego said, 'Fritsch, if I had that boy about I'd tan his arse till it was red, white and blue.'

'I somehow do not think you would,' said Fritsch. 'He is a *Wunderkind,* a genius. What can one do?'

'Is he learning the trade, at least? Is he useful?' Howgego asked.

Fritsch shrugged.

'What is he hiding?' Zobrany asked. 'There is a sad boy!'

Fritsch shook his heavy head. The boy came back with the bottle of gin and the screw of tobacco.

'Help yourselves,' said Howgego. 'And here's what my friend the Count wants. Only don't forget that he's just before he's generous, and knows Art, so let us have that much clear.'

'*Ah*-greed,' said Fritsch. 'Speak!'

'Go on, Count,' said Howgego impatiently, 'go on.'

Zobrany drew a deep breath and said, with many gestures, 'It is impossible to convey. This is for the Artist. An angel, and a cuckoo. Candidly, I have never seen a cuckoo. Perhaps my friend Howgego has seen a cuckoo?'

'No, I haven't,' said Howgego. 'Nor have I seen an angel, not yet. Fritsch, you know what a cuckoo is?'

'It is a bird,' said Fritsch, 'but I have never seen one.'

'Well, you know what an angel is supposed to look like?'

'Now *this* I know,' Fritsch said. 'A being celestial, winged, sublime.'

The old handicapper Howgego said, rubbing his hands, 'Four wings, two creatures, one bird – I'll lay seven to two Fritsch sorts it out; three and a half to one –'

Then the boy, who had been listening attentively, stood up and sauntered to the door. 'Forget it – I've got it,' he said, going out.

Howgego looked at Zobrany and said, 'Well – eh?'

Fritsch said, 'Give me a little something on account, and let me see.'

Giving Fritsch a sovereign, Zobrany whispered to Howgego, 'Let us go. We shall have our sign, my inner voice whispers.'

So the one-armed sign-painter settled down to his bottle of gin and his screw of red shag, while his clients walked home to Masham Court and the wild boy Hardy went flying away into Oxford Street.

Anybody who happened to notice Fritsch's mad apprentice rushing down Poland Street would have said, 'Here is one young man with a positive objective – here is a chap who knows his own mind.' Passers-by made way for him. Nothing but trouble could come of getting in this one's road, for he would go through an oak panel, to say nothing of fire and water.

Young Hardy was resolved, not to kill an enemy and rescue a heroine, but to walk across Hyde Park to Kensington and look up cuckoos in the Natural History Museum. And as he marched he thought how strange it was that although everybody was ready enough to talk about cuckoos, and people wrote to the newspapers every year claiming to have heard the first cuckoo in spring, and the Summer-Is-Icumen-In merchants had made specious songs about that monotonous bird for the past six hundred years, you never met anybody who had actually seen and handled a cuckoo.

How big was a cuckoo, for example? What was its colour?

It seemed to him that a cuckoo ought to be about five inches long, with a very large brown head, a knowing eye and a speckled belly. 'It lays its eggs in other birds' nests,' people said. *It*. Nobody ever thought of a cuckoo as being male or female; although necessarily the female laid the eggs and the male, most likely, did all the singing. He saw the cuckoo as a sympathetic sort of bird, poetic and improvident: it sang, had fun, condescended to visit birds of the middle class, said, 'Oh – mind the baby while we're gone,' and was off down the warm streams of the beckoning air. Hardy visualized the cuckoo with its claws on the mantelpiece, so to speak, drinking out of an acorn cup, taking life easy, spitting all over the place. (He remembered, as a matter of fact, that a certain frothy substance found in hedges is commonly known as Cuckoo's Spit.)

Even then, young Hardy liked to be knowledgeable in out-of-the-way matters, for he had already learnt that an ounce of valueless but amusing information is worth, conversationally, seven pounds of working knowledge. And, dour as he seemed, this boy liked to impress you, one way or another. Yesterday Hardy had been interested in the wanderings of the mad painter Monticelli; tomorrow it might be numismatics; today it was cuckoos. He made haste, for there was always the danger that his hurry might be over in midstride. For the city was full of sudden side issues, sideshows, sidetracks and distracting images inimical to talent on the hoof . . . A man goes to Kensington to look up cuckoos; but then a horse falls between the shafts of a cart, a bill-sticker starts pasting up a poster and must be watched until the last sheet is slapped home, a woman beats a man, a man beats a woman, a coalheaver disputes right of way with a milkman, an organ grinder's monkey is attacked by a cat – there is no limit to what may happen to wayward genius on the way to its objective.

For example: Hardy was very nearly diverted forever from his purpose by the sight of a policeman blowing his nose. Candidly: how often do you see a policeman blowing his nose? Still, Hardy walked faster, so that at the corner of Oxford Street he collided with a snub-nosed boy in a powdery apron, who shouted, 'Watch where you going, can't you?'

'Why, it's Gus!' cried Hardy.

'Tom Hardy! Wotcher, Tom!'

'What cheer. Where are you going?'

'Farringdon Road. Come with for a walk?'

'No, I can't. I've got to go to Kensington. I've got to find out about cuckoos.'

The other boy said, 'No you ain't. You don't want to go to Kensington to find out about no cuckoos. Come up Farringdon Road. I'll tell you about cuckoos.'

Hardy shrugged. Gus was an ornamental plasterer's boy, and there was no telling what might be learnt from him. But he said, 'You bloody little liar, what do you know about cuckoos, anyway? You never saw a green leaf in your life, let alone a cuckoo.'

'I bet I know more about cuckoos than what they know round Kensington, any road!'

'Get out!'

'All right. I bet a bob they never ate a fried cuckoo. I did.'

'You bloody little liar!' Hardy cried, delighted. 'You didn't!'

'Straight,' said Gus amiably. 'In Kent one summer when we was 'opping. I buzzed a stone at a bird and knocked it down. A gyppo gel says, "Ah, you dirty *gaja* cockney *chavvy*, what do you want to scale a stone at a cuckoo for? Thirty years' bad luck, and serve you right, and may you die in a bloody sweat, you sod!" So me and my brother Arthur fried it on a shovel and ate it.'

'Liar! . . . What did it look like?'

'Like a pigeon, with black-and-silver marks.' Gus said. 'I took the wings back to my mother and she put 'em in 'er 'at.'

Hardy said, 'Oh yes, I bet – a cuckoo in a hat! What sort of a beak did it have?'

'Curved.'

'Oh, what a terrible little liar you turned out to be, Gus!'

Equably, the other boy said, 'It's all the same to me, Tom, but I should think a gyppo gel ought to know a cuckoo.'

'Well, what colour were its eggs?' Hardy asked.

'Have a heart. You knock a bird down with a stone, and fry it on a shovel – Christ, you don't ask it to lay you a couple of eggs to go with it! But 'bout eggs: me and my brother went birds-nestin' one time and we got thirty-three swallows' eggs.'

'Yes, I dare say – and fried 'em on a shovel, eh?'

'Well, we fried twenty and 'ad ten each, but the other thirteen we took back to Mum, and she ate 'em all but five which was addled . . . Ever eat a live tadpole?'

'No. Did you?' Hardy asked, fascinated.

'Yes.'

'What was it like?'

Gus said, 'I didn't actually bite into it, but it tasted a bit like worms.'

'What do worms taste like?'

'Kind of like mould, sort of.'

'Did you bite into worms?'

'No, but live worms and bacon rind's a sure cure for a sore throat,' said Gus. 'Only you mustn't chew 'em.'

'Are you sure they don't charm warts?' Hardy asked, with a sneer.

'No, a maiden's piss cures warts – while fresh. Cold, it's no good.'

'You bloody little liar – did you ever try it?'

'No, but my father did.'

'And it cured his warts?'

'Well, no. Dad 'alf-killed my young sister when it didn't,' said Gus, imperturbable.

'Wasn't she a maiden, then?'

'She was entitled to be – she was only seven.'

'So your father's still got warts?'

'No, 'e died of enteric fever in the Boer War.'

Hardy said, 'I bet if they dug him up the warts would still be there.'

'Knowing the old man, I wouldn't be a bit surprised . . .'

So Hardy walked with Gus to Santini's sheds, near Blackfriars.

Santini the ornament maker was eating, without appetite, a black cigar. He frowned at them as they came into his powdery yard, and shouted, ''*Sto* bloody Gus! Whaffor you comea ina '*sto* bloody shop widda '*sto* bloody waster?' Then he said to Hardy, 'You – get outta my sight.'

Hardy asked, 'What have I done wrong, Mr Santini?'

'*Meh!* You get ona my nervous – go 'way!'

Always the one to smooth matters out, Gus said, 'It's all right, Santini, Tom only wanted to know if you could make cuckoos –'

'– Don't, Gus, don't – I told you Santini couldn't make a cuckoo coming out of an egg,' said Hardy, winking at the other boy.

Taking his cue, Gus said, 'And I told you Mr Santini could. A cuckoo. A cuckoo's like a pigeon or a dove, ain't it, Mr Santini?'

'Maybe yes, maybe no. Why?'

'I say, if a man can make a dove he can make a cuckoo,' said Gus.

Hardy shook his head, saying, 'No, no, not coming out of an egg, surely?'

Santini said, 'But whaf*for*, Jesusacrisake?' He shouted at Hardy, 'And fora you special – in sheet I makea cast. Ah, *shar*rap!'

Hardy said, 'You couldn't make a cast of an egg, hollow, I bet.'

'Hollow!' said Santini, with scorn, 'Ah, shar*rap*!'

'Now look, seriously, Santini,' said Hardy. 'Say I took a bladder and blew it up tight. Say you made a cast of it then, and afterwards let the air out of the bladder and pulled it out – what would you have?'

'I have sheet. Sharrap!'

'No, no – you're bound to have a hollow ball of plaster.'

'So? So it break. Finish. Sheet. Go 'way.'

Hardy persisted, 'Then it must be a special kind of plaster, surely, Mr Santini . . . Now look, take a balloon, the kind people fly in. Blow it up and cover it with this special kind of plaster.'

Santini was a stern, hard man, but he could not help laughing. He got out a great flask of wine and some cheese, and said, 'Fill you mout' an' sharrap, maestro, crissake! What comes is sheet, fool!'

Hardy went on, 'I don't mean an entire balloon, a whole balloon. Half a balloon, and you spray the plaster on in layers. A special sort of plaster that dries fast. You let the air out, and there you've got an igloo like an Eskimo. Eh, Santini?'

Santini was above all a craftsman. He said, 'An egg is an egg. Is an *egg* – right?'

'The strongest of natural forms,' said Hardy.

'That's right,' said Gus.

'You sharrap!' Santini warned him, eating hard cheese with a chisel. '. . . Listen you, Eskimo-eggs. How thick an eggashell?'

'That's neither here nor there,' Hardy said.

'Is, *is*! Gawdamighty makea limit: so much, no more. Other way, it crack.'

Hardy said, 'Never mind God – I wasn't talking about making houses out of eggshells.'

'An egg is to get out of, nota get into,' said Santini. 'So an egg is make strong from the outside, weak from the inside. An' widda limit. A certain size . . . An eggshell is strong for an egg, no more. You – balloons!' He laughed.

But Hardy said, 'Consider a bubble, a soap bubble. It's a Universe –'

'– Look, genius, maestro, snotty-nose – Gawdamighty makea limit. A bubble is a round. Blow a bubble too much, it go flat – and pop! . . .' He wanted to say, *An egg big enough to live in would want a shell six feet thick*, but his English wasn't up to it, so he said, 'You makea a good house from outside in. No bubbles, no eggs. Sharrap!'

Hardy sighed. 'Well, could I have another drop of wine?' Here was one of his peculiarities: he was proud, but he liked perversely to beg for unconsidered trifles. A mouthful of wine, a piece of string, the stump of a pencil – all was one to Hardy, so long as he had talked you out of it. Now, his restless eye was scanning the rubbish heap at the back of Santini's yard, and there he noticed a broken plaster pigeon. 'Santini, you don't want that busted out bird over there, do you?' he asked.

'Yes,' said Santini, pouring him some wine. 'Sharrap!'

Hardy looked at the flask. 'It's all very well to laugh at bubbles,' he said, 'and it's all very nice to talk about things being made from the inside out, or the outside in, or vice versa. But what is that flask but a bubble, Santini?'

'Take a cheese,' said Santini, enjoying his cigar and his glass of wine. 'Lissen, why you don' work asteady, makea regala pay money? You clever boy, you got hands – why not?'

Hardy said, 'It's all very well for you to talk about bubbles, and all that, Santini – but what do *you* know? The world is a bubble, and it was spun from the outside in. That Chianti flask is a bubble, and it was blown from the inside out. Honestly, given the right material, there's a balance of pressure; given the right pressure there's a balance of material . . . Santini, give me that broken old bird over there, will you?'

'What for you wannit?'

'Nothing.'

'Ah, take, take!' said Santini.

Now Gus put forward this observation: ''Ow do a chicken make an egg? Don't it kind of coat it with a skin and then plaster over that?'

'Sharrap!'

'I am shuttin' up. All I ask is, don't it?'

Santini cuffed his head. Hardy picked up the broken plaster pigeon, which had neither wings nor tail, and stuffed it into one of his tattered coat pockets.

'Why you no worka steady, makea regala wage? Why not, eh?'

''E's an artist,' said Gus, in his reasonable way.

'I am working,' said Hardy, touching his head. 'Up here.'

Then he walked out into the Farringdon Road, and as he went he caressed the broken pigeon from Santini's rubbish heap, and thought, *Talk is the secret – talk rings around 'em, that's the way* . . . He loved that long and dreary road, with its barrowloads of unwanted books and marvellously variegated junk. He looked up *Cuckoo* in a dictionary at a bookstall, and, sauntering on, stopped to look at the heaped handcart of a red-eyed old man who sold oddments of broken timber. There, half hidden by a spillikins-pile of assorted beading carved with meanders and guilloches, lay an object which instantly engaged his interest. Somebody had broken up some preposterous old Flemish sideboard, all angels and pineapples and cornucopias, which must have looked like half a Gothic cathedral; and here was one of its outcroppings in the form of a corpulent cherub, execrably carved, with a dove sitting on his head and a little tray on the uplifted hands.

Hardy said to the dealer, 'Hallo, Harry . . . My God, man, what d'you call *that*?

'That's a very wallible orlament.'

'Valuable ornament my foot! It's indecent. They could have you up for showing a thing like that in the open street.'

'Don't talk wet, young 'un – that's a religious orlament,' the old man said. 'It's a angel. See them wings?'

'Talk sense, Harry. Tell me honestly, did you ever see an angel with a prick like that?'

'Never you mind. Where's that ninepence you owe me for that shelf I let you 'ave?'

'I've got it here,' said Hardy, who had expropriated eighteenpence from Howgego's crown when he bought the gin. He knew that old Harry dearly loved a little gamble. 'I'll toss you double or nothing for it.' He pulled out a penny.

'Right you are, then. Toss, and I'll call when the coin's in the air. Let it bounce, mind!'

Hardy flipped the coin. It spun up, twinkling. 'Heads,' said old Harry, just before it tinkled on the pavement.

'Heads it is,' said Hardy affably, 'and that makes one-and-a-tanner I owe you.'

'Come on, lolly,' the old man said, holding out his hand.

'In a minute. What are you going to do with that thing there?'

'That wallible orlament? Oh, you can 'ave it for 'alf a crown, and chance it.'

'What are you talking about? You expect me to carry that thing through the streets for half a crown? Give me five bob and I'll get rid of it for you.'

'All right, all right, gimme two bob and take it away.'

'I'll give you eighteenpence,' said Hardy.

'Cash?'

'Cash . . . I'll toss you double or nothing, if you like.'

'All right, I'll toss. Call while the coin's in the air,' the old man said, flipping up a halfpenny.

'Heads, and chance it,' said Hardy.

The coin came to rest with Queen Victoria's head uppermost. The old man said, 'Oh well, better luck next time . . . Where's the one-and-a-tanner you owe me?'

'Wait a minute, Harry! Let's get it straight. We're all clear on the cherub, right? I owe you eighteenpence – right?'

'Right . . . Want to toss double or nothing?'

'Your call,' said Hardy, spinning his penny.

The old man called heads, and won. 'That makes three bob you owe me. Come on, lolly – lolly up!"

'I'll come back this afternoon. I get paid today,' said Hardy, lying with an untroubled face.

'Hey! Where you goin' with that orlament?'

'You just lost it, didn't you?' Hardy shouldered the wooden cherub. 'I'll be back later and pay you, and I'll stand half a gallon all right?"

'Honour bright?'

'Swear on my mother's grave,' said Hardy. Then he walked back to Santini's yard. The Italian had gone to dinner, and Gus was sweeping the yard.

'What's the purpose of that thing, Tom?' he asked.

Hardy – now that he came to think of it – had no idea. So he smiled his clown's smile and said, 'Gus, be a pal and help me get this thing back to Poland Street.'

'I can't leave till Santini gets back.'

'Lend us your barrow, then – just for an hour.'

'I can't. Santini'd murder me.'

'I'll have it back in an hour.'

'Swear?'

'On my mother's grave,' said Hardy; adding with reproach, 'you ought to know that a gentleman's word is better than all these horrible oaths. Doesn't every pickpocket kiss the Bible? I give you my word of honour.'

'Well, all right, Tom. Only 'ave that barrer back inside the hour, or Santini'll 'ave my skin. But what d'you want to do with that there naked statcher?'

Hardy was nettled, now; Gus had spoilt his mood. He had not the slightest idea what to do with that naked statue – in fact, the more he looked at it, the less he liked it. 'Mind your own business,' he said preparing to wheel it away in one of Santini's little handcarts.

'I been thinking about what you was saying, about blowin' up a balloon –'

Hardy had forgotten. '– Balloons? I've got no time for balloons,' he said. 'I'm thinking.'

'Don't fail to be back in an hour, Tom.'

'I gave you my word, didn't I?'

The euphoria gone, young Hardy was depressed and irritable as he trundled the handcart back to Poland Street. He was ashamed, now, of this potbellied and macandrous carving he had so joyfully acquired.

Why do I do it? he wondered. *Why?* Old Fritsch was obscenely facetious about it. The woman said, 'Oh, my!' and tittered into her apron. When Hardy took out of his pocket the crippled plaster pigeon, Fritsch threw back his head and shouted with laughter – as well he might, having a pound in his pocket, a pint of gin left in the bottle, and half an ounce of acrid red shag unsmoked.

'You wait and see,' Hardy said.

'*Wunderkind,* superman – I wait,' said Fritsch.

'How much is that man going to pay you for this sign he wants?'

'Dis depends,' said Fritsch. 'Ve must make a blan, a schcheme. Take a bit gin, boy, schmoke a pipe –'

'– Leave me be,' said Hardy; and then he went to work on the deplorable cherub with soft soap and hot water, and with sandpaper both coarse and fine. Fritsch marvelled at such frenetic energy. Five hours later, when Fritsch went to bed, Hardy was still working under the paretic yellow fingers of the sick gaslight – working as vigorously as if he had only just started.

When Tom Hardy was taken with such a fit he felt neither hunger nor fatigue. At ten o'clock next morning Fritsch came downstairs to find the cherub cleansed, scraped and painted flesh-colour, all but the wings, which were of silver touched with black. The wooden boy's nails and lips were rosy, and his protuberant eyes were ultramarine. His hair was golden, and Hardy had touched the nostrils with pink and pointed up the dimples. The bird on the boy's head was grey flecked with black and silver, and had yellow eyes. The effect was at once slightly shocking yet curiously attractive – quaint, arresting, bizarre.

'And what is dis bird on her head?' Fritsch asked. 'Vere is its vunction?'

Hardy, who was working on the mutilated plaster pigeon, said offhandedly, 'The bird? Oh, the dictionary defines it as one of the typical genus *Cuculus* – *Cuculus canorus*, the European cuckoo, which generally lays its eggs in the nest of the hedge sparrow, meadow pipit or wagtail. As anybody may see, it is zygodactylous, like a parrot . . .' Hardy had a retentive memory for juicy words like *zygodactylous.* He had painted the plaster bird golden-brown. 'When this is dry, I'll give it a good coat of varnish.'

Fritsch said, 'It is garigadure, but it is not ardt. Anadomigally it is monsdrous. Der belly is for a woman, bregnant. Der benis is disgrace-vul – it is not ardtistig, it is too human.'

'Shut up,' said Hardy. 'Did you ever see a human being with wings like that?'

And two days later, when Hardy wheeled his finished work into Masham Court, Zobrany said, 'It is striking, yes. Pray explain it, if you will.'

'It's a young angel with a live cuckoo on his head, of course. And on the plate, a roast cuckoo.'

Zobrany was delighted. 'This is Mr Fritsch's work?'

'No, it's mine. What you do is, have it fixed to the wall over the window on an iron bracket. People come from miles away to look at a landmark like that.'

'Yes, I like it. It has a certain . . . is the word *bizarrerie*? Only, since the English are a modest people, do you think, perhaps, a wisp of drapery?'

'Don't be silly,' said Hardy, 'it's Art . . . Now why didn't I think of doing you a kind of paraphrase of Leda and the Swan? . . . If anybody complains, simply say, "Lady, that cherub isn't nude. Those aren't bollocks, they're sweetbreads – this is a high-class restaurant, not a knocking shop." Say something of that sort. The price of a thing like that ought to be twenty guineas. But we'll take a fiver – cash on the nail.'

'Is that sufficient?' asked Zobrany.

The boy replied haughtily, 'As far as I'm concerned, you can have it for nothing. I'm not interested in it any longer. What's a fiver to me?' He caught Zobrany's glance as it passed over his ruinous clothes, and said, 'I scorn the niceties of the toilet, if that's what you're staring at. The sign's free of charge. With my compliments. Good day to you!'

'No, no – wait!' cried Zobrany, catching him by the sleeve as he turned to go. 'How like you are to a certain old friend of mine, with your fireworks and your pride! Calm, calm! I honour the paint-stained coat, the inky hand. Five pounds is not much, it is too little – I mean no more than that. Here is the five pounds for Mr Fritsch. And you must not be offended if I add a pound for yourself. You will allow me?'

'Oh, all right.'

'Will you let me offer you some refreshment, perhaps?'

'Brandy.'

'Yes . . . Forgive me; are you not rather young to drink brandy at this hour of the morning?'

'What's it to you? Who told you how old I was, anyway? And what hour of the morning d'you mean? If I've been up twenty-four hours, this is the middle of the night as far as I'm concerned. And as far as I'm concerned, is all that matters. Keep your brandy. So long –'

'– Wait, wait,' said Zobrany, pouring a glass of brandy for the boy and another for himself. 'Aie, aie – you might be my Little Napoleon's English cousin, if he had one! Only you are really talented. And your name is Thomas Hardy, the same as the celebrated man of letters?'

'Celebrated man of arseholes! Have you ever read a book by Thomas Hardy?'

'No, but –'

'– Neither has anybody else. Nobody has ever got to the end of a book by Thomas Hardy. Didn't you know that? And I'm sick to death of being associated with that old bore. No, my name is not Thomas Hardy. I'm plain Tom, henceforth. Is that clear?'

'Tom Henceforth? I beg pardon, I thought I heard you called Hardy. Forgive me . . . Will you not nibble a sweet cake with your liqueur?'

The pride of Lucifer wrestled briefly with the appetite of Youth, and lost. The boy ate three sugar buns. 'Tom Henceforth is a very good name,' he said thoughtfully, with his mouth full.

'Indeed, indeed,' said Zobrany, 'and I am sure that you will make it a famous one. I love all artists. I hope to see you again, often, after I have opened my restaurant. Come as a guest.'

'Perhaps I'll paint you a picture.'

'When?' asked Zobrany.

'When I can afford the time and you can afford my price,' the boy said loftily.

'Well, my respects to Mr Fritsch, and my felicitations on a brilliant pupil.'

'You flatter Fritsch and you insult me. His pupil, for God's sake!'

'Oh, I beg your pardon. Simply, my kind regards, then.'

But the boy took Zobrany's money and left town. A week passed before Santini got his handcart back. In the meantime, honest Gus was dismissed with a backhand slap in the face in lieu of notice, and for some time mourned his wayward friend, saying, in his simple-minded way, 'Tom must've lost 'is memory – why else should 'e let a pal down? Or it could be 'e got run over.'

But Thomas Hardy, thereafter to be known to the world as Tom Henceforth, was in the best of health and spirits.

FIVE

As the renovated café took form, Zobrany paid court to Alma Nollekens. Now Zobrany – himself of a susceptible nature – had sometimes been almost embarrassed by the effortless ease with which he could arouse the amorous in women of all conditions. Some of his companions in Hungary, Austria and Italy had told him that, for a man so endowed by God with presence and charm, working for his living might be construed as a kind of blasphemy. One of them, a Slovak, said, 'Look at me. To make a girl appreciate me, I have to give her a good hiding – one in the stomach, a couple in the face, tread on both feet before she can kick, then a quick shove under the chin, petticoats over the head; and *allez-oop*! But you, Istvan, you've only got to walk into a room and they bust their stays, they break out in nipples like nettle rash and go red as fire and shudder from head to foot. Go into business, fool, and I can show you how to make a million.'

'No, thank you.'

'If it's not women, you understand – the Other Thing – you can make two million a year, with blackmail.'

'How would you like a kick in the teeth?' said Zobrany. 'You outrage my feelings, you pig!'

Still, he knew that what this fellow said – allowing for the exaggerations to which such types are prone – was based on pretty accurate observation. Women were attracted to Zobrany; in general, by his powerful but graceful figure, his genteel manner, his brilliant eyes and his interesting pallor; in particular, by a certain quality of warmth which made them feel somehow completely secure and yet mysteriously in danger. They could rely on his discretion; but he would certainly give them something memorable to be discreet about.

This inspired him with a vague uneasiness in female company because he had discovered that while he had the power and the will to please most women, with this power went the ability to hurt them.

At thirty, looking back, Zobrany sometimes feared his realization of this fact had come too late. He was still vain enough to half believe there was no woman with whom he had consorted, whom he had not emotionally ruined. How many women were gazing haggardly into their punctured futures, empty now because of Zobrany? With how many unlucky men was Zobrany at the present moment being compared? His imagination peopled entire clinics with Zobrany-hungry wives and their hopelessly baffled husbands who could not possibly live up to the standard he had set, of what a gentleman and a lover ought to be.

And this self-congratulatory remorse had set a certain restraint on his emotions, so that for all his dashing manner, Zobrany was of withdrawing habit.

Now he was in love.

Alma Nollekens cast a spell. She had him in a web. Zobrany, a thoughtful man who had picked up the jargon of debate, said to himself, *In what way is this girl different from all other girls?*

He did not know. She was beautiful, certainly. But was Beauty a sum of perfections? No: Beauty was a total, the whole of which was greater than the sum of its parts. Alma's imperfections – if she had any – served only to emphasize the total effect of a stunning loveliness.

You have known several girls, more beautiful, better bred and accomplished?

Another silly question, Zobrany told himself. Beauty, in itself, is something merely to look at and listen to; accomplishments are acquirements, no more. According to such standards, the mind of (say) Aristotle in the body of Lily Langtry with the manners (for example) of Queen Mary, ought to be something to fall in love with. Such a mishmash, however, would make a man sick.

What, then, do you know of this girl? Reason asked.

Zobrany replied, with icy calm, that if he had first seen her jumping through a hoop in a circus, or dancing the can-can without drawers in a cabaret, or naked and painted with limewash in an Exhibition of Living Statuary, his feelings would still be of an elevated nature.

Then you must be crazy, Zobrany?

So be it. I am crazy. And what are you going to do about it?

In such cases, Reason is wisest when it turns a blind eye and takes a holiday; otherwise it is likely to be kicked downstairs. So the romantic Zobrany and the sensible Zobrany kissed and became friends. It was a case of 'If you can't lick 'em, join 'em.'

In his conversations with Howgego, Zobrany had likened Alma Nollekens to the creations of such masters of the something-to-get-hold-of types of beauty as Rubens, Titian and Ingres. But when he observed her at close quarters it seemed evident to Zobrany that even such artists as these could never have done justice to her. The greatest of painters can imprison only one beautiful fleeting instant. And the three-quarters of a degree of curvature through an eighth of an inch of elongation at each corner of her mouth – which was as much of a smile as Alma allowed herself – contained an infinity of fleeting instants, every one of which was worth a canvas to itself. Then there was her serious expression, which involved a hair's breadth of frown and an infinitesimal deepening of the faint indentation in her upper lip, upon which grew a half perceptible shadowy down and who in the world was to catch that?

It was when Zobrany looked straight into her eyes for the first time that he was sensible of a shock that made him start, blink and look again. For her left eye was blue and her right eye grey. Either shade was delightful in itself, but together in the same face their effect was indescribably disturbing – ever so slightly sinister. Alma's eyes fascinated Zobrany so that, even at the risk of being thought unmannerly, he had to stare. Perhaps Alma was used to being looked at in double-takes or perhaps it was all one to her whether you looked at her or not. There never was a calmer, a more indifferent woman.

But Zobrany noticed that although she seemed to be perfectly still, she was in constant motion, slow and steady as the minute hand of a clock. Watching with Zobrany's concentration you could see her stroking herself, ever so gently. The fingers of her right hand would lie easily upon her left wrist, and from there move to the first joint of the thumb in a gradual exploratory journey that took a full five minutes; what time, slow as a sundew aware of meat, the tip of that thumb would curve inwards to make contact with the middle finger, while the third and fourth fingers curled to explore the plump palm. She engrossed, she hypnotized, stimulating one of your senses at the expense of all the others – literally, she was entrancing to Zobrany. If his mind was not occupied with the movements of her fingers, then it tottered on the brink of one of the dimples near her mouth; or waited timelessly for her to finish a sentence, she spoke so slowly and so low. And she was often occupied with a piece of lace which she was making on a hard cushion of black velvet, drawing a fine white thread in and out of a confusion of tiny fat-headed pins – and then she might have been a spider, or one of the Norns blindly spinning.

Although he drove them hard the workmen liked Zobrany for his kindness, and because he evidently knew exactly what they were required to do. The café was cleansed and extended. The party wall on the ground floor was knocked down, and the kitchen installed in the basement. He told Alma all about it. 'It will not be a restaurant of the first class, or the second class, or of any class. It will be Zobrany's, that is all. Moderate prices, an intimate atmosphere, a decent luncheon or dinner for a shilling. A sound bottle of wine, to be sent across the Court for a noble wine, if you can afford it, but never anything mean; my friend Howgego stocks no bad wine.'

'It sounds nice,' she said, 'but it's going to cost a lot of money, isn't it?'

He said, 'That can't be helped. Let it cost.'

'I'm glad you've got a lot of money,' said Alma. 'You gave me that impression when I first saw you. "Here's somebody who's a Somebody," I said to myself. One can always tell a proper gentleman from a bit of brassy.'

Even her vulgarisms were pleasing to Zobrany, as they came out in her slow contralto voice. He said, 'Madame . . . Alma, if I may so address you?'

'Of course, that's my name, isn't it?'

'Alma. Oh, what a beautiful name! Alma, I would not for the world have you regard me in a false light. A gentleman, you say? Well then, if a gentleman is as a gentleman does, call me so; but of my birth I have nothing to say. Nothing. My family were not rich, only brave and honest. All the sisters were virtuous and all the brothers were valiant.' He twisted his moustache. 'My great-grandfather was a captain of grenadiers, and fought at Eylau. But I have not got a lot of money, and would never mislead you into imagining so. But I am wonderfully lucky –' Here, Zobrany surreptitiously touched the wooden table top and crossed his fingers. 'I had not been in London twenty-four hours when finance came my way, if I wanted it.'

Indignant with himself for even so tiny a superstitious implication of doubt, he stopped touching wood, uncrossed his fingers and wiped them on his handkerchief, saying, 'At first I thought Little Napoleon had cheated me. No, no – I am in his debt. He led me straight to you. This alone makes me glad. As for money –' Zobrany snapped his fingers.

She said, 'Little Napoleon. Was that the funny little man called . . .'

'Cseh. Yes. We called him Little Napoleon, in Rome.'

She said, 'I thought he was funny.'

'You liked him?' Zobrany asked.

'Liked him? No. He looked right through a person as if he didn't care whether one was there or not so long as you paid him his commission –'

'– Commission? You paid Cseh commission?'

She said, 'He did get me five hundred when I'd have been glad to get three hundred and fifty. He was entitled to a little something. Ten per cent – an agent's fee.'

'Napoleon by name. Napoleon by nature,' said Zobrany. 'Ah, if only he had had an army to desert or a republic to betray, my little Super-Busboy!'

'He was a baron, but too proud to use his title because he had been robbed of his estates by a steward who married his mother and then murdered her – why, what's the matter?'

Zobrany was off in a gust of laughter, slapping his knees, and saying,

'No, really – that boy is priceless, he is good for me, he is a cure for hiccups!'

'It doesn't matter much, anyway, does it? What I was going to say was, Mr Nollekens left me four thousand pounds, with insurance, not counting the property. At five per cent that would bring in four pounds a week, and I could do nicely on that. But I could invest some of it with you, if you like.'

Zobrany said, 'Dear lady, I cherish the hope that you will come to know me – to know me intimately. But I am a total stranger. And you say, "Invest"!'

She said, 'Well, I shouldn't invest any money with you unless you married me, of course.' She said this as a banker might say, *Unless you find two sureties*, or something of the sort.

'Are you serious?' Zobrany asked, blinking.

Completely at her ease, she replied, 'Why not? I'm not a girl with fancy ideas, though people do say I'm not bad-looking. I don't have any chance to go out and about to places where a girl could meet somebody nice. I like to stay where I am. And you're the nicest person I ever met, and a perfect gentleman, though you may be foreign. In a way, I'm foreign, too. I was born in Belgium. I don't see why not, if you like.'

Zobrany stammered, 'I assumed you to be penniless, I assure you – a penniless widow; although I could not imagine you were a heart-broken one.'

'Heartbroken? Well, I'm not properly a widow because I wasn't ever actually a wife, except legally. Mr Nollekens wasn't a healthy man, bodily. He lived on medicine. I only married him because if I hadn't I shouldn't have had anywhere to go.'

'You see, my English goes on two sticks, it is lame; I was trying to find words to say, "Alma, I adore you – let us go through life . . ."' Zobrany began to stammer.

'All right,' she said.

And now what the devil am I to do? Zobrany wondered, at once enraptured and frustrated. *Clasp her to my bosom and – and what?*

Alma continued, 'In a way, I'm like a tree. I hate being pulled up by my roots – I'm afraid of moving. We can be ever so comfortable, once the upper part is done up, can't we? And you'll let me be cashier. You'd be surprised how hard it is to find a cashier you can trust. You want eyes in the back of your head, and the wages they want are unnatural! My auntie told me that's why restaurant people generally marry their cashiers, on the Continent.' And she picked at her lace-making.

'You were Nollekens's cashier?' Zobrany asked.

'No, he didn't keep a till; he put all the takings in his pocket, such as there were. He ran the place down, you know – begrudged a lick of paint, and the coffee was all chicory, and the tea was stewed.' Abruptly, she got up and put her arms about his neck, and whispered, 'Will you give me a bath?'

'Sweet Alma!' said Zobrany, 'I shall bathe you in milk of almonds –'

'– I mean a bath with running water. I hate to have to go to the public baths every week or so. I was brought up very particular, and there's room for a proper bathroom. One gets so tired of jugs and basins.'

'Dear girl, you shall bathe in pigeons' milk if you like,' said Zobrany, kissing her. He was pleased to observe that she was as ignorant of the give-and-take of the kiss as a Polynesian with a hibiscus in her ear. 'Pocahontas!' he murmured, 'Saint!' Blood drummed in his ears, and he saw as through a pink haze her startling eyes, one grey and one blue, which seemed to throb and become iridescent and throw out sparkling rings like carriage lamps seen in a moist twilight. 'I love you!'

Holding him, she said, 'And I'd like a new WC. One that works with a chain. The one here works with a plunger, and gets stopped up.'

'You shall have a water closet of solid gold and a chain of rubies! Guerlain shall fill the cistern with *Mitsukuo*, and you shall dry yourself on a roll of brocade!'

'Mr Nollekens was very mean about paper, and things. Let's get married soon?'

'At once! Whenever the law permits!'

'Let's get the house nice first. And I'm afraid you'll have to get rid of the Sordics in the attic,' she said.

He thought, at that time, that the Sordics were a kind of termite, rodent or bug, and said, 'I shall exterminate them.'

She said, 'Whenever Mr Nollekens tried to kiss me his teeth fell out. You've got nice teeth, and you smell nice. Mr Nollekens had an ulcerated inside . . . I'm so glad! Somehow, I knew . . .'

Zobrany wondered what she somehow knew, and why she was so glad. Was it that she liked him especially, or simply that she hated to move?

And he was destined never to find out.

That Alma was a desirable woman and an exciting woman could not be denied. She moved in an esoteric aura of refined lust. Her sensuality was so profound, so all-embracing, that it was incommunicable as a mystic's ecstasy. It was an extrasensory sensuousness – a self-satisfying, self-fecundating, self-stimulating state of orgasm that went on day and night, self-renewing and inexhaustible. She could never be quite at home to Zobrany, though, but half-absent at an intimate rendezvous with herself.

She fired him with an inextinguishable, smouldering excitement.

He rushed across the court to tell Howgego, who said, 'I don't say that a gentleman like you mightn't have done better for yourself, Count; but you might do a sight worse. So hearty congratulations, and let's have up a bottle of champagne!'

'I deny that I could have done better. She is as clever and virtuous and prudent as she is well-bred and beautiful!' cried Zobrany. 'Do you know, she never was really married to the vile Nollekens.'

'There was a chapel ceremony and a licence, and they even had a bit of a breakfast, of a sort. After a fashion. I sent over half a dozen sound old Madeira at six guineas the dozen, but Nollekens wouldn't touch wine. He sent it back and said, could he have the money instead. So I gave 'em an aspidistra stand I happened to have handy, with a decent old plant in a Chinese pot. But you, Count, you shall have a slap-up breakfast in my dining room, by God!' Howgego rubbed his shiny red hands. 'I've got a few Nebuchadnezzars of good champagne I've been saving for my funeral – all my friends shall drink their fill, for there'll be no moaning at John Howgego's bar when *he* kicks the bucket – but I'll spare a couple for you, and all Masham Court shall drink your health and the bride's!'

'You are too good, too . . .' Zobrany shed tears. 'What is a Nebuchadnezzar?'

'Why, champagne comes in half pints, pints and bottles. Two bottles make a magnum, two magnums a double magnum, two double magnums a Jeroboam, two Jeroboams a Rehoboam and two Rehoboams a Nebuchadnezzar. I'll be your best man. I'll stand breakfast, and we must buy the bride a pretty present.'

'Ah, yes, I must get her a bathtub and a water closet with a chain.'

'I was thinking of a brooch, or something. But mention my name to George Warne over in Golden Square, and she shall have sanitation fit for a queen . . . Drink up! Count – the King!'

They drank.

'The bride!'

They drank.

'Death to the French!'

'My great-grandfather fought Napoleon at Eylau –'

'– My grandfather was at the Battle of Waterloo. Long live the King of Prussia!'

'Forgive me, dear Howgego, but I cannot drink that toast.'

'You don't like the King of Prussia? All right, down with the King of Prussia, then!'

They drank.

Assisted by a Frenchwoman from Kingly Street who called herself Madame Alice, Couturière de Luxe, Court Dressmaker, Alma Nollekens was working on her trousseau in the renovated sitting room over the café in Masham Court. Zobrany was banished: it was not only because there were garments in sight, of whose very existence an unmarried man was politely supposed to be ignorant; when thus engaged, ladies had things to discuss which they would have hesitated to talk about even to their doctors.

So Steve Zobrany, always something of a visionary, light headed now with love in its most hallucinatory form, had thrown himself into the business of completing the restaurant with such frenetic zeal that the workmen tapped their foreheads and exchanged significant winks. Even good John Howgego, who was glad to have this contagiously enthusiastic fellow as his guest, growled, 'Count, if you don't mind me saying so, you're carrying on like an eighteen-year-old boy. I'm glad it never took me this way. I wish –'

'– Oh, *tele van avàros,* tum-te-tum-te-tumtum!' sang Zobrany. 'The town is full of acacia blossoms, te-tum-te-tum-tetum!'

'I wish the honeymoon was over. But I will tell you something, though, my dear Count. I didn't have the heart to say so, because it would've been like telling a baby that was enjoying itself at the seaside it was wasting its time making patterns with matched pebbles on a sand castle. Candidly, when you started actually cleaning and pointing the brickwork, I thought to myself, "This is about as practical as dusting the coals." And as for the clear green you insisted on having the woodwork done in, I said to myself, "Why, he might as well have put on white kid gloves on a drayman." But honesty compels me to state that the place is turning out truly picturesque, and I'll be damned if I don't give the old Road To Hell a coat o' paint just to keep you company and live up to you. And we'll have a drop of cherry brandy on that.'

'Thank you, thank you! After all, the house is to be my home as well as my little place of business. And green is Alma's favourite colour.'

'As long as she likes it, that's all right.'

'Howgego, Miss Nollekens is a timid girl. She has not been used kindly by fate. Sweet child, how does she know what she likes or does not? Who has ever consulted her taste hitherto? She needs security, protection, love . . .'

'She'll get all that from you, Count.'

'*Pour elle mon cœur, pour elle ma vie!* Howgego, she is as modest as she is charming –'

'– You told me so before, more than once, you know.'

'She is as sensitive as she is modest, she is sensible as she is sensitive and pure as she is ravishing, she is as anxious to please as she is innocent, and as capable of pleasing in every imaginable way as she is exquisite!'

'Couldn't we cut out the poetry, just for five minutes?'

'I am not a poet. Alma is a poem.'

'Oh aye, I dare say. You've got educated feelings. One man looks at a sunset and sees roses, another looks at the same sunset and sees fresh-sliced York ham. It's the imagination that does it, and you're the sort of fellow that could warm his hands at a cat's eyes in a cold fireplace . . .'

'Baxter is putting up my sign tomorrow.'

'*That*'ll give 'em something to talk about,' said Howgego. 'Old Fritsch tells me that boy of his never came back. Now there's a German for you, every time! I asked him, "What, he nipped off with the money, did he?" And Fritsch said, "What money? It was the boy's idea, not mine. I did not raise a hand. I am paid for my paint he used. I am entitled to no more." Catch a Frenchman talking like that, eh? Just for that I'm going to let him repaint my sign.'

'There are good Germans,' said Zobrany. 'And there are bad ones. I do not like that barber Himmelstoss.'

'The Germans are the best barbers in the world, Count.'

'I find it hard to tolerate that Prussian *ish-ish-ish* way of talking. And I had to stop him almost with force from giving me a Kaiser Wilhelm moustache. "You haf der raw maderial," he shouts, "it is a grime to on der lipper gewaste in effeminacy der mannlich gifters of Gott." No, really – effeminacy!' said Zobrany, caressing his fine drooping moustache. 'Then, gagging me by sticking his shaving brush in my mouth, he starts telling me how to make liver dumplings.'

'I don't know about liver dumplings, but I bet you if he was a Frenchman he'd put frogs and snails in your mouth and say "Wee-wee". Dumplings or no dumplings, when I was in there getting shaved just now, old Himmelstoss was talking about getting his place painted up, too. I tell you, Count, you've brought class to Masham Court. I knew you would, I said you would, and so you have done. Say what you like about the Germans, they're a practical people. He's going to have his place done in a grained mahogany varnish stain that'll last twenty years – you'll redecorate three times to his once. But a French-man'd tie a few paper frills on, and say "Polly-voo", and leave it at that.'

'Dear Howgego, for your sake Himmelstoss shall have dumplings!'

'That's the spirit, my dear Count! I can't stand the sight of dumplings myself, but live and let live.'

'Except Frenchmen and frogs.'

'Well, you've got to draw the line somewhere.'

'And now I must go to see Letterea in Charlotte Street, about my saucepans.'

The old man looked after him, shaking his head. He had tried hard enough to take Zobrany's mind off the state he was in, and had nothing to reproach himself with. To Howgego, love was a fever that called for cooling medicines; allowed to burn itself out, it was apt to leave chronic weaknesses. He sighed. The discerning onlooker sees most of the game: he had been young and now he was old, and he had yet to see love making a bad man better or a good man happier . . .

SIX

Madame Alice was none of your phthisic spinster seamstresses, but a hard-eyed, soft-spoken, smart little woman, a woman of taste who had been maid to one or two fashionable kept women in Paris in the early '90s, and knew the world. She still had a gliding tiptoe walk and a habit of listening intently while you talked, holding her breath and parting her lips in a knowing and expectant smile, eavesdropping at your mouth as at a keyhole. She was ugly – not plain, anything but homely. As Zobrany had remarked, 'Madame Alice is like a Bulgarian goulash: the toughest bits of the beef in a sauce of liquid fire – all pepper and garlic and onion and dill and fennel and red wine. Once you have burnt out your taste buds with it, honest meat has no flavour any more.' She was probably about fifty-five years old, and looked forty, but gave it out that she was eighty – she had preserved her body and her power to attract men by the use of herbs and charms, difficult to prepare but available at a price. She could tell fortunes by cards 'in the secret way Napoleon brought back from Egypt'; or with tea-leaves 'by the secret Chinese method of the late Li Hung Chang'; or read palms 'in the mode of Abyssinia'.

Her interests were various. She knew all the ladies' maids in Mayfair and Belgravia, and did a steady trade in remodelled Parisian 'exclusives', slightly used tortoiseshell and silver combs and brushes, remarkable hats and evening slippers. She could remake corsets and invisibly darn silk stockings and cashmere scarves; diagnose a pregnancy at five weeks. Sometimes veiled women visited her little house in Kingly Street and stayed several hours; it was whispered that one of the brass plates on her door which said PATERSON: GENTLEMEN'S BESPOKE BOOTMAKER was nothing but a blind, and that she had a couple of curtained bedrooms upstairs from her showroom and workshop. It was hinted that if Madame Alice told a tenth of what she knew she could make a fortune; and, conversely, that she had already made a fortune by not telling a tenth of what she knew.

The tradesmen's wives of the neighbourhood liked Madame Alice, but feared her. Only one of them had ever ventured to quarrel with her – one Mrs Klingermann, married to a prosperous button-maker of Golden Square, who called her a witch to her face. Madame Alice said, 'You will make public apology to me for that, or I will take away from you everything you have, beginning with your husband.' Mrs

Klingermann made public apology: Klingermann was a steady man, and a conscientious husband, and a good father to their five children; but there was something about Madame Alice that suggested the home-wrecker – a vital ruthlessness, a calculated recklessness, a wanton heartlessness. Impossibly ugly as she might appear to the conventional eye, men found her (to quote the label on the sixpenny bottle of relish) 'piquant and appetizing'. She boasted of it, 'Prettiness is jam on suet pudding. It licks off one-two-three. I am ugly as a monkey, but in me males sense hot juices. I know the secrets of La Païva. Have you ever heard of La Païva? She was a flabby Polish Jewess with disagreeable pig's eyes, pink hair under her arms and a pasty skin. She wore a dress for twenty francs, had fingers like spring onions and bitten nails, and was so careless of her person that she had the odour of a shop where they sell horseflesh. Yet she was called Queen of Love in Paris, and millionaires paid her fifty thousand napoleons for one night. Why? Aha, aha! That is my secret. I taught it to a scullery maid from Montrouge with crooked teeth who was glad to sell herself for the price of a glass of *marc*, and in three years she was La Joyeuse with a four-horse carriage, an income of seven hundred thousand francs, and a Russian Grand Duke for a protector who smothered her with diamonds . . .'

As she cut and basted and draped, she talked in this vein to Alma Nollekens, looking disquietingly like a spider with a mouthful of pins for fangs and marvelling at the girl's calm indifference. 'But you are better than pretty,' she said, 'you are of a rare and distinctive beauty. Surely, my dear, surely this is something you must be aware of?'

'Mr Zobrany says so,' said Alma.

'Mr Zobrany says so, yes, yes, Mr Zobrany says so; and he is a very charming gentleman, and a handsome gentleman, and an educated gentleman, and he adores you, and he will no doubt make you very happy in bed –' She watched for a blush. The girl was impassive. '– And of course you think you love him. You think so, no? Tell me?'

'I suppose so.'

'In these matters you do not suppose; you *know* – there is no supposing. No, but you do not love him. How can you love someone and *suppose*!'

'Don't I? Perhaps I don't. I don't know.'

'She doesn't know! Do you care?'

'I don't know,' said Alma equably. 'I'm going to marry Mr Zobrany, aren't I? I like him. Isn't that enough?'

'Does he kiss you, embrace you?'

'Yes. We're engaged.'

'What do you feel when he kisses you, eh?'

Alma thought for a few moments and then said, 'I don't know.'

'A rage, a hunger, a desire to eat and to be eaten?'

'No, nothing like that.'

'A fury, an excitement?'

'Sometimes he tickles when he kisses me, but not in a nasty way.'

'Your nipples do not grow hard? You do not fight for breath? Your face does not burn? You are not aware of a trembling, a certain moisture and, down there, a twitching and a beating? You cannot hear your own heart beat?'

'I've never had a day's illness in my life, Madame Alice.'

'She never had – my God! Child, do you realize what you are?' Madame Alice was wildly excited. She grasped the girl by the arms and shook her. 'You are one in millions, you are the one absolutely perfect sacred courtesan! I know their histories, all of them. They were this, they were that, they were adored, worshipped; they were capricious, they were cruel, they were clever, they were rapacious, they twisted men around their little fingers. But all of them had one fault – somewhere, somehow, they *felt*, they had needs, they were women; and this was their ruin in the end. Tell me now: if it had not been Mr Zobrany who came along, but let us say the King of Prussia, would you have married him if he had asked you?'

'I'm not sure about that. I'd be afraid. A queen has to keep going out to receptions and parties, and hasn't got much time to herself, has she? I don't care much for going out.'

'Then if it had been an American millionaire with a gold mine, let us say, as handsome as Mr Zobrany but ten thousands times richer?'

'I don't know.'

'If he came to you and said, "Mademoiselle, here is a bag containing ten thousand pounds in gold, if you will sleep one night with me"; what would you have said then?'

'Money doesn't tempt me much, Madame Alice. I've got enough to live on.'

'She's got enough to – listen. We will say that you haven't got a penny piece to your name. Now I come to you – I am a millionaire, do you see? – and I say, "Alma, I have fallen madly in love with you. Sleep with me tonight and I will give you ten thousand pounds." Well?'

Alma said, 'What happens if I don't?'

'If you don't, child, you little idiot, I will buy your house over your head and have you thrown out to starve in the street! Well?'

Madame Alice saw a troubled expression darkening the serenity of the girl's face. After some hesitation she asked, 'But if I marry you can I stay here as long as I like?'

'No, you stupid, I cannot marry you because I have a wife and seven children in California. You must be my mistress.'

'Only once.'

'Once only.'

'For ten thousand pounds?'

'No, I have changed my mind because you are so foolish. Not for ten thousand pounds. I will simply agree to let you live here in this house you love so much.'

'I'm used to it, you see.'

'We are pretending that I am a millionaire who is amorous of you, remember . . . So; you will sleep with me and then I will let you live here. But if you do not I shall have you put out. Well?'

'Well, if I have no money, I'll have to go out to work, I suppose, or find somebody to marry me; so I'd better make up my mind to move anyway,' Alma said, laughing.

'Come, my dear, take a chance – sleep with me, and if you please me well enough you shall keep your house and I will give you ten thousand pounds after all. But first you must come to bed.'

'But what if I don't please you well enough?'

'Then you get nothing.'

'That's not fair, because I haven't had any practice pleasing people in that way. Give me a deposit, and come and talk the matter over again after I have been married a year or so.'

Madame Alice shrieked with laughter and said, 'She is impossible!'

'It's a silly game,' said Alma.

'Not so silly. It is played every day all over the world, for pennies and shillings, and loaves of bread and packets of tea, and roles in the theatre and diamond collars – this "unless you come to bed with me" game. You know you are worth millions? You know I could make a *grande dame* of you? Consider it this way: it is not that you are in love with your Mr Zobrany. Simply, he does not displease you and will be kind to you in this horrible house you are so attached to.'

'I'm used to it, Madame Alice. I can't tell you how the idea of moving upsets me.'

'Yes, yes, yes, your mama knocked this foolishness into your glorious head. One hope in life is all she had – that she might, for God's sake, not be put out into the street! For this she prayed, for this she worked, in this faith she brought you up. No? It is base, it is spiritless! For this you married with that evil-smelling Nollekens: though, mind you, many ladies de luxe I have known who owed successful careers to being nauseated by the embraces of somebody such as Nollekens at a tender age. Only he was too ill to touch you, you say. Consider then: you love to be left alone, eh? Then tell me, who is more her own mistress, to be alone or in company as she pleases, than an exclusive *femme amoureuse*? What does she give? To whom is she indebted? Upon whom is she dependent? . . . It is not that you are moral – you are too indolent. It is not that you have scruples – you are too ignorant. You give yourself to Mr Zobrany so that he will look after the shop for you and save you the trouble. Do you like cooking? No. Do you love babies? No. Is it your flesh that troubles you? No, it is not. It is simply that you are disgustingly lazy. I asked you in joke if you would marry the King of Prussia. No, say you, because to be a queen would be too troublesome, if you please! Would you sleep with a millionaire for ten thousand pounds? Yes, if he let you live here undisturbed. And you are not yet twenty; you should itch to see life and enjoy things. But no! "I'm used to Masham Court . . . I like Mr Zobrany because he has put in a new lavatory." Bah! I am not a one to have pity for men, I; but I am sorry for that one. He is head over ears for you, and it is a waste.'

Alma protested, 'It isn't only the lavatory.'

'No, it isn't only the lavatory – it is somebody who will go out and call the plumber. Eh?'

'But Madame Alice, why should you care, if I'm content?'

'Because you have no right to be content. You are too beautiful to be content, and it irritates me. And you listen once again, little girl: Mr Zobrany is a good man, and an ardent man; but a bold and an impetuous man. Also, not a very clever man. Who but a fool trusts a friend to buy a restaurant for him? Who but a fool looks once at a great red cat like you and says "Marry me"? Wait, the end is not yet. Say your husband fails here. Then they put him in prison, perhaps. And it may be that there are some babies. Then, perhaps, you will not think it such a silly game, this "come to bed with me or else"! Only by then . . . are you listening to me?'

Alma said, 'No. If I'm reading a book and I come to something I don't like, I just turn over the pages till it comes nice again. If somebody says something I don't think is nice, my ears close themselves the way my eyes do when I see something nasty. But go on, Madame Alice; don't let me interrupt you. I know you like to have a chat.'

'My God!' said the dressmaker. 'I give up, I resign. Let us try this *jabot* . . . Where are you going for your honeymoon?'

'I didn't really want to go anywhere, but Mr Zobrany says everybody has honeymoons, so I suppose we'll go somewhere. He says Paris is quite near. I don't mind, really, as long as we can be back in ten days.'

'She doesn't mind really so long as – For the love of God, the *jabot*, the *jabot*!'

Alma Nollekens liked to look out of the window and see the lamps being lit in the dusk. This afternoon being heavy with mist, the light in the centre of Masham Court came out like a black opal, but the one on the bracket in the archway appeared as a white dot in a pink disc ringed with yellow, like a cut blood-orange. The stained-glass windows of Howgego's saloon bar blazed briefly like a set piece before the plush curtains on their heavy brass rings were drawn with a clash; Smeed, the newsagent and tobacconist, let a little gaslight escape through his panes because he couldn't keep it imprisoned and still remain visible – he would not have parted with it otherwise; Himmelstoss the barber's pink gas globes popped; the demented Baxter, who repaired things, tinkered with a contraption of carbon rods and released a blinding glare of crepitant violet electric light. Last of all, the bookseller Maundy Pentecost made a pinhole in the twilight by putting an astral lamp in his window, not for illumination but as a sign that he was at home. Glancing sideways, she could see this dim light as it caught one of the bull's-eyes in the greenish glass; it reminded her of aquariums, which was convenient for a girl of sluggish imagination, in that Maundy Pentecost had a slowly swaying, gently wavering, loosely rooted look about him which it was difficult to associate with dry land.

He was a bookseller's bookseller: that is to say, he purveyed literature but read catalogues, and his was a repository and clearinghouse of books rather than one of those hospitable shops where readers come to browse and talk and sometimes to buy. Maundy Pentecost was vaguely offhanded with the few – the very few – who, coming into Masham Court by accident, walked into his shop to look around. Generally his door was locked, and bore a sign RETURN SHORTLY, which meant that he was floating about the countryside and entangling himself in parcelled lots at auction sales.

Alma was mildly surprised to see him come out now, wearing his bulbous brown hat and his iodine-coloured waterproof Inverness cape, and approach her side door. He knocked gently. She said good evening to him, and he faltered, 'May I come in?'

'Yes, do.'

She led him upstairs. 'Charming, charming,' he said, admiring the new wallpaper, 'most tasteful. A very graceful design, an exceedingly pleasant pattern, and the colours in perfect harmony. I congratulate you on your eye, Mrs Nollekens.'

'Oh, Mr Zobrany chose it. He knows I like green. Will you have a cup of tea? Or would you like some wine?'

'Wine?' Maundy Pentecost rippled with polite astonishment.

'Mr Zobrany brought it. I know he'd like me to offer you some.'

'You are very kind . . . Bless my heart, this is a remarkably fine oloroso! No, thank you, I won't have a biscuit. I am happy to see you blooming, Mrs Nollekens.'

'Thank you, Mr Pentecost. You, too.'

'Oh, I . . . I . . .' He waved a hand like a frond of kelp. 'The fact of the matter is, the late Mr Nollekens owned two or three books – *A Secret History Of The Vatican*, a folio edition of Law's *Serious Call* and *The Protestant Martyrs.* If you attach no sentimental value to these volumes, perhaps, I thought, you might care to sell them to me.'

'Why, yes, if you like. I don't read serious books very much. They're in the sideboard cupboard, I think. No, I left them in the wardrobe, where Mr Nollekens always kept them. He was at them every chance he got. Mr Nollekens was a very serious man. But Mr Zobrany isn't very fond of religion. I'll fetch them for you if you like.'

Maundy Pentecost watched her as she left the room. For a moment he changed. An egg sac opened and became an eye; a stem twitched and turned into a tentacle. Then she came back carrying three thick volumes.

'You have looked at these, Mrs Nollekens?'

'Mr Nollekens said he was going to teach me all about them, but . . .'

'Yes, yes; dear me, dear me; it was most tragic, most tragic. Well, perhaps Mr Zobrany would not like you to have these books, so I will pay you ten pounds for them if you like.'

'Really? As much as that?'

'Look,' said Maundy Pentecost. He laid a hand on the front cover of *The Protestant Martyrs,* and pushed. The leather spine of the book was flexible. The stippling on the front edge became a picture, delicately executed and indescribably obscene. He looked narrowly at the girl.

She said, 'Well I never! Fancy that.'

'It shocks you, perhaps?'

'It *is* rather rude isn't it? Are the other books like that?'

He showed her, repeating, 'It shocks you perhaps?'

She said, 'Is all that handwork?'

'It is by an Italian master of erotic subjects, Mrs Nollekens.'

'Then aren't they worth more than ten pounds?'

'Yes.'

'Then hadn't I better ask Mr Zobrany about them before I let you have them?'

He blinked at her. 'I think not, Mrs Nollekens; I rather think you really had better not. Let us change the subject for a moment, shall we?'

'If you like. Will you have some more wine?'

'Since you are taking some of the same, I will, I thank you, with pleasure. Mrs Nollekens, your marriage to your late husband was painfully short, I think?'

'He never was strong, and he was taken bad soon after the wedding.'

'You nursed him devotedly, I believe?'

'I prayed with him when he asked me to, and gave him his medicines.'

'Who was his physician?'

'He didn't hold much with doctors. He believed in faith, mostly. His friends called a doctor at the end, but it was too late.'

'Alas! I knew Mr Nollekens many years, many years. He was in his time bountifully endowed, copiously so, I may say.'

'Uh?'

'With virile force, Mrs Nollekens. As Blake puts it, "The lust of the goat is the Bounty of God." But in his later years I believe he was in the habit of taking tonics?'

'He never touched a drop.'

'I mean herbal tonics, drugs calculated to restore the manly powers.'

'He had a lot of different kinds of medicines; bottles, pills and all that. Why do you ask?'

'The physician diagnosed gastroenteritis, I think, complicated by certain intestinal disorders. Nobody but you and I know that the late Mr Nollekens was in the habit of taking white arsenic as an aphrodisiac.'

'I never knew that. Isn't arsenic poisonous?'

'Deadly poison, rank poison. And you were sole beneficiary by his will, I think. Dear me, dear me, Mrs Nollekens!'

'What do you mean, Mr Pentecost?'

'I mean that if somebody wrote a letter to the Public Prosecutor, and the body of Mr Nollekens were exhumed, the Coroner would probably find enough arsenic in his remains to hang you up by the neck, Mrs Nollekens.'

'I think everybody's going out of their mind today,' said Alma. 'The very idea of me poisoning anybody!'

'Perhaps. Nevertheless, I have it in my power to cause you to be arrested and brought to trial, and the evidence would be quite strong against you. In view of your youth you might, if found guilty, escape with penal servitude for life. If you were acquitted, you would be a marked woman; you would have to go away and change your name –'

'– I won't listen,' said Alma, covering her ears with her hands.

'You had better listen, I think.'

'I shall tell Mr Zobrany.'

'I shouldn't if I were you. Mr Zobrany is of the heroic type. He would make an affair of it. He would treat it in epic style. He would be so outraged that he would offer to fight people. For he would be convinced of your innocence, you see, and is one of those elevated souls that believe truth must prevail; that is to say, what they think is the truth. Innocent or guilty, you'd be ruined.'

'I didn't poison anybody.'

'Conceivably. But who's to believe you? And consider,' said Maundy Pentecost, looking at her narrowly, 'consider the months of imprisonment and mental anguish. Consider, Mrs Nollekens!'

'What do you want me to do, then?'

He was amazed at her calm. He said, 'I want it perfectly understood that I have it in my power to crush you. That in itself is a source of satisfaction to me. I could demand money of you –'

'– I haven't got it to spare.'

'You would have it to spare if I demanded it. You know you would. Luckily, I do not want money. But I like a certain sense of power. Mrs Nollekens, you are beautiful. You have a beautiful body – don't leap to conclusions, pray, for I have neither the desire nor the capacity to avail myself of your charms. My passions are entirely bookish. All I want to do is take your photograph.'

'Take my photograph?'

'Yes. I am compiling, for exceedingly exclusive circulation, an album, a certain album.'

'If you could wait until my new dresses are finished –'

'– You do not wear a dress, Mrs Nollekens.'

'Oh.'

'Does that shock you?'

'I don't know; I suppose so. And is that all you want me to do?'

'Yes, Mrs Nollekens.'

'Honour bright?'

'Yes.'

'I didn't poison anybody, you know, Mr Pentecost.'

'I am prepared to forget the matter if you do as I say. Mr Zobrany comes to see you of an evening. At what time are you expecting him?'

'Half past seven.'

'It is not yet a quarter to six. I will leave you now. Follow me, bringing these books, in a quarter of an hour. I will prepare my camera. Simply walk into my shop. It will take an hour. When you leave I will give you some novels to carry. You see that I am the soul of discretion, and that you may trust me absolutely. In the extremely unlikely event of anybody's asking questions, or seeing you come and go, you came to ask for something to read, and there will be your novels to prove it. I shall expect you. Until then, Mrs Nollekens . . .'

'These edge-paintings by Romano,' said Maundy Pentecost, 'really have a certain value, so by your leave, Mrs Nollekens, I will put them in my little vault before we go about our little business.' He led the way upstairs. 'I fancy that this room,' he said, opening a door, 'could tell strange stories, if the walls could talk. This house was the Earl of Olberon's *pied-à-tierre* in the 1770s, and he was one of the darker lights (if I may employ the phrase) of the Hell Fire Club. Dashwood has revelled here, and Bubb Doddington, and I do not doubt that Benjamin Franklin delivered himself of prudent aphorisms here, between indiscretions. Over there, as you see, are couches, sofas, carpets and what not. Here are my cameras, and these powerful acetylene lamps are ready to light. You may disrobe, if you please, behind that screen; for the mysteries of the toilet do not at present concern us.'

He took a bunch of keys from his pocket. 'This,' he went on, opening a padlocked door, 'this was a powder closet, which I have had enlarged and lined with sheet iron, so that it serves as a little strong room for my rarer books.' The door was of oak, also lined with iron. 'It is very heavy,' he said, straining against its weight as he pulled it open. 'And the floor is irregular, so that I have to fasten it to this staple in the wall with this little iron hook. So . . ."

He put Nollekens's books on a shelf and, stooping low, leant into the closet, patting them into their places. His head was against the jamb when Alma, with a tap of her finger, knocked the hook out of the staple. The iron edge of the ponderous door bit true as a paper cutter. The lamp fell and went out. For one second the old man crouched, gripped at the temples. In that second Alma turned and thrust backwards at the door with all the power of her loins and thighs. Something yielded with a soft crack. She pressed harder. Something fell with a clatter. There was a noise as of dried peas on the iron floor of Maundy Pentecost's little strongroom. *That'll be his false teeth, I dare say,* she thought.

There was a night light at the head of the stairs. She prudently blew it out before she went down. Then she picked up the novels the old man had left out for her. The shop door locked itself behind her with a sharp click. Back in her sitting room she stirred the fire and banked it with coal dust, for Mr Zobrany wanted to take her out to a theatre and supper, and she liked nothing better than a good fire to come home to.

'Has my darling been lonely?' he asked, when he came in glowing with love and the cold evening air.

'Not very. I got some books to read.'

'And do you really like your new room?'

'Better than ever.'

Maundy Pentecost had kept himself so much to himself that a month passed before his body was found. It was, they said, without meaning to be facetious, an open-and-shut case of accidental death.

But by then Alma Nollekens was Mrs Zobrany, and her husband the happiest man in the world.

PART TWO

SEVEN

. . . Zobrany smiles tenderly, remembering that evening at the theatre with Alma, just before they were married, so that Poppy asks him, 'What's the joke – or are your whiskers tickling you?'

He replies, 'I was only thinking, my sweet child. I was counting my blessings, and I lost count. It occurred to me that I must be the most fortunate man in the world. My only complaint is that I have not had my just portion of sorrow.'

'You've got an ingrowing moustache and it's touching your brain, that's what's wrong with you,' says Poppy. 'What d'you want sorrow for?'

'Chiaroscuro; shading, depth,' Zobrany murmurs, waving a hand at the pictures with which the walls are hung.

'Doolally!' says Poppy. 'Try sitting on a tack.'

'May I put it to you, for the thousandth time,' says Zobrany, 'that a cloth damped in water is better to clean ashtrays with than spit?'

He takes a feather duster, and flicks at the framed and unframed paintings, sketches, woodcuts, lithographs, lino cuts, mezzotints, dry-points and what-not, thinking, *The place has become a veritable Salon of Rejects.* There are, of course, the inevitable Toulouse-Lautrec posters – La Goulue, and Jane Avril, and Delysia – and a couple of bullfight bills such as no café proprietor of artistic taste can do without. And there are nudes of all kinds, in every possible attitude and all known media; and still lifes galore, with and without Chianti flasks; and abstractions, and pointillismes, and Impressions, and Post-Impressions; Dadaisms, Fadaisms, Gauginades, Van Gogheries, Chiricoid broken arches, Miroesque reveries, and an anatomically exact oil of a skinned grey-hound lying in a baking dish surrounded with onions.

But the wall behind the coffee bar is blank. It has been plastered and primed for a mural, and bears traces of ruled squares and faint charcoal outlines. The idea for the reception of which this wall is reserved is a stupendous one. This mural is to be unlike any other mural ever conceived – in fact the artist's original intention was to persuade some patron to build a high, wide cylindrical tower to contain it. It is to depict South American peasants, so hungry that their bones are bursting from their skins, lining up to work for two cents a day on a coffee plantation. Fat magnates with blonde mistresses giggle while overseers flog the peons to death, and stupendous stocks of coffee accumulate. Ticker tapes indicate that coffee prices are falling. The peasants are employed at one cent a day to throw the surplus coffee into the sea. They starve some more while the remaining coffee sells for ten times its normal prices. Now they are employed at half a cent a day in erecting a huge factory. Last panel: the pitiful remnant of the labourers line up begging to be employed for nothing a day at the door of the factory which is tooled for the manufacture of synthetic coffee out of sawdust.

This idea has been subject to certain variations in the past seven years. Sometimes, instead of coffee, it is wheat; gnarled North American peasants work themselves to death to fill the mighty granaries. Since the steel rollers of the mills won't take wheat germ, factories are built to extract the germ from the wheat. Starving peasants spend their last pennies to buy white bread, which makes their teeth fall out. Undernourished and rickety, they mortgage their farms to buy vitamin pills made from the wheat germ in pharmaceutical factories built nearby . . .

And so on, and so forth. Zobrany wishes the artist would make up his mind. He would long ago have had the coffee-bar wall painted, only he hates to hurt anybody's feelings – least of all that genius of the colossal concept, the wayward and incomprehensible Tom Henceforth, who has already drawn more than a little something on account.

Following Zobrany's glance, Poppy – whose eyes are never off him for long – says, 'Forget that one, he's a toerag.'

'Don't make me talk of matters you can't understand,' say Zobrany.

'Don't you try and make me understand matters you can't talk of,' says that irrepressible girl.

Young Tom Henceforth, to whom Steve Zobrany's heart went out because he was so like Gèza Cseh, could shed words glibly as a frog spawns, but he had an insuperable distaste for explanations of any kind. Pride, shame, uncertainty – whatever ailed him struck him scared and savage when his conscience locked horns with his vanity. He was not what is commonly known as a coward; he might have kept cool under a bombardment or before a charge of cavalry. But as a man may be bold and yet dread spiders, so Tom Henceforth shied away from criticism.

When he left Zobrany's the first time with six pounds in his pocket, he was beset by this terror: that Gus, the plasterer's boy, might come upon him from around the corner and say, 'Now, Tom! You know you gave me your honour to bring back that cart the day before yesterday. I forgive you, but you *did* give your word, you know . . .'

In such a case Tom Henceforth would not know what to do or where to look – he would even be at a loss for something to say. Similarly, if

Fritsch took it into his befuddled head to walk over to Masham Court for a drink and a chat, and ran into him while Zobrany's money was hot in his pocket, somehow or other all would be lost.

But nobody came up on Tom Henceforth, and nobody ran into him. Still, he hugged the walls and made a zigzag to Westminster, where he stopped at a post office with the intention of sending Gus and Fritsch a pound apiece. Having changed a pound to buy two registered envelopes he weighed the silver in his hand and went to a cheap coffee shop to think the matter over. Eating a meat pie, he thought that it would do to send them five shillings apiece in a suitably worded letter. Washing the pie down with tea, he changed his mind and decided to send Gus ten shillings, and Fritsch a postcard. Over another cup of tea and a coconut tart he asked himself, *But why?* Nibbling a jam turnover, he said, *All or nothing!* Topping off his snack with a yellow confection called a Conversation Pudding, he decided. *Nothing. Be strong!*

But it was a pity to waste the registered envelopes. So at another post office off Victoria Street he wrote on two slips of paper, ENCLOSED ONE POUND, LETTER FOLLOWS; TOM H., and put them without enclosures in the envelopes which he addressed to Gus at Santini's and to Fritsch in Poland Street. He mailed these envelopes punctiliously from the proper counter. It was in his mind that this was something that had to be done; but he shied away from asking himself why. A similar sickly instinct, no doubt, makes debtors send unsigned cheques, fooling nobody, fiddling for time to do nothing in.

But he had as little thought of time, now, as a windborne seed. Having nobody to talk to, Tom Henceforth was lost and adrift. He walked, as always, purposefully but without objective, into Lower Belgrave Street and out of it, and into Ebury Street, and around into the Buckingham Palace Road, and so by degress into Victoria Station where he found himself standing by a ticket office under a sign that said BRIGHTON–1ST CLASS. An old lady said, 'Pray make haste, young man.' A policeman looked at him askance. Tom Henceforth put down money and bought a ticket; after that there was nothing for it but to go to Brighton.

He found an empty first-class compartment marked NO SMOKING and got in. An inspector was after him at once, saying, 'Can I see your ticket?' Looking at it he said, Thank you, sir. Beg pardon. Some of the raff are always trying to go first on third class.'

'What d'you mean, raff?' Tom Henceforth asked.

'No offence.'

The engine hissed. Two detectives walked along the platform shouting, 'Card sharpers on the train! Warning! Warning! Card sharpers on the train! Sharpers on the train, warning, warning!'

As the train began to move an old man bounded into the compartment and sat back gasping 'Skin o' my teeth! Caught her by the skin o' my teeth!' He was a wiry, sunburnt old man with a blunt, bluff face fringed with the kind of whiskers they used to call Newgate fringes. His nose broke to the left, and his jaw appeared to have been knocked the other way. But his clothes were of good black broadcloth, and he grasped in one knotty fist a fine silk umbrella with an ivory handle banded and capped with gold. On one ring finger he wore a massive signet; on the other, a gold snake with ruby eyes. He carried a Gladstone bag and a box coat. Ignoring the sign on the window he lit a thick cigar with a fat wax vesta. Taking him all in all, Tom Henceforth regarded him as one of those tough-grained, cantankerous, law-breaking, eccentric honest men peculiar to England, whom everybody has read about but who are so hard to find in real life. Pillars of Church and State, they are somehow always in the Opposition; they hold up traffic, fight for rights-of-way and strike matches on NO SMOKING signs. Set them down in the Café Anglais and they demand tea and mutton chops; returned from Venice, they say, 'The foreigners apart, it's no different from Chiswick.'

His cigar well alight, the old gentleman said, 'I know this is a non-smoker, but I'm sure you don't mind.' Then he took out a T-shaped railway key and locked the carriage door, saying, 'I know you're not supposed to do this, but my name is James Goggs, and if they want to sue me they know where to find me. I'm sure you don't mind.'

Tom Henceforth said, 'I heard there were card sharpers on the train.'

Mr Goggs said sharply, 'This is a first-class carriage, you know. Have you got a first-class ticket?'

'Certainly.'

'I haven't,' the old man said. 'I'll see them damned first. When they provide first-class accommodation I'll pay first-class fare, not before. As for card sharpers, young man, I don't play. I can think of more amusing ways of going to the devil than playing cards with sharpers. Sharpers, indeed! I'm up to *their* games. But a sucker is born every minute, as PT Barnum said.'

Looking out of the window at the flying suburbs, Tom Henceforth said, 'I'm not fond of cards. It's a mug's game. Anybody with a few thousands to invest could make millions.'

This, coming from such a clownishly shabby specimen, made James Goggs laugh. 'Talk is cheap. Tell me how,' he said. 'Here, have a cigar.'

Tom Henceforth became fluent. 'London is overcrowded, and getting more so. It's expanding. I'd get hold of cheap land outside London – west as far as Uxbridge, northwest as far as Hendon, east out to Barking. Then build.'

'Build? What with?'

'I'd get the land on a small down-payment and float a company. Houses, shops, blocks of flats –'

'Who's going to live in 'em?'

'Londoners.'

'They walk there, presumably?'

'No. The Underground Railway people co-operate. The motor buses co-operate. New roads get built.'

'That's right. And then we have balloons and flying machines, I shouldn't wonder. Haha, what it is to be young! What's your calling, young-fellow-me-lad?'

'I'm a decorative artist.'

'Well, I hope you make your millions. I'm satisfied with rather less. You think in millions. I can make do with a couple of thousand a year in the Funds, a bit of land of my own, a yellow-and-black governess cart with a piebald gelding and a Dalmatian dog trotting between the wheels, and a good cigar to smoke. And my hobbies, my hobbies; for when I rest I rust. When I rest I rust.'

'You live at Brighton?'

'No sir, I live at Leigh in Essex.'

'And what are your hobbies, sir?' Tom Henceforth asked, in his most engaging way.

'In general, young man, making a confounded nuisance of myself,' the old man said, to his companion's great delight. 'My name's James Goggs!' There was a wickedness and a mockery in his eye which Tom Henceforth found extraordinarily attractive. 'I made my money in the British tobacco business.'

'I didn't know it grew here –'

'– No, young fellow, but it does in Jamaica, in Trinidad, in Burma, don't it? You can roll a cigar anywhere you like, I think? Who are the dagoes to arrogate monopolies of cigars, or the damned Dutchmen? I retired in '98. Since then I've been starting small businesses to annoy the combines, and letting them buy me out. It's instructive and it's profitable, and above all I amuse myself. Now I'm going in for fish.'

'Fish?'

'For the luxury places. Lobsters, whitebait, crabs, et cetera. I told you I live at Leigh in Essex. The best whitebait in the world come from the Thames estuary. The lobsters are very good, too. I simply cut out the middlemen, pack the best of the catches in seaweed and deliver direct to the hotels. Now I'm going to extend, and take in the restaurants and the larger private establishments.'

'Oysters, too?' Tom Henceforth asked.

'No, no, the Colchester men and the Whitstable men have got oysters by the short hairs. Lobsters, crabs and whitebait; and small superfine shrimps. James Goggs, the Essex Fisherman – that's me. Me, a fisherman!' He opened the Gladstone bag and took out a bottle of whisky and a little case of silver cups. 'Have a little Mountain Dew.' He filled two cups.

'Thanks . . . And your business takes you to Brighton, I suppose?'

'No. Not as yet. Just passing time. A friend of a friend has a nephew who wants a job, so I'll spend a weekend or so. I want a lively boy to work on wages and commission. It wouldn't suit you, not by a long chalk – there's no millions in it, nor anything like it. About eight hundred a year, perhaps. But not necessarily permanent, because I expect to sell out in two years – I'll get bored with it and want to find my fun elsewhere. My name's James Goggs.'

Now, Tom Henceforth conceived a passionate desire to sell whitebait and lobsters, to the mortification of the great fisheries. He said, 'I am not dressed like a salesman, because, like Dr Johnson, I scorn the niceties of costume.'

'So I see.' The old man was very dry.

'Why don't you let me sell your fishes?'

'True, you talk like a person of education, and have the manner. But who are you? Where's your fidelity bond?'

'What's a fidelity bond?'

'Don't you know? Why, it's like this: I trust you with the handling of a connection, a clientele. What's to stop you carrying it over to, say, Fortnum and Mason, for a consideration? So a fidelity bond is a surety that you won't. A legal document, a commitment undertaken by a solvent party – or by yourself, if solvent, through your banker or man of business.'

'Do I look like the sort of man who would take your customers elsewhere?'

'No. Do I? And my name's James Goggs.'

'Certainly not,' said Tom Henceforth.

'I know I don't. But that's how I got my start.'

'I haven't got any friends,' Tom Henceforth said.

'Money?'

'I have only about five pounds I can lay my hands on . . .'

Laughing, the roguish old man lit a fresh cigar, and said, 'Bless my soul, you're a funny boy! Look, I'll tell you what. Would you sign a form of contract categorically pledging yourself to the basic et ceteras?'

Tom Henceforth liked the sound of that. 'Categorically pledging myself to the basic et ceteras,' he repeated. 'But with reservations.' He liked legal terminology. 'With certain fundamental reservations in respect to a time limit with regard to the period of the contract . . .' He stopped, bogged down.

'You to pay legal costs?' said James Goggs sharply.

'Certainly.'

'Refundable after say six months, though.'

'All right. But what are the terms?'

'Your travelling expenses, three pounds a week wages, and ten per cent commission,' said the old man. 'You know my name!'

'I should stipulate that I had first opportunity to buy if and when you decided to sell the business,' Tom Henceforth said.

'Essentially so, young man, since that would make you in perspective a partner and so *in esse* cement your reliability. On terms to be mutually agreed, however. My name's James Goggs.'

'Of course.'

'Shake hands! Here's Brighton. We'll have a sandwich in the buffet and make a few notes . . .'

They ate soot-and-sulphur sandwiches seasoned with the remains of a delinquent ham that had died the Death of a Thousand Cuts, and took away the taste of them with a couple of bottles of Bass. And somewhere between the wording of memoranda in the pages of a notebook and certain interchanges of sentences garnished with words like *Whereas* and *Aforesaid* and even *Hereinabovementioned,* Tom Henceforth put down five pounds for legal fees – which Mr Goggs waved away and then pocketed with a shrug, saying at last, 'Well, well, we'll go to the Metropole and have supper, for I've booked a room there. My name's James Goggs. Be a good fellow and mind my umbrella while I step out to have a leak?'

Tom Henceforth drank his beer slowly, and ordered another bottle. He knew that elderly gentlemen sometimes take a long time over such functions; but after a while he began to think that Mr Goggs's leak must be something of the sort that, after a hundred years, makes stalactites. Himself aware of the pressure of accumulated liquids, he went to the urinal. Such was his artlessness – for there is nobody quite so gullible as an extremely clever boy – he really hoped to find his friend there, still leaking, or evaporating, or whatever he was doing. But there was nobody like Goggs in the places men stand at.

He ran back to the buffet, still grasping the silk umbrella by its ivory-and-gold handle. Goggs was not there. So Tom Henceforth had a glass of whisky to restore his faith in himself, and another to strengthen his conviction that nobody was to be trusted, and (with a giggle) a third to persuade him that he had known it all along.

This called for a fourth. And somewhere between the memories of repetitive meat pies and redundant coconut tarts, presumably forgotten but washing back on tides of coffee-shop tea with a flotsam and jetsam of jam turnover and a lagan of Conversation Pudding, Tom Henceforth had a bad dream . . .

He dreamt that he was talking to a woman-shaped object with banana-coloured hair, a vieux-rose bonnet, a purple feather boa, a turquoise blouse, an emerald skirt, orange gloves and high-buttoned slate-blue boots. She took him in her splintered claws and dragged him out into a lurid half-darkness under globes of mauve incandescence, full of whirling grit and the clashing of iron, dreadful with fire and thunder in a dome which threw back echoes of damned souls howling *Away, away – away, away!*

And there was a brass machine into which you put pennies. You pressed buttons, and a witch in a snood waved a disarticulated hand showing wire between the knuckles; whereupon the many-coloured woman cried, 'Opopanax, opopanax! Lily of the Valley, and Violet, Violet! Roses, Roses! Let's wash in it!' A miasma of foul perfume drenched him, and somewhere between the pit of his stomach and the crossroads of his pharynx bitter little efts swam in a black pool which rose . . . which rose . . . But just before he went down for the third time a giant's hand picked up the world and twirled it as one twirls a watch on its chain to amuse a baby; and the newts came out, and a hoarse voice said, 'Swine! Swine!' Whereupon the woman-shaped thing took him by the sleeve and dragged him into the realm of Chaos and Old Night.

I'll wake up, Tom Henceforth thought – and even as the thought came, it went, and the nightmare changed for the worse. Now he was a paper jumping jack with strings for nerves and no will of his own, dragged into the well of a titanic staircase. He was cold, but he could see the disc of a thunderstruck sun in a cosmos of deadly dust. The sun shrank. 'So cold, so cold!' Tom Henceforth cried, holding out his hands to the sun. But it dwindled and turned to brass.

'Let me in!' he sobbed.

An odiously knowing voice said, 'You don't know out from in, you innocent. But I'll save you from yourself.'

He was spun like a whipping top. The woman in the nightmare now had thirty shadows, and was multiplying herself to dance a black Carmagnole by the light of eight dreary candles. She was tearing herself to pieces. There flew a feather boa like a knot of vipers, and a shower of gaping slate-blue boots – away fluttered as many green skirts as there are flames at a witch-burning, and as many white petticoats as there are flakes of ash. The Night Mare was greenish-white, and reeked of penny opopanax mingled with sickly lilies and rotten roses; of candle grease, butcher shops, sour milk, violets, ammonia and pickled onions;

of sickroom odours prevailing over incense, and of forgotten vegetables. Now she stood on gargantuan cabbage stalks, holding in hands like bunches of carrots a pair of breasts like turnips with split radishes for nipples caught up in shopping nets of knotty blue veins. Her belly was that balloon house with the plaster still tacky on it; the mouthpiece of the balloon was where a human navel might be, only it protruded like a trumpet. Her toes were parsnips.

'Help!' Tom Henceforth cried.

'There, there,' said the Night Mare. Her several heads became one, covered with hair of seven different metals – brass, zinc, copper, iron, pinchbeck, lead and bronze – but the rest of her was lard, although she had a hand like a lemon squeezer when she took him by the scruff of the neck. 'I am going to eat you all up, every bit of you,' she said, undressing him much as one takes the carapace off a boiled prawn. 'Dilly, dilly, dilly, dilly – come and be killed!'

His stomach tied itself in a loose bow as he retched in reverse. Between finger and thumb she pinched out the light of the universe. There came into his mind a picture which had frightened him when he was an eight-year-old child, almost ten years ago – a print of an anaconda, its jaws open a good hundred and eighty degrees, swallowing a crushed fawn.

This is Sin – here is the Serpent, Tom Henceforth thought, in his dream. Then he was coated with saliva and swallowed.

But this is only a dream, the last thought came in a flood of relief before all went blank.

Awakening later he kept still for fear that his head might come off, letting only a corner of one eye take in the adulterated milk of a thinned-down daylight, thinking, *It was all those pies I ate. As nightmares go, that was a bad one.*

Thereupon he turned his head, and saw that he had not been dreaming. The Hag was still there, perspiring in a butyric dew like toasted cheese and exuding a miasma as of marinated feet, soused stomachs, devilled liver and hard-boiled eggs, with an over-all yeasty sweetness. He sat up with a muffled shriek.

She opened her eyes, which were large and grey, and said, 'Hush, dear.'

He leapt out of bed. Agile though he was, he was no match for her – she was swift and strong as a charging bear. His fright amused her. She rolled him up in a satin quilt, beat him with a feather pillow and pretended to suffocate him. He cried out, 'Go away!' Laughing, she released him and said, 'You shouldn't drink so much if you're not used to it, ducky. My word, it's lucky for you it was me you met! I'm your first girl, aren't I?'

He groaned. She went on, 'It's ever so early, but what's the odds? I'll make you a cup of nice strong tea. First of all, though, the best thing in the world for the morning after is a Skate's Eyeball.' She found a stone bottle of Hollands gin and a jar of pickled onions, poured out half a teacupful of the liquor and offered him a fat brown onion on a fork. As he recoiled she said, 'Chew up the onion good, but don't swallow it. Take the gin in your mouth and mix it with the onion – work it around, squidge it about – and *then* swallow . . . You can't? There's no such word as "can't". Come here . . .' She had him by the hair. 'It takes the nasty tastes away and does you the world of good. There now!' She took him by the nose. 'Get outside of that – all up, right down, there's a good boy! Oh, you lucky person – many a woman hanging around the London Road would have had your knackers off for cat's meat last night and given you something to make your nose fall off into the bargain. But I kept your money safe for you, and your umbrella, too –' That silk umbrella hung on her marble mantelpiece by its gold-and-ivory handle, next to a pitiful heap of silver and copper coins. She said, 'What in the world do you want to go stealing clergymen's umbrellas with their names engraved on 'em for? That's not sensible.'

'I didn't –'

'– I know, you didn't. You found it. Now let's imagine I'm the beak, the magistrate, you understand? You come before me charged with being in possession of this valuable umbrella. You say you found it. I ask you, "You found it, where?"'

'I didn't say I found it,' Tom Henceforth said. 'A man gave it to me to hold in the buffet, while he went to the Gentlemen's.'

She laughed. 'I'm the magistrate, and I say, "A likely story!"' – she had a knack of making a burlesque of intonations – 'I say, "Young fellow, since when did the Canon of Barchester hobnob with the likes of you in railway buffets and give you to hold in safe-keeping a gold umbrella presented to him by the Barchester Temperance Society while he went – forsooth! – to the Gentlemen's. Out of your own mouth you stand condemned, you ruffian, since the Canon has already notified the police that this same umbrella was stolen from him in the First-Class Waiting Room at Victoria Station . . . Lock him up!" That's what the beak says, and it's no better than you deserve, for petty larceny is no game for a boy of your education. And you a boy that wins scholarships!'

'I never looked . . . I don't know anything about the Barchester Temperance Society . . .' Tom Henceforth now felt indescribably foolish. 'And how d'you know I won scholarships?'

'Because you told me so, dear. You won a scholarship to be an artist. You said so. Now I ask you, child, what's the use of an umbrella? Where's the sense in it? How much did you think you could get for it – and you an educated boy! At the cushiest, it's a humiliation, ducky . . . Will you draw a portrait of me?'

'Yes, yes, but not now.' He clasped his head in his long wiry hands, which she observed were wide-spread and sharp-looking as five-tined pitchforks – wonderful hands for an abortionist, a pickpocket, a piano tuner or a card sharp; strong but genteel. He asked, with horror and morbid pride, 'Did I really – you know – last night?'

She replied, laughing, 'Did you really? I rather think you really did, my dear. To a woman, such joy can come but once in a lifetime. Like a honeybee you have left your sting forever in my flesh. If I don't have triplets, I'll be surprised, that's all I can say. Did he really? Oh crikey!'

Tom Henceforth's three-cornered smile was back. 'I hope I didn't hurt you –'

'– Said the organ-grinder's monkey to the brewer's horse. Don't worry your fat, child. I could accommodate you and the Barchester Temperance Society, and the Canon's umbrella – open. I'm not a loose woman, but I was in the mood, and I'm superstitious: I always think a cock virgin is lucky. What is more, I noticed you hanging about The Schemer Merton – him and his Gladstone bag!'

'Merton? I thought his name was Goggs. It was his umbrella I was holding.'

'I dare say he picked it up in the waiting room at Victoria. He can't resist a bit of larceny, that one, however petty. But he generally likes to give you a bit of paper, or something. He'd steal the pennies off his dead mother's eyes and leave a post-dated cheque for sixpence. You're lucky you came away with seven-and-six in your pocket. Make no mistake about it, you're lucky! As for the umbrella, well, I'll see you right about it. I'll tell Perp.'

'What'll you tell Perp?' he asked. 'Who's Perp? That's a strange name, Perp.'

'Perp is a strange man,' said she, deadly serious. 'Don't you dare smile when you say "Perp".'

'What does he do?'

'Perp? Everything. And look here – I'm not advising you, I'm telling you. What Perp says "Do", if you love your life you do it! Be warned by me.'

She must have been beautiful in her time, and still carried herself imperiously. While talking she had put on a Chinese gown, voluminous as a tent, embroidered with a gold dragon. Following Tom Henceforth's glance she said, 'This was a bit of loot out of the Summer Palace at Peking; so mind what I say. I'm Perp's friend; I look after things for him once in a while.'

'You are an actress?' he asked, with a friendly smile.

'I have been, in my day. I played Aladdin to Dan Leno's Widow Twankey, and the Duke of Manchester won a thousand pounds concerning the measurement of my thigh, which was twenty-five inches. My bust was forty-four and my waist was twenty-nine. Hips forty-six. But I was so built you'd never guess I weighed twelve stone ten. I was deceptive –'

'What does Perp do?' Tom Henceforth asked.

She said, 'Perp does everything and anything. And I'm telling you: if you've got anything to do in Brighton, you do it through Perp. If you've got anything to get, better tell Perp. You're an educated boy. Did you ever see *The Tempest*?'

'I've read it.'

'Then you remember Prospero? That's Perp. Prospero.'

'I'd like to meet him,' he said. He was cowed, but he could adapt himself to a frayed tangle of circumstances faster than a sailor could splice a rope. He really did want to meet Perp; such a meeting was somehow essential to the development of the tortuous Original the world was to know as Poor Tom Henceforth. So when he spoke, his words had the unmistakable ring of sincerity, and so had his manner.

She said, 'My name's Molly Irving, and I can generally read men like a book; but I can't quite make you out. You may well be an artist, for all I know. I'm a theatrical person, and I've got ears. You naturally talk like a gentleman, but you're trying to slur. Somewhere or other you've been well brought up; because it's harder for a gentleman to talk like a guttersnipe than it is for a guttersnipe to talk like a gentleman. You're dirty, but not naturally so – you put it on like a nigger minstrel puts on burnt cork. Your hair would wash out sandy mouse, your nails would dig out elegant, and about two swipes with the handle of a razor'd bring your face up sweet as a baby's bottom. But you've got a funny face, and I can't read it. You don't make expressions – you sort of slip a kind of cord, and let it go like wet linen. But it doesn't fall down; it falls *up*.' A thought struck her. 'You're *not*, for God's sake, some relation of the Canon of Barchester's?'

Tom Henceforth shook his head. 'I'd like to meet Perp,' he said. Thinking of the name, and repeating it in his mind, he saw Perp as a chubby man with a florid complexion and a jolly little round chin, an amiably pouting mouth and a comfortable stomach; a clean pink man with fluffy hair and a manner of cocking his head and twinkling merrily over gold-rimmed spectacles. Probably he would lisp a little and chuckle a lot – it seemed to Tom Henceforth that there was no other way for a man to look, who had a name like Perp.

Molly Irving said, 'Well, so you shall.'

EIGHT

Now the carpeted stairs creaked under some great weight slowly climbing. 'Watch out, mind!' said Molly Irving. Then Perp came in without knocking and kicked the door to behind him. Thinking in studio jargon, Tom Henceforth wondered, *Is this fellow complete but unfinished, or finished but incomplete?* Perp might have been made of the best-preserved scraps of half a dozen broken-up bodies knocked together to kennel a stray spirit, yet there was a certain complacency in his bearing. His manner said, 'Just look here – with these two hands I made myself. And talking of hands, feel these. I got the left off Tommy Burns when Jack Johnson was through with him. The right, a bargain, I got off Madrali the Terrible Turk. Do you see these shoulders? I picked 'em up off a drayman with a broken leg. Look at these legs. I scrounged 'em off a stevedore with a broken shoulder. Bone, sinew and nerve, alone I done it. I'm nothing fancy, I don't deny – a hobby, a labour of love – but I wouldn't swap bodies with Sandow or souls with Jesus Christ!'

Only Perp had no face.

Twenty years or so previous, when he might have been about thirteen, Perp probably had a profile; but this must have been before he learnt in the hardest way possible that, just as only a fool works, so nobody but a man born to be beaten does his own fighting. Circumstances had made a target of the youthful Perp's face as the cannoneers made a target of the face of the Sphinx – and like the Sphinx Perp could show nothing of an expression but a strange blasted smile, half catlike and half womanish, chipped at the corners and pitted at the curves. Seen sideways (and he seldom let them be seen otherwise) his eyes were watery, almost colourless. His forward glance was grey, glacial, incurious, self-sufficient, strangely limpid yet seemingly without depth: it was the way his eyes caught the light; you could see your reflection there, nothing more.

And about this man Tom Henceforth sensed something like an aura of overwhelming power. If ever one man held the freehold to himself, that man was Perp. Slouching, ramshackle, inimitably slovenly, he carried himself with an air of supreme proprietorship and sublime indifference.

Dragging his heels, he crossed the room. 'Let's have a look at this,' he said, in a hoarse bass voice. Then, so gently that Tom Henceforth could find nothing disagreeable in it and so swiftly that he could have thought of nothing to say or do if he had found it so, Perp took him by the waistband of his trousers and the slack of his shirt and lifted him half a yard off the floor.

Tom Henceforth, who had read tales of unarmed travellers surprised by bears, kept still.

'That's right,' said Perp, nodding. 'That's quite right. I want you to understand me, that's all, see? This is only to remember me by –' He slapped the boy in the face and threw him into an easy chair. 'No hard feelings, kid. That's my card, like, with my compliments. That spells *Perp*. Got it?'

And as long as he lived, Tom Henceforth would remember that moment; and the memory of it would never be tinged with resentment. This proud mountebank of a boy who was to grow into the touchiest of men, of whom it was to be said that he was motivated by pure malice in everything he ever did, never thought of Perp except with an admiration beyond wonder. He always felt that he came out of the affair with credit . . . That wasn't a slap in the face; it was no more a blow than a pat on the back is a punch in the spine . . . No, no, that was a caress, coming from Perp! Now, even as he bounced on the plush cushion with the sting of the hand on his cheek, his quick wit told him that Perp measured men by their reaction to the shock of meaningless violence. There was a sort of greatness in this, he felt: a flavour of Chaka, of Tamerlane and of Jenghiz Khan. Rancid, acrid and smoky – the very smell of the man evoked images of the great kraal and the high veld and the irresistible Impis; the felt tents and the dung fires and the galloping hordes!

He said, 'I understand. Benvenuto Cellini's father hit him on the head when they saw a live salamander, just so he wouldn't forget. No need to repeat the compliment. I've got it.'

Perp made no reply. He could not decide whether this stranger was some new type of genius, or an unfamiliar variety of a common kind of idiot. He offered a feeler, 'We're friends now, so tell me; what's your idea of the value of that silly old umbrella, eh? Tell us, what's it worth?'

Tom Henceforth replied, 'If we're friends now, you tell me. I know nothing of umbrellas, and care less.'

'Good again! If you don't know something, say so straight out. And even if you do know, say you don't, because that way I might tell you something more than what you already know . . . To the ignorant everything is told. So be ignorant. Now then; is that old brolly worth something? If so, what? Speak up.'

'The gold on it –'

'– The gold on it, broken up – which it will be, you know – could be worth a couple of shillings. Take off labour costs, and so forth, call it ninepence. When I say *worth*, I mean what it'll bring me in, not you.

Handle and frame, a couple of bob. Not to you – to me. All in all, what have you got there to risk your liberty for? You'd be a lucky kid if I gave you a shilling or fourteenpence. I talk to you like a man because I like your manner. You've come to the wrong shop for petty larceny, young 'un.'

'Have I?' said Tom Henceforth. 'You were talking petty larceny. I wasn't.'

Molly Irving said, 'Don't be cheeky, dear.' But Perp said, 'You shut up . . . Go on, kid, say some more.'

'All right. How much gold is there in a sovereign?'

'Less than a pound's worth, naturally. There's silver in a gold quid, there's copper, there's tin and all that. There's less than twenty shillings' worth of gold in a sov, just as there's less than twelve pennorth of silver in a shilling. Well?'

'You get a lot of gold I dare say, one way and other?'

'Well?'

'And you pay next to nothing for it.'

'Well?'

Discomfort and danger were nothing to Tom Henceforth now: he had an idea. He said, 'You talk about petty larceny! Ha! Why, a match-seller is a timber merchant to you.'

Perp lounged towards the fireplace and picked up a long iron poker. 'You and your bloody pick-ups,' he said to Molly Irving, pushing her into the boy's lap. 'Don't move.'

'Perp, no! No, Perp!' she said, 'Perp!'

'Be cosy,' he said, always smiling. Then, without noticeable effort he bent the poker so that it encircled Tom Henceforth's neck and hers, pressing them cheek-to-cheek. 'Be cosy, and I'll show you a trick.'

He poured some gin into a teacup and took a pickled onion out of the jar. Holding the cup in his left hand, he flipped the onion up to the ceiling with his right thumb, much as a boy shoots a marble. As the onion fell he slipped a razor out of his waistcoat pocket, cut it in two and caught the halves in the cup. He licked the vinegar off the blade before he closed the razor and put it away, murmuring, 'You ain't worth my personal attention just yet, but I could gut you like a herring, you know. What d'you mean, talking to me like that? Eh?'

Tom Henceforth said, 'Come off it.' He was frightened now. 'If you meant to gut me like a herring you'd gut me like a herring, not play about with pokers and pickled onions.' Wildly excited, he shouted over the woman's shoulder, 'Why don't you go on the music halls?'

His voice rose. 'No, you're not good enough. Bill Bankier could twist that poker into a corkscrew –' His breath came short. 'Cinquevalli could balance you and your poker, too, on the tip of his nose – Rastelli could juggle with you, gin and onion and all – No, a Saturday night singsong at the Old Brown Bear's your style, you . . . you . . .' At this point he became silent, and closed his eyes. In awful shame and wild delight, Tom Henceforth was experiencing his first conscious orgasm. 'Take this poker away and I'll tell you what I mean,' he said, in a broken voice, limp and spent. 'Take this poker away . . .'

It is easier to bend an iron bar than to straighten it, so that Perp had to exert himself to let them loose, and by then Tom Henceforth was calm again. The woman, trembling, helped herself to gin and gave him some. Crossing his legs, he said, 'What I mean is, if you can get gold, why not *make* money? Considering what your raw materials cost, why, you could make a good pound for ten shillings. Whereas, I bet you sell twenty shillings' worth of broken gold for fifteen.'

Smiling his defaced smile Perp said, 'Kid, I love you! I can't help it, I just love you. Molly, let's have another drop o' gin. Give the kid another drop.' She obeyed. Perp sat close to Tom Henceforth and laid a huge, cold hand on his knee. His bass whisper, now, had a soothing, soporific quality; it was drowsily musical, like the buzzing of bees on a lazy afternoon. It seemed to the boy that he had been listening to this voice since the beginning of time; there was no other sound worth listening to. '. . . That's all right, I know you feel strange, and there's no use you trying to tell me different, because you don't want to tell me different, you know, because I like you and you like me and we're friends, you know, and you're comfortable and safe and nice and sleepy, you know, because you've missed a night's sleep, but you can rest now, you know, so take your time and rest a bit and Perp'll put you right, you know, so catch up with a bit o' lost sleep and then tell Perp all about it . . . That's right, good, good, all's wrapped up snug and safe . . .'

Molly Irving watched, her mouth square with terror. Perp took a cup of gin from her nerveless hand, held it to the boy's lips and said, 'This is coffee, you know, a nice hot cup o' coffee to make you feel at home and all nice and easy, so drink it nice and slow and take your time, take your time, it's hot you know so drink it slow . . . all up, all up . . . good, goo-ood, gooo-oood . . . that's the boy . . . and now I ain't Perp, I'm you, you know, and you can talk to yourself to your heart's content.'

He handed Tom Henceforth a teaspoon, and the boy stirred the cup of gin and began to drink it in short sips. As he drank he whispered '. . . Petty larceny twopenny-halfpenny snotrag swipers. Broken gold. There's a law against counterfeiting, yes. Yes, but where's the law against making a sovereign with twenty-two shillings' worth of gold in it? Don't change it in England. Take it abroad. Buy with English gold in France, Italy, Germany, Spain, Belgium . . . Antwerp; buy diamonds. Buy works of art. Buy silk, buy spices, buy lace, buy ships, by God! . . .

Make good gold pounds, gold napoleons, gold twenty-mark pieces, gold eagles – better than the Bank. Don't *de*preciate coin of the realm – *ap*preciate it. Gold medallions exactly like real money. Don't even *call* it money – put it down and let it talk for itself. Buy, buy, buy . . . and sell for good paper, and buy more . . .'

'Ah,' Perp whispered, 'but where does Perp's gold come from?'

Tom Henceforth murmured, 'Perp is the thief. You are the creative artist, Tom Hardy.'

'Tom Henceforth?'

'Henceforth henceforth. Yes.'

'An artist, and to hell with gold and all that muck. That's not Tom's line. It's gone, forgotten – out, spark out, blank.'

'Gone, forgotten.'

'Now we go bye-byes . . . ah, what a lovely sleep . . .'

Tom Henceforth sighed, half smiling. Sleep blurred the precocious angles of his grasshopper's mouth. A lock of hair fell over his forehead, and now he was the most artless boy in the world. Molly Irving said, with a shudder, 'I've seen it done a hundred times on the halls, but the way you go about it gives me the creeps. Thank God you never did it to me!'

'That's right, thank Gawd.' said Perp. He lit a cigarette. He was thinking.

'You wouldn't do that to me, would you, Perp?'

'That's right.'

'What are you going to do with the kid, Perp?'

'He might come in handy. Then again, he might not. I'll see.'

'He's a clever kid, though. Isn't he, Perp?'

'That's right . . .' Perp was thinking, *Maybe a bit too clever by half. Say 'gold' and there he is, lengths ahead and still running. Yet I'll swear he never thought of gold till the word came up.* He said, 'Get the kid something to eat. And coffee. Go on.'

She laid a violent hand on a chipped porcelain bell-pull. Somewhere in the lower distance a cracked iron bell tinkled, and a fat little woman wearing an apron over a tall thin woman's cast-off red silk dress came in and said, 'Well?'

'What's in the larder, Rita?'

'German sausage, tongue and brawn.'

'Make up a nice big plate, then, and a pot of coffee.'

'Make up two nice plates,' said Perp. 'And bring some pickled cabbage. And look sharp.'

When she was gone Molly Irving said, 'You wouldn't even try to do a thing like that' – she nodded towards the sleeping Henceforth – 'not to me, would you, Perp?'

'That's right.'

'You never *did* try. You didn't, did you?'

Perp said, 'You wouldn't know if I had, would you?'

She was silent. Soon the servant returned with a tray. Then, having dismissed her, Perp said, 'Wake up,' and the boy opened his eyes. 'Why,' Perp went on, 'you dropped off right in the middle of an interesting little chat. Come on, have some breakfast and tell us some more about gold.'

'Gold? I don't know anything about gold. What d'you mean? Oh,' said Tom Henceforth, 'you mean that umbrella?'

'That's right,' said Perp, his mouth full of sausage and pickles. 'Never mind. No more do I know nothing about gold. I'm a racing man, you know. I'm a –'

But Tom Henceforth had snapped at the word 'racing', caught it in mid-air, and was away with it. 'Now take racing,' he said, in the tone of one who, having argued thesis and antithesis, comes triumphantly to cast-iron synthesis. 'It stands to reason that it's a mug's game. It's dependent on chance. Only a fool depends on chance. A clever man depends on absolute certainty.'

Perp said, with scarcely perceptible irony, 'That's right. Like backing every horse in a race to win, kind of style, eh?'

Even he was taken aback when Tom Henceforth said, with the bright air of a schoolteacher encouraging a backward boy, 'Right, quite right!'

'I judged you to be a smart kid,' said Perp softly. 'I'm a gentle-hearted sort of man, but I can't bear being proved wrong when I size somebody up. Say something clever, sonny, and say it quick, because I never warn a person twice.'

'For God's sake don't tease him, child!' cried Molly Irving.

'You can shut your trap,' said Perp.

Tom Henceforth continued, 'Firstly; where's the really heavy betting done? On the course? No. The millions go through the big agents, like Weatherby, say. That kind of betting is done on credit, by telegram from the course if need be. Am I wrong? No. All right then. Now you know there's lots of noblemen and gentlemen with good names and absolutely spotless reputations nowadays who are so hard up they don't know where to turn for a measly thousand pounds or so. Ruined, but nobody seems to know it, since the Boer War. First of all, by one means or another, you get hold of two or three of these. You put it about that they have made, or better, inherited a few thousand pounds. And you open accounts for them with five or six of the biggest bookies in England. Limit – say, two thousands.'

'That's nice,' said Perp.

'Oh,' said Tom Henceforth, 'they don't bet much. Twenty-five here, a hundred there, you see. In the course of three or four months they play with a matter of five hundred, no more. Their names are good, their credit is established, *and they always bet by telegram from the race course.* Now we come to telegrams. How much does a telegraph operator earn? Two pounds a week? Two pounds ten? I don't know, but it isn't much. Well, what you have to do at this point is, scout about for a telegraph operator who's in trouble, and hard up. They're mostly married men with families – these steady-job fellows generally are, don't you see. And you find one who is desperate. In fact' – Tom Henceforth smiled affably and with candour – 'if I were you I'd arrange it so that one or two telegraphers really did get into a bad scrape of some kind. His wife could break a leg, or an arm, or something like that; or his house could burn down. *You* know. And you say to this poor bugger, "Look here, my friend. How would you like a thousand pounds, free and absolutely without risk?" So he jumps at it.

'I hope you follow me. The procedure now is simple as ABC. One day, betting from the course, Lord X, or Sir George Y, or the Honourable Mr Z hands in to the telegraph operator, say, sixteen telegrams, each betting a thousand pounds on a horse in a race where there's sixteen runners. The operator stamps all these telegrams as having been handed in five minutes or so before the start. You know the result comes to the telegraph office a matter of seconds after the judges' decision. So the operator sends the telegram backing the winner, and tears up the other fifteen. The wires are always heavy just about then. The telegram with the bet arrives simultaneously with the news from the winning post – perhaps a quarter of an hour later. But the time stamp being in order, the bookie must pay. That's what I mean by backing every horse to win in the same race, don't you see; and if you don't try it too often you can clear two hundred thousand pounds a year, allowing twenty per cent or so for overheads like bribery, and the gentlemen's split, and so forth. Now d'you see?'

Perp's laugh was like the beating of a drum with a loose parchment. He cleared his throat and spat with tremendous force into the cold fireplace. 'And what book did you read that yarn in?' he asked.

Tom Henceforth protested, 'I swear I just made it up – it's my own idea, honour bright!' He was embarrassed to feel his voice rising thin and plaintive.

'Stand up,' said Perp.

Tom Henceforth stood.

'Drop the round-the-'ouses.'

'What?'

'Take your trousers off.'

'Go to hell!' Tom Henceforth shouted; and then he took off his trousers. 'What's – what's –'

'I'll give you what's what's,' Perp said dispassionately. 'Now don't you look lovely? Eh, don't he look lovely? Those eyes, those nose! Oh, I could eat him up like custard! Gimme a spoon, gimme a spoon! Oh, I could take him into a corner like Little Jack Horner! Stick a bit of holly up his bum and call it a Christmas pudden! . . . You, Molly, take the coals out of the bath and hot up some water and give him a wash. Wash his head –'

'– You know very well I keep a clean bath,' she said.

'Yes, you use your biddy-pan for pickling gherkins. You never had a bath since you last stained a rag twenty years ago. I said give him a bath, right?'

'All right, Perp.'

'Diddle diddle dumpling, my son John, one shoe off and one shoe on,' said Perp, picking up Tom Henceforth's coat. Economical of gesture, before he straightened himself he caught the boy by a foot, overturned him into the upholstered chair, wrenched off his shoe and swung it by the lace like a pendulum. 'Dickery dickery dock, the mouse run up the clock. Don't go away, whatever you do,' he said, throwing the garments over an arm. Carrying them thus, and still holding the dangling shoe, he went out.

'Begin to see what I mean?' Molly Irving asked.

'I knew you'd wash out nice and crisp,' she said, half an hour later when, bathed and combed and wrapped in one of her kimonos, Tom Henceforth sat and admired his fingernails, feeling wonderfully at home in the world. 'Yes, you come up sweet as an apple.'

'But what's Perp's game?' he asked.

'You never can tell. Admit, now; you can't help being scared of Perp, can you now?'

'I'm not afraid of Perp. What I want to know is, what does he want with me?'

'I don't know, dear, honest I don't. He took a liking to you. You never can tell. He might take you into the TPA.'

'And what's that?'

'The Turf Protective Association. Perp has all sorts of businesses, you know. Property – he owns this house, and others. He's got shares in things. The TPA's a sort of insurance company. Like the Prudential, only unofficial, and fairer. If people had their rights,' said Molly Irving, 'there wouldn't be one law for the rich and another for the poor. But that's the way things are, and that's where Perp comes in. It's like this.

Say you put a pound on a horse and it comes home at twenty to one. You trust your bookie like the Bank of England to pay you that twenty pound. Better than the Bank! A banker can go bust, and turn round and say, "There's the City for you, gentlemen – unfortunate speculation – circumstances beyond my control. Here's sixpence in the pound, and fare thee well." And he'll get his discharge, and be none the worse thought of, and drink his wine in the Savoy, and they'll make a knight of him.

'Ah, but when that banker goes down in the *Gazette,* is his bookie entitled to put himself among his legitimate creditors? Oh no. So Perp steps in and says, "There's no dead loss here, friend. The TPA will collect for fifty per cent of the total, plus expenses. Fifty per cent of something is ever so much better than a hundred per cent of nothing." And so it is; that's arithmetic. So Perp does the collecting.

'You'd be surprised what a rough business the turf is. There's all sorts of nasty people hanging about to make the bookies' lives a misery. So they have to join the BBS – the Bookmakers' Benevolent Society, that is – and Perp looks after 'em. They pay a subscription, according to their means, and that insures them against rough stuff from common extortionists. The BBS works either way, dear: it not only insures the bookie against violence if he pays his dues; it guarantees that he'll get violence if he doesn't, you see. And what's more, if the bookie has a bad run, as bookies do sometimes, he can borrow money to tide him over from the BBS.'

'At interest?' said Tom Henceforth.

'At a fair rate of interest,' said Molly Irving. 'A bookie can't go to the City and float a loan, can he? A bookie can't sell shares in his business on the Stock Exchange. A bookie pays for cash, on the course. So the BBS lends him money without any security, not even a signature, and he simply pays it off in instalments at the rate of five pounds a week for every four he's borrowed. The BBS doesn't press for the principal, as long as the bookie pays his interest regularly plus expenses. He pays; Perp takes good care of him.'

'And if he doesn't?'

'In that case, Perp takes good care of him. Perp does a lot of good all round. I can tell you, there's not many around the race meetings that don't owe their safety to Perp, dear – from owner to tipster to tic-tac man; let alone the entertainment people, from the sideshow proprietors down to the lowest form of life which is the "Piddle-or-Poop-a-Penny –Wash-'n-Brush-Up-Tuppence" person in the Ladies' and Gentlemen's Convenience tents. And a word to the wise, love: you mind what Perp says, for if you cross Perp, regardless of age or sex or time or place, he'll look after you. I shouldn't be surprised if he had something genteel for you; you're not good-looking, but you've an attractive manner.'

Then the street door slammed. Perp was back. He slouched in, carrying a portmanteau, and proceeded to talk as if he had been there all the time, in the tones of a mild and reasonable man moderating an acrimonious argument, '. . . Now then, considering my mind was made up an hour ago, where's the point in arguing the toss? I know just what I'm going to do with *you*, kid.'

The boy answered boldly, 'You think you know, you mean.'

'I know I know. Come here,' said Perp, taking him by the chin. 'Can you look me in the eye and tell me I don't *know* I know? Can you look me straight in the face and tell me *you* don't know I know? Eh? Eh?'

Tom Henceforth tried hard to answer, but no words came. He would have given his left hand for the power to return Perp's awful pale gaze, but it couldn't be done; he had to look away; a man might as well try to stare down a pair of acetylene carriage lamps. He saw Perp take out his razor. 'Not in here, Perp!' the woman cried. But the man stretched a long arm to the washstand, picked up a damp face rag, moistened the boy's cheeks and shaved them in half a dozen light and dexterous strokes. Then he opened the portmanteau and took out a complete change of clothes.

NINE

'Dress yourself up in these here, from the skin out,' said Perp.

The underclothes were of silk. As Tom Henceforth put them on, while Molly Irving looked the other way, Perp murmured, 'How many times have I seen a feller giving himself away by not dressing proper? Put an eight-guinea suit of clothes on a yob, and anybody can read *Yob* on his face as clear as print. It ain't what you wear, it's what you feel that makes you look right. You're a bit of a gentleman? Feel like one. Only the likes of Molly-O there can put herself on a satin dress over a shitty chemise and think she looks like Mayfair – whereas anybody with half an eye can tell she's a bit o' brassy undercut. Detail, detail, that's what counts. Now dress, like I told you.'

Everything fitted Tom Henceforth exactly as it was proper for clothes to fit him – with a kind of baggy elegance, a negligent modishness. The shoes bore the stamp of an Italian bootmaker, the shirt was French but the suit had no labels to identify it. Perp looked on, nodding. He said, 'I don't know why it is, but that pepper-and-salty kind of Irish tweedy sort of stuff always inspires confidence, if it ain't too new. Tie your tie loose. And here' – Perp took out an old silver watch with a worn leather guard – 'this goes in your breast pocket. We couldn't do without a watch, you know; we travel a bit, we've got to catch trains and all that. Now a hat –' There was one in the portmanteau; a crushed bottle-green German felt, battered but clean. '– There now! Light overcoat, gloves, and you're a gentleman, barring a haircut. Look at yourself in the wardrobe mirror, and you'll see what I mean.'

Molly Irving cried, 'Why, he's a real toff!'

'You shut up. You've never been in the same room with one, not by daylight . . . Well? Now you look like a gentleman, don't you?'

Tom Henceforth said, 'I don't know. What does a gentleman look like?'

'That's the proper answer. A gentleman doesn't look like nothing. A gentleman is at home and on home ground wherever he is, whatever he's got on. Don't look at me – I'm like that, but I ain't a gentleman, I'm a king. What Perp goes about in is Perp's regalia. Never measure yourself or anybody else by me; I'm different . . . Now, you know, you can pass anywhere as you stand, and if you put your hand in your pocket to change a sovereign, nobody's going to look at you twice.'

'What's the idea, though?' Tom Henceforth asked.

'In case anybody wants to know, you're studying to be an artist, and kind of looking about you.' The portmanteau yielded a little Gladstone bag. 'Detail, detail! In this here bag is a change of underwear, a sponge bag, some handkerchiefs and a pair of dirty socks, a pair of clean socks, two shirts clean and one soiled. And here's a little book of drawing paper and some pencils to put in your pocket. And here's a purse, a nice pigskin purse, not too old but not too new, with nice compartments for silver and gold and coppers . . . And now tell me what you think of these here.'

Perp felt in a greasy waistcoat pocket and drew out five gold coins. He threw them down and watched impassively as they bounced, ringing, on the table. 'Pick 'em up, feel 'em, and tell me what you see and feel there.'

Tom Henceforth said, examining the money, 'They look like gold sovereigns to me. They're all dated 1908, though.'

'Good. You've got sharp eyes. All dated 1908, eh? Well, well, well! All right. Now put them sovereigns in that purse, and go out and change 'em, and bring me back four pound ten in half sovereigns and silver. Go to the barber in Ship Street and get your hair cut. Change a quid there. Get yourself a chop at Sweeting's if you like, or go and have tea at the Chelsea Bun Shop; break your second quid and ask for a sovereign's worth of change for another. That makes three. Go to a chemist's and ask for a box of peppermints. Change pound number four. Get a packet of cigarettes and bust the fifth. And be back here in two hours with the change. I'll be waiting for you.'

Tom Henceforth said, 'I take it this money is –'

'Never you mind,' said Perp. 'Do as I tell you.'

'What do I say if I'm stopped and questioned?'

'Ah, that's something I'm going to leave entirely up to you. It's a test, like. Get it? *Psst!*'

Perp jerked a thumb towards the door.

The fat little servant let Tom Henceforth out. He found himself in a forlorn crescent of pillared stucco-fronted houses. Nearby the uneasy shingle said *hush, hush* to the restless sea. *I'll chuck his damned fake money right into the water,* he thought, walking towards the sound. On the promenade he stopped to look at the last of the season's holiday-makers. They walked with resignation, like prisoners at exercise, ignoring the donkey boys and the imploring old man who cried, 'Ride in the goat cart! Ride in the goat cart!' *I'll go on the pier and put pennies in the slot machines, and then I'll toss Perp's purse into the sea, and . . .*

And there he was, not on the Palace Pier, but in Ship Street, gazing at his reflection in the plate-glass window of a barber's shop. He went in, hung up his hat and coat, sat in a chair and said, 'Just a trim, not too short.' Then, 'No brilliantine, thank you; a friction. Not violet, eau de cologne.' And, opening the pigskin purse, 'I'm afraid I must ask you to change a sovereign. I have nothing smaller. Thank you, good day.'

It was as easy as that.

I'll try it just once more, he thought, at a tobacconist's. There he asked for a box of Hamid's Selected, opened it, lit a cigarette at the little gas jet, flipped one of Perp's gold coins in the air, caught it and threw it nonchalantly on the counter. The shopman gave him his change without a murmur. As he went out Tom Henceforth reasoned, *It's probably always as easy as this the first few times; later they remember you, and put two and two together.*

But although he felt free, reckless and light as air, he was vaguely angry. He asked himself, *Who's Perp, anyway, that you should do what he tells you to do? Who's afraid of him and his . . . his . . .* His what? Tom Henceforth didn't know. 'Go to Sweeting's and have a chop,' Perp had said. It was almost as if that overwhelming man had looked into his memory and had caught him peering curiously through the window of Sweeting's in the City and promising himself a stockbroker's lunch there, as soon as he had a decent suit of clothes to his back and five shillings loose in his pocket. Perp had commanded him to do nothing he did not already desire to do. On the one hand, this was comforting; on the other, oddly disquieting.

Let things take their course. Tom Henceforth walked to Sweeting's with his customary resolute stride, and went right in, and sat confidently at a corner table and demanded menu and wine list, although he knew exactly what he intended to order. He had thought it out months ago: a glass of dry sherry and a little smoked salmon, a grilled sole and a glass of light white wine, a bloody double rump steak and a glass of good burgundy, a bit of Stilton and a glass of tawny port, a cup of black coffee and a thimbleful of sound brandy. And so he told the waiter; was served accordingly, exactly as he had hoped to be served, and ate and drank like a little hero. When the cheese and port were brought he felt free to look about him.

The restaurant was half empty, lunchtime being past. A cloud of cigar smoke drifted to him from a table nearby. He looked towards it, sniffing; somebody was burning up a good two shillings' worth of the best Havana there, he decided, full of well-being. Then he heard a humorously cantankerous, jolly voice saying, '. . . A bit of land of my own, a yellow-and-black governess cart with a piebald gelding and a Dalmation dog trotting between the wheels, sir, and a good cigar to smoke –' He looked again. The cigar smoker who was talking had a sturdy black broadcloth back, and he was gesticulating with a broad hand on the ring finger of which was a gold snake with ruby eyes.

'– And my name's James Goggs,' said Tom Henceforth, tapping him on the shoulder.

The old man was on his feet in an instant. His eyes flickered with recognition, but only for a moment. He said, 'Who the devil are you? I don't know you? What's your business, damn your impudence?'

'I thought you said your name was Goggs.'

'Goggs? Goggs? What d'you mean by Goggs?'

Tom Henceforth said, 'Perp sent me.'

It was a firecracker of a name to drop. The old man started violently, and his ruddy face became dull and mottled. He faltered, 'My name . . . my name's not Goggs, young man.'

'I know it isn't,' said Tom Henceforth. 'It's Merton. I've got a message for you from Perp. If your friend will excuse you a moment, better come over to my table.'

The old man followed him. Seated at Tom Henceforth's table, he took a glass of brandy, and some of his composure returned. 'Now what's all this?' he asked, forcing a laugh.

Letting his expression become blank and staring straight into the old man's eyes, the boy thought hard of Perp's terrible head. Fifty muscles in his flexible face jumped at the image. (*My God, he looks like Perp!* the old man thought, with a fluttering heart.) Scarcely moving his faintly smiling lips the boy said, 'Perp has a bone to pick with you, Mr Schemer Merton. You're to go and see him in two hours, at half-past four. And Perp doesn't mean twenty-five minutes to five. He means half-past four. He wants to have a little chat with you about the fish business. Also, there's the matter of the Canon of Barchester's umbrella.'

'I was only having a bit of a lark. You know that, don't you? That fiver – I was going to give it back to you, so help me God I was –'

'That's all right. You can give it back to me now.'

'I will, I will!' The old man took out a wallet. 'Have you change for a ten-pound note?'

Taking the banknote Tom Henceforth said, 'I'll get Perp to change it, so I hope it's good.'

'It is.'

'I'll owe you the change. You're to be at Miss Irving's place at four thirty.'

'Over in Pitt's Crescent? There? Oh Lord!'

'It's not an affair for the TPA, and it's outside the jurisdiction of the BBS. Perp will deal with it personally; you know Perp and how he is about detail, detail, always detail.'

'Put in a good word for me, will you? Remember the fable of the lion and the mouse. I could perhaps do you a good turn some day.'

'You're not a bad sort, really,' Tom Henceforth said, finishing his coffee. 'What you do is this. Give Perp a fiver and say, "This is to buy little Tom a new suit." Have you got that? It's a password from me.'

'And may I ask who you are, sir?'

'I'm Perp's nephew.'

'I thought I saw the family resemblance. A wonderful man, your uncle. He pretends to be a rough diamond, but it's easy to see that he isn't one of the common herd . . .'

Tom Henceforth paid his bill. On the way out he changed the fourth of Perp's 1908 sovereigns.

For this boy, *away* was a direction and *anywhere* a destination. While he yearned unaccountably for the presence of Perp, he itched to be somewhere else. Attracted to the man, he automatically hated him. He had faith in Perp, and therefore he renounced him. If Tom Henceforth stayed with Perp nobody could hurt him; if he went, nobody would help him.

He ran away.

Molly Irving said to Perp, 'I suppose you know what you're doing.'

'That's right.'

'It's not for me to ask questions.'

'You never said a truer word in your life.'

'I was seen with that boy, you know. I must have been seen with him in the buffet.'

'Don't mix me up in your bits o' nookey. Who cares?'

'If they pick him up the trail leads straight back here to me.'

'Well? They got nothing against you but your looks, and you can't help them.'

'I wouldn't have given a green kid five queer quids to smash.'

'No more would I,' said Perp. 'Them five pounds was good 'uns.'

'*What?*'

'You heard. Good 'uns.'

'I don't understand.'

'You wouldn't.' He ate a pickled onion. 'You. How often have you known me to sum a man up wrong?'

'Never.'

'That's right. I sized that kid up. He's better than fly and he's cleverer than smart. I got no use for him yet, but I'll have plenty later. You think from your mouth to your arse'ole; I think ahead. I've had my fivers' worth out o' him already. If I guess right, he'll bust them five quid and hook it in his nice new suit, and think he's passed bad money and – worse – robbed me. That's the way I want it. When I need him I'll find him, and when I find him I'll forgive him, and when I forgive a man

I've got him by the balls – a man like that one, I mean. Meantime, let the kid grow up on his own and save me the trouble o' nursing him. Let him brew, let him ferment, give him his own time. That way's always best.'

'And if he comes back with the change?'

'Then he ain't my boy, and I'll chuck him out.'

Later, when The Schemer Merton came and stammered his excuses, and paid a five-pound note 'to buy little Tom a new suit', telling of the encounter in Sweeting's, Perp astounded him by giving him a friendly slap in the face and a glass of gin.

'That's my boy!' he said.

'Your nephew? A remarkable young man, and remarkably well-spoken, sir.'

'He takes after me. Have some more gin. No, wait a minute, you like whisky, don't you?' Perp got out a bottle of Monk's Very Old. 'Let's see, your father was a parson, wasn't he?'

'You know everything,' said The Schemer Merton.

'That's right. You go to church.'

'Not every Sunday, Perp – just occasionally,' Merton said, with a deprecatory shrug.

'An educated man, a religious man,' said Perp with disgust, 'and he don't know Southern Railway and the South Western belongs to me! Ignorance is no excuse for working my railways without a licence, you know. All right, I let you off this time.'

'I meant it more as a joke,' said Merton.

'I know all about such jokes, you know.'

'Your nephew is an artist, sir; he took me in completely.'

'That's right. I was talking about religion. That brolly you half-inched off of the Canon of Barchester. I got it here.'

'It was more of a mistake than anything. Our umbrellas were standing side by side, and –'

'You're a liar. Now I been looking up this here Canon of Barchester. What *is* a canon, anyway?'

'A dignitary of the Church, sir, who possesses a prebend for the performance of divine service in a collegiate church, or cathedral.'

'That's nice. What's a prebend?'

'An allowance, a stipend –'

'Wages. Well this Barchester one don't live on his pay.'

'Some canons are rich.'

'That's right. This one's got a collection of Greek and Roman coins. Hang on to that fiver for expenses. You're going to Barchester to return that there umbrella. Come the independent retired gentleman – your old tobacco line'll do – dropping off to pay his respects on the way to

Salisbury. I'll loan you a few old coins to ask him an opinion of. He'll ask you to tea. Spot the collection, take notice of locks and windows. Draw me a map. Get it?'

'Yes sir.'

'I dare say the Canon'll be offering a reward for that brolly – it's a presentation, you know. Tell him to give to the Temperance Society – though I lay you a horse to a hen he opens a bottle of wine, and even money that's Madeira or East India sherry. For the stomach, not to drink. Drink educated. I want that map accurate as the Ordnance Survey, not only the house but the garden. For the roads and the town, bring back one o' them Walking Tourists' Guide Books. All right? Right.'

'I dare say,' said Merton, with some diffidence, 'I dare say, all being well, knowing you to be a very fair and just paymaster –'

'Listen, old man' – there was no friendly familiarity in the way Perp said this; he was simply calling Merton an old man – 'how old are you, sixty-five?'

'Sixty-five next birthday.'

'Remind me to send you a clockwork train. Sixty-five bloody years old, and he ain't got the common savvy to fluff that I'm not a cheap crook! Paymaster? By Jesus, I'm the general and you're the private! All being well or all not being well, *you* get *your* bully beef and bloody cocoa, and when I win you get your little bit o' loot, don't worry. And it's always Active Service, mind; and you know what to look forward to if caught spying, deserting, betraying, or mutinying, or being a coward in the face of the enemy. And, day or night, drunk or sober, if Perp says "Do this", or "Do that", you drop whatever else you're doing whether you're in the middle of a shit, a shave or a haircut, and you jump to it. Then Perp looks after you. Any mistakes made around here, I make. You do just like I tell you, and you do that dead right. If you do it wrong, I don't say you was mistaken; I say you didn't do what you were told. And I disciplines you. Get it? There's always luck, but I'm the judge of what's luck and what ain't, you know; and if you come a cropper doing just what I tell you – which ain't likely – I blame myself, not you, and I see to it you don't lose by it in the long run.'

'Yes sir.'

'Perp. Call me Perp. There's millions of Sirs. "Sir" means nothing.'

'Perp.'

'Help yourself to some more of that whisky. It's thirty years old. It costs fifteen shillings a bottle,' said Perp, affable now. 'So I'm sending you to Barchester. What my plans are, never you mind. I may follow 'em up, or I may not. You'll do like I tell you. I've had my eye on you, you know. You're in the estate agency business in a small, one-man way.'

'I'm in a small way in every respect.'

'That's right. You're what I call the little general shopkeepery style o' thief. The penny-here-and-a-penny-there kind; the it-all-mounts-upper class o' fiddler, like. Eh?'

He cocked an eye at Merton who, seeing that he was expected to reply, said, 'I am unassuming and respectable by nature, sir – I mean Perp. A man can't escape his upbringing. The rector of a poor parish, with a family, has only one worldly ambition, sir – to remain healthy and make ends meet, putting a few pounds aside for a rainy day. In this regard alone – for a more honest man never lived, rest his soul – I resemble my father. In this alone he failed. In this alone I have succeeded. If I had presumed to be ambitious I should have failed miserably. As it is, I have lived forty years on the wrong side of the law and have only once been charged; and that charge fell through for lack of evidence. I know my limitations and keep rigidly within them.'

Perp, magnanimous, said, 'That's all right. It's nothing to be ashamed of. It's the best thing a man can do, know his limitations. I bet you if I had limitations *I'd* know 'em and live within 'em. The point you raise is the one that interests me, though: forty years a tealeaf – petty, I grant you, but a tealeaf – and hardly known to the police except as a sharper over leases and all that, which don't count. What d'you make a year?'

'On the average, about six hundred pounds.'

'O' course, you've got money in the bank.'

'Yes sir. Yes, Perp. I have a thousand pounds to my credit at the London and Sussex Bank.'

'And?'

'And seven thousand in gilt-edged.'

'It's like being well-dressed,' said Perp. 'It gives a feller a manner you can't fake, a bit in the bank and a few stocks 'n shares. That's the way everybody that works for me is going to be. I don't like your whiskers.'

Merton's Newgate fringe was part of his stock in trade. It framed in silver, sanctified, set off and lent virtue to an otherwise questionable face. Thus bewhiskered and properly displayed in a suitable light, Merton had deceived experts. He had been known to say, caressing that venerable hair, 'I wouldn't part with it for a thousand pounds. I like it; it has *grown* on me – ha-ha-ha!' Now he said without hesitation, 'If you don't like them, that's good enough. I'll cut them off.'

Perp was satisfied. He said, 'No, you can keep 'em. I don't like 'em for Barchester. Where's your sense? Cut them whiskers off, and you're conspicuous; you're well known for 'em round here. For Barchester they're too peculiar and not educated enough. You don't cut 'em off –

you add to 'em; moustache and chinwhisker, like a professor. In that character, you book through to Salisbury, and what's more you go to Salisbury, and you come back from Salisbury. Like I said before, something may come of this, or then it might not; but with me you put as much science into pinching a toffee apple off a barrer as you do into knocking off a million. You map every last detail.'

'If you please, I'd like to go up to London and look at the Coin Room in the British Museum. Also, in the library, some works on numismatics.'

'What's that?'

'Coins.'

'You do that. I want you here the day after tomorrow at three o'clock for a dress rehearsal, like. You can go now.'

Thus, one Monday six weeks later the morning papers bore news of a 'daring daylight robbery at Barchester'. While the Canon, the Reverend Dr Amyas Baldhill, and all his household were at divine service the previous Sunday morning, thieves broke into his house and stole twenty-five trays of ancient Greek and Roman coins, comprising one of the five most important collections in England, insured for thirty thousand pounds but in point of actual value priceless. The Criminal Investigation Department of Scotland Yard confidently expected to make an arrest.

But Scotland Yard confidently expected nothing of the sort. There was a brutal simplicity about the affair, a blank and trackless straightforwardness, a featureless obviousness. It seemed to be exactly as reported: between nine and eleven o'clock on Sunday morning, some person or persons as yet unknown just broke in and carried away twenty-five trays of rare coins. A gang must have done it, because each tray was twenty inches long, sixteen inches wide and almost three inches deep and weighed about five pounds, with frame and glass. The whole business was somehow out of order. If the thieves had known exactly what they were after, why had they not skimmed the cream of the collection, which would have consisted in not much more than a large pocketful of gold and silver coins? But they had encumbered themselves with several cubic feet and a hundred and twenty pounds' weight of valueless wood, cardboard and glass. True, they had left the cabinets of bronze, copper and brass coins untouched. Still, something didn't quite fit; something somewhere was out of keeping with the robbery as a whole. It was too neat and yet untidy.

The thieves had spent no time searching for what they stole. An electric burglar alarm had failed to work simply because somebody had disconnected the dynamo in the tool shed from which it drew its current. Then they had come in by the kitchen door, using a skeleton key, leaving no fingerprints or footprints. They had torn off locks and broken open doors and cabinets with a plumber's wrench and a cold chisel. The entire operation could not have taken more than forty-five minutes. But, carrying the heavy bulk of all those trays, how could they have got away unseen?

The Rector, a sensitive and worldly gentleman, offered five thousand pounds reward for the return of his coins; no questions to be asked. The British Mutual, with whom he was insured, offered as much again. The underworld was silent. At last, with that air of good sportsmanship which insurance companies adopt when they cannot break a contract, British Mutual paid up. Dr Baldhill went up to London, drew his thirty thousand pounds, put it in the bank, and started back to Barchester. At Waterloo Station something odd happened: a seedy little man touched his cap and begged for the price of a cup of tea, and on receiving a threepenny piece said, 'Don't forget the box seats in the summer 'ouse, your reverence.'

'What's that?' the Canon asked; but the man had disappeared in the crowd. Box seats in the summer house? He wondered about that all the way home. It came between him and *The Cornhill Magazine*, took the zest out of *The Westminster Gazette* and vaguely disturbed his light dinner – a little clear soup, a salad, a chicken and a sweet omelette – he was not a trencherman at the best of times. He took six ounces of port in a graduated medicine glass, and then, reasoning that the air would do him good, put on a black mackintosh, took a stable lantern and walked out into the garden. This was a gracious piece of ground, well planted with flowering shrubs and handsome old trees and furnished with pretty little groups of eighteenth-century statuary. There was a Grecian Temple of Meditation, and a grotto, and even a neat little seventeenth-century maze of high, clipped box hedges – nothing labyrinthine, but amusingly baffling – in the centre of which stood a small octagonal summer house. Here were several carved wooden chests designed to contain cushions and folding chairs, disguised as benches. These were the 'box seats', of course.

Dr Baldhill lifted the lid of one of them and looked in. He uttered a low exclamation. The light of his lantern shone on the glass of a familiar frame, in which glinted certain battered discs of dull silver. And then a deep voice said, 'All right, Dr Amyas Baldhill, we were waiting for you.' He turned and saw two tall men standing by the open door.

'What . . . What . . .'

The bigger of the men, elephantine in a great raglan overcoat, said, 'I am Detective Inspector, retired, George Hunt, late of Scotland

Yard, presently investigator for the British Mutual Assurance Company of Leadenhall Street, London. This is my colleague, of the same company, Charles Woodward, Detective Sergeant, retired, also late of the Criminal Investigation Department. We've been keeping an eye on you for some time, Dr Baldhill.'

'What is the meaning of this?'

'Conspiracy to defraud is the matter, I'm afraid, Dr Baldhill.'

'I don't know what you're talking about.'

'By your leave, we'd better go into the house. Don't worry about your coins,' said Hunt, as Dr Baldhill looked back, 'they'll still be there where you had 'em put. If they haven't run away this past few weeks, they're not likely to do so now.'

'I don't know what you mean!'

'You'll explain that in court, I dare say. We've got the man you hired to steal your coin collection last September, and he told us exactly where you arranged for him to hide the stuff while you collected the insurance money.'

'This is monstrous!'

'We'd better go inside, sir. It's a cool sort of night to be standing in summer houses. But I expect you generally come out with a lantern about this time of the year to look at the garden?'

Numb and silent, Dr Baldhill led the way back to the house.

'Before we proceed any further,' said Hunt, when they were in the doctor's study and the baize-lined doors were closed, 'our credentials.' He took out a wallet, and so did Woodward. 'You ought always to ask for credentials,' he said. 'You never can tell who we might be.'

'I give you my word of honour that I know nothing of this, nothing at all!' Dr Baldhill cried.

'Firstly, sir, do you recognize this photograph?'

The doctor looked. 'I have seen the face before,' he said. 'He was here, in this house, last September, I think. Yes, his name is James Whelan Duffy, and he is a –'

'Pardon me. His name is John Wheeler, better known as "The Parson", and he is a notorious criminal, sir, as I rather fancy you must know. He specializes in queer burglaries. That is, burglaries with the connivance of the so-called victims, with a view to mulcting the insurance companies.' Hunt seemed to like the word. He repeated it, 'Mulcting the insurance companies. What was he doing here September last, sir?'

'He came to return an umbrella I lost in Victoria Station.'

'All the way out here for that?'

'He stopped on his way to Salisbury.'

'Very likely. Eh, Woodward?'

The other man said, 'Very.'

'This is horrible, horrible! A nightmare!'

'Yes, sir. Anyhow, he owned up; confessed. You paid him five hundred pounds to screw – which is *their* term for break and enter – your house, and steal your coin collection. He told us where you'd arranged to have him put the swag, sir. Otherwise how could he have put it there? That maze would take a stranger an hour to thread. That's why we were there waiting for you. We had our suspicions, don't you see; and they were justified, you'll agree, I think. How else do you explain being out there looking in those boxes in the summer house at this hour of a nippy November evening?'

'A beggar who wanted the price of a cup of tea –' the doctor began; then stopped, hopeless. He tried again, 'Somebody, apropos of nothing, mentioned –' Then he said, more calmly, 'Appearances are against me. I believe I am the victim of some incredible, some monstrous conspiracy.'

'Very likely, sir. Eh, Woodward?'

'Very.'

'And your endorsement scarcely dry on our company's cheque,' Hunt said. 'You oughtn't to have done it, sir, you really oughtn't. As it stands, it's an open-and-shut case. Larceny, sir. Wheeler's unsupported statement – or James Whelan Duffy's, as he is known to you – would be worth nothing. Even if the coins were where he said they were, that mightn't mean much without corroborative evidence of your collusion; he might have planted 'em there to pick up later at his leisure. But your going right to the boxes? That looks bad, that really does look bad, sir. Eh, Woodward?'

Woodward said, 'Couldn't look worse.'

The stolid, laconic officer, rigid in a black ulster, was unspeakably terrifying to the Reverend Dr Amyas Baldhill. He cried, 'I am the victim of some fantastic concatenation of circumstances, I assure you! I'll simply make restitution of the money, and explain the case!'

'Your Mr Wheeler has confessed, though.'

'Let him withdraw his confession. I won't prosecute.'

'And that's an offence in itself. That's compounding a felony, you know. British Mutual couldn't he a party to that, don't you see,' said Hunt. 'Not officially. Never.'

'It's this rascal's word against mine,' said Dr Baldhill.

'It'll look bad, sir, very bad, in the Sunday papers. We believe you – eh, Woodward?'

'Absolutely.'

'But I can see it in *Reynold's*,' said Hunt.

'Then what am I to do?'

'Doctor,' Hunt said, 'you might be surprised if I told you how often we insurance people have to smooth things over and hush matters up. Sometimes we bend the law without breaking it, as the saying goes. You understand that you can't make restitution of the money officially?'

'I suppose I understand. Perhaps my solicitor –'

'Doctor, I'd recommend that you kept your solicitor out of this. He's a sound man and a steady man, and a first-rate country family businessman, but he might find himself a little out of his depth here. Better let us have the British Mutual's cheque back before you pay it into your bank tomorrow –'

'– But I banked it in London this morning! I bank with the London & Provincial.'

'Well, let us have your personal cheque for the amount, drawn to bearer. Better write a covering note to the manager, to the effect that the sum recently deposited must be withdrawn forthwith for purchases in connection with the renewal of your coin collection. Which won't be untrue, you know, and you know why. There's your coins in your own summer house. As for Wheeler, better give him a couple of hundred, and we'll get him loose and kick him out of the country with a warning. These things are done more often than you know. Our own et ceteras – call it five hundred in all, over and above . . . It wouldn't look half so bad, you see, if you weren't a canon, and a gentleman of very high connections – you're Lord Balsam's second cousin, I think? – with an archdeaconship in sight, and maybe a bishopric after that. And (it's our business to know little things like this) you *did* start negotiations for a property in town, near Eaton Square; and you *did* say to Sir Howard Brocklebank that you'd gladly put down ten thousand, only you'd either have to sell some of your coins or draw on your capital to raise it, and you said you'd let him know. Eh, Woodward?'

'Correct, Mr Hunt.'

'The hideous part of this is, that I'm absolutely innocent!' cried the Reverend Dr Amyas Baldhill. 'It's preposterous!'

'We believe you implicitly, but we're servants of the company, sir; and you haven't got a leg to stand on. You should thank us for our help.'

'I do, I do. But . . . Would it help if I spoke with one of the directors?'

'Doctor,' said Hunt, 'don't do it. You've got your coins, and you very nearly got the money too. You'll get precious little sympathy off any of our directors, I assure you. Let sleeping dogs lie – or let lying dogs sleep. Be advised by me.'

'What am I to do? What am I to do with the unhappy coins now? What *shall* I do?'

'Put 'em back one or two at a time, I should,' said Hunt. 'In two or three years, there you are again, aren't you?'

'I suppose so . . . Oh, what an unbelievable horror!'

'Well, I hope this will be a lesson to you, Doctor. You can't play with pitch without defiling yourself.'

'I give you my sacred –'

'– Don't do it, sir! You're a churchman and I don't like to hear it. As for that five hundred extra, I put it to you: Woodward and I save the company hundreds of thousands annually. What do they pay us? I get three hundred and fifty a year, and Woodward gets two hundred and seventy-five. We're loyal, as you see. But a man must live. And we'll handle Wheeler – or Whelan, as you call him.'

'I'll write a cheque, a separate cheque. The other sum – it's very large – had I not better draw it from the bank myself?'

'It might be just as well. We'll come with you first thing in the morning, if you like.'

'It will be a load off my mind.' Dr Amyas Baldhill clutched his aching head. 'Oh, what an age we live in, what an age we live in! And Whelan was such a decent-seeming sort of man . . .'

Everything went smoothly. A month passed before he discovered that at least ten thousand pounds' worth of the rarest of the coins were gone from their frames, including some irreplaceable masterpieces by Myron, Polykrates, Kimon, Eukleidas, Herakleidas, Euainetos and the Aetna Master.

'These here coins will keep,' said Perp. 'For the time being, forget 'em. By and by they'll turn up out of nowhere, in Philadelphia maybe, and now we've got 'em they're so much the rarer. Meantime, let's settle up. There's thirty thousand pound here. This I divide in four lots of seventy-five hundred. The first quarter comes straight off the top; that goes into the general fund for expenses and emergency. So that I put aside. Right? Right. The second seventy-five hundred is mine, personally. Any objections? No? That's a relief. That leaves fifteen thousand. Jack cracked the place and planted the stuff, but Kevin and Fred talked the old parson out of the –' Perp made a bank teller's gesture with thumb and middle finger. 'So I call that even work. The three of you get forty-five hundred pound apiece. That leaves fifteen hundred. Merton gets one thousand. All right?'

The men nodded. Merton said, 'Perfectly, perfectly.'

'That leaves five hundred over. I'm splitting that two ways; two-fifty to Merton, for having the gumption to mark the three trays with the rarest stuff, and two-fifty to Jack for bringing the coins away. Is all fair and square?'

They said that it was.

'I should just about hope so,' said Perp. 'You know what a good screwsman earns on the average, all in all, as long as he lasts at the game? About three pound ten a week, if he's lucky. The Accountant worked it out – burglary and thievery in general is the most underpaid skilled trade in the world. But not with me it ain't. Look at yourselves for instance. Merton's an estate agent, Jack's got a bicycle shop, Kevin's in the novelty business, Fred's got a sweet-stuff shop. You'll put money in the bank and live comfortable and quiet till I want you again. It's better than the Cooperative Wholesale Society, and one of these days when I work it out with the Accountant, strike me blind if I don't start a proper Pension Scheme!'

Kevin, the laconic man, said, 'I couldn't help feeling half sorry for the old clergyman.'

Buttoning up his money, Merton said, 'Couldn't you? My father was rector of a poor parish, and a worried family man, but he'd have gone to the gallows before he fell the way that canon did. I hate rich clergymen.'

'Everybody's got a crooked bone in his body,' said Perp indulgently. 'Never mind your father. Ain't you got me? Be thankful, shut your jaw and go home.'

Later he went to Pitt's Crescent. Molly Irving, who knew nothing of this stroke of business, was surprised and delighted when he tossed twenty-five pounds into her lap.

'Why, Perp! What's this for?'

He said, 'Nothing. When I was a nipper my mum used to cut into me with a copper-stick when she came home with a gutful o' blue ruin. "Take that, you filthy rotten little swine! And that! And that!" If I said, "What's that for? I ain't done nothing," she'd say, "It's a little bit on account, you ugly little bastard, against you do something." Then she'd batter the piss out o' me. I take after the old mare. Them twenty-five quid's for nothing you've done right – it's against what you might do.'

'You're one of the best,' she said.

'That's right.'

'Whatever I'd do, I'd never beat a child with a stick. She must have been a horrible woman.'

'Oh, I don't know. What with being too old and ugly to go out whoring except on a foggy night, and too bloody lazy and dirty to take in washing, she done the best she could, all things considered.'

'You bear her no grudge, Perp?'

'Much use that. She's dead and gorn. Let her lie.'

'If she was alive I bet you'd look after her, Perp.'

'Yes, that's right. I'd send her a barrel o' white satin and a box o' salt kippers. I often wondered what's she'd be like if she had all the gin she could get down. You can't judge a person till you've seen what he looks like when he's happy . . .'

TEN

Full of good food and wine and triumph, delightfully titillated by a sense of danger, pleasantly electrified by the feel of crisp silk between his clean skin and the best suit of clothes he had ever worn, with more money in his pocket than he had ever owned and a well-packed bag in his hand, Tom Henceforth walked in glory.

At Brighton Station he bought a first-class ticket to London, for from London he could go wherever he liked. He felt so strong and light that if he jumped for joy (which he was almost impelled to do) the air would support him like water, like warm water in a dream, and then a flick and a wriggle would send him swiftly gliding to the high glass roof, free as a big fish among minnows. And the glamour of that moment was never to leave him, so that he could say, long years later, 'Give me the compost of the Railway Terminus! Because it is a physiological fact that when people are *going*, they exude certain essences of excitement, which are irresistible. That's why the best place to pick up a swift lay is on a boat or a train, or in a station. I love stations. For months, I haunted them, living from hand to mouth, nourishing myself mainly on noise and smoke – getting fat on the steam of stewed people the way cooks get fat on the steam of the kitchens . . .'

As he pictured himself, Tom Henceforth, after he left Brighton, was a kind of wraith – something disembodied that sported in the wind of the guard's green flag and cavorted with the pea in his whistle. And for the purposes of Henceforthian narrative, this was just as well. The sordid details of how he breakfasted and dined at Zobrany's place, and picked up pocket money by such artistic subterfuges as promising to paint people's portraits, are neither here nor there: he really did enjoy the sweaty dissolutions of the great termini, and loitered in those places – always carrying Perp's Gladstone bag, and never without a clean shirt.

So it happened that, one evening, having borrowed a few pounds on account of God knows what, and lusting after the peculiar pleasures of the melancholy mists that always haunt the neighbourhood, he went to Euston, and sat down on a bench next to a girl.

'Is this seat taken?' he asked.

'I suppose it is, now that you've taken it,' she said.

'Do you mind if I sit here?'

'It's a public place, I suppose.'

'Have you any objection to my smoking?'

'I don't see any sign that says SMOKING PROHIBITED.'

'But do *you* mind?'

'It's a matter of indifference to me, so long as you don't smoke a clay pipe.'

He took out his box of Hamid's Special. 'Lots of ladies smoke, nowadays. May I offer you one, ma'am?'

'No, thank you.'

He looked at her closely as he lit his cigarette. She sat erect, but at her ease, genteel in a grey costume and a white blouse, with no jewellery but a little golden cross set with seed pearls at her throat. She had laid aside a grey cape trimmed with fur and an umbrella with a silver-mounted handle. Her black-gloved hands rested on a plain leather handbag in her lap. Tom Henceforth observed that the suitcase at her feet was old and battered. Her hat was severe, without compromise. She had pale ash-blonde hair, gathered at the nape of her thick neck into a ponderous plain knot.

But when he looked at her face, Tom Henceforth froze, staring.

Here – as he chose to phrase it – Nature had turned artist. He took out Perp's sketching block and a crayon and began to block in her head. As he had expected – since no human being can see a stranger drawing his portrait and remain entirely disinterested – she said, 'Are you sketching me, by any chance?'

He replied, with enthusiasm, 'I wish I could. I handle a pencil the way a gypsy handles a fiddle – all Roman candles and skyrockets. That's what my teacher used to say. Whizzbang and sparks, and down comes the stick . . . Don't move . . .' She shrugged slightly. He went on, 'Whoever made you said to the world, "Damn your Venuses, let me show you what can be done with a handful of contrasts and a little good taste!" They said, "This bulgy forehead, children, I make the best of by pushing out these cheekbones . . . the nose, which is nothing much to speak of, I make exciting with a kind of savage flare of the nostrils. The sweep of the jaw may stand. The chin's beyond reconstruction, being short and a bit receding. Ay, but we emphasize it, d'you see, with this dimple and make it and the nostrils complementary to the mouth . . . And here – oh, here, children! – working on this heavy pale mouth, I let my fancy run away with me. Never mind Burne-Jones and all that romantic rabble with their slack-lipped skivvies. Who could imagine kissing a pre-Raphaelite beauty without getting a mouthful of spittle? Probably flavoured with fish and chips and tea. No, no, no! Here's a big mouth. Let's make it bigger! Make it obscene! Just for once, a teeny touch of Aubrey Beardsley, if you like, in those sneery great curves," . . . That's what Nature said, when he put you together, lady. "As for those eyes. They're narrow and long? Lengthen 'em, turn 'em up at the corners a fraction of a degree, and for God's sake let those irises stay heavy and rusty as old iron! There you are," said Nature. "Now put this one next to Lily Langtry and just you see which one men'll run crazy after! Dolores, our Lady of Pain."'

She laughed, and then her pallid and undistinguished face changed. The thick, curved lips curled back, uncovering large white teeth; her mouth opened, exposing a moist red tongue; the long eyes glittered. In a flash, she became revolting and desirable. Then she was plain and expressionless again.

She said, 'You have a remarkable flow of conversation. I will have one of your cigarettes, I think, if I may. May I see what you've drawn?'

'It's not very good . . . Do you live in London?'

'No. Let me see that drawing, won't you?'

He gave it to her, explaining, 'The noise of the trains . . .'

'I think you've caught my eyes rather well.'

'Oddly enough, they're almost the same colour as this red crayon. I've never seen such a colour.'

'But you've made me look like a mixture of Ophelia going mad, and Lady Macbeth.'

'You read Shakespeare?' he asked.

'Sometimes. I'm an actress,' she said.

'I thought you were a governess, or a lady's companion.'

'So do lots of people. I'm an actress just the same.'

'Where do you live?'

'My home is near Manchester. You are an artist, or an art student?'

'Not exactly. I do all kinds of things. I turn my hand to this or that as the mood takes me, you know. Will you be going home?'

'Yes, I'm going north. I was with Scabright's Company for the season in Hastings. But it turned out badly. He couldn't even pay us at the end. All of twenty-eight shillings a week! I'm fortunate to have my return ticket. But that's the theatre.'

'What name do you act under?'

'Era Moon.'

'Have you been on the stage long?'

'Seven years. Since I was fourteen.'

'Are you married?'

'No. What a curious boy you are!'

'I'm not a boy. I'm older than I look,' said Tom Henceforth, blowing smoke through his nostrils. 'When are you going to Manchester? I have a reason for asking.'

'I'll stay in town overnight and go on tomorrow, I suppose. What reason?'

'As it happens, I'm going to Manchester, too.'

'Really? Where in Manchester?'

'I have to see a man on business. Where are you going?'

'I stop with a friend in Windwood,' she said. 'But they may have something for me. My friend wrote and told me there's a famous Austrian impresario in town, starting something new and looking for talent. New things excite me.'

'What's his name?'

'The Baron de Say. Have you ever heard of him? Gèza de Say.'

Without hesitation Tom Henceforth cried, 'What, de Say? Heard of him? I should think I have. I know him well. He's the man I'm going to Manchester to see. He's a friend of the family. I'm half Austrian myself.'

'Not really? What's your name?'

'I don't tell everybody,' he said slowly, thinking furiously. The only Austrian or Hungarian name he could think of was Mozart. 'But . . . well, I don't mind telling you' – he had one now – 'my name is Zobrany, Tom Zobrany.'

'What a most extraordinary thing,' she said, her eyes shining. 'Why, if you know him well you could introduce me to him.'

'Of course,' said Tom Henceforth. 'I think you're the most beautiful creature I ever laid eyes on. Introduce you to old de Say? Be delighted, Miss Moon.'

'Call me Era. May I call you Tom?'

'Please do.'

'Zobrany is such a melodious name, though. Is your business with the Baron theatrical?'

He parried this. 'It's rather confidential for the moment.'

'You're not a performer yourself, by any chance?'

'No. I'm a free agent, an independent man.'

She took out a newspaper cutting. 'My friend sent me this,' she said. It had been clipped from the *Manchester Evening Opinion*, and conveyed the news that Thurstan Preston, the great cotton broker, had breakfasted that morning with the Baron Gèza de Cseh, the well-known theatrical impresario, at the Grand Canal Hotel, that justly famous rendezvous of the rich and the mighty . . . Asked if he proposed to devote a moiety of his native genius and self-made fortune to a theatrical venture, the magnate Thurstan Preston, renowned for his native Lancashire wit, convulsed the *Evening Opinion*'s correspondent by replying, 'Ah, if I told thee what I meant to do, tha'd be as wise as mysen!' The writer was one John McErroll.

Era Moon said, 'The Royal Canal is as expensive as The Grand. Where will you be staying in Manchester?'

Tom Henceforth returned the cutting, muttering, 'I haven't decided, yet.'

'The Baron –' she began.

'You note the accent over the *e*? That means his name is pronounced "*Gazer*" not "Geezer", you know. It's a good name for my old friend de Cseh, though.'

He spoke with complete authority. A less credulous person than Era Moon would have thought, *This boy has known the Baron de Cseh all his life*. 'Will you really introduce me?' she asked.

'Yes. We'll go north together.'

'Where do you live in London?'

'I don't. I live in Brighton; Pitt's Crescent. We own some houses there. I've finished my business here, so if you're free, why not dine with me?'

'I'm not dressed –'

'– Neither am I. We'll go somewhere informal. Pagani's? Romano's? The Café Royal?' He had heard of these places. She knew them well, by hearsay.

'Wherever you please,' she said.

'Where are you staying?'

She laughed. 'At the Provincial Jeune Première's and Understudy's Residential Club.'

'Where's that?'

'Here. The waiting room at Euston Station.'

'I think we can do better for you than this,' said Tom Henceforth.

Many years later, recounting the incident in one of his glittering, satanically hyperbolic monologues – diamonds by lamplight but paste in the morning; champagne to hear but heel taps to remember – Tom Henceforth was to say:

'. . . It was first love at first sight, and you know what that's like – acute discomfort – if you went to the doctor with such symptoms, damn my eyes if he wouldn't slap you onto a table and open you up for it! All the blood in your body goes to your head, your face swells up, your heart goes off like a pump in a drought, you get pins and needles in the soles of the feet, your spine turns into a damnation thermometer and a swift chill sends the marrow down with a rush to fill a whacking great bulb just behind your bladder, so that you can't pee. At the same time your arsehole winks, your toes curl up and your lips go black. She was ordinary enough till she smiled, but then – my God! Listen – may I be struck dead this minute if I tell you a word of a lie – I heard paper rustling on the seat next to me. I'd brought some fruit to eat, and the noise came from the bag. I looked, and may I be deprived of my eyesight if two bananas hadn't stood up on end and peeled themselves! I swear upon my mother's virtue, I was leaking semen like an incarcerated bull elephant in *musth*.

'So we went for dinner to the oyster shop near Victoria, and she got outside of twenty-four oysters and a fecundating great red cow-lobster shedding eggs like a burst bag of beads bedevilled in a yolky sauce blazing with red pepper, preparatory to sucking off the flesh of a pair of sizzling chops of which she crunched the bones, washing all this down with gulp after gulp of that rasping wine of Capri which smells of sweat and sulphur and yeast and crushed pumice! Then a jam pudding gory as the head of John the Baptist on a hot plate, and a wedge of Camembert cheese that ejaculated spermy drops from its gashed flesh as she sent the knife home; to say nothing of coffee and rum. If what I say diverges from God's truth by the breadth of one hair, let me be castrated with a sickle and buried in shame – when she left, oozing protein, she stopped at a baked potato machine and asked for a King Edward twopenny one! The potato man had hands like coal shovels, but even he had his difficulty taking a spud out of the ashes. He split it with his talons, and sprinkled it with salt. By the Body and the Blood, it blazed incandescent in the night! Yet she buried her cool face in this obscene tuber so that it burst into steam, and in three seconds by the stopwatch licked out its pulp and swallowed the skin, and called for more, and with her ravenous lips drew the bowels out of another two-pound potato in one kiss, as if it were a miserable grape. Then she said, "It's past ten o'clock. We have only a few short hours before we catch the train at six-forty-five tomorrow morning. Don't let's go to a big hotel where we'll be conspicuous. Time's short. Let's go to a smaller place near St Pancras or Euston."

'So we went to the Northampton Hotel, and I took a double room – gas bracket with a Welsbach mantle under a pink globe lit by a pinpoint of concentric half-lights and penumbrae; dressing table full of rusty hairpins; washing stand with a drawer choked with sodden red newspaper parcels, supporting cracked jug, chipped basin, slimy soapdish and a thing like a vase for nobody knows what; slop pail with a straw handle and a busted lid, ringed like a five-thousand-year-old redwood tree section with the detritus of half the kidneys in north-west London, by God; and a two-gallon pisspot in a bas relievo of gilded violets, into which somebody had been sick after eating tomatoes. But what did we care? May the Almighty God spit in my upturned face when I beg mercy at the Last Judgment – we were in that state, we'd have coupled at the bottom of a cesspool on a mattress of live rats, between blankets of lice under a counterpane of red bedbugs, and called it a love nest!

'Before the door had closed we were in each other's arms – slap-bang! Listen. What, you may ask, happens when two moving bodies, both irresistible, rush together? Why, they violate a law of Nature which says that no two objects may occupy the same space at the same time, and the result of this God-awful blazing concatenation must be a cosmic explosion. So it was with Era and me. We violated every law of Nature. In our first get together, all four brass knobs flew off the bedposts and went hurtling downstairs in a volley to smash to smithereens a thirty-six inch Benares brass dinner gong and short-circuit the tramlines for the entire neighbourhood. To this I swear by all I ever held sacred. The poor old grey coiled springs of the mattress parted like hair under shears as we (now two snapping halves) bit into it, thrashing and drumming our heels like people strangling on a live electric cable! The building rocked – the manager threatened to call the police – but we went on and on and on, hour after hour.

'By dawn I was raw and sore as a squeezed-out pimple on the neck of a City clerk waiting for a slow train on the platform of Stepney Station in the middle of a rainy evening in February. Vitiated! She lay smiling in her sleep, plastered with glairy plasma and sprinkled with the shattered wreckage of the bed; a succubus, a vampire!

'I dressed, intending to get away quietly. Her clothes were neatly folded – I am prepared to swear that they had folded themselves of their own accord, since with these two eyes I had seen her burst out of them, sending them flying in thirty-two different directions, in one throb. There were her coarse little linen drawers with lace at the legs, and her dinky little chemise, and her stays (one of the laces of which, I swear, uncoiled itself and opened its metal tag and hissed at me like a snake), and her petticoat, and all that. These garments smelt faintly of the theatre and the boarding houses connected with it. Yet they were clean, notwithstanding!

'I felt the foot of her stocking. It bent without cracking. This touched my heart. In the face of adversity, she remained sweet and dainty. I said aloud, "You *shall* meet the Baron Gèza de Cseh!" At the whisper of this name she opened her eyes and said, "I trust you, Tom." Astounding girl! She said, "Why, you're all dressed! I'll dress, too, and we'll catch the six-forty-five." I was bruised from head to foot and chewed up like a stick you throw for a dog. She slithered out of the debris of a pillow she had torn up in her ecstasy and, covered with feathers, glided at me like a bloody Lamia, wound herself round me like a bleached python and withdrew from me the last driblet of my vitality in one wiggle, pinning up her hair at the same time, holding me with one leg like somebody in an Indian sculpture.

'How the devil I was to handle this Baron de Cseh business I didn't know. I planned on giving her the slip in Manchester. So runs the world away.'

And so ran Tom Henceforth's story.

It was true, to this extent: he did take Era Moon to dinner at the oyster shop in Victoria; and after a supper of oysters and lobsters and lamb chops, of which she unquestionably ate her share with excellent appetite, they did share a room at the Northampton Hotel. It was a decent room, since the Northampton catered for a steady, middle-class sort of bona-fide traveller, and there was a clean bathroom in the passage only two doors away. (But Tom Henceforth was a raconteur of the Naturalistic-Gothick school, and had his artistic conscience as such; he hung gamey reminiscence high and ripe, and cooked it spicy.) Era Moon's disrobing really was swift and gymnastic; but she managed it by sleight of hand under a nightdress like a conjurer's cloak – there would have been nothing exceptionable about such an undressing if it had been done in broad daylight in the open street.

She said, 'How nice everything might be if we both weren't so tired, and I wasn't unwell, and we knew each other ever such a lot better!'

'What, aren't you well? Was it the lobster?'

'No, not the lobster; something else. I'm indisposed.'

'Is there anything I can do?'

'I don't think so. Aren't you awfully tired?'

He was. They slept side by side, hand in hand. Next morning he asked if she felt better, and she said, 'In two or three days.'

After the Northampton Hotel's invariable breakfast of mixed grill, toast and tea, they caught their train to Manchester.

Tom Henceforth was later to asseverate: ' . . . Reeking great glabrous sausages cracked between her teeth and the bacon splintered, while gouts of kidney gravy spurted out of the corners of her mouth and dribbled blood and fat into the hollow of her throbbing white throat, making little scummy pools just behind the collarbone, what time she pronged her huge red tongue into the yellow bellies of frazzled eggs, by God! Frightful great mouthfuls made bulges from her Adam's apple to her navel under her white skin, like eggs going into a snake's belly, as she gulped; but she cocked her little ringer as she lifted her cup, and drank her tea in tiny sips. She swabbed her plate with soggy toast, and grinned, and so help me Jesus she now had three mouths – one pink, one orange-colour, and one blackish purple! . . . All the way from London to the Liverpool Street Station in Manchester I had to lie on my belly while she kept trying to turn me over like a great pale ravenous bird trying to get a worm out from under a rock. If I exaggerate, let me never rise from this chair! . . .'

An elderly couple travelling to Crewe mistook Tom Henceforth and Era Moon for brother and sister, and gave them mint humbugs to suck. Her friend was at the station to meet her – a square-cut blocky woman with sulphurous little blue eyes and a hitched-up chin.

'Jo is more like a mother, or an aunt, to me,' Era had said.

But mothers do not kiss their daughters and nieces do not embrace their aunts as Jo and Era did.

'Jo, may I introduce Mr Tom Zobrany?'

The woman offered Tom Henceforth a harsh, uncompromising hand and a glance he could almost hear, like the flame of a blow-lamp.

Era explained, 'Mr Zobrany is a friend of the Baron de Cseh. He is going to introduce me.'

'To introduce *us*,' said the woman called Jo. '*Us*, Mr Zobrany. I know you and I know your sort. I can read you like a book. If you're trying to seduce *my* Era with fairy tales you've come to the wrong shop, for you can't bamboozle me. *I* know your tricks, and I'm up to 'em, for I'm in the theatrical profession myself. You're no professional. What's your business, eh? What's your business?'

'My business is *my* business,' Tom Henceforth managed to say, with an offended air. 'Meet me tomorrow morning at ten o'clock at the Grand Canal Hotel.'

'Why, what's a whippersnapper like you to do with the Baron de Cseh? You aren't his valet – you're not gentleman enough to be even a gentleman's gentleman – I can see through *you* like water. You're a schoolboy, a nasty little schoolboy –'

'– No, Jo, he's kind,' said Era Moon.

'Tomorrow at ten,' said Tom Henceforth, turning on his heel; and strode away in a white rage, out of the clangorous stinking station and into the raw and dripping Manchester evening.

Whippersnapper! Schoolboy! The worst of it was, that the woman was right: he had come to the wrong shop, and he couldn't bamboozle her. But if she thought she could read Tom Henceforth like a book why, there, he swore, *there* she was wrong.

As usual he walked aimlessly but at a swift and resolute pace, briskly turning every corner as he came to it. The smell of Manchester, he decided, was like an old woman in wet rags frying fish over a fire of coal dust in a disused railway coach on a steaming rubbish dump in a heavy mist . . . On the basis of this impression alone he felt he could write an amusing and instructive Guide to the City. Then he caught the odours of hot ink and damp paper, looked up and saw a sign:

MANCHESTER
MORNING STAR
EVENING OPINION

Destiny had guided him. He pushed open the door and walked into the dim lobby. An old man in a glass box asked, 'Aye?'

'I want to speak to Mr John McErroll.'

''E's gone. Tha'll find him i' t' Bull, most like. 'E'll be standing near t' cheese, I dare say.'

Sure enough, there he was in the Saloon Bar of The Bull in Bull Yard – inky-fingered like a clerk but not of the business quarter, business-like in his manner but not like a tradesman, sly as a pickpocket but not of the underworld, decisive as a detective but not of the police force, surreptitious as a tout and brisk as an auctioneer, yet with the absorbed look of an innocent bystander – helping himself to a cut of crumbly Cheddar, and looking into a pint pot with the moody air of one who knows that only three inches of flat beer stand between himself and a long thirsty evening.

Tom Henceforth heard the landlord say, with fatalistic sarcasm, 'That's reet, go on, help thysen! Why don't 'ee tak' t' bloody cheese and gi' me back t' slice, Mr McErroll?'

'Peace, ticklebrain!'

Tom Henceforth said, 'Pardon me, am I addressing Mr John McErroll, the dramatic critic of the *Evening Opinion*?'

The man stared at him. He had a broad corrugated lip like a scallop shell and a thin sidelong nose, sad sidelong eyes and a disillusioned chin. 'You are addressing John McErroll the scavenger pertaining to a journal of that name, and therefore not a dramatic critic but a go-between for the paper manufacturers and the privies in which that so-called newspaper is generally to be found hung up with suitable perforations – where it might be found useful, though not worth the halfpenny they charge for it, if it were not so polluted with bad ink and worse editorial matter that it is apt to render doubly offensive that which it scrapes away,' he said, in one breath. 'What can I do for you?'

'I read something in your paper about the Baron Gèza de Cseh, and I wondered if you could spare a moment. May I offer you –'

'– You may, young man, you may. At exactly this hour of the evening I am in the habit of taking half a quartern of Power's Irish in a little water, hot. Only it is my duty to warn you that I shall not be in a position to return your hospitality until tomorrow when the cashier's till opens across the way.'

'Twice,' said Tom Henceforth to the landlord. '. . . It's a great pleasure, Mr McErroll, I assure you; and as for returning what you call my hospitality, please don't think of it –'

In something less than four minutes he had caught the other man's manner of speaking; in five minutes more he would have the cadence.

'– The fact is, that I'm concerned in a way with the Baron de Cseh, and since I like your way of writing and all's grist that comes to your mill as a gentleman of the Press, I thought I'd like to give you such news as I have, rather than just let it loose.'

'Are you Irish, by any chance?'

'No,' said Tom Henceforth.

It would take him a good hour in McErroll's company to pick up a decent brogue.

'No, I'm nobody in particular. I'm here on business, actually, with the Baron. He has found what he's looking for, here in Manchester, as it happens – a great new talent. The Baron has found a new actress. She looks like a pale saint. But when she opens her mouth and laughs, she looks like – well, it's like Mary Magdalene, Before and After; only in reverse. You never saw anything like it. And here's where your paper comes in, because she's a Manchester girl, from out Windwood way, and her name is Era Moon. You have my authority to say that the Baron de Cseh is thinking of making her the leading lady in a new production, although as yet that bit's a poetic fiction –'

'– The hell with your poetic fictions, man! Where's the great truth that didn't start as poetic fiction? Seven items out of ten in those deplorable pages of ours are only put out because the paper must be filled. Give us the story, then' – he took out pencil and paper – 'let's have the names. I'll do the rest. "*On dit que . . . tralala-tralalee . . .*" I can still slip it in in time for the *Morning Star*, for she has yet to be put to bed, the whore. Come on, now . . .'

'Keep my name out of it, if you don't mind.'

'I forgot to ask your name. Never mind that now. "A famous actor-manager from London" – that'll do.'

'Doesn't your editor check news items?'

'What for?'

'In case they might not be accurate.'

'Oh man, *man*!' cried McErroll, writing and laughing at the same time.

'The same again,' said Tom Henceforth to the landlord.

'Wait till I come back – I'll not be gone a minute – don't go away, whatever you do!' McErroll ran out, and the rush of his departure made the gaslights flicker.

'Eh, he's a funny one,' the landlord said. 'He gets t' sack regular three times a week, but always cooms oop wi' summat and they taks him on again, like.'

'An intelligent man,' said Tom Henceforth.

'Aye. I wish he was a rich 'un. Here 'a cooms! Dig for thy brass!'

'We're in,' said McErroll. 'Where's that whisky?'

They sat at a table. 'How well d'you know the Baron?' Tom Henceforth asked.

'Know him? I don't, man. As far as anybody knows, he's some crony of old Thurstan Preston's, and they knew each other in Rome. Now everybody knows all about Preston. He's the cock of the dunghill. Just a common old working man – he started life as one of a family of seventeen, and all of 'em syphilitic, myopic, anaemic, diabetic, rachitic and generally buggered up. He went to work twenty-six hours a day starting at the age of nine, at elevenpence a week, upon which he supported the entire family. Saved up his money and bought out the boss, and that's how he's where he is today – King of Lancashire, owner of seventeen mills and a multimillionaire. But no side about him, mind you, for he still smokes tobacco, eats chicken eggs and wears no more than one pair of trousers at a time like a man of the people as he is. Never touches a bite to eat except when he fancies it, and is abstemious in his drinking, for he invariably puts down his glass when he opens his fly to piss. A moral influence, by God and by Jesus! "The naked every day he clad, when he put on his clothes" – touching the matter of which, he's shocked beyond endurance at the high incidence of nudity among savages, and believe me when I tell you that he lies awake at night worrying that a hundred million chocolate peni and twice the number of ebony tits are waving in the breeze uncovered by fifth-rate cotton printed in five colours with the signs of the zodiac. Just a horny-handed old Lancashire toiler, puffing his soft clay cutty-pipe.

'"Horny" – pardon me while I sermonize, for theology is in my blood – brings me to my Secondly, which is Rome. The old hypocrite likes his bit of nookey, and he likes it young and barely nubile, and he likes it wrapped in silk and scented, and so he goes to Italy for it – and it's my guess that there's where our Baron de Cseh comes in, for I never yet met an impresario that wasn't half a pimp. And hence, we will assume, Thurstan Preston's interest in theatrical enterprises – if interest there be on his part. For into this queer picture comes a figure who is none other than Salomon Samoon! . . . Better call for another couple of glasses. I'll stand treat tomorrow.'

'Let me lend you a pound or two until then.' Tom Henceforth had three pounds left.

'I will, and thank you . . . Here, curate, drawer, tapster! Bring the bloody bottle! . . . Now let me tell you something. The Bradford woollen men think they're sharp, but they're afraid of the Manchester cotton men. And both the Bradford and the Manchester men shiver in their shoes when they hear the names of the Stockport Armenians. But the Armenians of Stockport bolt their doors and pray to whatever fish-tailed dog-faced gods Stockport Armenians worship, when they hear the name of Salomon Samoon, who is half Welsh and half Baghdad Jew and comes from Bolton, but is by religion a Quaker, with a branch of the family in Belfast and another in Hamburg. Samoon and Preston are deadly enemies, you see; and all of a sudden Samoon appears to have a finger in the Baron de Cseh's little pie. There is my Thirdly, my dear boy . . . And the gossip is that your little Baron is buying leases on theatres all over England. And now you come with the news that he is to produce plays. Let us have another drink, and then talk of higher things.'

'–Yes, do. But what have you heard about the Baron? What sort of impression is he making here?'

'Och, who cares? Look: if Preston is seen even kicking you up the backside, your credit is good in this city. If Samoon lets you have what they call "the reek of his muck" hereabout, you are assumed to be a person of consequence. Your Baron lives in a suite at the Grand Canal. The staff at the hotel tell me that nothing but the best is good enough for him, and he sends that back five times before throwing it in the waiter's face. As Alexander the Great always had a wild boar on the spit in case he wanted to dine, and as Napoleon always had six capons on the fire against his being in the mood for lunch, so this Baron of yours always has champagne at a certain temperature, and a supply of those sickening sponge-cakey biscuits dirty old men seduce small girls with, always fresh and warm. Yesterday he asked for wild strawberries. There were no wild strawberries. He said, "Let there be wild strawberries." And there were wild strawberries.'

'Will there be something in the paper tomorrow about Miss Moon?'

'My dear, your young lady is assured of immortality for just about as long as it takes a man with nothing better to do to read a dozen lines of blunt five-point type.'

'I admire your conversation,' said Tom Henceforth, 'but you must excuse me a minute. I've got to . . .'

'Let Nature take its course,' said McErroll graciously.

But Tom Henceforth did not pause at the ammoniacal iron enclosure in the yard. Much as he liked the Irishman, Era Moon and her friend Jo were on his mind. He had to get them in their cells, each with its drop of bitter honey and its seal, and put away in his past to sleep and grow in the dark. Present, they encumbered the future.

He took a cab to the Grand Canal Hotel. The man at the desk said, 'I'm afraid the Baron de Cseh will see nobody tonight, sir.'

'He'll see me,' said Tom Henceforth.

'I'm afraid not, sir. If you'd leave a message?'

'No message. Say, Mr Zobrany. Send up word. Tell him, Mr Zobrany from Rome, if you please.'

'I'll send up a message with a page, if you say it's personal, but the Baron –'

'– It's personal. Zobrany, from Rome.'

As the clerk later told a colleague, 'There was this young man, dressed like a gentleman, but with this wild look in his eye and a certain *manner*. I thought to myself, "He looks as if he's going to murder the Baron," and I said to myself, "And a jolly good job if he does!" Anyway, I sent a page boy up with a message: Mr Zobrany from Rome. The boy came down white as a ghost. As soon as he knocked, the Baron flew at him like a wild animal, the way the Baron does, with "How dare you?" and all that. Then the boy said, "It's Mr Zobrany from Rome." The Baron went pale as death and ground his teeth and cried out, "Oh my God, my God!" Then he got hold of the boy and shook him, and said, "Tell him I'm not in, you little beast! No, tell him to come up! No, say I'm out! No, bring him up; yes, bring him up; no, no; yes, conduct the gentleman up, show him in. Zobrany, oh my God! Oh yes, oh no! Order champagne, damn bloody bugger! Quick!" – like a person demented, picking up handfuls of air and knitting with 'em, so that it seemed murder was certain to be done. And I, for one, shouldn't have broken my heart, I do assure you! But when the waiter fetched up the wine, there was the young fellow, cool as you please, sitting by the fire and eating ladyfingers; and the Baron pale and set like a cold blancmange, trembling but quiet for once, and in a dew of perspiration. The waiter, Luigi, said, "Mark my words, the young man is of the Camorra – he has the Black Hand on that one. Let him say his prayers." But no such luck . . .'

ELEVEN

Like a bacteriologist's specimen when the dye takes hold, Gèza Cseh had become distinguishable as something more than a faint smear. He had twisted into focus, popped into a category and was characteristic. It was possible, then, to guess in what circumstances the little fellow might bite, and the pathology of the conditions he might be expected to bring about when he began to feed.

So, that fanatic urgency which had been unseemly in the waiter, and that *maître d'hôtel*'s air of careworn authority and preoccupied condescension so ludicrous in the busy little busboy, combined most marvellously to suit the character of the Baron Gèza de Cseh. Incongruities became congruous and airs were transformed into graces, as fifty grandiose mannerisms fused in one Grand Manner. If his old friends of the Hungarian colony in Rome could have seen him in clothes by Poole and shod by Lobb, barbered by Penhaligon and hatted by Lock, they would have called him Little Napoleon in a very different tone of voice; and not to his face, either, for he no longer had the look of a man to crack a joke with. Only the diagnostic eyes of very experienced old waiters detected something in him that did not appertain to the aristocracy – something in the way he had of beckoning with half an eyebrow, pointing with only the last joint of one finger, cursing them without moving his lips and expressing displeasure with one nostril. But even they said among themselves, 'Most likely he's the pampered son of some millionaire hotel proprietor who bought a title in Romania back in the '70s.' They reasoned that no true nobleman *hochwohlgeboren* could know, with such awful exactitude, the mechanics of being served.

He had not lied to Howgego when he said that he was going to America. His passage was booked (he had to pay cash for that) and he was on his way to Liverpool to take the liner, when, idly turning the pages of an illustrated magazine, he saw the name of Thurstan Preston on a coloured advertisement. Now people might say what they liked about the Cotton King, Preston, but nobody could accuse him of not knowing what was what when it came to Art. Like the soap-boiler Pears, Thurstan Preston paid Royal Academicians to draw his posters; but where Pears appealed to the public through the homely whimsey of bare babies in baths groping for dropped washballs, Preston preferred thoughtful, spiritual themes. He had paid Robert Grinling a cool eight thousand for this one. Grinling was the most lifelike painter of draperies in the world. If you took a magnifying glass – which many people did – you could count the stitches. Buyers from St Paul's Churchyard, brought to Grinling's exhibitions, looked at the canvases and said, 'Why, here's Lyons velvet at three guineas a yard! There's a lovely bit of Milanese shot taffeta! And *that* piece of shantung wasn't bought off a barrow in Petticoat Lane!'

The picture Cseh contemplated was of the Nativity – a subject of which the drapers have never tired – and Grinling had done it all in cotton. The original had excited the admiration of the entire trade when it was unveiled in Manchester. It was almost impossible to believe that it had been done with brushes. You could read the lines on the uplifted palms of the shepherds if you had the skill – no two hands were alike – and count the hairs on the oxen if you had the patience. But this was nothing. The fabrics were the thing. Looking at the Virgin, delighted experts cried, 'That's a first-rate piece of long-staple superfine Egyptian in fast royal blue!' And there was Joseph in a sound hard-service medium-count tropic-weight Indian duck, off-white with a faint blue stripe; and the farm girls in washables, various. From the Magi to the shepherds, there was a length of Lancashire goods to suit every taste and condition. You could almost hear it rustle.

No caption or slogan marred the tone of the picture. Simply, THURSTAN PRESTON COTTONS. Below, the reader was invited to send sixpence in stamps to cover cost of packing and posting a free copy mounted and ready for framing, together with The Thurstan Preston Mills Fashion Book and a selection of patterns.

Now Gèza Cseh knew Thurstan Preston. He had his card, which, being by instinct a collector of such souvenirs, he had picked up off the floor when he was helping to carry out the glasses after the Cotton King had given a party in a suite at the Albergo Magnifico in Rome, a year or so before. It was a highly select and discreet party, paid for by Preston and arranged by that inevitable pair of Roman good companions – the plump blond prince whose eyebrows turn down at the corners and up in the middle while his mouth turns down in the middle and up at the corners; and his cousin the dark count whose mouth turns up in the middle and down at the corners; both very tired and tolerant of everything. It was a most respectable party, to which ladies could – and did – bring their twelve-year-old daughters. The children were allowed to stay up extremely late. For their entertainment, presumably, there were also present two ladies dressed as gentlemen, and two gentlemen dressed as ladies, and a female midget. Cseh found the card in assorted debris which included broken glasses, crushed pastries, cigar butts, a corset, a quantity of empty bottles, a silver-mounted dog whip, a handful of small change, a hair ribbon and a young girl's drawers.

He kept the small change and the visiting card. (He had a visiting card of his own, now, beautifully engraved, *The Baron Gèza de Cseh*, with a coronet above.) Even if old Preston had noticed him, which was unlikely, the odds were a thousand to one against his recognizing him. *One way or another I am certain to get something out of him*, Cseh thought, rummaging in the grab bag of his imagination for a catchpenny scheme of promising shape.

Among other properties Thurstan Preston owned a pit of rare clay, known to the building trade as Rose o' Lancaster, which digs out warm pink but bakes to the colour of a red-hot, rusty iron stove. It holds the deadly dull glow of the kiln. Some of the most conspicuous public buildings in the north of England are built of Rose o' Lancaster bricks, which are guaranteed to last forever. Ten thousand years hence, when everything else is gone and forgotten, archaeologists digging in the dust will find whole railway stations of Rose o' Lancaster as good as new, still dotted with indestructible enamelled iron plates advertising Bovril, Virol and Beecham's Pills.

Then of what should a man like Preston build his own mansion, if not Rose o' Lancaster? As for the house itself, the least said the better; words cannot convey the tone of delirium, and this was gibberish in brick, raving in stucco and foaming in cast iron. We used to laugh at the story of the California gold miner who struck it rich, rushed to the nearest town, dashed down a sack of nuggets and ordered a thousand dollars' worth of ham and eggs. There would have been something human in such an extravagance – the man was hungry for ham and eggs, and really felt he could eat that much. By the same token, a thirsty man thinks not in glassfuls but in lakes. That same miner probably yearned for a soft bed, too; but it is doubtful if, having eaten his dinner, he went to a hotel and booked three hundred and sixty-five bedrooms. That would have been sheer madness. Yet some cotton men went crazy like that in the days of their glory: bustled into builders' offices, hurled down chequebooks and ordered two hundred thousand pounds' worth of assorted architecture. Preston had stipulated that the place must have billiard rooms, ballrooms, conservatories, salons, studies and a library. 'The rest I leave to you,' he said. They built him a house that combined the more noticeable points of the Cathedral of St Basil, Strangeways Gaol and the Albert Memorial. In its way it was almost sublime – it stood just this side of the physically impossible.

But nobody laughed at the Thurstan Prestons then. The laughter was to come much later when the Slump caught the cotton kings short, and hungry children could be seen playing jacks on the cobblestones of the silent mill towns with droplets from cut-glass prism chandeliers out of ballrooms nobody had ever danced in, or having games of catch with crystal doorknobs for balls, or looking at one another through bits of Flemish stained glass, taken from the ruins of mad moorland mansions abandoned half-built. And then the laughter was, as the saying goes, at the wrong end of your teeth.

Not that Thurstan Preston himself ever went broke. You had only to look at the man to see that this could never be. Here was the type of the old North British Viking – the raider, the trader, the huckster with the knife in his sleeve. He double-crossed Alfred the Great; he was Quisling of Haardrade; he sold out Harold; and when he couldn't lick William he joined him and bided his time three hundred years or so and swallowed him, and Normandy, and France, India, Africa, America, Australia. By 1911 his teeth were in his own tail, but he had not yet swallowed himself, and was still having his skalds sing alliterative monosyllabic sagas of himself and what he had to sell.

Cseh was prepared to bully Thurstan Preston. 'I am a friend of Prince Damiani d'Aretini; we met, you will recollect, one charming evening at the Magnifico, in Rome' – this was to be his opening gambit. At which the sly old hypocrite would shuffle, and stammer, and come to heel. But the man he now confronted was not the hung-over Silenus of the jockey stools whom he had last seen in a dressing gown and slippers with an engorged face bloated and fixed in the satyriac grin of a man hung up by the heels. Here was somebody dry and impregnable, with a head formed in overhanging slabs like glacial rock, a sunken cross-stitched mouth and eyes harsh and grey as coke under shaggy asbestos brows. There was cokey grit in his voice, too, and something cinderous and crunching in his snatching handshake. This one was beyond fear; his soul was safely laid by in the chapel, and his money was secure in the bank. He was of the Elect; he couldn't be made bankrupt, and he couldn't be damned if he tried.

So Cseh changed his mind and said, 'We met very briefly at a reception given for Monsieur Coën of the Somali Development Company at the Hotel Excelsior, Mr Preston.'

'Oh aye? Sit thee down and 'ave a cup o' tea, Baron,' said Preston. Not one man in a thousand will recognize a busboy out of the restaurant. Of this perceptive few, not one in a hundred could successfully pretend never to have seen that busboy before. Thurstan Preston was the thousand-and-first man, and one in a hundred thousand. Half tempted to say, 'Ah left ten bobs' worth o' change in Italian money on t' floor in t' Magnifico. Fork up and I'll gi'e thee a couple o' bob for tha honesty,' he kept still and waited. '– Or happen tha'd like coffee?' he said.

'You are too kind.'

'Whurt 'ee stoppin', Baron?'

'Pardon?'

'Eh, excuse me gi' ah talk broad. Whur dost 'ee live, like?'

'Ah, yes. At the Grand Canal Hotel, Mr Preston.'

'Eh, but that's dear!' said Preston, shaking his head.

I have him impressed after all, thought Gèza Cseh; while Preston said to himself, chuckling inwardly, *By gum, t' lad's better than a poppit show!* He settled his stone chin into his alabaster collar with a rasping sound, dropped a portcullis of splayed teeth in a kind of smile and sat back to listen while Cseh talked. At last, moved in spite of himself by the little man's blazing energy and fascinated by the vigour and variety of his gestures, he said, 'Baron, in a nutshell: plan is to lease theatres all over Midlands and t' North for variety shows fro' t' Continent and Yankee moving-picture shows? Thurstan Preston Cotton to sponsor local talent and print gummed labels, one for every sixpenn'orth of my goods purchased, two labels being equivalent to a pass for two persons to see t' show?'

'Yes,' said Gèza Cseh.

'Sitha; that's like trading stamps, and they're older than t' hills. But what o' that? So's pie, and what's nicer than pie? Nay, see, Baron: t' idea has summat to recommend it, but tha wants thy trading labels on stuff quicker consumed than Thurstan Preston Cottons – happen a bar o' chocolate, a bottle o' pop, or happen a block o' stickjaw toffee. A pin to see t' peepshow; a label to see t' show, like. Eh, 'eck – dost 'ee know t' life on *my* goods? Nay, be still, lad – Baron, I mean – ah don't say nay to t' idea, mind that. It's a wheeze that wants thinking on. But – tell 'ee what – Thurstan Preston's a name to conjure wi' in Lancashire. Hast 'ee heard on Rothschild, t' financeer? A man said to Rothschild, "Gi' us twenty thousand pound, Rothschild?" Rothschild says, "Nay, lad, I'll do better. Tak' my arm and we'll go for a stroll i' t' City." Man takes Rothschild's arm, and they go for stroll i' t' City, and by noon next day man's list is oversubscribed. I'll not put out money as yet, but I'll lend thee my arm to be seen on, and it'll cost thee nowt. Eh?'

'But –'

'– Don't 'ee worry, Baron. I'll breakfast wi' thee tomorrow. After that, say nowt, and if somebody asks thee owt, like, "What's to do wi' thee and Thurstan Preston?" – smile and howd tha tongue, and happen tha'll see what tha'll see . . .'

Preston's reasoning was lucid, businesslike, economical and sternly moralistic: *If I poison a cake and offer it to my enemy, I am culpable.* But *if I happen upon a cake I don't like the smell of, and label it* PROPERTY OF THURSTAN PRESTON, *and my enemy takes it and eats it and makes himself ill thereby, he has nobody to blame but himself.*

'You are not yourself interested in investing?' Cseh asked.

'Happen ah am, happen ah'm not. We'll see. Do lak ah tell thee for t' time being, Baron.'

'I will, sir, and with profound gratitude!'

Thus, the news getting about that the Baron de Cseh was Thurstan Preston's cake, a dozen curious speculators came out of their holes and waited for the crumbs to fall. A larger predator, Salomon Samoon, watched their movements with cool curiosity; and he was, perhaps, the one man of all men Thurstan Preston feared and hated. Old Simeon Samoon had come staggering down the burning roads of Mesopotamia under a load of rugs heavy and hot enough to suffocate a donkey, making himself understood in a lingua franca composed of the detritus of a dozen dialects, selling from door to door and café to café; impervious to heat and cold, threats and blows, insults and injuries; patient as a beggar, watchful as a thief, never taking No for an answer. He boarded a stinking steamer at Galatz in 1863 and came to Cardiff, where he became a moneychanger, then a moneylender and hence a financier with a finger in a dozen adventurous enterprises. He sent his son Salomon to Cambridge to get to know the right sort of people. The boy came down fastidious as a great cat, polished of manner and capable of talking about books and pictures with the best, a Bachelor of Arts who had boxed for Jesus College and had an interestingly broken nose. The old man said, 'I am sharp as a knife, but Salomon is a circular saw. He can make black white. While he is talking to you about Rembrandts he is with the other hand unscrewing your arms and legs off.' By 1911, when he was only forty years old, Salomon Samoon had quadrupled his father's capital, and still felt that he was only beginning.

The aged Simeon, blind with cataracts, asked, 'What's with this new business of Preston's?'

Salomon laughed. 'A child could see through Preston's little game. This fellow Cseh's an unmitigated fraud, and a fool into the bargain. Preston is pretending to be interested in him in order to let him catch us.'

'So what are you going to do?'

'Be caught, Father.'

'What are you talking about?'

'I'll let us be caught for a couple of thousand, perhaps. Then, when they see that we're in, Elvey and Foley will dash in, too. Elvey can't afford to lose just now. But he'll speculate and lose. And we'll get Elvey and Foley's for five or six thousand pounds instead of twenty or thirty.'

'And what if Preston has got the same idea?'

'I hope and trust the old rascal has. For, if you remember, Father, Maclehone holds a debenture for Elvey. And we hold Maclehone. And do you know what? That little Austrian has a good idea but doesn't know it? That's why I said he was a fool as well as a fraud.'

'Yes . . . In 1898 a Russian counterfeiter came to me with some sovereigns made of a heavy metal that was not gold. I let him cheat me at a fifty per cent discount. The ignorant fellow had cast the money in platinum. Aram Arabian made his fortune by being cheated into buying a farm nothing would grow on. Of course nothing would grow. It was an oil field.'

'Oh, this Baron, as he calls himself, has nothing to sell we want to *buy*. I merely said he had a good idea. I've already got *that*. We're playing with a few pounds to get Elvey and Foley's, nothing more . . .'

So Gèza Cseh found himself in the centre of a group of clear-headed businessmen with no nonsense about them, who knew just what they wanted and had made up their minds to get it. What they wanted happened to be a foothold on the ground floor of British and International Enterprises. His suite at the Grand Canal Hotel was already littered with papers – forms, prospectuses, estimates, letters. He was delighted, but somewhat frightened. He had hoped for nothing more than a few hundred pounds to snatch and run away with. Now he had fifteen thousand pounds in hand, from three investors, and fifty thousand more to come. He was reminded of an occasion when, quietly opening a pilfered bottle of champagne for a surreptitious drink in one of the hotels he had been dismissed from, he was stunned by an explosion, struck in the eye with the metal-shod cork, and drenched in a deluge of wine. Here, he had drawn a stopper and let out a genie. Enough was enough, he decided; Italy before Austerlitz; Napoleon knew when to withdraw. He would slip away with what he had, and gather himself for the big killing.

His mind made up, the plan formed itself. One portmanteau of his very best suits, a business trip to London – five days only, gentlemen, for a conference with Mr Stollthen, a cab from Euston to Victoria, a train from Victoria to Newhaven, a boat from Newhaven to Dieppe, a car from Dieppe to Le Havre, and from Le Havre a liner to New York. Then –

– Then, dear God, then somebody announces Mr Zobrany!

A great man may hire servants to pick up after him, but he must drop his own litter; he may employ people to remember for him, but he must do his own forgetting. Without a well-caulked past no ego can remain unpunctured. So when Gèza Cseh heard the name of Zobrany he repeated it in an incredulous hiss that seemed to let out all the air in his thin body, so that the same name sucked back in three breaths could not restore the comfortable state of inflation into which he had lately pumped himself. For he had yet to master that useful feint of mnemonics which may be termed Forgettory.

There was Rasp still unforgotten; and the memory of Zobrany scarcely skinned over. Having taken five hundred pounds of that affable man's money he congratulated himself on his magnanimity, thinking, as he had thought in the case of old Rasp, *Another man would certainly have taken the whole lot.* Then he struck himself on the forehead and asked himself, *Why the devil didn't you, then, while you were about it, you fool?* From this it was an easy step to the conclusion that Steve Zobrany owed him five hundred pounds, to say nothing of the potential value of certain desirable leaseholds in Masham Court, W1.

But between Gèza Cseh and his argument came an image of Steve Zobrany, murmuring, 'Poor Little Napoleon, I blame myself for having trusted you. It is no triumph, Gèza – it was like taking pennies from a blind man. Go your way; desert, betray – from Egypt to Moscow to Waterloo is the path of the Little Corporal. Look me in the face, say you are sorry, take the money and go with God!' And this image blurred the Vision Splendid. He knew he could not bear to look Zobrany in the face, because he was indeed sorry; and sorry for himself because he suffered through being sorry.

There was more nerve in him than – judging him according to his actions – his enemies would ever know he had. Cseh would rather have faced the hangman on the scaffold than Zobrany at this moment. But he shouted, 'Tell them champagne, champagne and ladyfingers! What are you waiting for? Show the gentleman up, confound you, show the gentleman up!'

And in came Tom Henceforth.

Many years later, Tom Henceforth's story of that encounter, which gained richness with every repetition, was recorded for posterity by the same young man out of University College who had been caught in a raid on Zobrany's sign. Fascinated by Henceforth's account, young Ody marvelled that it played back thin and sour, and no more like what he remembered having heard at a Chelsea pub than an eructation is like the spicy meal which preceded it. It had something of the tedious bathos of an aftermath; which led the former medical student to wonder if one ever really hears what one thinks one hears. There was the mellow, modulated, mocking voice with all its overtones of pity and its undertones of disgust in contrapuntal disdain, playing variations on a leitmotif instinct with malice and scorn; there was the solid smack of the phrasing and the clatter of images hit dead centre and cracked like so many coconuts. But what in the world was all the noise about?

Edited and expurgated it went like this:

'. . . And so I got to the Grand Canal half sozzled, and the attitude of the poor buggers downstairs led me to expect God knows what sort of Transylvanian translation of *Wuthering Heights* – as sure as I sit here, I really and truly looked forward to something truly Baronial. I expected to hear a bellow and see him come out shouting, "Stuff me a matron with paprika and put on another kettle of schnapps! Skin me a small boy! Heat me a brazier!"

'And what do I see but a pinheaded drip with a face exactly like that specimen in Lombroso who got ten years for bestiality with a six-month-old pig, gaping like a fish and making fizzling noises in Hungarian like a bottle of soda water: *Mogdiptych horogorgy ogeorgy horoporgy ogororory Zobrany pish?* – or words to that effect; and I have no hesitation in telling you I felt let down. He stands there goggling, with his hands kind of frozen in the middle of a gesture, and he said, "You are not Steven Zobrany" – and I can see that he was very happy to observe that I wasn't. And so I say, "No, I'm not, as a matter of fact; I'm just a very dear friend of his." And he says, "Be seated. Let me offer you a glass of champagne. Won't you have a sponge cake?" And as God is my judge, he clicks his heels in his emotion, and throws a napkin over his arm, and I say to myself, "Baron be damned, my friend – if you aren't a bloody waiter in disguise I'll eat my hat!" And he was in disguise – diamond studs, wine-coloured velvet smoking jacket and all. And then when the waiter came up shaking like a leaf, Cseh goes for him like a wildcat, spitting and screaming, "What do you mean? What is the meaning of this outrage? Are you insane? Are you drunk? Are you syphilitic? How dare you bring Cordon Rouge when I ordered Mumm? Take it away! Bring it back! How dare you bring Mumm when I ordered Bollinger? What is the meaning of this outrage? Take it away! Bring it back! Put it down! Pick it up! Bring it back and take it away again! Call the manager! Call the police! Open the bottle! Close the bottle! . . ." and so on and so forth.

'And at last he offers me a Partagas as fat as a rolling pin, and takes one himself and stands there nibbling at the end, and says, "What can I do for you?" To tell you the truth I hadn't the foggiest idea what he could do for me, so I said nothing and sat still, staring at him and smiling. Then he says, "You have come from Zobrany? But how did he know I was here?" And I say, "Ah!" and drink my champagne. "And is Zobrany well?" he asks me. "But why did he send you, and what – and what – and what –" He sticks there like a wonky gramophone, and it doesn't take Sherlock Holmes to work out the fact that Zobrany has got something on this half-portion who says he's the bold bad Baron de Cseh. So I shrug like an expert and say, "You ask what. Don't you *know*, Monsieur le Baron?" – putting just that extra little emphasis into the title – and he says, "I can, of course, explain everything." "Oh, of course," I say, "of course you can." Then he says, "I am glad Steven sent you – you have a sympathetic air. Let us discuss. Let us be good friends. It is, I take it, a matter of a certain little sum of money? Pooh pooh! That is nothing, is it? Between gentlemen, what is money? I spit me of money! What is it my dear old friend Zobrany wants? But what is your name?" I tell him, Henceforth, and he repeats it to sound exactly like Anusfart. "Is it fifty pounds, a hundred, Mr Anusfart? Speak." This is all very well, speak; but what am I to say? So I pull down the corners of my mouth, and look sideways at him, and shake my head, and he says, "What, the whole five hundred? But there were expenses. Still, between friends, what is a pound here, a pound there? Come, let us be gentlemen, let us have no *scandale*" – the poor little bastard is terrified of me! – "Zobrany shall have the entire five hundred pounds. There! But what is your Christian name?" I tell him "Zobrany." "But what do you mean, Zobrany?" "Zobrany Henceforth," I say, "he's my uncle." Then he says, "But he never told me he had family in England! Why did he never tell me?" I answer, "I suppose because you never asked him," and I have him there. He says, "The matter shall be arranged tomorrow in the morning. Pray take more wine, Anusfart." "The name is *Henceforth*." "Oh, pardon: Hans Fuff." He's getting quite tiddly himself, and as for me, the champagne and the Irish whisky are beginning to work on my imagination.

'Something or other being, as it were, off his little mind, he started to talk, and let all the saints be my judge, never was such a load of unqualified wild ass's shit dropped from the lips of one small Hungarian since the thunderbolts smote Ananias! He regurgitated crap like a stopped-up ladies' lavatory on a rainy Saturday night at a six-day bicycle race in Marseilles; about the money he had made and the women he had laid, and the duels he had fought and the jewels he had bought, and antres vast and deserts idle and anthropophagi that do each other eat, until I said to him, "Gèza, you're too confiding. You don't know me, really. How do you know I'm not an investigator for Thurstan Preston?" That shook him, and he said, "What? What do you know about Thurstan Preston?" I said, "Oh, you know, you know," remembering what McErroll had told me, "Old Preston? Why, I know him well," I said, "a nasty old man, a tin chapel wallah, who sacks his factory girls for immorality and every Wakes week, having purified himself with an annual bath and fortified himself with prayer, goes abroad on business and is to be seen in the high-class Continental knocking shops drinking crème de menthe frappés out of the private parts of little dagoes. But what can you expect? Nature must take its course, and we pass through this world but once. After all, until he was thirty he never had it with his pants off, and didn't get to take his socks off until he was past caring much." "– No!" says the Baron, "not truly?" "Yes, truly!" I tell him. "I know the Prestons well. And Salomon Samoon, too." "What? You know Mr Samoon also?" I said to him, "I know practically everybody, my dear Gèza; I am an artist and a citizen of the world."

'If he could hand the stuff out, so could I, don't you see; but I was watching him more closely than he was watching me. I have the eye, my friends, the eye! And I saw how he twitched at the names of Preston and Samoon like a stung horse. "You are going in for theatrical production," I said, "and I'll tell you something more. You are going to discover a brand-new actress, a Manchester girl what's more, and her name is Era Moon; she has the face and figure of a Botticelli Venus, but when she laughs – so help me God in Heaven, Gèza, all the devils of Hieronymus Bosch and Breughel and Felicien Rops come pouring out of her throat! You'll see your name coupled with hers in tomorrow's *Morning Star*." "– How is this? –" "– You'll see, Gèza, you'll see. She'll be here tomorrow at ten. I've made an appointment for you," I said. "I told her I was working for you. So while you're about it you might as well give the nephew of Steve Zobrany a job, and have done with it."

'He said, "A job? You want a job? Yes, yes, a job; you shall have one, my dear. Take it. It is yours. What job?" I said, "First things first. Shall we discuss Steve Zobrany?" He was taking the name more easily now. He said, "Very well, let us get it done with. There is a small debt outstanding. As a gentleman I acknowledge it. I must make a short voyage to London in a few days, and I will pay him in person. Did he tell you the amount?" I said, "You know the amount as well as I do." "There were expenses, expenses extraordinary; he does not understand, he is not a man of affairs; a property such as that in Masham Court is not got just like that," says the Baron. I said, "Come off it. It's a slum. Dear Zobrany was robbed, sir, robbed!"

'He said, "Enough, my dear, enough. I will deal with it personally. I give you my word of honour that it was my intention, anyway, to call on your uncle, my best friend, when I came back to London. There, that is settled, eh? Now, you are a clever young man, and my friend's nephew, and you wish to work for me? –" "– Not for you, with you, Gèza, with you. You haven't got a Personal Assistant?" "No, but you may assist me if you please, Mr . . . ? –" "– Henceforth." "– Hen's Foot. Let us have a little more wine." He rang the bell like a maniac, and terrified another waiter. Then, "Tell me more of this young lady, my dear Hen." I said, "The matter of salary we can settle once and for all. I want ten pounds a week and expenses, and a hundred pounds in advance to replenish my wardrobe." He thought a bit and said, "Very well." And thus I knew he was a crook. I said, "And board and lodging, of course." "– Why not? I shall want you near me here in the hotel." I knew then that he was going to do a bunk. To deal perfectly plainly with you, I didn't mind a bit: I was having fun. My chief preoccupation just then was with that girl, that diabolical girl. She sucked at my soul. She was like a rat in the wainscot of my spirit.

'I said, "Let's have the hundred, and I'll tell you a great new idea you've just had." He took out ten tenners without another word, smiling at me with all his teeth, and I felt that this was just a trifle too easy to be perfectly comfortable. But the girl Era Moon was working in my system. Exactly what this great idea was, I didn't know; but I was certain I'd have one as soon as I started to talk . . .'

TWELVE

'. . . I said to our little Baron, "Now just you pay attention to me. You just keep the glasses filled and listen. As I gather, you are interested in theatrical matters. You're going to take theatres and put on all kinds of shows, including, as a special attraction, cinematograph programmes. A special attraction, forsooth! A special attraction, I ask you! Man alive, hasn't it dawned on people yet that these Bioscopes and Orpheums and Kinemas and Cinemas represent a coming industry? In America they're already big business. Millions are being made out of these flickering little shows. Hasn't it occurred to you yet that if it's possible to make a number of little moving pictures it is possible to make a number of big ones? Complete plays, entire dramas, with dramatic effects hitherto undreamt of on any stage? Has nobody realized just what the moving picture camera may be capable of? Or are we all Chinamen and Mayas?"

'He asked me what a Maya was, being under the impression that it was either a functionary in a cocked hat or a female horse. I had to tell him that the Chinese discovered gunpowder but used it only to make squibs with, and that the Mayas of Mexico had the wheel, but never thought of doing anything with it except make toys to amuse the children. I said, "And here we have the art form of the century, and all we do with it is photograph cowboys shooting revolvers and fat men falling on their arses. Yet the time will come when the moving picture will be a more powerful influence in the world than the printing press. Immense dramas will be photographed. Millions will pay tens of millions to look at them. They'll shout for them, they'll live for them. The theatre as we know it will become extinct. Who in his right mind would go to a stinking provincial theatre to see a troupe of broken-backed strollers play a third-rate piece, when he might for the same money watch the greatest actors in the world performing in drama on a gigantic scale? And that is bound to come. It hasn't been done yet, but the time has come to attempt it.

'"Think of what can be done with the cinematograph camera. It can show you fifty different scenes in fifty different parts of the world in fifty minutes. It can show you armies on the march, history being made, entire wars, love scenes, orgies, dreams, elephants, locomotives, anything, everything! Only the other day I saw a French thing about people going to the moon in a skyrocket. Your idea of a series of theatres is well enough in its way, but it's pusillanimous. We must think on a worldwide scale. Your idea is largely a retailer's idea. We must think wholesale, Gèza. Offer world-famous actors and actresses thousands to perform in just one play, and then show that one moving picture thousands and thousands of times. Arrange popular romances for the cinematograph screen – Charles Dickens, *The Count Of Monte Cristo*, *East Lynne*, Marie Corelli –"

'He said, "It is a thought. Marie Corelli is a very popular writer, and so is Ouida."

'"Ouida, too, if you like," I said. "And speaking of Marie Corelli, don't touch her. She'd expect to be paid, and she'd want to have a finger in the business. No, let her keep her finger where she's most accustomed to it; not in our affairs. Take one of her most popular books, *The Sorrows Of Satan*; keep the general idea, but turn it back to front. Instead of Satan as a man, have him assume the form of a woman. I should hope he can assume any shape he likes, for God's sake! The Devil comes to earth in the form of a girl who looks something like this –" I drew him a sketch.

'"Who's this?" he asks. I tell him, "The young lady I was talking about just now. See what a face she has for a man who knows light and shade, like a good photographer! As for her other attributes, well. She comes to earth to tempt people. We simply alter *The Sorrows Of Satan* a bit, and make an hour-long picture show of it. That would do for a start. Later we could do something more ambitious, like the Old Testament, or the Trojan Wars, or the Battle of Waterloo –" And then he asked me, "– Did Napoleon really lose the Battle of Waterloo?" Now when a bloke about five feet high with a lock of hair hanging over his forehead puts a hand inside his waistcoat before asking you if Napoleon really lost the Battle of Waterloo, there's only one thing to say, and I said it. I said, "He was betrayed, but even so he wouldn't have lost if it hadn't been raining at the time. Or we could do a Life of Napoleon. Anything is possible! Why should the Americans have to be first with this kind of thing? If we did Napoleon, I have just the right girl for Josephine. Or if a biblical subject, like the Queen of Sheba, I can suggest just the type. Or Rider Haggard's *She*. Or *The Beautiful White Devil* by Guy Boothby. Only we keep the basic idea and redo the things. Why waste money? I can do it myself for half the price."

'. . . But all this is under the bridge. You've got to remember that it happened when all the world was young, my friends, and I was barely eighteen. Horse buses were still running over Waterloo Bridge, radio wasn't known, Karl Marx was an intellectual parlour game, you could tell a Socialist because he wore a red tie, Britannia ruled the waves, the Liberal Party was getting strong, aeroplanes were barely hatched, my

God! – whisky was three-and-six a bottle, women wore stays and long drawers and long hair and long skirts, nobody had ever heard of Freud, Sex meant Gender, Bloody was spelt Dash, tanks were pipe dreams in the notebooks of da Vinci, there were "things nobody talked about", you didn't sweat but perspired, little boys who played with themselves went mad with softening of the brain and died in agony, little girls never did, women couldn't vote, you didn't know how babies were born – to cut a long story short, I repeat, it was long, long ago and I was very young; and my heart and soul were in everything I said and did, and I was running on all eight cylinders. The Baron wasn't much more than twenty-five or -six, either, and as wild a little bastard in his way as I was in mine.

'I have no pity for the torments of youth, so-called – no sympathy, absolutely none. You're young; that's enough. What do you want, for God's sake? A pension for being young, or something? So I sold Cseh the idea of the Main Feature. I invented it on the spur of the moment just because I had a hard on for that girl Era Moon. If she had been diabetic I'd have invented insulin, if she'd been a stripper I'd have invented zip fasteners. She wanted to be an actress – I crashed Cseh's suite, got myself made Personal Assistant and invented the full-length motion picture and sold him the idea, all in forty-five minutes by the clock, and if I tell you a word of a lie, may I never rise from this chair.

'Next morning at ten o'clock Era Moon turned up sure enough, in a black costume with bits of dyed rabbit on it, and a little black veil, and may God damn my soul to hell, but as she came into the lobby of the Grand Canal, every man's trousers became a tent, and a marble Venus in the vestibule turned green with envy as the fig leaf flew off a plaster Apollo with a dull crack and a full-length portrait of Prince Albert looked sheepish and covered its fly with its hat! She was chaperoned, by that female called Jo, who used to do a strongwoman act on the halls, driving nails through oak planks with her fist, breaking horse-shoes, letting loaded carts run over her chest, and all that. She had swapped hand grips with Tom Inch, and broke three of his knuckles. She had wrestled with Ali The Turk, and cracked his ribs. She was about five feet high and five across the shoulders, with a chin like a cobble-stone and a man's haircut, and eyes you could fumigate a bug-ridden house with.

'She came in with a smile that said, "Now you just mark my words, my dear – that whippersnapper was telling you a pack of lies. Just wait and see." It was a pleasure to see her face when I stepped out from behind a palm tree and gave them a Continental kind of bow, and kissed Era's hand and conducted them upstairs to the Baron's suite. Little Cseh, who had a figure precisely like a wax dummy made to show off gents' natty suitings, was in a morning suit. No jewels; one black pearl in his cravat. Introductions effected, coffee was served. Jo sat glum while Cseh gave the girl the once-over.

'He didn't know exactly what to make of her; which told me that he knew bugger all about the theatre. He didn't know what questions to ask, even. She had a wretched little scrapbook with her, and some photographs. I was dead right – the camera picked up the real girl – she photographed ravenous, and her red eyes came out bright jet black. I said to the Baron, "You must see her laugh to appreciate her properly, Monsieur le Baron." Jo asked, "Who *is* this young man, sir?" And the Baron said, "I thought you knew him well, madame. He is Monsieur Hen, my personal assistant." "I thought he said his name was Zobrany." "His first name is Zobrany, madame; he is the nephew of a very dear friend of mine; I am in *loco parentis* – a friend of the family." I must say that he carried it off very nicely indeed, not being rattled. But they didn't have the Indian sign on him, and I had, you see.

'"Laugh!" I said to her. "Show the Baron how nicely you laugh." And she laughed. That did the trick. Cseh's eyebrows went up into his forelock and his ears twitched. He asked her to walk up and down. She did. The long bell-shaped skirt practically pealed. She had this quality: even her ankle was a bit of sexual apparatus. Your imagination ran up her leg like a spider and then went off bang.

'"I have a new project in hand, an extremely ambitious project," says Cseh, "and I believe that you may be suitable to play a very important role in a production I have in mind. Eh, Hen?" I said, "Most positively, Monsieur le Baron. I take it you are thinking of Salome?"' At this, Jo chimes in with, "Oh no she doesn't – I can't have her undressed on the stage." And Era gives her a deadly look; absolutely doused her like a shovelful of wet sand. But Cseh, smooth as silk, says, "Madame, the production I have on hand is a cinematograph production of hitherto unheard-of proportions"; and then I really had to admire the little sod, because he went on from there with a scheme, a layout, practically a *fait accompli*, that made my general sales talk sound hollow as a dead nut. You would have thought he'd dreamed of nothing else all his life; had all the techniques at his fingertips. Pathé, Lumière – he knew 'em all. He was using the girls to try it out on, don't you see, and it went down like so much jam – they licked it up like an electuary – even the lesbian Jo softened a bit, and said, "Of course, in the nature of what's purely professional . . . I appear in tights myself, but not to attract men or excite their disgusting susceptibilities. Feel that arm!" And she flexes an arm the size of a bolster, and I take hold of a handful of it and it was like trying to dig your fingers into the inflated tyre of a five-ton truck. The Baron felt it too, and looked aghast at me. I looked aghast back at him. Then we both looked aghast at Jo. Cseh had the right idea: you can't get along in show business without somebody to look aghast at. If I were a high executive or administrator in that racket I'd employ two, one to sit on each side of me; I'd look aghast at them, they'd look aghast at me, then at each other; back again to me and then, as the case might be, join me in a headshake, a nod or a burst of incredulous laughter.

'I should say at this point that we didn't know what a lesbian was back in 1911. Common or garden buggery was an open book to the upper classes and the lower, if not to the middle; there was always Oscar Wilde to fall back upon; and anyway, in the Army and the Navy and the public schools and the reformatory schools and so forth, sodomy was *de rigueur*, practically. Besides, it was a criminal offence, and got into the papers. But lesbianism was something kind of vague – there was no law against it, and nobody seemed to know exactly what it was – you couldn't sin except with a man, was the general idea. What could two women together *do*? was what the general public wanted to know. I confess, even I believed it had something to do with urination. We called 'em Sapphists, if at all. They were good times. *The union of man and woman is half bestial and half angelic; the union of two men is wholly bestial; the union of two women is wholly angelic* – that kind of thing. Such matters simply weren't talked about. We would have been outraged at the sight of a painted twank cuddling a permanent civil servant, which nowadays we take for granted. But a big bull-throated dyke publicly feeling around a debutante we thought of as sort of sisterly.

'The Baron invited them to dinner. The dog wished Jo off onto me, begging me to hold her off. I laughed up my sleeve because I knew Era was mine; and besides, Jo aroused something like curiosity in me! As I say, I'd never seen one of them before. And it was a good dinner: everything of the best, and this wasn't anything like good enough for Monsieur le Baron Gèza de Cseh. He kept apologizing to these two women, whose idea of a blowout was a chump chop and chips and a hunk of roly-poly pudden with golden syrup . . . "What can we do? We are at *Ultima Thule*, we are among the Corybants of the Philistia of the Provinces, bless my heart! *Ach, barbarismus!* . . . Waiter, take this filth away, give it to the dogs! Bring it back! Put more pepper in, take more pepper out!" It was a treat to hear him, better than a snake-oil salesman's patter, and the ladies adored it.

'Jo nodded to me, as if to say, "There's a man who knows what's what," and Era Moon's foot was in my groin under the table while she gazed at him with adoring eyes. He kept the wine going, all the same. Later on, when he was showing Era something in an album, and she was playing tunes on the piano in the suites – she played exactly like an eight-year-old child who, after six lessons, is taught "a piece" at her mother's urgent request – Jo, who wasn't accustomed to wine, cracked brazil nuts for me three at a time between four fingers of one hand, and poured out her heart, telling me there were friendships between women that no man could ever possibly understand. "A man has only got one thing I haven't got," she said. I asked, "A vote?" She said, "It's proved that a woman is superior to a man in every possible way. She is the perfection of mankind. Men have breasts, undeveloped. Women have the same, perfected. Men have clitorides, out of proportion. Women have peni, in proper proportion. Men have no wombs. Women have. Men have disfiguring beards. Women haven't." And so forth. She wasn't a bad sort, actually. I liked her, on the whole. "I come from Intack Shaw" – it wasn't enough that she was a professional strongwoman and a lesbian, she had to be a Yorkshirewoman, to boot! – "and nobody ever liked me because I wasn't a little bit o' fluff. But I've my feelings under all this brawn . . . When I was only a girl I could pull against a plough horse and pin the Champion of the Dales wrestling Northumberland and Westmorland style." Which was very instructive and interesting, only I wanted Era so badly that my spermatic cord was playing, like old Joe Chirgwin on a one-string fiddle, strange glissandos of love and frustration.

'And still Era and the Baron stayed in discussion, and still Jo told me of her passion and her loneliness . . . Ah me! And all the while Jo was telling me of the mishaps that had befallen her on account of her unnatural physical strength: if she picked a flower its petals fell off, if she squeezed a bulldog his eyes came out, if she stroked a horse his teeth fell out, so that nobody loved her but Era, who brought out all the latent gentleness in her. "If you do anything to hurt Era," she said, "I'll tell you what I'll do. There are three hundred bones in the human body. I'll prove to the doctors that I can break every one of those bones into three pieces, and still leave you alive to regret it. And don't think for one second that I couldn't and wouldn't," she said, tearing a thick bronze ashtray into thin strips and nervously plaiting them into a braid. She said, "But luckily Era doesn't like men, least of all you. She told me so. But what's the Baron making sheep's eyes at her for?" She went across the room, crawled under the piano, lifted it on her back and walked away with it, saying, "I can do this and carry a solid mahogany table in my teeth at the same time."

'And at this point the party broke up, and I saw the girls to a cab. I had a chance to ask Era, "When?" She said, "Soon, soon. Thank you for everything – everything!" Jo shook me by the hand, taking care not to break it, and said, "You'll see to it that if Era goes on the pictures I go, too?" I said, "Absolutely."

'I said to the Baron, "Look here, you lay off that girl or I'll tell my Uncle Zobrany." He said, "What is she to me? I am engaged to be married to the Countess Ursula von und zu Leibeshohle-Sussurusky of Potz" – or something like that – "and I dare not compromise myself. But the child has promise, and we must see whether she can be of any use to us. Let us have some champagne and sponge cakes. I am most pleased with you. I think I shall ask you to go to Liverpool on Wednesday, and obtain details of the latest motion-picture equipment from Pelican, who has an agency there in Lime Street. The longer you know me the better you will understand that with me to decide is to act."

'So I went to Liverpool, and what happened to me there would fill a book. However, not to fill a book: when I came back five days later on the following Monday, the Baron wasn't at home. He'd had to go to London, they told me, for a conference with Stoll, and wasn't expected back for several days. All his largest trunks were in his bedroom – costly French luggage – and half a dozen suits hung in the wardrobe, along with a lot of shoes and stuff. I stayed on in the suite. The night I got back, Jo turned up, and she was something terrible to see. She took me by the throat and shook me like a rat and called me a swine. Era had run off with the Baron – simple as that! Packed a suitcase, left a farewell note saying she couldn't stand it any more and just vamoosed. All Jo wanted was to get her hands on Cseh. I said, so did I.

'Her grief was absolutely awful. "She was all I had, she was everything," she kept saying. "What am I going to do? Oh, what am I going to do?" You know, I never was one to mourn the fate of Sodom, not being in the least that way inclined; but I couldn't help feeling sorry for the woman. She made a kind of broken, lowing noise, half human, half cow; but couldn't cry. As you must have read in all those books people read, that kind of grief is aphrodisiac.

'All of a sudden . . . Well, look: have you ever been raped in a baronial suite in the Grand Canal Hotel by a lesbian professional strongwoman on a windy autumn night in Manchester? No? Then you haven't lived.

'All being over she picked me up and brushed me off and asked if she'd hurt me. "*You* are all I have now," she said. "Don't worry, I'll work for you, and we'll have lots and lots of babies." The girl was stone crackers, quite round the bend. "Never mind Era," she said, "I've got you and you've got me." I said, "Oh, definitely." "It's not as if you were actually a *man*," she said.

'Before dawn I hopped it; strolled to London Road Station, dived into a train and scarpered. I came away with some bruises on my heart inflicted by Era, some contusions on my back inflicted by Jo, and slightly over a hundred pounds in my purse. Oh yes, and a pair of diamond studs the Baron forgot to take out of a shirtfront. He'd got clean away with a cool fifteen thousand of canny Manchester money, and good luck to him! Old Preston simply laughed. The shonk Samoon – now Lord Cragsmoor – moved in on two co-investors, and snapped up a brokerage and a clothing factory.

'What happened to Jo I never knew. But do you know, I never heard such desolation in the wind and strings of a human voice as she conveyed in that tearless keening she sent up when Era ran away . . .'

. . . *At least there was that one tiny touch of compassion*, Ody thought, putting the machine away.

THIRTEEN

Perhaps a few of Tom Henceforth's dithyrambs concerning this Era Moon had hit Cseh in some particularly vulnerable spot: he had read some stories by Guy de Maupassant, and it may be that he saw, in Era Moon, one of those queer nymphs that occasionally occur in the works of that master. Boneless, bloodless, all but invisible except in the kind of layered light that comes through church windows, they marry cynical men about town, boulevardiers of property, saturated with pleasure – insatiable roués whose gnu-horn moustaches dangle, quivering, from lips like bladders full of blood. 'Don't weep, it must be,' witnesses tell her weeping mother, who stumbles away to pray while the best man shakes his head, thinking of the devil knows what exploratory drillings, sanguinary strikes, unmentionable impalements and stoppered gurgles of anguish between spattered bed curtains. A month later he goes to visit his newly married friend and is met by a tremulous old gentleman with the pouched face of a toothless bloodhound and a hand like a dead fish, who plucks him by the sleeve and calls him Georges: it is the girl's husband. He explains – the child was brought up in a convent, and never learnt the facts of life. Sinless as a babe, she has dealt with him as a child deals with a glass of cream soda – sucked him dry, *parbleu!* as with a straw – drained him of his manhood until there's not enough of it left to make a gurgling noise with at the bottom of the empty vessel that is himself; and still she draws and draws, thinking that the first nuptial embrace should go on and on forever, *nom d'une araignée*! She is an innocent nymphomaniac . . .

Or it may be that Era Moon reminded Cseh of some cool and inaccessible lady whose glove he had picked up, or of some actress who had tipped him a krone for carrying slops to her poodle, or of a blonde girl in a tobacco kiosk who had called him a 'snippet'. Or it may be that, as an outlander pretending to dignity in a strange city, he was attracted to her as a simple answer to the simple question: *How does a gentleman find a healthy young woman in this town?*

Era Moon, according to his trained observation, being ready and willing to be seduced, Gèza Cseh decided to go to bed with her.

No words were spoken. Her eyes said, *Yes, yes, yes – I can hardly wait!* Her foot under the table said, *Beyond this foot there is an ankle, and beyond that ankle a knee, and above that knee a thigh, and . . . Stop it, or I'll go up into the air like a skyrocket!* Her handshake said, *Soon?* The expression of her lips said, *Alas, impossible!*

They were never alone together for more than half an hour at a time. The woman Jo was obtrusive and stolidly hostile in a way Cseh found nightmarish – it was as if somebody had given him a very ugly and ponderous piece of furniture which he didn't want, but it kept following him about on its mighty oaken legs. And was always at his elbow. And if Jo was absent, there was Tom Henceforth, with his lowering triangular smile and his tangled skein of talk. The girl was preying on Cseh's mind; and time was running out.

Then, one afternoon, when Jo was absent and Henceforth was in Liverpool, she came to his suite. Cseh snatched her to his bosom with a rapid burst of kisses aimed point-blank at two feet, which missed her face but creased her scalp, leaving her otherwise untouched.

'No,' she said.

'We must, we must!'

'Not now.'

'Not now, not now! What do you mean, not now? What, not now? When then, not now? Now, now!'

'Not like this.'

'Not like this? Not like what? What do you mean? I adore you! So what do you mean?'

'I'd hate it like this.'

He said, with the realism of a man accustomed to grappling kitchen-maids between shifts, 'It will only take five minutes.'

He was strong in the arms, for his weight, but he might as well have tried to hold a seal. She was free of him in one experienced writhe. 'No, it's too sordid,' she said.

'Sordid? What does she mean, sordid? Where, sordid? Sordid!' He was mortally offended. 'And it is I who will give you everything. Everything! Listen to me; I will give you a career, money, diamonds, all you want to eat, champagne, pearls, I will make a great actress of you, I will put the world at your feet!'

She smiled, then, and said, 'Will you give me your luggage?'

'What do you mean, luggage?' he asked, suddenly quiet.

'Behave yourself, and I'll tell you.'

'My luggage? What luggage?' – he pointed to the open door of the adjoining room, where half a dozen trunks stood, for all the world to see – 'there is my luggage. What are you talking about?'

'The trunks and things you ordered from Hitchcock's.' She went on in her wonderstruck jeune ingénue's voice, 'You had two cabin trunks specially made for you by Mr Hitchcock. Then, when he and one of his men came here to deliver them, you made a terrible scene, and sent them back after an hour's argument. The whole hotel heard it. Only you just pretended to send them back – you paid for them, and while you were making all that noise, you packed them with your best things and *then* had them taken away. So it appears as if all your clothes and things are here in your rooms; whereas they're in the cloakroom at London Road and you've got the keys to them in your pocket.'

It was true: those trunks, and Hitchcock's connivance, were the only things Cseh had bought and paid for. 'Who told you this?' he asked.

It happened that she numbered among her admirers one of the trunk-maker's journeymen who, being jealous of Cseh, warned her not to trust him, and confidentially told her why. But Era Moon was not such a fool to say this; she simply smiled and shook her head.

'And so what of this?' Cseh demanded. 'A gentleman may not store part of his wardrobe in order to have breathing space in this dog kennel of a hotel, no?'

She shook her head again. 'The hotel would have put them in their store room if you'd asked. I believe you're going to run away.'

'You have got a, a, a, a touch of the sun.'

'It's pouring with rain. It always is, in Manchester. I believe you're going to run away, and I want you to take me with you.'

'But,' cried Cseh, laughing, 'that is exactly what I wanted to do! That is what I meant to do, hoped to do, longed to do!' He lied reflexively, as a boxer feints.

'You are going to run away, then?'

'No, of course not. But in my business there are a thousand things that require to be attended to without preambulatory discussion, and so – it not being in my nature to enter into explanations with the vulgar – I do things in my own way. So . . .'

'Where are we going?'

'We? We are going to New York.'

'When?'

'When? Today is Monday. I go on Thursday.' Thursday would be as good a day as another. 'But you must get rid of your Jo.'

'Fortunately, she's got an engagement at the Darwen Hippodrome. Poor Jo!'

'And this Henceforth. What is he to you? Eh?'

She laughed. 'He's only a boy, just a friend, nothing more.'

'We will go first to London, then to Paris, and afterwards to America, yes?' *I'll ditch the bitch in Paris*, he thought. 'And now –' He lunged, thinking to catch her off balance. But she was a veteran of five hundred defensive battles – could take on a priapic stage manager twice her weight, in a clothes closet, and still emerge without a scratch – and, for all his speed, Cseh was outclassed. He abandoned the idea of stunning her with some not-too-heavy object, and simply shrugged.

'Not now. Later,' she said.

But when was 'later'? It takes two to make love, in the most favourable of circumstances. In the train to London she got grit in her eye; in the Grand Hotel, Trafalgar Square, she felt too sleepy; the boat train to Dover was too crowded; and between Dover and Calais there was no time for dalliance, even if she hadn't said that she thought she was going to be seasick. A retching woman would turn aside a charge of heavy cavalry, let alone a man singlehanded. The mal-de-mer lasted until they reached Paris, where Cseh took a suite at the Grand Hotel. (Nothing but Grand Hotels for Gèza Cseh!)

But there, first of all, she said that she couldn't because she was too excited. Her excitement abated by three days of shopping and going to the theatre, she found that the water didn't agree with her, and got diarrhoea and, as it seemed, stopped defecating only to try on dresses. An enraged Cseh called a doctor who gave her a draught of medicine. 'Well?' asked Cseh.

She said, 'It's much better now, but I'm awfully sorry – I'm indisposed.' Cseh tore his hair; she made some more purchases.

Five days later, Cseh said, 'I have spent fifty thousand francs on you. *Well?*' She made a helpless gesture. Two days after that, he said again, 'WELL?'

She said, 'I can't help it, it must be the change of air', and burst into tears. 'A change of air often affects me like that,' she explained.

After ten days of this, Cseh expostulated, 'God damn it all to hell! I don't believe you. A hippopotamus could not contain so much vital fluid as you say you have been losing, strike me blind – a hippopotamus with his throat cut, by God! Enough of this. Do you take me for a complete fool?'

Then she said, with infinite tenderness, 'Gèza, my dear. I have something to confess. I am in love with you.'

He howled, Then take off your drawers, your abominable drawers!'

'I'm in love with you, Gèza, and I don't want to spoil things by having a . . . a sordid affair –'

'– Sordid, sordid, sordid, sordid – what does she mean, *sordid*? Sordid, ha-ha! What the devil do you want, curse you? Don't I love you, too, bugger you?'

'I want it to be . . . something lovely, something *forever*, something –'

'– Something, my arse! I have spent two thousand pounds on her, and she wants something lovely!'

'You can take back your gifts, Gèza –'

'– What am *I* to do with your corsets and your gowns?'

'– But I can't let you touch me until we're married.'

He said something in Hungarian which, freely translated, would mean 'Twenty-seven thousand million bombs full of excrement', and rushed out of the hotel. Then he rushed back again and tore one of her chemises to pieces. She said icily, 'Ring for the maid. I want to pack. I'm going home. Now that you have revealed yourself in your true colours . . . Thank Heaven I found out in time! . . . I'll confess everything. I was a party to your crimes, but I was infatuated . . . I'll confess . . .'

'You'll confess? She'll confess? What confess, confess what?'

'That I helped you to swindle –'

'– And this is the woman I hoped to marry!' cried Cseh, quick as a weasel. 'A traitress, and I wanted to make her the Baroness de Cseh! A slanderess – I, a swindler! *Oi!*'

'I wouldn't have you if you were the last man in the world!'

'Oh now please, darling Era!'

She melted. 'Now I'll tell you another secret. I didn't want you to . . . do anything to me before we were married, because I'm still a maiden. No man has ever touched me.'

'No!'

'It's true.'

'Let me see.' He offered a polite forefinger.

'Afterwards.'

Immediately after their marriage, which was formalized forthwith, Cseh discovered that she spoke the truth. She was not merely a virgin – she was a super-virgin. Nature had endowed her with something like a burglar alarm, so sensitive that a fly could spring it: a certain point being passed, a current was broken, a clamp closed and a siren went off; her entire respiratory system was affected, she turned blue in the face, her eyes watered and her very pores revolted in a perspiration that smelt of cats. Nothing could be accomplished without chloroform.

'But isn't it a proof that I kept myself pure for my husband?' she asked, inhaling ammonia after her first convulsion. 'Be patient. I dare say it'll wear off. I would if I could, you know.'

'A fine damn bargain *I* got,' said Cseh.

They sailed from Le Havre in the *Marguerite de Navarre*. Cseh let it be known in the first-class saloon that, as far as he was concerned, the Cunard-White Star Line could go to the devil. 'I had intended to sail in April,' he said, 'on the maiden voyage of the *Titanic*. I demanded such-and-such a suite of staterooms. They tell me, "No, you may have such-and-such another." Bah!'

'I hear,' said an American gentleman, 'that the *Titanic* is the last word in shipbuilding.'

'Sir,' said Cseh, in his most portentous manner, 'there is no such thing as "last word". If there were, progress would cease. There is always something better. There is always room for improvement.'

'I meant, the last word to date, of course.'

'Ah, but the calendar has many leaves.'

'And may I ask if you're going to the States for business or pleasure, Mr . . . ?'

'Cseh; at your service.'

Cards were exchanged. The other man said, '*Baron* Gèza de Cseh!'

'Mr Lewis Morris Davis: how do you do?' They shook hands and Cseh went on, 'I am travelling mainly on business. That is to say, I am interested in the cinematograph business, and wish to study it at close quarters.'

'Well! So am I. I'm interested in exhibiting and distribution.'

'Without efficient distribution there can be no profitable production,' said Cseh; this being a perfectly safe comment to make, in any circumstances. 'Let us have a bottle of champagne.'

'I don't know a lot about wine. If you order it I'll gladly pay for it.'

Then Cseh rose to the occasion, and gave the wine steward such a tongue-lashing in English, French and German that even Mr Davis, a suspicious and masterful man, was dumbstruck with admiration. 'We must sit together at table. The Baroness and I have our own table. We prefer to choose our own company –'

'– Oh, your lady is with you? So's mine. I'm sure she'd be happy to meet the Baroness, and so should I.'

'Then I will tell your dining-room steward, I will give him orders.'

'Fine, fine. Mrs Davis is a little under the weather right now, Baron.'

'I am very sorry. There is no need to call me by my title. I am thinking of living permanently in America – I am a republican by conviction, and seldom use my foolish, empty title; I shall drop it altogether.'

'That's very democratic of you, though I should have thought it'd come in handy, in business.'

'How, sir? Only fools are impressed by titles, and I have no interest in doing business with fools.'

'There's another man on board who might interest you, Baron, only I can't understand a word he says. As far as I can gather, he's on the production side, or something, but he only talks German.'

'I speak German fluently,' said Cseh. 'Also French, Italian, Hungarian, et cetera, et cetera.'

'That's him over there, reading a book. His name's Bessermann. Would you like me to bring him over and introduce him, Baron?'

'Call me Cseh.'

And it transpired that the melancholy Bessermann was a persecuted man and a man of sorrows, as well as a dedicated artist. He was an innovator, an inventor of fresh techniques. Heartened by champagne, and by the sound of his native language, he poured out his soul.

'The man with the camera,' said he to Cseh, 'is as a god. He alone, selecting from an infinity of possible angles, can catch the *Augenblick* and tell it to stay. He alone of all human artists can compose with the shadow and the light in motion. This is the art of the future. I am a martyr to it, I am its slave . . . I put on film two dramas for the Aleko Company. They were magnificent. They lost money. Aleko went bankrupt. I worked with Oriflamme. We produced a masterpiece. It was a commercial failure. Oriflamme committed suicide by soaking himself in amyl acetate and burning himself to death. Then Harz went to America and said he would send for me. He did. He sent me my first-class ticket and expenses, and said, "Come. A great new company is formed." I packed up and started. At Le Havre I received a cablegram saying, "Don't come. The new company is *kaput.*" I came anyway, having my ticket. In America I shall look about me . . .'

'Look no further,' said Cseh. 'Sign me a bit of paper, a form of contract, and you shall see what you shall see, my dear Bessermann.'

'Yes. I will. You have the look of a man of destiny,' said Bessermann. 'Make out your paper, and I'll sign it. After all, what have I to lose?'

To Davis, Cseh said, 'Bessermann is a great artist, and he has a lot of fine ideas. I have contracted him to me, in case I decide to go into business.'

'You have capital, then?' Davis asked.

'Oh, I am prepared to risk twenty, thirty, fifty thousand dollars.'

'Oh, you are? Then look, Baron, why not let's talk business?'

And so Cseh bought an interest in one of the minor film distributing companies. He reasoned that, in the last analysis, it is the salesman who dictates to the manufacturer, the circulation pusher who dictates to the editor and the distributor who has the last word in matters concerning film production. Matters were made easier by the strangely intimate friendship which had sprung up between Era and Mrs Davis. 'Women are funny,' said Davis. 'Elinor hasn't taken much interest in anything much since our Irving was born. Not even in me, if you know what I mean. She certainly has taken to the Baroness – I never saw anything like it. They go around arm-in-arm like sisters. It's kind of touching. And I'll be darned if I know what they can find to talk about all the time, locked up in the cabin.'

'Clothes, no doubt, or babies,' said Cseh.

Bessermann said, 'My interest in the Baroness, Herr Baron, is passionate but purely academic. As you must know, her face was made as if expressly for my camera. If only her position permitted her to act for the camera, I could astonish the world with that face!'

'All things are possible,' said Cseh. 'I will put the matter to her as delicately as possible, and we shall see what we shall see . . .'

And he thought, *Women are two for a penny. What the hell? Taking one thing with another, I didn't make a bad bargain at all. My instincts were right; I was a fool to doubt them . . .*

A few years later, the best-dressed and most fascinating of all the Hollywood actresses, Erabella Luna, was to say to Gabriel Chess, high executive of Immortal Artists, Inc., 'Gèza, I think I'd better have a divorce.'

'Have a divorce, have two divorces, for God's sake! See if I care!'

'I'll divorce you, then.'

'Go ahead.'

'Now, about a settlement.'

'What? You think I'm going to pay you alimony?'

'I didn't say that. I don't want alimony.'

'Fine.'

'Alimony stops if you marry again. I said, settlement –'

'– Why, you disgusting little beast, I made you what you are today . . . I give her fame and fortune, and she wants settlements! Go to hell, you snare and you delusion, you!'

'All right, I'll sue for annulment on the grounds that you couldn't consummate our marriage. I talked to my lawyer about it. Also, I shall accuse you of unnatural habits.'

'You are the one with the unnatural habits, you vile creature!'

'Prove it. It'll look well in court, won't it? And if it comes to who made whom, you owe more to me than I owe to you. I'll put it out that you're impotent and a homosexual.'

'Ha-ha! *Me?* I can prove –'

'– Prove it, then, and I'll add adultery. About the settlement . . .'

'What grounds, then, do you want to divorce me on?'

'Mental cruelty.'

'Suffering Jesus! . . . What d'you want a divorce for, anyway?'

'I'm a vamp; it'll be more in character if I'm not married.'

'By the bleeding hands and feet of . . . Oh well. How much?'

'We'll go into how much you've got, divide it in two, and I take half. That's fair, isn't it?'

'WHAT? Over my dead –'

He settled for one-third. Several times before then she had given him occasion to say to himself, 'I should have waited, and sailed in the *Titanic.*'

Now (always excepting the official Histories Of The World) there never was such a stupendous mass of literature, so consistently fabulous in character, as that which has been inspired by, excreted from, squeezed out of or dreamt around people connected with the movies.

And in the course of nature, Gabriel Chess had his share of this mess of bunk and counterbunk.

Thus, in due course, Alma Zobrany, turning the pages of a magazine devoted to the more printable carryings-on of film stars, could say to her husband, 'Look at this photo, Steve. That man shaking hands with Wallace Reid. Doesn't he remind you of what's-his-name?'

'Of who, darling?'

'The little man who bought the restaurant – the one you sent.'

'What, Gèza? Let me look . . . "Producer Gabriel Chess and . . ." There *is* a resemblance, certainly. But Gèza's face is easily mistakable – now it has one expression, now another. And in white riding breeches? My Gèza? "Producer"? It seems most unlikely.'

'I only wondered. I've got some more magazines here, and there are other pictures of him.'

'What,' said Zobrany, laughing, 'you keep a file of this sort of thing?'

She had, in fact, acquired a liking for the cinema: there was so much to be so cosily looked at, and so little to read. Later, when the talkies were to come in, she would even experience something like enthusiasm. 'Yes,' she said, 'I like looking at them. They pass the time . . . Here's another one of him with Nazimova –'

'– There is a *likeness*, yes. But here he is with a little moustache. Yet the name sounds similar, in a way: Gabriel Chess – Gèza Cseh. Still, with a man like Gèza, you must see him in motion to know he's there. I've never seen him still. But if it amuses you, why not? Listen, the next time I'm out I'll buy you a scrapbook, and you can cut out pictures and gum them in. I will also get you a bottle of gum and a little brush. Would you like that?'

'If you like . . . It says that the most fascinating woman in Hollywood is Erabella Luna. Also the best-dressed. She and Gabriel Chess were married, once, but she divorced him for cruelty.'

'Ah, in America "cruelty" is when a man snores. I heard a funny story', said Zobrany, overcome with laughter, 'about a woman who asked for a divorce because her husband blew smoke rings through his nose. "Still, there are no grounds here," the lawyer said. And she said, "Yes, but don't you understand – he *doesn't smoke*!"' Mirth strangled Zobrany; he became blue in the face.

'Then how could he blow smoke rings in his sleep?'

'You are absolutely priceless!'

'. . . She's younger than me, but she's been married and divorced three times.'

'Which one is this?'

'Erabella Luna. But Gabriel Chess never married again. It says here, DOES GABBY'S SMILE MASK A BROKEN HEART?'

'If so, my dear, it is even less likely to be Gèza, because whenever he was hurt I can assure you that he kicked up the devil of a row. I have seen him cry like a child when he lost a game of dominoes, and if he cut his finger he would put on bandages enough for a cut throat. But if he broke his heart, believe me, there would be a real commotion. Still, who knows?'

'Then you don't think it was your friend?'

He said, 'It is not at all likely. You see, making pictures is a skilled business. It must be like putting on a play, only even more complicated. I don't know much about it, but so it seems to me. I don't know precisely what a film producer does, but he is a very important man, in charge of everything; and I am told that these productions cost thousands and thousands of pounds. A man does not simply go up to somebody and say, "I have had some experience as an under-waiter; therefore give me thousands and thousands of pounds and I will make moving pictures."'

'I suppose not,' she said, picking at her embroidery. 'How do you get to be a producer, then?'

'I don't know,' he replied, baffled. 'I'm blessed if I know!'

'It says how Samuel Goldwyn was only a glove salesman, and Mr Mayer was a rubbish collector.'

'Yes, yes, but these men are *commerçants*, business-brains. If it had seemed to them that there was a lot of money to be made quickly out of, for example, books, they would be book publishers; or if it were paintings, they would print works of art, or what not. It happens to be cinemas, so they are film men. Buyers, sellers, executives, administrators. I can't see my little Gèza . . .' He paused, feeling that his argument was growing weaker and weaker.

'It says here how Erich von Stroheim used to be a dishwasher,' she said. 'So did Rudolph Valentino.'

'Of course, my sweet; and I am talking nonsense,' said Zobrany. 'You are right and I am wrong. I might just as well say, "A poor farmer's son doesn't go out and make motorcars," or something equally stupid. And I hope it *is* Gèza, if it amuses you to think so.'

He was not annoyed; only nettled. Here was Alma's first spark of interest in life outside of Masham Court, and Cseh – or somebody who looked like Cseh – had to be the one to strike it! Then he reproached himself: *Pig! To begrudge the girl this harmless recreation!* and, having to go and see a tradesman in Swallow Street, went to the Burlington Arcade and bought her a fine scrapbook bound in morocco, with her initials stamped in gold on the cover.

And he said to himself, *A man does not simply go up to someone and say 'I have had some experience as an under-waiter; therefore give me, et cetera, et cetera' – oh no? Bite your tongue, Zobrany! All he had to do was say to you, 'I have had no experience whatsoever; therefore give me a thousand pounds and I will buy a restaurant' – and you couldn't get to the bank fast enough! . . . Devil of a Gèza! . . . If Gèza really* is *Chess . . .*

Without knowing why, and wishing the little rascal all the luck in the world, Zobrany hoped he wasn't.

PART THREE

FOURTEEN

Watching Poppy as she comes up from the kitchen balancing a pile of clean plates, Zobrany feels all the anguish sensitive people experience at the circus, when the comic acrobat acts drunk and pretends to lose his footing. It gets him every time. The girl seems to have no sense of peril. One of these days she will drop the lot; and if Zobrany were given to serious self-examination he would be half ashamed to learn that he almost wishes she would. To make matters worse this morning, she is suppressing a fit of the giggles.

'For God's sake, child, take care!' he whispers, resolving to install an upstairs scullery and a dishwashing machine. *No, absolutely – it's final*, he says to himself, for the hundredth time. 'And now what's the joke?'

'Old Sordic. He just called me a fourpenny prostitute.'

'Is that amusing?' asks Zobrany indignantly.

'Well, it was the way he said it: *frostitute*. A fourpenny frostitute! Next time somebody asks what's for dessert I'm going to say, "Try a fourpenny frostitute." "What's a frostitute?" "Why, a cold tart, of course."'

Zobrany finds this extremely funny. 'You must be a remarkable girl, to get comedy out of Sordic.'

'Who wouldn't laugh at somebody that calls fish and chips "piss in sips"? You say their name like "Shoreditch". Is that the right way?'

'It is a Serbo-Croat name, or something of that kind. I-C, with an accent like a little *v* over the *C*, is pronounced *itch* . . . Talk about something else. I am drinking coffee. We know that the Sordics are here; we know that the contents of our intestines are here: there is no need to talk about them while one is drinking coffee.'

'Can you imagine 'em in bed together?'

'Silence!' cries Zobrany. 'It is an order!'

'*I* don't mind 'em,' says Poppy. 'I sort of like 'em.'

'You sort of *what*?'

'You can't help kind of liking somebody you're sort of sorry for.'

'That is a pernicious philosophy, my dear, and I advise you to get it out of your head at once . . . You are sorry for the Sordics? Why?'

'I came down early one morning, and I saw 'em crying.'

'You were still asleep. You were dreaming.'

'No, they were crying. And it wasn't onions. He was sitting at the table with his head in his hands, crying, I tell you, and she was stroking his horrible old head and tears were running down her horrible old face. I don't know why.'

Sympathetic tears gather in Zobrany's eyes. 'Why didn't you mention it to me before?'

'A person's entitled to cry if they like,' Poppy says. 'Look at you, with your face as long as a fiddle!'

'*Et ego in Arcadia,* Poppy.'

'Meaning what?'

'Perhaps they were homesick.'

'I don't believe they ever had a home.'

'That has nothing to do with it, my dear child. Neither had the man who wrote "Home Sweet Home". One is homesick for a dream, always, not a place.'

'How long have they been here?'

'Twenty-five years, Poppy,' says Zobrany. 'It was like this: the previous tenant of this building, a person called Nollekens, left them behind, so to speak. He could not very well take them with him; occasionally they have aggravated me into wishing he had; he died, you see. They rented the attic for five shillings a week. I wanted my house to myself, and so I gave them notice to quit. They refused to go. I was firm, I was brutal –'

'– Har, har, har!'

'– They locked themselves in. I laid siege and cut off their water supply. They capitulated. I was much relieved and decorated the attic. Even Mrs Zobrany, who has the patience of an angel and a heart of the purest gold, was glad to see the back of them, for they seemed to permeate the house – one was aware of the Sordics as of an escape of gas – they made one uneasy. I said to myself, "That is that."'

'But they came back?' Poppy asks.

'Not exactly. Two or three weeks later, hearing suspicious noises, I went downstairs in the dead of night and discovered that – God knows how – the Sordics had dismantled their brass bedstead, carried it piece-meal to the old back cellar and set it up there. It must have been a labour like that of Gilliatt in *Toilers Of The Sea* – a feat of engineering. And so the business started all over again. In the meantime, how could I see human beings living with the rats in the dark down there? I had the cellar dried out and floored, whitewashed, et cetera, and let them have the use of some pieces of furniture which I should have given away in any case. And in a restaurant there is always something left over to eat, still fit for human consumption, which would anyway be thrown out. "So, be my dustbins," I said to the Sordics, "eat eggshells and cabbage stalks, and be damned to you!"'

'I can just see you,' says Poppy, with a laugh.

'And in short, here they still are, still detesting me as I detest them. I discovered that they could peel vegetables and even cook a little. But oh dear me, I never knew that they had it in them to cry! Could I have misjudged these Sordics? I was young and in love – I still am, though no longer young – and young men are hasty and harsh in their judgements, too angry with that which hasn't the good fortune to be as beautiful as Mrs Zobrany is; impatient of anybody who isn't as lucky as I have always been.'

'Mrs Zobrany's lucky, too,' Poppy says. 'They don't give your sort away with a pound of tea, I don't mind telling you.'

'Be quiet, Poppy, and don't talk nonsense. And do you know, believe it or not, the Sordics have twice stood by me in a fight. Once, when some students tried to steal my sign, for a joke, and once when some people smashed my teeth with a brick –'

'– I wish I'd been there then,' cries Poppy, flushing darkly. 'What did they want to do that for? Who done it? If it's anybody I know –'

'– It was before you were born, my dear child, in 1914, when the Great War broke out, after the retreat from Mons.'

'Was it Germans that done it?'

'No, I wish it had been. It was Englishmen.'

'The dirty dogs!'

'Not at all. Ordinary nice people, startled, hurt, frightened for the moment. Somebody had spread the word that there was a German spy in Masham Court.'

'It was them Sordics, I bet.'

'No, I think it was a man named Smeed, a newsagent. It doesn't matter. I was across the Court, talking of the war with my dearest of friends, old John Howgego, who used to keep the public house there.'

'I don't like the feller that's got it now, do you?'

'He is all right, but he is not John Howgego. There was a man!' Adjusting the tea urn, Zobrany thinks of his first night in London. 'You would have liked him, Poppy,' says Zobrany, and tells her of the old man's hospitality.

She murmurs, 'I can't make you out. You'll put your hand in your pocket for every lousy layabout, and say, "It's nothing, don't mention it, it's a pleasure." But somebody offers *you* a glass of rum and a bite to eat, and that makes *him* a great man. It don't make sense.'

'It's hard to explain.'

'I bet it is.'

'John Howgego, I say, was my dear best friend. He was a world-defier. He defied the Brewer's Combine, the Income Tax, the Defence of the Realm Act; he defied the police, the Church, the sanitary inspector, the Army, the Navy, the King and Parliament; he defied sickness and health;

he defied riches and poverty, life and death, God and the Devil. There was an Englishman, my dear girl! And he hated the French. He could not believe that we were at war with Germany, because he liked the Germans. We were having a glass of wine, and he was telling me how England and Germany, with Austria's help and Turkey's co-operation, were bound to crush France and Russia, when the mob came roaring into Masham Court: *German spies! German spies!* They were going to lynch a barber named Himmelstoss who had his shop here in those days – a disagreeable fellow with whom I had quarrelled –'

'– He must have been a real beauty to get *your* back up.'

'Well, he called me a *Zigeuner*, a *Schweinerei*, a Hungarian stinker, and what not; for then, as now, the Germans were convinced that they were the master race.'

'I hope they chopped his bloody head off, the fat pig!'

'No. I ran over to mind my café and look after Mrs Zobrany, first and foremost, and then somebody shouted, "There he is!" and a baker from Carnaby Street, whom I did not patronize because I didn't like the bread he sold, threw a stone at me, and missed.'

'I'd have murdered the sod!' says Poppy.

'Ssh! Then a handyman called Baxter called out, "That's not him! We want the blooming barber!" And so they rushed on Himmelstoss's shop.'

'Good for them!'

'Not good for them. Bad. I disliked Himmelstoss, as I say, but it is impossible to stand by and see one man torn to pieces by a mob. I got in the way and shouted, "Stop! He has a wife and children! Do Englishmen make war on women and babies?" At this, somebody in the crowd cried out, "Pro-German! Pro-German! Down him!" and threw half a brick, which hit me in the mouth and broke my front teeth. I caught him by the throat with one hand, and the baker by the ear with another, and knocked their heads together.'

'Good for you! I wish I'd been there.'

'Then the Sordics came up, he with a rolling pin and she with a meat chopper, yelling some strange war cry. It is true that they had come to regard this house as not mine but theirs; still, I was outnumbered thirty to one, and they *were* there with me. Luckily the police arrived and the crowd dispersed. There is the whole story.'

'What happened to the barber?' Poppy asks.

'Himmelstoss? He was put in an internment camp and locked up until 1918.'

'The poor thing. I hope you sent him a nice bunch of flowers?'

'What? Oh, a joke. No, I sent his wife a few groceries, nothing much; that's all.'

'You didn't!'

'Why not? One does not make war on women and children. She was a good woman, as such types go. Good or bad, a woman is a woman and a child is a child. Live and let live – especially children . . . The idiot Himmelstoss – nothing that man ever did was right, somehow – wrote me such a grateful letter that they almost put me in jail, too. I was summoned to Whitehall and cross-examined, and it was very harrowing. Poppy, will you for God's sake go and put a clean apron on?'

'In a minute. Where was Mrs Zobrany while all this barney was going on?'

'Ah, another woman would have screamed, had hysterics, fainted – the devil knows what. But Mrs Zobrany remained perfectly calm; an example to all of us. She sat at the window embroidering me a satin tie with a design of roses – I have it still, and would not part with it for a thousand pounds. When you talk of Mrs Zobrany, you talk of one lady in a million!'

'You know what you ought to have? Half a dozen kids.'

'Poppy, I just told you to go and change your disgusting apron. I don't know how you manage to get so dirty.'

'All I can say is, if I'd been there at the time –'

'–Yes, yes, you'd have made an exhibition of yourself, and a nuisance; but you were not there at the time, you were not born at the time, so go and put a clean apron on. Must I tell you a hundred times? Will you never do the least little thing I ask of you, Poppy?'

'You'd get the surprise of your life, what I'd do if you asked me.'

'And wash your hands for luck while you're about it.'

'Say the word and I'll stop biting my nails and picking my nose, and get my hair cut,' says she, going out.

A man would have to be made of stone not to give this girl's highly manoeuvrable bottom a gentle pinch as she passes. Zobrany is not made of stone. 'Oo-oooh!' she moans, on a dying note. 'You gorgeous beast – kiss me quick, I'm coming!'

Then she is gone. *No, I mean,* thinks Zobrany, *'Stop picking my nose and get my hair cut!' . . . 'Kiss me quick, I'm coming!' No, really! . . . 'Gorgeous beast!' What next, I wonder? . . .* A few seconds later he hears Poppy's voice raised in song and going full blast, high and sweet, strong and clear.

Zobrany knows that he has no need to look at the time: if Poppy is singing aloud, Alma is awake; and if Alma is awake it must be eight o'clock. Still he checks; turns on the radio and, sure enough, catches the last two pips of the signal. Alma is a gem of a woman; you could cook, you could catch trains by her. With her bodily functions and a sextant, you could navigate a ship. When she yawns and closes her eyes it is midnight; when she opens her eyes and yawns it is eight in the morning. If instinct and your watch say that it is eight o'clock and Alma is not yet awake, then it must be Sunday, on which day, like any working girl who treats herself to an extra hour's rest, she sleeps until nine.

Preparing her coffee tray, Zobrany sees himself in the polished curve of the urn, all nose and moustache. *'Half a dozen kids' – no, really, I mean!* he says to himself. *But still, it is a kind thought, and healthy. With most of them these days it is, 'Who would bring a child into a world like this?' And all they think of is pessaries and pessimism and proletariats . . . Half a dozen? Two would do nicely: a dark one like my mother and a red one like Alma . . .* And he wonders, but without bitterness, at the whim of chance which has so ordered matters that two such fine specimens as himself and Alma should remain childless – she, with her gentle heart overflowing with love and her superb body oozing all the salty perfumes of fecundity, and he by no means despicable.

Then Poppy returns, beautified, in a fresh apron and a clean collar. 'Okay?'

'Absolutely charming. I will take up Mrs Zobrany's coffee.'

Twenty-five years of Zobrany's cosseting and pampering would have turned an ordinary woman into something like a peach-fed sow; but Alma has absorbed affection as wood takes in wax and the exudations of caressing fingers, and acquired a certain subcutaneous glow, an underlying texture, a look of quality, a feel of value. Coming in with her coffee, Zobrany pauses to admire her from the doorway. She sprawls, half in and half out of bed, waiting for the monitor in her head to tell her to go and make water. Her nightdress is rucked up to her waist. 'And poor Jason thought *he* found the Golden Fleece,' says Zobrany, putting down the tray and patting her between the thighs.

'Good morning, Steve.'

'Good morning, dear Alma.'

'Have you opened?' She has asked the same question every morning for a quarter of a century, it suggests that she didn't know how late it was, and that if she had known, it would be she who would bring him coffee at eight o'clock.

'The restaurant?' says Zobrany, who is thinking about something quite different. 'Just now. Have you slept well? Is there anything I can do for you? I have brought you the paper.' She likes to see the pictures in the *Daily Mirror* as she sips her morning coffee, and has even taken an interest in the adventures of Pip, Squeak and Wilfred in the comic strip on the Children's Page. She doesn't actually read the big black headlines; she contemplates them, and has discovered that if she looks at them long enough and then closes her eyes tight for a few seconds, she can see those same headlines on the ceiling.

'Thank you, dear.' She sits up, pulling down her nightdress.

'You know what somebody said just now?'

'No, what?'

'That we ought to have six children,' says Zobrany, with a chuckle.

'That would have been nice, but . . .' She does her best to look sad. 'Never mind, dear.'

'No, no, no! I mentioned it because I thought it was absurd, for fun. Like the male tiger, I should be jealous of my young.' Zobrany looks predatory.

'After I've drunk my coffee, would you like to make love to me?'

'Very much indeed, darling, but Poppy is all alone in the accursed restaurant,' as if Alma didn't know. 'Perhaps later, when I rest after lunch?' he says, knowing that Alma will be at the cash register between four and six; and he sighs, thinking, *Accursed café business!*

'That would be nice,' says she, well aware that it is out of the question.

He gives his moustache an extra twirl, rearranges his hair and changes his tie, putting on a red-and-gold brocade cravat with a knot as big as a duck's egg, and goes, as he says, back to the chain gang. She, dipping croissants in coffee and enjoying her breakfast, thinks over the matter of six children, or rather lets the thought go unmolested into its hiding place.

Zobrany doesn't know it, but she was pregnant twice in the first three years of their marriage. It was a matter of indifference to her, until Madame Alice took her in hand.

One day, when she was trying on a hat, the Frenchwoman said, 'My instinct tells me that you are *enceinte.*'

'Am I?'

'"Am I?" My God, don't you know? Haven't you noticed anything? The time of the month, the nasty-pain time?'

'Nasty pain? Oh, that. I don't have nasty pains. It's nothing.'

'Has it been late?'

'Now that you mention it, yes, I think it has. I'm glad you reminded me, Madame Alice. It's been weeks.'

'You are usually regular?'

'Every new moon.'

'Have you ever been late before?'

'Once.'

'When?'

'About a year ago. I forget. Not really late, actually. It was a mistake. I was looking at last year's calendar.'

'My God! . . . She was looking – Listen. You are too young and pretty to embarrass yourself with babies. I still have hope for you. There are women whose spirit comes late. You are one of these, and you are lucky: it means you will stay young and pretty forever. Ninon de l'Enclos developed late, and she was seduced by her own great-grandson without knowing it.'

'Wasn't it illegal?'

'Wasn't it illegal! Now look: do you want to swell up like a balloon, vomit every morning, be wretched for months, squeeze out of your pretty belly a lump of meat weighing nine pounds? You have seen a lump of meat weighing nine pounds? Well then. And this lump of meat will spew and make pee-pee and ca-ca all over you, and scream at you all night, and kick you in the stomach, and bite your nipples until they bleed, and stretch you so that your husband will not want you any more and go and waste money on prostitutes who will give him frightful diseases and which he will bring home to you so that you come out in sores and your nose falls off. And if this lump of meat is a girl, for twenty years she will be a curse and a burden to you, and you will never dare turn your back for fear that she will rush out and get pregnant by God knows who, and bring you home more lumps of meat. And if it is a boy, he will eat you up for twenty years and then run away with a hussy. And in the meantime all your teeth will have fallen out, your hair will have turned to string, your bottom will be choked up with engorged piles, your beautiful white legs will be something to make one spit at them, for they will be covered with black veins, your hips will have spread like a tub of dough in a bakehouse, your skin will be pasty. How would you like all that?'

Alma said that she would not like this very much, she rather thought. Madame Alice, who loved wickedness for its own sake, said, 'I'll charge you nothing, because I still hope to make something of you. There is no need for your husband to know. What a man doesn't know never hurts him, and a man never knows anything, anyway. Besides, he is amiable and handsome, but stupidly in love with you – which is the way for a husband to be. If he caught you in bed with the postman, and you said to him, "I am only posting a letter," he would believe you. Come, let's look at you . . . Oh, la-la! What sinful waste! It's like using a Gobelin tapestry for a dishrag, what you do with this charming thing. In one month exactly, then, we'll *ferons sauter* this nuisance.'

'If you say so, Madame Alice.'

Later, showing Alma something like a morsel of crushed beetroot on a piece of lint, Madame Alice said, catching a sigh, 'All the same, it's marvellous! This could have been Rothschild.'

The second time, she said, 'I see that you are hopeless. Look: love is nothing to you. If I say to you, "Come to my house for two hours and entertain a respectable old gentleman there, and he will give you fifty pounds" – well?'

'I don't want fifty pounds. I've got fifty pounds.'

'Then be damned to you, idiot! Give me fifty pounds, or go to the devil with your bellyful of Hungarian goulash!'

'All right, Madame Alice.'

'Where are you going?'

'Home.'

'Wait a minute. Give me twenty pounds.'

'No.'

'Fifteen, then.'

'No.'

'Ah, *flute alors*! Give me –'

Alma shook her head – that is, swayed it, like a tortoise.

'Then take this muff and neckpiece, which was the property of the Countess of Gunnersbury, for fifteen guineas.'

'All right.'

'Next time this happens I wash my hands of you, do you understand?'

'All right, Madame Alice.'

A chain rattled, water rushed, and there went the dark girl or the golden boy of Zobrany's dream. And what he didn't know never hurt him.

. . . *Now!* says the time signal in Alma's mind; and, faintly smiling as always, she goes to the toilet as a girl might go to meet her lover after a bitter-sweet separation.

Tuesday morning is generally quiet, except in the way of ructions, which somehow tend to break out then. Zobrany has time to remonstrate in German with the butcher about the veal; to demolish the greengrocer in Italian in a skirmish over radishes; to upbraid the coffee man in French concerning Kenya berries; and to issue an ultimatum in official English to the fishmonger, in the matter of a broken treaty relating to haddocks. After that he must commiserate with the cook, a Swiss who has lost all hope, in the lingua franca of the kitchens, which is made up of the chewed and spat-out gristle of half a dozen languages, and may not be spoken in ordinary tones because it has evolved in yells through tubes. Zobrany's customers have picked up a taste for the strictly proletarian dish known as Toad-in-the-Hole – sausages or chops baked in batter – and the cook feels that he has sunk low enough without that.

Zobrany is afraid that he may hang himself again (he had to cut the cook down, once before) and goes out of his way to comfort him on Tuesday mornings.

Then, Poppy's colleague Violet, having recently 'left to better herself' – Zobrany really had to dismiss the girl for soliciting among the customers; ten shillings with knickers off, fifteen in the Altogether, fancy stuff half a crown extra – he must interview applicants for the vacancy. And where, he wonders wildly, where are those two million unemployed he keeps reading about, who only want a chance to do an honest job of work? Where does the Labour Exchange find these sticky dregs and heel taps of humanity? He wants a Waitress, Young, Good Appearance, Experience Unnecessary if Willing to Learn; to whom he is prepared to offer Good Wages, Gratuities, Good Meals, Laundry and Reasonable Hours. Apply 8-9am. It is useless to telephone and protest, 'Really, I am a restaurateur, not a pathologist; I am running a café, not a haunted house at a fairground. Have you nothing at least half human on your books?' They reply that they're doing the best they can. The agencies are just as bad. He wants a waitress: they send him waitresses' grandmothers. He repeats, he wants a waitress, young, good appearance, et cetera: they send him a one-eyed Cypriot, a half-witted dwarf, a youth just out of Borstal and a creature that looks like a coal miner with dermatitis.

'I want a girl here, a girl!' he shouts at the agents. 'Why didn't you say so?' they ask; and send him a succession of women so unmistakably fallen that he expostulates over the throbbing wire, 'This is Masham Court, not Buenos Aires! This is a café, not a Lock Hospital!' Now come a few more, all hopeless. This little misery looks like the howl of a dog made visible; that chlorotic misfit sounds like the white of an egg made audible; the third is young and of good, if frightened appearance, and she is willing to learn, but she has one little failing – when spoken to by strangers, she wets herself. 'I'm sorry,' says Zobrany, giving each applicant two shillings for her fare home. The fourth that morning is a burly girl with woolly blonde hair and a peremptory manner. 'I am a Cherman refutchee in *dis* country. I haf not been long in *dis* country. By profession I am a ski insdrugtor, not in demandt in *dis* country . . .' The last today is a little lady who says she isn't used to this kind of thing, but will accept the post to augment her old-age pension; before her marriage, she tells Zobrany, she was on the stage, her *metier* being the art of diving into a deep tank and smoking a cigarette under water, but she had to give it up because her lungs got wet.

When she is gone Zobrany says to Poppy, 'I can imagine hell as an endless repetition of interviews like this. To every one I must say No . . . But then again, an endless repetition of anything, even an exquisite pleasure, would be hell.'

'Never mind, here comes somebody you can talk about philosophy with.'

'Ah, Mr Ody!' cries Zobrany, coming forward with his friendliest smile. 'Good morning.' He has a great liking for this nice clean boy, who is old enough to be his friend but young enough to be his son, and is pleased that he has taken to coming in for breakfast every day, when he is in town.

'Ah, Steve.' Ody takes his place near the window and puts down a pile of notebooks. 'I'll just have coffee and a roll, I think. I don't feel very bright.'

'You have a hangover?'

'I think I'm poisoned. I was at a party last night in Fitzroy Square, and they had cider.'

'Cider matured in old sherry casks is a dangerous thing, if you're not used to it. A Norman, or a Somerset man, or a Devonian can drink it all day long. But the children here have found that it is fourpence a pint – it is like Gin Lane, only you may say "Drunk for a shilling, stupid for one-and-fourpence and sick all over the place for eighteenpence." I am not going to sell you anything. I am going to give you something. This morning, be my guest.' Zobrany brings a cup of coffee laced with brandy. 'Drink this, and afterwards you must eat what I give you . . . Oh, and remember something: never, never eat mushrooms with cider. You did not, I hope?'

'We did have mushrooms on toast.'

'Good, now you know better. A moment.' He goes, and returns presently with a copper dish of scrambled eggs and ham. 'Eat this up. It is York ham. And there is only one way to scramble eggs: use a lot of butter and a lot of eggs; no milk, no nothing . . . You are writing an article for the papers?'

'As a matter of fact, I am. These' – Ody nods towards the notebooks at which Zobrany has pointed – 'have nothing to do with it. These are something else. The article – I'm not actually writing it; it's a symposium, as they call it.'

'On which subject, if I may ask?'

'*Would I Live My Life Over Again?*'

'Hah!' cries Zobrany, amused. 'Good!'

'I've got to get comments from the Dean of Westminster, Marie Tempest, Bernard Shaw, HG Wells, Gracie Fields and a woman who's been forty years in a Poor Law Institution; Stamford – the man that's just out after doing ten years for espionage; Ivor Novello; some athletic has-been – preferably an old heavyweight boxer; Professor Haldane; Professor Joad; a Liberal politician; and a burglar named Freddie Ford.'

'But who wouldn't like his life over again?' Zobrany wonders.

'In all its details, I mean,' says Ody.

'But why not? It would be better the second or third time. The plot is the least part of a good story: it improves with rereading, does it not? Or else Art would be wastepaper. Do you say, "I wouldn't read *Don Quixote* over again because I know what happens to the hero"? Do you say, "Paint the window black, I have already made myself familiar with the landscape"? No, no, no. A book is more than the sum of its incidents, a man is more than the sum of his parts, a life is more than the sum of its events. I feel, therefore I am. I evoke, therefore I feel.'

'May I quote you on that?'

'But why me? I have no place in such a symposium.'

'Oh yes you have,' says Ody. 'You're the only really intelligent man I've ever met who is happy, who speaks no evil of anybody, and whom everybody loves. You may not know it, but you're a phenomenon.'

'No, a phenomenon! No, really!'

'Steve, could you name any incident in particular that you'd especially like to relive?'

'Oh, many, many; but they are private – not scandalous, not scabrous, simply personal. My dear Ody, certain holy instants are particularly a man's own . . . But how quickly you write! Is that shorthand?'

'Yes. Do go on.'

'– Unless, of course, you understand, a man is a poet or a musician, and then he is not ashamed to try and convey . . . Was Keats the only man who ever loved the nightingale? Was Shakespeare the only man who ever saw life as a dream within a dream, or Bach the only one who heard the morning star singing and all the sons of God shouting for joy? No, no, it is because we have all felt these things that these men are so great. Life would be better the second time around; one's ear would be better attuned, the palate better adjusted, the eye more focused.'

'What about the bad moments?'

'The sense of proportion being in alignment, one would see them for what they were worth. Whatever occurs, my dear fellow, *forsan et haec olim meminisse jubavit* – some day even this may be pleasant to look back at.'

'Would you have everybody live his life over again, Steve?'

'It would not be a bad idea.'

'Take, for example, Hitler.'

'Hitler? I know Hitler. I've met Hitler.'

'You have?' cries Ody, thinking that perhaps Zobrany refers to some encounter years ago.

Zobrany says, 'Yes. So have you. Sometimes you have seen as many as three Hitlers in this café of an evening; and two Mussolinis, and at least one Stalin. Hitler is the artist *manqué*, and the lover *manqué*, and the god *manqué*. I have an idea that it all comes down to his not being able to paint. A little talent, a little recognition . . . but I had better speak for myself alone. In a way, everybody lives his life over again – at least people live for the same reasons that lives have been lived before. That's why history repeats itself – because men repeat themselves. I think they always will. People will always have to survive, and to do so they must always love and fight, make and break. There is no easy formula that I ever heard of, my dear Ody.'

Ody suggests, 'Communism?'

'Ideal, but it presupposes too much, you know. "From each according to his ability; to each according to his work" – do you know what that means? It means that about eighty per cent of us are unnecessary, my dear fellow.'

'Scientifically speaking,' says Ody, 'eighty per cent of us are.'

'But this I have heard. I'll tell you something: it is not for Science to tell Man what is necessary or otherwise – it is the other way round. Science was made for Man, not Man for Science. Are we crystals? Are we square roots? Science tells me that I am made up of carbon and hydrogen and all that, to the value of five shillings. So be it. My chemistry I give to Science; but my Self belongs to me, and I belong to you, and you belong to God – and waste no time, my dear Ody, making me a questionnaire concerning the Nature of God, because I don't know anything at all about it.'

'You don't believe that mankind may be saved through the proper appreciation of Science?'

'I keep an open mind. There are machines, I am told, that will play a piano as accurately as Schnabel. I am not impressed by this: I am waiting for one that will interpret me a mood. There are X situations in fiction, I am told – somebody has invented a Plot Chart to prove it. Well, stick me this chart onto an engine which, when you pull out the "Ungrateful Children" stop, writes me *King Lear*. When you have done this, I will be in love with Science. Come on, now; I'll be easy on Science: make me a gadget with a sense of humour – nothing but that – and I'll buy it if it ruins me! . . . You see, my dear Ody, sociologists fit people to sociology, and living people won't have that for long. Sociology is a science – it may warm my water, but what about my blood? Science is exact, and so you get used to it. Science shows you short cuts. It is handy, but the soul of a man is roundabout, inefficient. Still, give it a chance, I say! Man is young, Science is a toy, and there is nothing so grave or dictatorial as a child at play. One of these days there will be a cosmic wedding – Learning will marry Knowledge, and may you live to see what will be born of it! Meanwhile, since you must concede that the likes of me are economically valueless, I like Democracy because of her faults, of which I am one.'

'You're not valueless, Steve, economically or otherwise.'

'Scientifically speaking, I am redundant. I am strong enough still to shovel my eight cubic yards of dirt per day, yet all I do is pour water over tea and coffee and sell it by the cupful at a profit. Also, I'm a lackey; I wait on people. And a saboteur: if a man is broke I say, "Pay me some other time," thus delaying the Revolution. I believe in Live And Let Live; this is unscientific. So be it. The man to talk to on this kind of topic is Tom Henceforth. Now there is a man who has a point of view, a new approach to practically anything. I haven't seen him just lately.'

Zobrany glances automatically at the place where his mural ought to be. Ody unconsciously lays a hand on his notebooks and says, 'I saw him last night. He was at that party in Fitzroy Square.'

'He was the life of the party?'

'He always is.'

'A man of tremendous personality, a genius,' says Zobrany warmly. 'An artist, a poet, a critic, a man of ideas, a modern Leonardo!' Poppy, who has been listening from a distance, sings:

''Arder, 'arder, Leonarder,
Do it with the poker –'

'Poppy!' says Zobrany, in a terrible voice.

'What's the matter? It's a song about firemen on a ship.

'Crack the clinker, you lazy stinker.
Call yourself a stoker?

'What's wrong with that?'

Ody says, 'Poppy, would you come and sing some songs at the Jingle Club one of these evenings?'

'Har, har, har. Would you like a frostitute?'

'This had to come out sooner or later,' says Zobrany.

'What's a frostitute?'

'A bit o' cold tart.'

Ody comes right back with, 'You'll feed me up to gastronomical proportions.'

'No, really!' says Zobrany, vastly amused. '. . . I wish Tom Henceforth would not make such a stranger of himself these days. But no doubt he is working hard at his novel.'

'I don't see a great deal of him either,' says Ody. 'He's making researches; "getting raw material" as he says "out of the political quagmire".'

'An artist must be everywhere. I expect great things from Henceforth.'

'You've known him a long time, Steve, I think?'

'Off and on, twenty-five years or so. Did you ask him if he would live his life over again?'

'As a matter of fact, I did. It turned into a kind of party game, in the end . . .'

FIFTEEN

It had been what Tom Henceforth described as 'the typical arty-farty party . . . Some tall girl with bulging eyes comes up to London to learn all about art on three pounds a week from Father, and she goes like a homing pigeon to the Fitzroy Tavern and is picked up first time out by a hollow-eyed layabout who tells her he's a poet, and she'll be good for him and help him cure himself of homosexuality. And the next thing you know, this County gel who belongs in Guildford High Street – dressed in good tweed badly cut, with one foot on the running board of a two-seater in the gutter and the other in a teashop doorway, and her cowish hips at sixes and sevens and a fanny-pad waggling out like a rabbit in a sack, having conversations with people on the other side of the street in a voice like a coal heaver – this bony daughter of Anaemia breaks it off with the half-arsed Dulwich College rugger-bugger she's been engaged to ever since they used to play stinkfinger on the towpath and goes to live in a couple of rooms off Charlotte Street, happy as a pig in shit. She buys a secondhand divan for fifteen shillings and pays somebody twenty-five to saw the legs off it; and she gets a sixpenny orange-crate from the greengrocer and covers it with two pounds' worth of brocade and calls it a bookcase, and fills it up with poetry books; and she sticks a candle in a beer bottle and buys a barrel of Henekey's cider and says, "Let's have a house-warming." So she and her Peter John, or Robin John, or Michael John, or Christopher Robin – they always have names like that – go and scrape the pubs and the cafés for guests. "We have a bar'l of Henekey's cidah and a bar'l of Benskin's beah – *dooo* come!" And up pops the same sad rabble of dirty old women who used to model for Epstein and Gaudier-Brzeska, or sleep with Hemingway and Sherwood Anderson, and the man who got locked in the Gentlemen's with Gide and Proust, and the Yank with the Oxford accent, and the spiv with the Yank accent, and the society girl turned Communist, and the inevitable crush of panders, pimps, parasites, flagellants, sodomites, lesbians, hermaphrodites, pick-pockets, deserters from the Army, touts, chalkers on walls and such-like men of letters; plus the Peace Pledge Union, and a riffraff of venereal old veterans – the man who lost his memory at Mons, the man who lost his balls at Bailluel, the man who lost his penis at Poper-inghe, the man who lost his head at Hazebrouck, the man who caught the syph at Soissons – and revolutionaries galore . . . The barrel of cider goes *psst!* and so does the beer, and the wine, and the gin, so they mix up all the heel taps and drink that, and then send out for more, and some sausage rolls and meat pies, and everybody spews his guts out all over everybody else; and the Tiger Woman, who must be seventy if she's a day, takes off her drawers and dances a gopak; and Epstein's model, all beslobbered with vomit and snot and tears, strips to prove that she's kept her figure, although she could throw her tits over her shoulders and wipe her back on them, if she ever wished it, which she hasn't this forty years; and two fairies fight with fingernails over a sailor they picked up in The Plough; and Christopher Robin, or whatever his name is, "says" – not reads, *says* – a little thing he's just "done". And it's all too bloody intellectual for words . . .'

But Ody, in a marginal note, wrote, 'Daphne and Bridget gave a party for Fritz Tamrodt and Sylvine. I got ill, but Z says it is my own fault for mixing cider and mushrooms . . .' He liked that young couple. Fritz Tamrodt was a cameraman in documentary films, and Sylvine a serious young actress fresh out of the Royal Academy of Dramatic Art. Being in love, they got married, and were going to live out at Beaconsfield; they were as simple as that. It was whispered that until her marriage Sylvine had remained a virgin, and so people said that she was frigid or a lesbian. Tamrodt, for his part, had a distaste for what he termed 'alley-cat promiscuity', and therefore women who found him attractive said he was either impotent or a pederast. It was observed that Tom Henceforth was unaccountably irritated by this marriage. It was known that Henceforth had paid court to Sylvine in his backhanded, ambiguous way. But she had said, 'Frankly, there is something about you which repels me.' She was a wholesome, earnest, candid girl. 'All that talent, and . . .' she made a gesture which conveyed an impression of smoke thinning out and blowing away. 'No tenderness,' she said. Tom Henceforth pretended to laugh it off, saying, 'I'll be a brother to you, then', and bided his time.

So, after the guests had drunk the health of Fritz and Sylvine, he said, in his strong, soft, compelling voice, 'I was thinking of one thing and another last night, and I thought I'd compose a little epithalamium for these nice people. But it must have been something I ate. Instead of a Scatter Ye Rosebuds affair, up popped something like Gray's 'Elegy', only different. You could call 'Girl's Elegy Written In A Beaconsfield Bedroom'. I didn't write it down because I had no time –' He had spent weeks putting the verses together, and memorizing them. '– But it goes something like this:'

Everybody was silent. Tom Henceforth pitched his voice low and solemn and in his precise diction he declaimed:

'He promised me a most important part
And so I went to bed with Tommy Rot.
His Tarts are not worth mentioning, dear heart!
At last the dawn has come. But I have not . . .

A writer wishes that his story'd earn
Enough to pay his rent, for live he must;
An actress gambles – she must live and learn –
Against long odds her Animated Bust . . .

Let Cleopatra weep, Lucrece coquette
And proud Thamar lie sprawling on her back!
Let Sylvine spread her thighs! What will she get?
A little zigzag on a Sounding Track . . .'

There were sixteen verses, and a snarl in every one. But when he came to:

'Banish remorse! I sparkle like champagne.
I see last evening through the eye of lenience.
My belly's smooth and white as porcelain –
But so is every Gentlemen's Convenience –'

gentle Fritz Tamrodt bounded across the burlap-covered floor and struck him an open-handed blow in the face. Tom Henceforth, grinning like a gargoyle, said, 'Aha! My shaft went home, did it?'

The cameraman clicked his heels, bowed to Tom Henceforth and said, 'I beg your pardon. That doggerel is the best thing you have ever done, and it is poor; but you put your little heart and soul into it, and so I apologize. Sylvine . . . ?'

There was a moment of uneasy quiet as the young couple left. Then Ody, to ease the tension, told the company about the symposium he had been commissioned to put together, while either Daphne or Bridget – and which was which Ody, after a few drinks, could not tell – gave Tom Henceforth an especially strong glass of gin and hoped he had not been 'upset by that whey-faced tart, Sylvine, and her pitiful little Rilke-and-milk shake, Fritz Tamrodt . . .'

The few who, later, sheepishly admitted that they enjoyed Tom Henceforth's company when he was the life and soul of so many bohemian parties in the 1930s remembered him as being almost fastidiously unkempt. He was never dirty; his wiry white hands were always neat, and his hairless face seemed to have a labour-saving synthetic surface – a wipe with a damp cloth brought it up fresh as paint. But as to his clothes, they might have been checked by a script girl whose duty it was to keep constant a certain characteristic state of precariousness. Certain buttons were always hanging by one maddening thread; and for years the world had waited for his elbows to break through the worn places in his sleeves, or for his helpless-looking tie to come undone, or for the ribbon to fall away from his wilted black hat.

An old scar at the left-hand corner of his mouth still looked only half healed: he said he had got this scar in Ireland, in 1919, when a sergeant of the Black-and-Tans had pistol-whipped him on the way to jail; it added a dash of the sinister to his habitual ventriloquist's-dummy grin, and women were very fond of it. This scar, together with a slight but noticeable limp, made his hypnotically dangling buttons and his general appearance of half-decent neglect curiously attractive: some girls were drawn to the frayed edges of Tom Henceforth's cuffs as nail biters to jagged thumbnails.

'I used to get myself up like a pox-doctor's clerk,' he would say. 'When I was a promoter I spake as a promoter, I dressed as a promoter. (I carried my clothes well, too. I always had a wire-clothes-hanger figure, all anatomy.) But when I became a man, and discovered my destiny – which was to be a novelist – I put away bucket-shopkeepers' broadcloth and took to tweeds. But I was a natty son of a bitch when I came up from Manchester. One or two people still remember me as a kind of Piccadilly Johnny, hanging around the West End cafés and looking a bit like Max Beerbohm, only taller and healthier . . .'

This was an exaggeration, of course; but Zobrany could remember the afternoon, not long after he had opened the restaurant, when he completely failed to recognize, in a well-turned-out young man who came sauntering into Masham Court lashing about with a thin ivory-headed Malacca, the grotesque clown who had been the sign-painter's boy only a few months before. The young man had stood, looking up at the sign and admiring it from every angle, and said, 'You know, painted up like that, there's a kind of sublime vulgarity about that little monster – like the figurehead of an old ship, or the Guildhall Giants. You could never achieve such a perfection of crudity in carving nowadays.'

'It is the work of a young genius –' Zobrany began.

'– How much would you take for it?' Tom Henceforth asked.

'Take for it? It is not for sale at any – Good God! Is it you?'

Over coffee, Zobrany asked, 'Have you inherited money?'

'No. I cleaned up a little on a theatrical deal, down in Lancashire . . . Why don't you have some nice lively murals in here? I don't mean views of Naples Bay, with trees like umbrellas, like they have in the spaghetti places. Something original.'

'Like, for example, a pictorial map of Piccadilly and its environs, with Masham Court as its centre?' said Zobrany, thinking of Cseh's mad chart.

'Perhaps. I'll think about it.'

'Will you paint it for me?'

'When I have time.'

'You are very busy now, Mr Henceforth?'

'Well, I have plenty on my mind.'

'How much would it cost?'

'That would depend,' Tom Henceforth said. 'It would depend. Upon factors, various factors.'

'Would you like me to pay you something on account?' Zobrany asked diffidently, glancing at the boy's well-cut clothes.

'No, no.' Tom Henceforth had money in his pocket for the time being. 'But when I want it I'll ask for it.'

'Promise?'

'Word of honour,' said Tom Henceforth; and he kept this promise most scrupulously.

SIXTEEN

Social significance ran strong and turbid in the 1930s. Protest became vociferous. The Inside Story came into its own. The only point of view worth printing was the Worm's Eye View, which magnified the underside of things, and the editors were not slow to discover that there was money in it. Eminences were levelled and obscurities exalted; mountains became molehills, pimples became volcanoes. A few years previous, an author could generally sell a novel about (say) William Shakespeare. Now, offered such a subject, a publisher was likely to demur. 'Yes, but what about Robert Greene? He debunked Shakespeare. Greene was an Oxford intellectual who, because he wouldn't lick the boots of the ruling classes, was reduced to living on the earnings of a prostitute whose brother was a pickpocket, "The Cutter" Ball. There's a terrific scene where Greene swells up and dies, covered with blotches because of eating decayed pickled herrings washed down with Rhine wine in the company of Nashe and William Monox. Look, why not write your novel about a poor man's son, a talented playwright, who can't get into the Shakespearean theatre because he won't become the homosexual lover of a lord, turns back to his own class, evolves the first Trades Union and is hanged, drawn and quartered for high treason – as seen through the eyes of "Cutter" Ball?'

The 'stark human document' became the order of the day; the 'unadorned personal narrative'. Shepherds left their sheep and artisans their benches, wives deserted their husbands and soldiers their regiments, to write 'heart-rending accounts, full of brutal candour, with moments of pure beauty'. Boys just out of school, with the toffee still sticky on their cheeks, put out 'sensitive and haunting' exposés of canings and burnt porridge in the academies.

Most working writers kept on the alert for interesting – that is to say startling and improbable – biographical subjects in the market places and the coffee shops. Among these was Ody, and the object of his professional curiosity – which was later to become an obsession – was the wayward, perverse, sardonic, unpredictable and morbidly fascinating character of Tom Henceforth. Fortunately, Ody had a small private income: if you elect to dedicate yourself to charting mirages you have got yourself a full-time job – no salary, and pay your own expenses. His parents had wanted him to be a doctor; but he discovered that he could write saleable articles, and there was the end of that. Then he met Tom

Henceforth, whose conversation shocked and delighted him. To his mind, this pungent character was perfect raw material for a Profile, an exhaustive character study, to be productive of profit and prestige. The ex-medical student was by habit a conscientious taker of notes. After a month or two of writing what he called 'Henceforthiana', he found that he had acquired an unbreakable habit. It was not affection, admiration or respect; it was addiction.

One of Ody's old medical friends remonstrated with him. 'What the hell's come over you? What's got into you? If you've got to be a hanger-on, for God's sake find somebody worth hanging on to, but what's so extraordinary about this Henceforth fellow?'

'I'm interested in him.'

'You act as if you were in love with him, or something.'

'Don't be a fool,' said Ody. 'I don't even like him.'

'Brilliant, I grant you, and funny as hell. But to be taken in small doses. Soho's full of his sort. Drop him, old boy, drop him!'

'Jack, when I want advice you'll be just about the last man in the world I'll come to for it. You're just the sort of bloke who'd tell Pasteur to stop wasting his time on ridiculous little microbes. Let's say I'm reading Tom Henceforth for a thesis, and mind your own business.'

'What thesis? The bloody clown! He's one solid antithesis from ear to ear.'

'There's got to be a reason for him, somewhere. I want to stain him and mount him. I want to try him on the rabbits,' said Ody. 'He might be the Common Cold, for all I know – psychologically, I mean.'

'You can sterilize your glass after he's been at it, but you can't very well go and boil your head, old man. I mean, a bacillus runs true to type, more or less; but that one just bamboozles. I don't blame you for chucking Medical – it's a mug's game. But if you want to go in for Psycho – and that's where the money is, old boy – why not come back to UC and finish your last year?'

'– Oh, go and get your degree and stop worrying about me.'

'– The fact is, though, you're simply enjoying yourself.'

'I'm engrossed.'

'You're morbid.'

'You're a fool.'

'All right, Ody . . . Would you like to lend me a couple of pounds till the end of the month?'

'Oh, all right,' said Ody, handing over the money.

'Thanks, old man.'

'If you're short, you know, I've got another pound or two.'

'Bless your heart, old boy, that's all right. I spent an evening with some fellows from Trinity, and flogged the microscope . . . They're going abroad, and drew an eighty-pound kit allowance, and I was helping 'em drink it up.'

'How much did you hock the mike for?'

'Two pounds.'

'Well, you'll need a little extra for a homeopathic hair of the dog. I'll lend you a fiver and you can stand me lunch.'

'Oh, all right.'

So they went to a chop house in Panton Street; and there Jack found some of his companions of the previous night – The Horse Coogan, and The Bull Grogan, and Dog Concannon – all hungover, repentant, full of wise hindsight and hard up, so that the luncheon took a whisky-fied, beery, philosophical turn. Aching from the affable back-slappings of The Bull Grogan and the bone-crushing handshaking of The Horse Coogan, Ody had to listen to the affectionate but sententious effusions of his old friend Jack, publicly analysing him 'for his own good'.

'Ody's soul is corroded with guilt, but it is not of his own making. He was born into the plush-lined strongbox of the bourgeoisie. In a period of depression, dole, means test, universal malaise – three million unemployed in Great Britain, ten million unemployed in America – the solid middle-class Ody puts on a weatherproof mackintosh and galoshes and, umbrella in hand, goes out to learn the meaning of the wind and rain!'

'*Strepitumque Acherontis avari!*' said Dog Concannon. The roaring of the hungry stream of Death. *Et penitus toto divisos orbe Britannos* –'

Ody shouted '– What the hell do you mean, "*toto divisos orbe Britannos?*"'

'Estranged from the world, Englishman, estranged from the world.'

'Living vicariously,' groaned Grogan. 'If he has money to chuck about, he ought to let *us* take him around.'

'Thank you,' said Ody. 'I've already seen the inside of a knocking-shop at the back of Dame Street, and drunk a gallon of draft Guinness at Mulally's –'

'– Which is more than your Tom Henceforth has,' said Jack. 'The bloody gasbag!'

'*Horresco referens*,' said Concannon. 'The Eyeties are using mustard in Abyssinia.'

'In case of a mustard gas attack in the Abyssinian jungle or desert,' said Ody, 'be sure to wear an airtight rubber suit and to carry with you several thousand gallons of water to spray over contaminated areas. In this way you may live to make a report – that is, suffer vicariously. In the event –'

'What are you talking about?' asked Coogan.

'He's being funny,' said Jack. 'He is indicating that following the war in Abyssinia and following Tom Henceforth around Soho are fundamentally one and the same thing. Eh, Ody?'

Ody said, 'Not a bit of it. I'm a researcher. You're a bunch of barbers.'

'If I had money of my own, I'd be a researcher, too,' said Grogan.

'*Damnosa hereditas!* A small private income is the ruin of a young man,' said Concannon.

'If I were Mussolini I'd send Haile Selassie a thousand Irish medical officers,' said Ody. 'It'd come cheaper than air raids and kill more wogs.'

'A false economy,' said Grogan. 'In twenty years there'd be thirty thousand ginger-haired bastards for you to cope with. The Eyeties never occupied Ireland the way they did England for five hundred years –'

'– Unclench your hairy great fists,' said Jack, 'and don't get acrimonious. Change the subject.'

'To come back to it,' said Ody, 'one man wants to reach the South Pole. Another man wants to find the source of the Nile. A third man wants to find out about Arabia Deserta. A fourth wants to climb a mountain; a fifth wants to climb down into a pothole. I want to go through Darkest Tom Henceforth with gun and camera. For the last time; so what?'

'*Ex Henceforth semper aliquid novi,*' said Concannon.

'John Donne was all wet,' said Coogan, suddenly gloomy. 'Every man is a dark continent entire of itself.'

'Some more than others,' said Ody.

'He's making mental notes,' said Jack. 'Watch it, boys. He has systems of mnemonics, private kinds of shorthand, and he fiddles with wire recorders. He's a voyeur and an eavesdropper in the name of Science –'

'Me and Aubrey; me and Pepys; me and Freud,' said Ody.

'Not forgetting Suetonius and Walter Winchell,' said Concannon. 'He is a Corybant of the keyhole. Let him be, let him be!'

'You are an unscientific lot of buggers,' said Ody.

Grogan sang:

'He knew all about Etymology,
Hebrew, She-brew, Jujuology,
Syntax, Tintax, Hobnails, Boot Jacks –
He was as full as a Pickford's Van
Because he was a Sci-en-tif-ic Man!'

'Come, a man's entitled to study stagnant water,' said Jack. 'Besides, he's a guest at my table, and I won't have him ribbed.'

So Ody did not invite them to the party at Fitzroy Square – which, as a substantial contributor to the commissariat, he had a right to do – and felt that it was all for the best, especially when something in the atmosphere called for a diversion. 'Darling, would *you* have your life over again?' a dishevelled brunette asked, sitting on the arm of Tom Henceforth's chair and shoving a plump shoulder against his cheek.

He didn't say yes, and he didn't say no; emptied his glass, held it out to be refilled and started to talk . . .

. . . You know, I came back from the north with quite a bit of money. My God Almighty, I was what they call nowadays a Business Consultant, before the milk was dry on my lips. Sir Augustus Bracegirdle – *Sir* Augustus, if you bloody well please! – 'the genius of pre-fabricated building construction': I gave him the idea for the Collapsible Concrete Foundation back in 1911, when he was plain Gus, barrow-shoving for a wop plasterer named Santini over at Blackfriars. Demonstrated it with a rubber football bladder and some plaster of Paris. Suburban Developments, Limited – paid-up capital thirty million pounds – that was mine, too. I could tell you things you'd find it hard to believe. Who ghost-wrote *Riceyman Steps* for Arnold Bennett? Never mind.

As I was saying: I used to get in a little reading at the British Museum, and so I ran into this Mehmet Zudd in Ye Olde Englishe Tea Shoppe.

Ever see a hunchback seven feet tall? Seven feet tall and black as ink, humped back and front like Punch. Humped back and front, with a woolly head and his face cicatrized with tribal markings, four to a cheek. Thin lips, not thick, and a mouth from ear to ear. Black lips, from ear to ear; and speckled teeth like a box of dominoes. I looked under the table to see if he had any feet, because I was prepared to see a spiral of smoke and a brass bottle where his boots should have been. He was eating a ridiculous boiled egg; it should have been an ostrich egg.

While I'm taking a good look at him out of the corner of my eye he catches the waitresses exchanging whispers and giggling. One of them comes over to take my order, and he says to her, measuring out about fourteen inches on the table top, 'About like that.'

The girl blushes red as fire. I tell her to get me a pot of tea and some buns, and this black man says to me, 'It is not difficult to read white women's thoughts.'

'You're a man after my own heart,' I tell him. 'What's your name?'

He makes three clicks, two gulps, blows a raspberry and sobs four times, and says, 'But, for convenience, I spell it Z-U-D-D. I am a businessman and a politician. Also, I am a spiritual leader.'

'What kind of business!'

'Consolidated Africa, Limited.'

'Politics?'

'African consolidation.'

'Spiritual trends?'

'The consolidation of Africans.' He has an eerie way of talking, this geezer; like Morse code on the low string of a double-bass; no punctuation, no expression in his voice and none on his face.

I say, 'I take it Consolidated Africa, Limited, is some kind of trading company?'

His humps must be full of extra lungs, or something; he can go on for about ten minutes without stopping for breath in this wog tom-tom Morse, telling me what he trades in, beating time with a finger, *Tum tata tum-tum, Tata tata tum-tum* –

'– Cocoa and copra,
cola, piassava,
tin, ore, ivory,
oil seed and ground nuts,
hardwoods, obeche,
copper, gold and rubber,
castor oil, diamonds,
bauxite, piassava,
cocoa, cocoa, cocoa,
iron, piassava –'

I thought piassava was some kind of juicy fruit – it sounded kind of squashy and yellow. I didn't find out until later that it's a palm fibre they make brooms out of. If he wanted to emphasize something he just said it two or three times. Cocoa-cocoa-cocoa meant a hell of a lot of cocoa. I knew there was money in that, but I'd never considered oil seed and ground nuts – they went into margarine, apparently.

I ask him, 'Did I hear you say gold and diamonds?'

'Oh yes,' he says, and takes some brown pebbles out of his waistcoat pocket. These are diamonds uncut.' In another pocket he had a cigarette tin full of little nuggets. 'But we do not say anything about that. They are illegal. So these things we keep secret until the right time comes.'

'What right time?'

'The time of consolidation.'

'You have diamond mines?' I ask him.

'Oh yes. But the white men would take them away if they knew. So they are secret. Secret-secret. Also gold also secret-secret. Tin and copper, too and lead and iron and bauxite. But my country is in the hands of the Imperialists. First I must win independence for my people. The only one way to do this is by legal trade. Consolidated Africa, Limited, will pay the producer more and sell for less to the consumer.

Also we know where there is oil-oil-oil. We know where the elephants go, when they are old, to die. We know where are the diamond mines of Solomon. But now it must be secret. Secret-secret. If what we know were told there would be blood.'

I say, 'Blood-blood-blood, and then some blood.'

'And so Consolidated Africa, Limited, will fight the United Africa and Unilever companies by legitimate trade. So I am in London to begin business. In good time there will come out our gold and our diamonds and our ivories. And then if there is to be blood then there must be blood but it shall not be our blood oh no-no-no.'

'As I see it, Mr Zudd, you're a kind of accredited representative of a group of independent traders.'

'I am Chairman and Managing Director of Consolidated Africa, Limited. Also I am Chief of the Porro. Also I am Head Man of the Night Leopard Men and of the Silver Face Men and Mask Maker of the Nyamibebua Men. I am High Priest of the N'Gagan'gor. These are things few white men have ever heard of. So if I say a certain word at Boma in the morning then such and such a man as far away as Mombasa will die before midnight. For you have telegraphs but we have the drums-drums-drums. I am a spiritual leader. So if I say, "You shall not sell your cocoa to United Africa but you shall deliver it FOB at such and such a place for shipment to me," then that thing is done. Because if it is not done I shall say a certain word in a certain place and then the person who has not done what I have said shall be done will die before midnight. You will tell me please what is your trade.'

I tell him I'm a business consultant, recently engaged in theatrical ventures of an ambitious nature. And I ask him, does he know many people in the City. He says, 'Nobody.' And I ask him how much capital he's got to go into business with over here. He says, 'None. God will provide.'

I say, 'If it's not an impertinence, which god happens to be the one you say your prayers to? I ask only to be informed.'

And he says, looking me straight in the eye, 'As Chairman and Managing Director of Consolidated Africa, Limited, I naturally assume divinity. I say my prayers to myself therefore.'

'And where are you living?'

'I have been staying at an hotel. It is not good. I shall look for a private room in a house.'

'The landlady where I live has a room to let,' I tell him.

'Then I shall go and live there.'

'I'll find you some capital,' I tell him. 'Only I want a broker's commission.'

'It is yours.'

'Ten per cent.'

'It is granted.'

'Expenses, of course, both ordinary and extraordinary.'

'It is agreed.'

'Tell me all about the Night Leopard Men.'

'I may not do that unless you are initiate.'

'You can initiate me if you like.'

'First you must fast twenty-eight days. Then you drink Omolo tea. Omolo is a bark the elephant eats when he is constipated. After that I circumcise you with a stone knife and slash your face four times on each side with leopard claws. Into these wounds I rub red pepper but you must not cry out on pain of death. Then you may eat – but not before you have gone out alone and killed a leopard with a spear. You eat the heart of the leopard raw. After your circumcised parts are healed by dipping in hot pitch you may marry.'

'I'll think it over,' I said.

We walked to the dump he was living in, in Marchmont Street. The landlady said, 'What about that two pound you owe me?'

He said to me, 'Pay her', and so I did. Of course, if that had been now, instead of twenty-odd years ago, I could have shown him how to make capital out of the Leopard Men initiation alone – with modifications: fast twenty-eight hours, take Eno's Fruit Salt, dip penis in chicken's blood and make four marks on each cheek with a celluloid leopard's claw, go out and strangle a kitten, eat a pink heart-shaped sponge cake; and then you get a diploma and a tube of white Vaseline and a coupon entitling you to the embraces of one publisher's reader. It costs you fifty pounds. Ladies half price only they've got to wear a leopard-skin-type dress to meetings; which sets 'em back thirty guineas. Rent of bedrooms would bring in a pretty penny, to say nothing of the bar business . . .

However, here was this poor harmless crackpot, all set to take on United Africa and Unilever and the chocolate combines singlehanded – just the sort of nut your average, inimitable, straight-faced English bloody humorist loves to have a bit of fun with, bull-baiting now being illegal. I could just see the God-damned stockbrokers' clerks having the time of their lives with poor old Zudd around the City teashops – Christ Jesus, he'd be better than misdirecting a blind cripple! I could just hear 'em: 'Anything doing, Chawley?' 'No, old boy. Old boy, haven't gypped a widow or an orphan these past three days. Let's look up Zudd and give him a letter of introduction to Lifebuoy Soap. Send him haring down to Port Sunlight what, what?' . . .

And so I said to myself, *We'll see who has the joke with whom!*

I had it all worked out in five minutes, you see. I told Zudd, 'I know something about Big Business. Go to a bloody English businessman with a straight and above-board proposition and he'll laugh at you first and swindle you afterwards; go to him with an out-and-out crooked scheme and he'll swindle you first and laugh at you afterwards; but approach him with a wheeze whereby he can make money by altruism, and you've got him.'

'Explain to me the meaning of "altruism",' says Zudd.

I say, 'Altruism is raising a million pounds to build a poorhouse, taking twenty per cent off the top plus working expenses, and getting a knighthood for it. Altruism is cutting off a dog's tail, eating the meat, and giving the bones to the dog. Altruism is making a fortune out of dead turkeys to celebrate the birth of Christ, and making a fortune out of cocoa to make chocolate Easter eggs to celebrate the death and resurrection of Christ. I, Brother Zudd Almighty, am going to look up a couple of rich do-gooders, and put it to them that they cast a little left-over bread upon the waters, on the tacit understanding that it's cocoa-bait. And piassava – we mustn't forget piassava . . .'

Zudd nods a head like a coal scuttle overflowing with horsehair and says, 'You have my leave to proceed.'

'It's a pity we haven't got some kind of documentary evidence to show,' I tell him; whereupon he drags out a bundle of telegrams, all to Zudd, Victoria House, St Alfred's Close, Bishopsgate, London.

They're from various parts of West Africa, and they say TWO THOUSAND SACKS COCOA READY SHIPMENT BEACH ACCRA, and FOUR HUNDRED LOGS MAHOGANY READY SHIPMENT FOB BEACH FREETOWN, and EIGHT HUNDRED BAGS COLA BEACH LOME READY SHIPMENT CIF, and EIGHTEEN HUNDRED POUNDS PRIME IVORY IN TUSK IN BEACH BINGERVILLE PLEASE ADVISE. All that kind of thing, signed WILSON.

I ask him, 'Who's Wilson?'

He says, 'Babatunji Akamolo Aridada N'Kaka Wilson is one of my agents between Grand Bassam and the Congo Basin.'

'And what's this "Victoria House, St Alfred's Close" stuff?'

'I have taken business premises in the middle of the City of London.'

I ask him, 'Are you allowed by your religion to drink whisky?'

He takes out a little round mirror and looks at it; then nods. 'It is permitted,' he says, and puts the mirror away, and downs half a pint at a gulp without winking.

I say, 'Once I get a few philanthropic souls interested, it might be a good idea, just for the sake of appearance, to say you're a good Christian.'

He says, 'Oh. I am a Doctor of Divinity by correspondence of the Christian Theological Institute in Detroit USA. One must subscribe to a popular superstition. Also I am a Mohammedan and circumcised. This latter I can prove –' And he sticks his hand inside his shirt, just under his collar. I'm absolutely aghast. One hears stories, of course, but

. . . well, after all . . . ! He undoes a button and pulls out a locket. '– I have here my prepuce preserved in camphor,' he says, somewhat to my disappointment.

I tell him, 'I think the cables will be credentials enough.'

Then he looks around my sitting room and says, 'You have many books.'

'I am a writer,' I tell him.

'You will have little time for literature for the present.'

I say, 'That's quite all right, Lord Zudd. Anybody can write a satire, but it takes a real satirist to live one.'

So I went to work. That kind of thing is easy as pie. I dug out the Socialist MPs and all that. Jesus God, I got a pukka Lady with a title for a buckshee secretary! If I had a son (that I knew of) I should say to him, 'My boy, to get rid of any inhibitions you might have, the best thing is a Polish-Buriat-Hairy-Ainu-Formosan-Scandinavian hybrid that has been locked up to ferment for seven years. But the next best thing, involving you in small risk of venereal infection or marital involvement – the effects of both of which are grave and far-reaching – get hold of a Lady with title with Liberal tendencies, for a real roll in the mud.'

Did you ever cohabit with the nobility and gentry on a heap of half-cured monkey skins to the rhythm and noise of seventeen sewing machines in a dressmaker's loft overhead, under a desk on a sweltering afternoon full of thunder clouds in Bishopsgate? Then you haven't lived.

But to return to business: in three weeks I got a dozen interested parties together, and we had a semi-formal tea party at the old Cosmo . . . Let's have a bit more gin, and drink – To hell with British benevolence, and may our altruistic businessmen hang themselves on their own phylacteries! . . .

One of my likeliest marks was a Jew moneybags named Benoni Bararon – one of the messianic sort with a look of meek dismay that seems to say, 'Could you please direct me to Calvary?' Family had been here since the time of King John. Obliged Richard Lionheart with substantial advances; was in the mercury supply business for alchemists when Fugger had the monopoly; supported James I, Charles I, Oliver Cromwell, Charles II; baronetcy from George III.

Our Benoni had picked up a kosher kind of Christian socialism at Oxford, and had taken up Africa. *Mister* Bararon – he wouldn't use the 'Sir' – had picked up a Yank named McClure, who was supposed to have been with Stanley on one of his expeditions. McClure was a pal of Frank Harris – which ought to have been enough to put any sane man on his guard – and he was one of those serious, humourless, deep-set, moustachioed characters whose every last piddling word is a bleeding pronunciamento. A voice like a bassoon, hellish impressive.

He wanted Bararon to finance some kind of humanitarian goings-on in the region of the Upper Kasai. *Conman* was written on his face in letters of fire, but Benoni Bararon had taken a fancy to him; admired his conversation no end. I knew that if McClure had his way we'd be *kaput* as far as that source of revenue was concerned. But by the luck of the Henceforths this geezer was delivered into my hands just when he was on his way to our tea party.

'How are you?' I asked him, and he said he wasn't feeling too good: a touch of ague, a smidgeon of dengue, a soupçon of breakbone fever, rat-bite fever, the Congo Skitters, the Nyanza Squirts, malaria both malignant and benign – all the things you get in those parts. So I say, 'Come and have a pick-me-up.'

'I gave it up years ago,' says he, 'it disagrees with me.'

But if I choose to put myself out to be persuasive, it takes a tougher cookie even than McClure to resist me for long, and so I steer him into the Southampton bar and whisper the waiter to get us two John L Sullivans.

. . . Ever had a Sullivan? It's as follows: a double dry gin, a double curaçao, a glass of brandy, a glass of calvados and the juice of two oranges. Stir well into half a pint of champagne and serve freezing cold in a frosted glass . . .

'This,' I tell him, when the Sullivans come, 'this is practically a tee-total drink – it's got oranges and things in it for the stomach.' So he says, 'Your health, sir,' and downs it like so much lemonade – which, if properly mixed, it rather tastes like. I keep 'em coming. They have no effect on me, of course: I couldn't get really drunk if I wanted to; it can't be done; I've tried. But after about four of these I see a kind of maniac look in McClure's eye, though his hands and voice are steady enough.

'Now I feel better,' he says, giving me a poke in the ribs. 'And I'll be about my business.'

'What kind of a little speech are you going to give us?' I ask him. 'I understand you're going to say a few words at tea.'

'Some bullshit about twenty-four carat arseholin' Brotherhood of Crap,' he says. 'My creepin' Christ-killer of a sheeny's worth a hundred God-damn thousand pounds to me. What's your nigra worth to you, on the hoof?'

I say, 'You have another while I run along. See you at tea.'

I nip off, and tea has started, and the cucumber sandwiches are being handed round when McClure turns up. He looks sober as a judge, though, and is the soul of courtesy in the Southern style. Somebody says a few words here, and somebody else a few words there, and then our sensitive little Benoni Bararon suggests that Mr McClure, associate of the late HM Stanley, say a little something.

Up bobs McClure, and in a voice big enough to fill the Albert Hall he says, 'My name is Henry Manure from Shittick, Nevada, but they call me Shit for short!'

Uneasy murmur, and an exchange of glances. He goes on to talk of the Brotherhood of Man, and says that in the dark all cats are grey. He gives the company, in minute detail and with copious references and asides, an account of the sex habits of certain Central African tribes, some of which are so revolting that anthropologists writing of them put them not merely in Latin, but in Greek. He reassures such coloured people as are present; tells them not to worry, for he is with them all the way, and then some, asseverating that as for himself he will copulate with anything that is hot and hollow, from a hen's arse to a glowing stovepipe.

When Benoni Bararon pulls him by the coattails to make him sit down, he turns on that inoffensive man with the snarl of a tiger and requests in the coarsest imaginable terms that Mr Bararon take his fingers out of his bottom, adding that if Mr Bararon wants some faeces he (McClure) will be glad to provide him with a teaspoon.

Observing a Hindu lady of high caste among the guests, McClure asks her how her Little Pink Lotus is getting on, and that reminds him of an incident about a female porter of the dirt-carrying caste with whom he spent an interesting hour in a disused mineshaft.

He offers to buy the wife of an Abyssinian diplomat for three cows and a shotgun.

Then he is conducted out, singing 'A Man's A Man For A' That.'

That was a good mixture I had fed McClure. I had prompted Zudd to give Bararon a look of horror and disdain, and he gave him one all right. What can the poor little bugger do but stammer apologies and express the extremest mortification, I ask you? And his willingness to stand by our African Co-operative – magic word, co-operative; I stuck it in myself – to the tune of five thousand for a starter?

So old Zudd makes his speech, and hands round his telegrams, and in the end that little party netted us a matter of seven thousand seven hundred and fifty pounds; seven-seventy-five to me as my ten per cent. Good old Zudd gave me a promissory note for the amount plus five per cent interest, and started to cable instructions about all that cocoa and stuff. Of course, I knew what was going to happen – or I thought I did. The cocoa and all that didn't turn up. Zudd sent more cables. Then one day he called a meeting of patrons and investors, and said, 'Oh, People. My agents have been remiss and I am regretfully compelled to go to Lagos and say certain words. I must act. The time for talk is past.'

And did they call the police, or otherwise cut up rough? Altogether about fifteen thousand pounds of their money was in Zudd's hands.

And believe it or not, they went to the station to wave their handkerchiefs when they said goodbye to it.

The secretary and I hung about the office, listening for the telephone and scrupulously stacking up bills for things like furniture and what not, that Zudd had paid for with those promissory notes of his.

One wire came. It said: CONSOLIDATED AFRICA LIMITED VOLUNTARILY LIQUIDATED AGENTS ALL PASSED AWAY CONTRIBUTIONS WILL BE REFUNDED ZUDD. And shortly after that some men came to take the furniture away.

And here's a pretty irony; one of the broker's bum bailiffs who I split a bottle of beer with told me he was a veteran of Ashantee. He said, 'I helped carry away Nana Prempeh's golden stool.' And he said, 'I helped capture Kronje, and he made as if to hit me in the face with his sjambok. See what an old soldier comes down to.'

I don't know exactly how it is; certain things move me. Three things I know not, nay, four things are too wonderful for me: a lost dog patiently waiting, a child playing with a piece of string and talking to himself, one egg being cooked in a little tin saucepan and dust in a sunbeam just after furniture is dragged out of a room . . .

Oh well, I had had my fun. All my money was spent, but what the hell? I went on my way. And the only remarkable part of this story – the really marvellous part which I'm not going to tell you – came to pass a little later; and then I could paraphrase Baudelaire when he saw the Polynesian idol. I said to myself, 'Don't laugh too soon – it might be that Zudd really *was* God!'

Poor old Ody and his *Would I Live My Life Over Again*!

Ask a bloody silly question and you'll get a bloody silly answer . . .

SEVENTEEN

The homeless have their dosshouses, the paupers have their poorhouses, the very tramps have their benches or doorways or arches. A man must have somewhere to go. But it was Tom Henceforth's fancy to let it be understood that he lived nowhere at all.

So when the party in Fitzroy Square broke up at about three o'clock in the morning, Tom Henceforth's hostesses told him that they would be glad to make up a bed for him on the sofa. But he said, in the exaggerated Cockney he chose to affect when he was tired of being amusing in his own right but still whimsical, 'No thanks, ducky – I got to go 'ome and empty the mousetraps. Lend us a tanner for me tramfare to Tottenham.'

And there, again, was another of Tom's eccentricities, the ladies thought, exchanging smiles. He liked to embarrass you by borrowing the pettiest sum he could think of, and then put you out of countenance by paying it back with interest in the form of a flower or a book. Daphne and Bridget had nothing smaller than half a crown, so he accepted that. 'Be seeing you,' he said, and went out, running downstairs swift and purposeful as a spider.

'Amazing man,' said Bridget. 'I think Fritz made a perfect fool of himself.'

'Though Tom *did* go rather far.'

'Oh, nonsense! He was having fun.'

In fact, Tom lived ambiguously, in the craziest of old houses at the back of a cut with a double entry, behind the most inaccessible turning in a secretive and decomposing neighbourhood, an aneuritic rupture in a tortuous thoroughfare called Turnagin Alley.

He knew at least a hundred different ways of walking there from Fitzroy Square, but tonight he chose the shortest. He wanted to work; felt keyed up to it. It could not be said that Tom Henceforth was a masochist; he neither feared violence, nor invited it. But he did play host to one of Algolagnia's poor relations – a shameful kind of worm that lived on Outrage. When hungry, the worm bit, and a predatory Henceforth went foraging for it. Fed, it slept; and he felt free to be himself – a man of slick reflexes, delicately poised, in the rippling pink of fighting condition, and deadly with either hand – and then he preferred to be alone.

He lit two candles, admiring the play of shadows among the bunches of newspaper cuttings in the hundreds of spring clips that hung from nails in the walls. Twenty thousand, thirty thousand strange or contradictory items, every one with its pencilled note, and every note a sting. From screw-eyes under a shelf that ran the length of the room dangled hook-topped invoice files upon which were impaled pieces of paper of all shapes, sizes and colours – envelopes, menus, corners torn off blotting pads, the margins of newspapers, the covers of magazines – all covered with jottings, comments, memoranda of things overheard. When all this was co-ordinated, Tom Henceforth would produce The Novel Of All Time.

But now he had some articles to write, for which he had drawn money in advance. As usual, he was late for deadline. He owed *The Socialist Tactician* a satiric parable about lemmings, or ostriches, or owls, or opossums – any notoriously stupid bird or beast to which it was convenient to liken a senior statesman. He was known to the readers of the *Tactician* as 'Shchedrinson'. Then there was a piece to finish for *The Occidental* – which was said to be financed by Goebbels – on Jewish influences in modern painting. His pen name here was 'Primo Walter'. Left, right and centre, Tom Henceforth wielded his scourge impartially.

He arranged his candles on the writing table, put out a clean writing pad and a supply of cigarettes and sat down to work. But as soon as he put pen to paper, it was as if he had touched a spring which opened a valve at the back of his skull: his head emptied itself, and there he sat, mindlessly drawing faces. He drew a Tamrodt with a nose like a figure 6 and Chassidic side curls; a Sylvine, chinless and slack-mouthed; an idiotic Ody with question marks for hair; an Era Moon, cruelly scarred by the years, with a front tooth missing.

Then, half dreamily, stroke by abstracted stroke, he drew another woman's head, a Gorgon's head classically debased and suggestive of a frozen, beastly beauty, of desire and disgust, craving and revulsion, nausea and appetite. 'Oh God damn Ody and his twopenny symposia!' he said, between his teeth, and tore the paper into tiny pieces, which he dropped into a saucer and burnt to ashes with a match.

'To hell with Tricia d'Ordinay!'

All the same, he drew that head again, with greater care; pointed up and conventionalized its salient angles, erased its human contours, reduced it to a curiously virulent-looking group of asymmetrical polygons; held it at arm's length, liked it, wrote BITCH'S HEAD below it; looked at it again, disliked it, tore it across and threw it into the fruiterer's bushel basket he used for waste paper. 'This is what comes of mixing gin and cider,' he said.

She wasn't a memory; she was a symptomatic pain in the mind to be associated with a disordered liver, a furred tongue, evil aftertastes, hot foreheads and sour stomachs.

There was something about Lady Patricia d'Ordinay, daughter of the 9th Earl of Calicoone and voluntary secretary to Mr Zudd of Consolidated Africa, Limited, that challenged even Tom Henceforth's powers of ornamental overstatement. She would have made a spicy titbit for the gossips of any town, at any period; but to London Society just before World War I, Tricia d'Ordinay was worse than an Untouchable, she was an Unmentionable. Her name might have been a foul word of four letters; a decent woman, seeing it chalked on a wall, would be expected not to know what it meant. The most scurrilous lady scandalmongers, exchanging rumours behind closed doors, referred to her as P— D—.

If, as the legend said, there was an ancient curse on the warlock Calicoones of Cumberland, she was an awful manifestation of it. There was bad blood in the family, whose history for the past eight hundred years was an almost unbroken record of violent crime. Occasionally, a virtuous Calicoone came to the title, and then he was a monster of respectability – invariably red haired instead of dark, which was the family colour.

She was one of the true-bred Black Calicoones, with eyes of fire, brows of soot and hair like the smoke of a burnt offering. Tom Henceforth was captivated by her. He saw a tall, sway-backed woman with insistent breasts and impatient buttocks, uncorseted, dressed in stuff that cost two shillings a yard, perfumed with something at two guineas an ounce. Dark circles of shadow made her eyes seem feverish and old, and she had a habit of chewing her voluptuous lower lip, showing a row of very white, slightly prominent teeth.

'Come and have lunch,' she said impatiently. Whatever she said came out preoccupied, irritable.

Over devilled crabs washed down with white wine, he asked, 'Does your father mind your working for a black man?'

'Mind? I should say he does mind! That's why I'm here; I hope it gives him an apoplectic fit; I hate him. He can't stand niggers. I've given it out that I'm living with Zudd. In sin.'

'But you're not, surely?'

'Why "surely"? I'd ask Zudd to come to bed with me, but I'm afraid he'd refuse.'

'You'd . . . ? You're afraid he'd . . . ?' Tom Henceforth was astounded.

'I'd go to bed with him for the pleasure it would give me, thinking about what my father would say if he could see me. He'd refuse, because he'd know that was why I wanted to go to bed with him. Refuse me something and you make an enemy of me, and I may as well warn you in advance that I'm a bad person to have for an enemy. And I rather like Zudd, so let him be.'

'And how are you as a friend?'

'Bad either way, and proud of it.' Her tone implied that this was something every schoolboy knew.

'Best leave you alone, then?'

'Unless I fancy otherwise.'

'Why do you hate your father so much?'

'Because. Because he's a Red Calicoone, and a hypocrite. I could tell you hundreds of reasons why. I learnt the dictionary hating my father. You know that old game, "I love my love with an *A*, because . . ." and so on? I used to play, "I hate my father with an *A*, because . . ." all through the alphabet. I hate him *because.*'

'What did you find under X?' Tom Henceforth asked.

'There's xenogenous. A festered finger you get from a splinter under the nail is xenogenous in origin. He's xenogenous. And I hate him with a *Y* because he smells yeasty. And I hate him with a Z because he's zumoid.'

'What's zumoid?'

'A diseased state that comes through something fermenting. He's horribly zumoid, the pink-haired Moote.'

'What's a Moote?'

'One of the Calicoones married some woman named Moote in the sixteenth century – some Tudor bastard, I believe, with that disgusting ginger hair they had – and the wretched strain simply won't die out. If ever I had a pink-haired child I'd take care it didn't live two hours. Do you believe that?'

Tom Henceforth looked at her, and believed. 'You're not married?' he asked.

'Yes, I was married when I was eighteen. By my grandmother's will I was to have eight hundred a year on my marrying, so I got married to somebody. Then I left him, and haven't seen him since.' This, as she said it, was a matter of course; it couldn't be otherwise.

'What was he like?'

'A fumbler. He was supposed to be in love with me. I dare say he was; lots of people are. You will be, too. What did you say your name was? Henceforth, eh?'

'Why should I fall in love with you?' he asked, unaccountably confused.

She dumbfounded him by saying, 'Give me a cigarette. Would you like to come to bed with me?'

'Eh?'

'Now, Henceforth, let's have no hypocrisy – what I call Mootery. Do you, as an unattached man, make bones about this sort of thing? Or, for that matter, as an attached one? Do you say – if you happen to feel an urge for a chambermaid, or a shopgirl, or a waitress, for instance – "Let there be decent preliminaries? " As an *homme moyen sensual* – do you?'

'Well, no, but –'

'Well no but what? So if I, as a *femme moyenne sensuelle* – let us say a little more than *moyenne* – think to myself, "This manwaiter, shopman, errand boy, postman, gentleman, or what not – is available for the asking; I think I'll have him tonight"; haven't I the right to ask him if he'd like to come to bed with me?'

'Well, yes, certainly you have the *right* . . .'

'All he has to do is slap my face and say, "How dare you?" Or, "I'm a respectable married man"; or, "I'm not that kind of a boy" – isn't that so? I asked you a straightforward question. Would you?'

He gulped and said, 'Yes.' Then he recovered himself: people might say what they liked about him, he thought, but nobody should ever charge him with being slow on the uptake when it came to catching the spirit of a joke. He added, 'If you'll promise to stand me a hot supper. And not to look when I undress, or you'll laugh at my torn underwear. After all, it's only human *nature*, and it *is* in the Sight of God, *ain't* it?'

'You're laughing at me,' she said.

'Well, you're laughing at me, aren't you?'

'No, I'm inviting you to spend the night with me.'

He was sure that the beating of his heart must be visible through his waistcoat, but he replied, with his normal grinning composure, 'What time?'

'Will eight o'clock suit?'

'Where?'

'403 Hertford Street, first floor.'

'Oo-er! Oh crikey! I couldn't, mum. I dursn't be seen ringing the front-door bell at sich a slap-up address as that 'ere, mum. Or shell I come in at Tradesmen's?'

'I shall be cross with you if you don't answer me seriously.' She was angry, and took it out on a roll – which she pulled to pieces.

'What, do you mean to tell me nobody's ever laughed at you before?' he asked.

'I asked you a simple question. On equal terms. I offered you a simple invitation –'

'– No, you didn't, not simple at all. Not equal. In theory, if you like, equal; simple in principle, but actually not at all simple. A man says to a waitress, "Come to bed with me." All right, why shouldn't a woman say the same thing to a waiter? No reason why not. But if she wants to play the *homme moyen sensuel*, a little more than *moyen,* and all that, she ought to be prepared to take what goes with the game.'

'I hate idiotic jokes,' she said.

'Why should you? A waitress has to laugh off a man's proposition a dozen times a day; a good-looking barmaid fifty times a day. If the customer took umbrage, and went red all over and rolled his eyes, and ground his teeth the way you're doing, he'd be regarded as a kind of lunatic.'

'I am not in the least –'

'– Because who's he to regard his invitation to bed as something absolutely not to be refused? Then, things being equal, who are you? It sounds all very equal, and all that, but when it comes to the point you still hide behind your petticoats and make a face like a woman scorned, don't you?'

'The fact is, I have a very quick temper,' she said.

'The fact is, you take yourself too seriously. You can't take a joke, and I can't help making a joke. Shall we have some brandy?'

'Yes. And you're lunching with me. I invited you.'

'That's something I'm not going to argue about,' said Tom Henceforth. 'Let me take you to dinner in return.'

'Not this evening. We'll have something cold at my place,' she said, and added, 'Seriously. Be serious. Please.'

'I'll be there at eight. Half past seven, if you like.'

'In fact any time after six, if you're free.'

'In that case, it would be simpler if I went home with you from the office at five.'

'Then I might as well take the rest of the afternoon off, mightn't I?'

'You might as well.' His knees felt uncertain.

They found a taxi. '403 Hertford Street,' she said to the driver. *'Hurry!'*

And so began an involvement out of which even Tom Henceforth couldn't extract a lively anecdote, however tranquil or euphoric good food, drink and listeners might make him.

He would say, 'If that was a love affair, gallstones are jewellery,' or something of that sort. Or he might allude to it by generalizations like, 'To certain women, the act of love is in fact an Act of Darkness.'

It was not gentlemanly reticence that prevented his talking of Lady Patricia d'Ordinay, or even mentioning her name: once he was in a reminiscent vein there was nothing sacred to Tom Henceforth, who had a pinch of salt for anybody's wounds and a pin for everybody's image, not excluding his own. In this latter regard: if he happened to feel that he had not done right by himself, he was capable of speaking of himself so scathingly that even people who only half-liked him were impelled to come to his defence; though, like a staunch old servant, he would allow nobody but himself to talk lightly of Tom Henceforth. So it was not shame.

It seemed that she could only keep her shape in the lower deep; fished up, she would burst. And there she swam, seven miles down, in the dull glow of her own phosphorescence; a memory pertaining to No Man's Land; something beyond perspective, a one-and-a-half-dimensional figment, defying discussion.

Ody was not far wrong when he wrote, in his private shorthand: *Whatever happened to Tom Henceforth in the early years of the Great War must be something to which distance can't lend enchantment, nor time justification.*

Sprawling naked on a white fur rug and smoking a cigarette, she said, 'You laughed at me when we were having lunch, didn't you? Now do you find me funny?'

He shook his head and said, 'Not funny at all. Wonderful.'

'*Monsieur est content?*' She bowed her head in mock humility.

'Overcome,' he said. 'What are you laughing at?'

'I wish my father could see us now.'

He pleaded, 'Oh please, can't you forget him for a little while?'

'And think of you instead, is that it?' She clapped her hands. 'He's in love with me, he's in love with me – I told him so, he's in love with me!'

So he was. He said, 'Well, when we were . . . just a little while ago you said you loved me.'

'Oh, then. What one says *then* doesn't count. It's just talking. Love *you*, good God! . . . There, I've hurt your feelings, haven't I? It serves you right for laughing at me.'

Tom Henceforth shouted, 'I'll laugh at you as often as I like! I'll laugh at you to your face and I'll laugh at you behind your back! And I am not in love with you.'

'Oh yes you are. Go on, though – laugh at me. I like it when you laugh at me; it irritates me, and that makes me amorous. And don't be in love with me – be in hate with me; I find men make love better out of hate than love. Open another bottle of that champagne. You do it so well. I'm sure you must have been a waiter. Or a cellar boy, at least. Fill us some glasses, and then laugh at me some more – laugh right in my face. Tell me about *your* father, whatever he is – and I imagine him as something very ordinary – he couldn't be worse than mine.'

'Open your own damned champagne,' said Tom Henceforth.

'A butler? A discontented butler? Is your father a butler? That's exactly the sort of thing an ill-conditioned butler always dreams of saying, but never says, "Open your own damned champagne."'

She sat up and squatted cross-legged. Keeping his voice steady, Tom Henceforth said, 'You could almost convert a man to celibacy. From where I'm sitting I can see exactly how one is conceived between urine and dung, just like the theologian said.'

'Of course. Now open a bottle of champagne.'

He rose and said, 'I'm going', and went to where his clothes were thrown over a chair. She watched him, and when he was half dressed said, 'Tell me some more about theology. My father is a great churchgoer – except twice a year when he comes up to London and goes on the loose. Don't go yet: tell me about . . . oh come, I apologize. I'm wicked, I can't help it. Come and tell me you forgive me; but not in your shirtsleeves and braces – let's be on equal terms in that way, at least. I really do want you, you know.'

'No.'

'Come here and tell me you forgive me.'

'No.'

'Oh, don't keep saying No, No, No, like a parrot, when you mean Yes. Do either dress or undress. You can't imagine how silly you look with your waistcoat buttoned wrong. Let's kiss and make up. Please? I said "Please".'

He could not resist her. Throwing off the clothes he had angrily crammed himself into he came and sat beside her. 'I' – it stuck in his throat, but he got it out – 'I love you.'

'I know you do. Let's drink to it.'

And what could he do but open that bottle of champagne after all? Ten tempestuous minutes later, contemplating her, he said, 'And still Caruso sings.'

'What d'you mean?'

'That theologian had a dirty mind. That song comes out sweet between a stomach full of macaroni and a nose full of –'

'– Oh, I understand. My father is a hypocrite, too.'

'I wish you could stop thinking about him. Did you hear what I said just now? I love you' – it came out easily, this time – 'I wish you loved me.'

'Leave well enough alone. You can do anything you like with me. Isn't that enough? Tell me to do something for you, something menial. Tell me to clean your boots . . . Now you're laughing at me again, damn you! You'll pay for that!'

'It was the way you said, "Tell me to clean your boots": you ought to have added, "It's an order!" One of the Misses Borgia doing a penance: "I'm under oath to wash the feet of every stinking beggar from here to Compostela, so off with your toerags, damn your eyes!" *Tell me to clean your boots, for God's sake!*'

'I have an abrupt manner. I want you to do whatever you like with me.'

'Such as what, for instance?'

'First of all fill the glasses.'

He filled one glass and then dashed the cold wine into her face.

'How's that for something I wanted to do with you?' he asked. 'Pour your own damned wine!'

'Yes . . . Yes . . .'

Walking home to Finsbury through a fine warm rain at three o'clock in the morning, Tom Henceforth thought: *A few nights like this could kill a man. The girl is mad. It's all experience, but once in a lifetime is just about enough. Never again!*

He was to repeat this resolution some thirty-five times – about three times a week for the next three months. Then Zudd went back to Africa, and the men came to take the furniture away, and there was the empty office in St Alfred's Close, and the lonely sunbeam, and the dust motes. His landlady, Mrs Fell, who was with a group of investors who came to the station to see Zudd off, said, 'I do hope he comes back.'

'He's done a bunk,' said Tom Henceforth.

'I hope not,' said Mrs Fell. 'I invested eight hundred pounds with him. Oh, and Mr Henceforth; I don't like to mention it, but there's a matter of eleven weeks' rent outstanding. I wish you could manage to let me have at least something on account.'

'Zudd owes me money, too.'

'It's very unfortunate, but . . .'

'I'll get some money, Mrs Fell, don't worry.'

'Mr Fell's always laughing at me for trusting people. I shouldn't know where to hide my face . . . You know, Mr Henceforth,' she said, as they went back to Fiennes Street, 'I wish you'd take more care of yourself. You're young to be neglecting yourself the way you do. You're not looking a bit well, and that's a fact. You're all edgy, and white – why, my goodness, there's no blood in you –'

'– Ever hear of vampires?'

'I don't remember that I did.'

'They come out at night and bite you in the throat, and suck you dry. Well, I'm being bitten by a vampire.'

'Not in my house, unless you brought them with you.'

'Do you know, Mrs Fell, that's very funny!'

'Well. Do try and let me have something on account, or . . .'

'I will, Mrs Fell. Tomorrow.'

'For certain, Mr Henceforth? Because I'm afraid I can't . . .'

'For certain.'

Damn her, he thought, *she's seen me leave with bundles and come home without them: she knows I've pawned my clothes. No blood in me! If it were only blood Tricia sucked. But she's burnt all the temper out of me. Where's my spring? Where's my resilience? Where's my nerve? Where's my spirit? Where's my will?*

He walked westward, brooding. Today was Thursday, and on Thursdays she required him to be at her house at six o'clock. She required him to be there. And he realized, sickly, that if she had required him not to be there he would have gone just the same, and begged to be let in, if only for ten minutes.

He found her in a strange, mad mood, pacing the carpet and laughing to herself. 'Oh, it's you,' she said.

'It's Thursday. We saw Zudd off. I thought you'd be there.'

'What on earth for? Let him go, and good luck to him. He fooled them all, and serve them right.'

'Everybody believes he'll come back.'

'Some people believe in the Second Coming of Jesus Christ.'

'I don't.'

'Oh, you. Who cares what you believe, you conceited puppy?'

'Tricia, what's the matter?'

'There's some wine over there. You may have a farewell glass.'

'A farewell . . .'

'Yes. I'm leaving England. I've nothing more to keep me here. Nothing I could ever dream of would hurt him any more, now. You may sit down and I'll tell you.'

'Hurt who?'

'My father, of course. I've told you of his habits, his mean little underhand habits. Twice a year he comes to town to see his agents, get beastly drunk and pick up a girl. A brunette; he likes dark girls. Last night a prostitute friend of mine – don't look so shocked; most prostitutes hate men – called to tell me that he had got drunk at the Alsatians and had been taken home by a girl I know named Molly to her place in Jermyn Street. I told my friend to tell Molly to give him something to put him to sleep, and I got in a cab and went over there at five this morning. Are you listening? This is better than merely a good story: it's perfect! Perfect!'

'I'm listening.'

'The old pig was undressed and snoring in bed. Molly and I are much of a size, and similar in colouring. I changed into her négligé, hid her in another room, and simply waited, sitting in a chair. At seven o'clock – nothing on earth will keep him asleep later than seven – he woke up, groaning, "A cup of coffee, get me a cup of strong black coffee", and rubbing his eyes, and feeling about for his spectacles . . .'

Laughter overcame her. 'Go on,' said Tom Henceforth.

'I brought him a cup of coffee, then, and I said, "Here you are, dearie – Oh *my God*! YOU!" and dropped the cup and saucer with a terrific crash. And he screamed, "Oh my God, my God, what have I done, what have I done? Oh, what have I done?" He thought that he had lain with his own daughter while drunk, like Lot in the Bible.'

'What happened then?'

'As they say in the novels, "He rushed blindly out" – dressing himself as he went, and I looked out of the window and saw him running up Jermyn Street with his coat and waistcoat over his arm and his hat on the back of his head. And now . . .' she sighed with pleasure '. . . now I'm at peace with the world. Let him pray his knees to the bone, he'll never pray *that* off his beastly little conscience. And as for you, I shan't be needing you any more. You may go.'

'Eh?'

'Are you deaf? You're dismissed.'

'But Tricia!'

'Be off with you! But first, a glass of wine. I owe you a full glass of wine.' She filled a goblet with champagne. 'This – my own damned wine – with my own fair hands –'

She threw the wine into his face and flung the goblet after it. He felt the glass splinter against his teeth; struck out wildly and knocked her down. She bounded up, hissing with rage, and hurled the bottle. It glanced off his head and burst against the wall with a great frothy splash. Then she tore open a bureau drawer; her fury saved him, for the drawer came away bodily, letting fall a mess of papers in which she groped, stooping, for a little silvery revolver.

As he staggered out, salty with blood and sour with wine, he heard a shot and saw a blue Chinese vase in the hall start as if with surprise and fall into three pieces while its lid went rolling drunkenly away. Then he was reeling down the street, and he remembers the lights shining through green, red, mauve and blue bottles in a chemist's shop, and something that stank and stung, and a voice saying, 'That's a nasty cut. Better get a doctor to put a stitch in it . . .'

After that he was under a red lamp, and in a room that smelt of iodoform, where somebody sewed up the corner of his mouth with a curved needle and told him to go home and rest. It seems to him that he began to sob, and said, 'I have no home, I am henceforth homeless . . .'

And it would appear that he went into a public house and drank a lot of whisky, and tottered out into a heartless maze of streets, streets, streets, alleys and passages and lamplit squares; and he must have gone into an old-clothes shop, because the fetor of it comes back with the memory of Tricia d'Ordinay, and there he exchanged his smart broadcloth suit and his box-calf boots for a pair of secondhand shoes, thirdhand trousers, a fourthhand jacket and ten shillings in cash.

Somewhere, a newspaper boy with an ear-splitting voice yelled, 'Paip*yer*!' *Star*! Paip*yer*! Suicide of Earl, Earl commits suicide, suicide of Earl, suicide, suicide, *Star* paip*yer*!' A man in a shattered billycock hat and a red muffler said, 'Yers, yers, bloody chucked 'is self under a train, the bloody aristocrack, and serve 'im bloody right! Dahn wiv 'em!'

Somebody said, 'Hurt yer face, mate?' 'Champagne party,' Tom Henceforth said, he thinks; and there were roars of laughter, laughter unending, and after that the world became an intolerable abstraction in an alien geometry in which it was somehow possible for a triangle to consist of three obtuse angles and a cube to have nine sides, all made of concave mirrors . . .

And then . . . ?

EIGHTEEN

Early one morning in the autumn of 1915, between the setting of a bombers' moon and the rising of a watered-down wartime sun, Steve Zobrany – dressed, as he believed, like a working man, in a navvy's moleskin cap and a sky-blue scarf tucked into an old black frieze jacket – walked to Covent Garden to see a man about potatoes, which were becoming increasingly difficult for a legitimate buyer to come by honestly. They weren't rationed; only scarce, and likely to get scarcer. It was prudent to keep in touch with a wholesaler, and it was Zobrany's harmless conceit that he fancied himself as being exquisitely adapted to the tricky business of such relationships.

The man he knew being named Jacobus van Dyn and looking as if he might have just got up and waddled out of some second-rate Dutch daub of Boors Drinking, Zobrany always armed himself with a handful of certain exceptionally vile cigars called Rotterdam Orange Blossoms, and primed himself with a smattering of Dutch history – Holland's proud heritage, from the Union of Utrecht to the 'glorious succession of the present young queen, the lovely Wilhelmina', Van Dyn, whose family had been around Covent Garden since Nell Gwyn sold oranges in Drury Lane, regarded Zobrany as a scientist of our time might regard a visitor from another planet; literally, from out of this world.

'Let us have four sacks of potatoes,' said Zobrany, striking a free and easy attitude, in which he was somewhat less convincing than a curate playing Bill Sykes in a charity performance of *Oliver Twist*.

'What are you talking about, four sacks? Ask me for my right arm, why don't yer? Four sacks! I'll give *you* two, and chance it.'

'Four.'

'Lemme finish. Two, only you've got to take a couple boxes 'yacinth bulbs.'

'Hyacinth bulbs? What am *I* to do with hyacinth bulbs?'

'Comes to that, what am I to do with 'yacinth bulbs? If they was tulips I could sell 'em for onions, mixed in. Well? Don't waste my time. Eh?'

'Have some cigars . . . Look, give me four sacks and I will take the hyacinth bulbs. I could give them away to customers to plant for Easter. But I must have potatoes.'

'*You* must! Oh, all right, I'll let you 'ave three, only you must take two o' swedes, and chance it.'

'Jacobus, *no*! Turnips, perhaps. Swedes, no. Give me four of potatoes and I will take one of swedes. There. Eh?'

'It can't be done, it just can't be *done*! . . . Look, I tell you what. There's a war on. Right? Right. Take the swedes while the going's good – put 'em in a dry cellar – swedes you might be glad of next year. Three of spuds is final. Take 'em or leave 'em, and chance it!'

Zobrany said, 'Jacobus, you are an honest man. If you say three, let it be three. If you say swedes, let them eat swedes. Hyacinth bulbs? All right. Give me the potatoes. Only may I have a few carrots?'

'Oh Christ! Take spuds, take carrots, take your dog's face out o' my shop and good luck to you! . . . And I'll give you a tip.'

'Yes?'

Van Dyn whispered, 'D'you want some leeks? Go to Marks and whisper in 'is ear a certain party from Bow Street knows what there is in 'is cellar. Right? Right. I'll get a boy to shove your stuff 'ome.'

He yelled, 'George! Four spuds, two swedes, two 'yacinths and one carrots on a barrer! Fetch a boy forrard! . . .' An attenuated loiterer got up off a heap of sacks. 'Keep your eye on 'im – make 'im go in front – them spuds is diamonds,' said Van Dyn.

Then he began to shout at a female greengrocer wearing a man's tweed cap fastened to her back hair with a baroque pearl hatpin, 'Spuds, spuds, spuds! All I 'ear is spuds! . . . Don't blame me, blame Admiral Jericho, blame Beatty, blame the U-boats – *I* can't invent spuds! Ask the Kaiser, and chance it – don't ask me! George! Give old Mother Nature 'ere one spuds – one spuds and one swedes. Five? Five? Does she think I'm *made* o' spuds? One spuds and *two* swedes – say another word, and God strike me blind . . . You'll *what*! Oh, George! One spuds and *three* swedes to old sweetlips . . .'

Zobrany said to the young man who had hold of the handles of the barrow, 'Are you strong enough to pull this to Carnaby Street?'

'Yes.'

'But my dear fellow, you are lame!'

'Say where to, will you mister?'

'Have you breakfasted, at least?'

'No. Where to?'

'Stop for five minutes at The Sun. Eat a sandwich and drink a cup of tea,' said Zobrany. 'Excuse me, but have you much experience of this kind of thing? Better pull than push, *I* think, over these stones . . . Four sacks of potatoes, two of swedes . . . a cargo, no light load. I'll help from behind, eh? One, two, three, and a–aie, aie, aie! What have I done?'

'You shoved me off my feet, that's all. Give a man a chance to start, can't you?'

'You are too light for this kind of work, my friend. Have something hot to drink first, at least, and a bite to eat. When we get home you shall have a proper breakfast.' They stopped at the corner of Bow Street and Long Acre. 'If you must starve, then starve on a full stomach, as the saying goes,' said Zobrany.

The young man muttered, 'All right, Bishop Myriel – let's have the cup of tea, and save the silver candlesticks for later on, will you?'

It was daylight now. 'But my God!' cried Zobrany, looking at him more closely, 'I know you. You made my fine sign!'

'So I did,' said the other, with a weak laugh, 'and you're Zobrany. Well, well, well.'

'No, but my dear fellow, this will never do! No, upon my word of honour . . . whoever you were, you understand, you being a little uncomfortable in one leg, I meant to take the weight of this cart from behind. But Mr Henceforth, I never –'

'– Buns, buns, give me buns,' said Tom Henceforth dreamily. 'Stay me with tea, comfort me with buns, for I am sick of . . . I am sick of . . . I am sick of . . .'

Zobrany dragged him into The Sun, and called for hot tea, Bovril, coffee, brandy, anything. The latest war news was in: the Allies weren't doing well in Salonika, but Sir Douglas Haig had succeeded Sir John French as GOC on the Western Front. Somebody was saying, 'It's chins. The War Office picks 'em for their chins. If you want evidence, look at the photographs. Roberts was all chin, Kitchener was all chin, Joffre's all chin. French didn't have enough chin, so they chucked him out. And Haig has got more chin than all the rest put together. If Punch didn't have a hump they'd make a general of *him*. Thank God we've got a navy!'

Zobrany said, 'I'm sorry, my dear Henceforth, but a taxi is not to be had for love or money. You must put your pride in your pocket and jump up on the barrow and ride with the potatoes.'

Tom Henceforth tried to sneer, 'The least I can do to repay you for your cup of tea is to let you make a display of yourself as a Good Samaritan, I suppose.' Then his face twitched, and he said, 'I beg your pardon, I didn't mean that.' He coughed, and added, 'At least, I didn't mean it to . . . The fact is, I don't quite know what I meant. I mean, I can walk. I could have pushed your barrow home with you on top of it, if you hadn't been so bloody . . . so bloody . . .'

'Let's go then, old fellow.'

'Where to?'

'To my house, where we can have breakfast and a rest in a clean bed. You are exhausted.'

'What do you want to pick on me for, to be benevolent to?'

'I am not picking on you. That I happen to know you makes it so much the better. It makes no difference to me that you are you. Somebody wants breakfast, I offer him a bun. I see somebody lame, I offer him a ride. You are making all the philosophy, not I. Enough, I am in a hurry. Will you get up and ride? Or follow? Come.'

Tom Henceforth bowed his head and said, 'I'll ride.'

'Up with you, then.'

When Zobrany trundled the barrow into Masham Court, Tom Henceforth was asleep, his tousled head on a sack of potatoes. The Sordics came out to carry in the vegetables. Aroused, Tom Henceforth blinked, looked up at the sign and down at the barrow, and muttered, '. . . And that reminds me. I promised young Gus I'd bring Santini's cart back; and I think I owe Fritsch a pound or two . . .'

'But poor Fritsch has hanged himself,' said Zobrany.

'What for?'

'Why, in 1914 Fritsch said, "If England has not sued for peace by Christmas, by God I'll hang myself!" He was a man of honour, in a Teutonic style. On New Year's Eve he took a last drink of gin and hanged himself from a hook . . . I have no eggs, but there is some good beef stew, and so you must be content with that. Come in, come in.'

The last of the night prowlers, steaming in what smelt like the first stages of spontaneous combustion, came by to pick up a neatly wrapped paper package from the lid of the dustbin. 'Wait a minute,' said Tom Henceforth, exploring his pockets. He found a halfpenny and three farthings, which he threw down with a gesture. 'There's always somebody to patronize,' he said, with a half-smile rendered sinister by a red scar at the corner of his mouth. 'So give me stew.'

'Aie-aie, such bitterness!' said Zobrany, leading him in, 'I don't patronize – I pay tribute, my dear fellow.'

Having talked a little, sporadically, between mouthfuls, Tom Henceforth drained his third cup of coffee and said, 'That's just about as much as you need to know about it all. Is it a breakfast's worth? Have I sung for my vittles?'

'I asked no questions,' said Zobrany. 'You are upset and angry, or you wouldn't talk like that. I am a person of good faith, and you do me an injustice, Mr Henceforth.' He was almost indignant. '. . . But then, I'm condemned out of my own mouth. In one breath I make allowances for your being tired, and in the next I blame you for a thoughtless word. Excuse me. Rest in the spare bedroom, and –'

'– I'm sorry, I'm sorry.'

'Not at all, not at all . . . You mentioned a certain affair of the heart –'

'– Of the *heart*?' said Tom Henceforth. 'You've got your anatomy all wrong. I went off my nut, and that's about all there is to it. It's happened to me once; it'll never happen again.'

'No, but let me finish,' Zobrany said, pouring two little glasses of brandy. 'First of all, though, will you taste a compôte of fresh plums? And here is another thing for a man of your inquiring mind: why is it that any national crisis, in any country whatsoever, has a stimulating effect on the growth of plums? When King Alexander and Queen Draga of Serbia were murdered in 1903, there was a bumper harvest of plums, especially in Slovenia. Plum brandy – slivovitz, or szilvorium – of that year is exceptionally good. In Russia in 1905, plums grew on every bush, as the saying goes, after the assassination of the Grand Duke Sergius. When King Carlos of Portugal was shot in 1908, Portuguese plums were a drug on the market in Lisbon. In Greece, in 1913, I am told, when King George was murdered, people had to go about with umbrellas to protect themselves from a heavy fall of fine plums. And now, in England, in these dark days, plums, again, flourish like weeds. Why is this, I wonder? Plums and apples. There must be a reason for it . . .

'But as I was saying, in a way I envy you; I really do, my dear Henceforth! As man to man, I have had my share of romances, but only one *grande passion* – and then everything went as merry as a wedding bell; there was nothing but clear bliss, which does not diminish but goes on and on, carrying me with it. I feel I have missed something. Or do you think, perhaps, there is something lacking in me? A divine fire? A magic flame? Something? I feel such an ox . . .'

Abruptly interrupting, Tom Henceforth said, 'I don't know whether I ought to curse you or not. When you turned up this morning I'd made up my mind to do myself in. I had it all worked out.'

'Oh, that's quite all right,' said Zobrany. 'Practically everybody has contemplated suicide by the time he's your age. He who doesn't think of killing himself at twenty will do so at forty – it's dangerous then.'

'But nothing's possible without privacy,' Tom Henceforth went on dreamily. 'Without privacy you're everybody's dog. The whole world is there to stop a man dying. Never mind about his living; he mustn't die. Suicide is where a person kills himself and is therefore the homicide of one of His Majesty's subjects, and is a felony –'

'– Oh, come now!'

'– The attempt to commit suicide is a misdemeanour at common law. I had it all worked out, only I wanted ten shillings – eight for rent of a room, and two for gas . . . Don't imagine for a moment that I'm afraid of heights or depths, or what people like to call "leaving a mess". And you'd be surprised how many people pretend to tidiness after the event. They see themselves as pink-and-blue guts in a slobber of strawberry jam, and put themselves in the position of somebody who has to do the scraping-up. Squeamish! There's nothing like that about me, I swear. It's about as specious as being shy of using a bedpan in a hospital it's perverse pride. How many living offences to the nostrils of mankind have I seen, who "didn't want to make a mess" – themselves open shit-pots under the sky, by God! No, no – oh no, no! –

> *'And throughout all eternity,*
> *I mop up after you, you after me –*

'Oh no no! Believe me, they won't leave you be; that's the long and short of it. Just you try to climb up to within dead-sure dying distance of the pavement and jump, man, and you'll see! The rat has his hole to die in, but not you – oho no, not you! Without a place of your own, I dare you to cut your throat or poison yourself – come on, I dare you –'

Tom Henceforth began to laugh; kicked off a series of sobs like a motor bike, went shuddering from hiccup to hiccup, hawked as the thing took hold and was about to have hysterics when Zobrany took him by the arms and shook him until his head rolled loose on his neck. 'Nothing personal – nothing, nothing, nothing personal –' he said, handling the boy as a laundress handles washing.

'Don't,' said Tom Henceforth. 'Don't. I'll be sick.'

'Oh no, pardon me. Pretend me – no scruples – before the event –'

'– Stop it!'

Zobrany slapped his face, more noisily than painfully, and said, 'Will this hold you?'

'Leave go . . .'

'Then stop laughing.'

'I wasn't –'

'Then stop crying!'

'I didn't!'

'Then be calm, my dear fellow.'

'I am calm,' Tom Henceforth said, shuddering.

'That's the way to be. Drink more coffee and listen to me. You are – excuse me – perhaps twenty years old? It is a serious age, very dangerous. Twenty takes death as a matter of course. Twenty is terrible; twenty knows everything. But I am getting on in years. I'm thirty-five. When I was twenty it seemed to me that after thirty there was nothing much to look forward to. Then I saw as through a glass, darkly. I thought as a child, I understood as a child; I could talk about life as a matter of cells, and corruption was only bacteria – why, God forgive me, I thought of history as a science and cookery as colloidal chemistry –'

'– So it is,' Tom Henceforth said.

'It is not! Dietetics is chemistry; cookery is an affair of sympathy. Hence the expression, "Better a meal of herbs where love is."'

'History *is* a science.'

'No, it isn't. It is a tale and a dream. Look here, at your age I thought as you think, in a way, more or less. Then all of a sudden I looked through a pinhole in the screen, as you might say, and what did I see? A disc without a rim. I knew then that everything we think of as definite is only a story. Something of the imagination. I said to myself, "No, really, if even the geometrical circle is nothing but the multiplication of a transcendent ratio – *pi* being a purely speculative figure – surrounding an area without an exact boundary, then for God's sake what is what? The circumference of a circle is where the wheel touches the ground to take you where you have to go. Enough? The ultimate dimension is not for me" – that's what I said to myself. "Tree leans upon tree, and man upon man," I said. "Be decent, take all you can get and give all of what you have; live with dignity, from hand to mouth; wait your turn, share and share alike, don't spit in the dish, live, and let live – this is science, and all the rest is dust and shadows." You'll be surprised when you learn how much there is to live for, my dear fellow. You are lucky to be able to feel, even to feel discomfort. It's indecent to imagine that you want to die. So you have been humiliated? Then what? Have patience; the flood goes, but the sand remains, as the peasants say . . . But perhaps I don't make myself clear?'

'You don't. There's no need to. If you like talking, then talk. I'm better now. Lend me five bob and let me go.'

'No, rest first. There is a bed. Then you can have a bath. What size collar do you take? Fourteen?'

'I suppose so. I don't know.'

'And after that a clean shirt.'

'Zobrany,' said Tom Henceforth, 'you're a meddler and a busybody, and a bit of a fool. You give me a pain.'

'All right . . . And you were writing a book, you say, but your landlady seized your books and your papers and all your clothes? I'll go and have a word with her –'

'– I didn't say "seized". I owed rent and I did a flit, and that's all there is to say about it.'

'I speak to you as a friend. Return me that little compliment, and stop barking at me. How much do you owe her?'

'Five pounds, six pounds, something like that.'

'You should have said to her, with a nice smile, "Mrs So-and-so, let us –"'

'– Oh, for God's sake! I didn't say this or that simply because I didn't choose to. Thanks for the stew. Good morning.'

'Sit down. You didn't choose to. And so you chose to be a vagrant around the markets, living like a lost dog?'

'Yes.'

'She is a very severe woman?'

'No, quite ordinary. But who the hell wants pity?'

'Why, everybody wants pity. What's the matter with pity? How could we live without it? Only the word is wrongly used to imply condescension, like charity. Pity is humble, not condescending.'

'Be humble at somebody else's expense, then; not mine. I forbid you to go and have a word with anybody on my account, do you hear?'

'Yes. If you have any more hysterics I shall have to hit you again . . . And this African man ran away with all your money?'

'I didn't say that, did I? I said he shot the moon owing me some. Ah, but I helped that nigger take a bite out of the arses of a few benevolent characters around the City, though! I knew him for a crook from the very beginning. I had my little bit of fun.' Tom Henceforth smiled. 'I don't begrudge it . . . Look here, you've been kind to me, and I didn't mean to insult you. Have you got a few pounds to invest? Seriously, I mean: I can show you how to make a lot of money. Lend me a pencil and a bit of paper, will you?' All at once he was fresh and eager. Zobrany watched with interest as he sketched the outlines of something that looked like half an egg attached to four lengths of tape. 'Now this is real honest-to-God Applied Psychology.'

'What is it?'

'Think. Where is a man most vulnerable?'

'I don't know. It depends. Do you mean physically? Then there are his eyes, of course, and –'

'– Soldiers have helmets to shade their eyes. What about their silly testicles? Have you ever been to a museum to look at the armour? Balls are the first thing soldiers' wives think of – always have been. The knights used to have hammered steel jockstraps –'

'– No, really! Hammered steel jockstraps!' said Zobrany, laughing. 'I have seen them, mind you, but it sounds funny the way you put it. Yes, of course, every soldier is afraid of being caponized. But he is also afraid that his wife will be unfaithful to him while he is away at the wars, and often with good reason. Why not draw me a girdle of chastity? For I take it that this is some kind of protective apparatus for men only?'

'It's good for morale. A man's twice as good in a battle if he thinks his knackers are bombproof, and this is turning out to be a war of splinters – a high-explosive war's bound to be. Now my idea is to have these things made up of compressed paper with a cotton cover. It actually might stop a small flying fragment of metal; but what's more important, people will *believe* it'll stop it. It's the thought that counts.

Actually, the odds against a man's losing his bollocks are astronomical – you'd be safe selling the contraption with a thousand-pound guarantee. You could manufacture it for about a shilling, and sell it for five. Six! No, six and eightpence-halfpenny; women like fractions of pennies, and they're the ones that'll buy the thing to shove in the parcel they send, along with socks and cigarettes. In three sizes: large, medium and small. No! Cut out "small". Bad psychology. Have only two sizes. Normal and Extra. "Super" a shilling more. They'll all buy Extra or Super, to impress the neighbours. The same model, in metal – De Luxe – half a guinea. Good God, if I had connections I bet a thousand pounds I could sell it to the War Office!'

'Similarly,' said Zobrany, 'ladies protect their breasts. What about brass bust-supporters for Red Cross nurses and WAACs?'

'And here's another,' said Tom Henceforth, drawing a rounded oblong.

'And what is that?'

'It's to be carried in the breast pocket on the left-hand side. It's a metal shaving mirror, guaranteed to turn a bayonet thrust. It has the soldier's number stamped on it, and an unconditional guarantee. Also, a few words out of the Bible, or the Lord's Prayer, or something. It –'

'– What unconditional guarantee?'

'Why, that if the wearer of this piece of goods is killed in action through the failure of it to protect the part of his body it covers – that is, his heart – his widow, on presenting the perforated bit of plate to the company, is awarded five thousand pounds. Now don't get excited! It has to be a legitimate casualty; it has to occur in action against the enemy; it has to make a hole in the plate. What with belts, pouches, and all that, a soldier is pretty well invulnerable in the region of the breast pocket, and when it comes to bayonets it stands to reason he'll get hurt in the guts or the throat, or perhaps the leg or the shoulder. Even so, how many men get hit right over the heart? We could sell a hundred thousand at a pound apiece; it wouldn't cost more than eighteen-pence to make, complete with cloth cover, and the buyer would get an insurance policy thrown in. Actuarially speaking, it's a snip! What do you say?'

'I'll think about it, and you get a little rest. As a matter of curiosity, where were you living at the time of this African affair?'

'Eh? Oh, Number 11, Fiennes Street, Finsbury Square. Why?'

'Nothing, nothing . . . And you were writing a novel?' said Zobrany wistfully.

Tom Henceforth shrugged, and said, 'Oh all right, show me your spare bed and I'll lie down on it for an hour.'

'There's a good fellow.'

Falling asleep in the guest room, Tom Henceforth murmured, '. . . And there's a packet to be made out of commemorative stained-glass windows . . .'

'Poor child,' Zobrany whispered, covering him with the blankets, and he went upstairs to dress. Then, having stuck a yellow chrysanthemum in his buttonhole, he took his walking stick and went to Finsbury Square.

'Oh my goodness gracious me!' cried Mrs Fell. 'A friend of young Mr Henceforth's? Come in, do, sir. We've been looking for him all over. Thinking he'd joined the Army I wrote to the War Office, but . . . let me take your hat and coat. Won't you have a cup of tea? Do have a cup of tea.'

'You are very kind, ma'am,' said Zobrany, in his most persuasive tone. 'I have not a great deal of time, but since you are so good, thank you, I will have a cup of tea . . . You were looking for Mr Henceforth? Quite right, very natural. I believe – let us face the fact – that there is a little matter of rent outstanding?'

'Oh, that? Well, yes, but not really.'

'Please?'

'Oh, I mean, yes, eleven weeks at twelve shillings, but that don't signify, you know.'

'No?'

'Well, yes, but not really, I'm sure. We're much obliged to Mr Henceforth, actually. Sir Benoni Bararon advertised for him in the papers, on account of Mr Zudd.'

'Oh?'

'A gentleman of colour, but quite a gentleman. It's only skin-deep, after all, when you come to think of it, isn't it? But though Mr Fell laughs at me for it, I've got second sight, being partly Asiatic, and something always tells me who to trust. Where *has* Mr Henceforth been keeping himself?'

Zobrany made a gesture which said, 'Here, there; what do I know?'

She went on, '. . . Although I don't mind telling you, that would have been one thing I'd have tried to keep from Mr Fell, because eight hundred pounds is eight hundred pounds, war or no war, and this was just before.'

'I understand, dear lady, that this person Zudd made off with –'

'– Oh dear no! That's what people thought, but *I* had faith. Being partly Asiatic, I've got second sight, you know. "Mark my words, Mr Zudd'll come back," I said.'

'And he did?'

'No. But he did settle all his debts – *with twenty per cent interest*! Twenty per cent. And would you believe it, he sent a form of apology:

circumstances over which he had no control prevented him paying a hundred per cent, as he had told his investors they might expect. There!'

'And you had invested –'

'– Eight hundred pounds. And got back nine hundred and sixty.'

'I am rejoiced, dear madam, to hear it! Then certain sums owing to Mr Henceforth . . . ?'

'Care of Sir Benoni Bararon, all paid up, every penny. Say what you like, it's only skin deep. White is as white does. That's why Sir Benoni Bararon advertised for Mr Henceforth in the papers, only it was my thought that he'd joined up, being such a lively young gentleman.'

'Then the matter of his rent is not a serious consideration?'

'Oh my goodness, no! I knew he was a little short towards the end, between you and me, because his clothes began to go. Into pawn, I mean. But . . .'

'Has he any clothes left in your care? And papers?'

'Well, I needed the rooms, you see, so I packed everything up and put it all away safe. Papers galore, and a lot of books. Only one suit, an old green tweed; but a dozen shirts and a dozen and a half of collars, sixteen pocket handkerchiefs and three coloured silk –'

'– Oh, excellent, excellent! And may I take them with me? Mr Henceforth has been poorly. I will gladly pay any outstanding –'

'– Oh, he could have had them any time, for the asking. I'm sorry to hear he's not been well, though. Take him his clothes by all means, if you like. He owes a matter of six pound twelve, but that's all right – he can pay me when he comes by. And you mustn't forget to tell him to get in touch with Sir Benoni Bararon, a perfect gentleman in spite of his religion. But religion is as religion does, and it's only skin deep, after all. Being partly Asiatic myself, I'm broadminded. Are you a Congregationalist sir, by any chance?'

'No, I am an agnostic.'

'Well, that's only skin deep, too, I dare say.'

And so Tom Henceforth was awakened by Zobrany, effervescent with delight, crying, 'Celebrate! Celebrate!' and offering him a hot Cornish pasty.

'What's the matter?' he asked, and then caught sight of one of his portmanteaus at Zobrany's feet.

'Who asked you to shove your nose into my affairs?' he demanded. 'Why can't you mind your own bloody business?'

'You are talking in your sleep. Listen; your African has paid up, and Sir Benoni Bararon is holding a sum of money for you. Your papers are safe. Here are your clothes. And now are you going to tell me to mind my own bloody business?'

'Good God!'

'Now you can finish writing your book, eh?'

'Oh, sure, sure . . . How much?'

'He repaid Mrs Fell with twenty per cent interest, and all other creditors likewise,' said Zobrany. 'And so you can finish writing –'

'– I was to be found, if that sheeny bastard wanted to find me,' Tom Henceforth said.

'Never mind, my dear fellow. Now you can –'

'– Now I can mind my own business. This isn't the time to write books. It's a time to make money. I'm going to make some money.'

'Listen to me, my dear fellow. Seriously: your ideas are brilliant, but there is a trace of (do forgive me) sharp practice at the back of them. Armour-plated et ceteras, psychology, stained-glass windows – no, really! It is amusing, but it is likely to end badly. You remind me very much of a friend I had, whom I admired. Well, I liked him; he was my friend, and lonely like you. "Little Napoleon", we used to call him: he might not have the price of a glass of wine in his pocket, but he couldn't talk in anything but millions. And he ended robbing his best friend and running away. It is always like that: in theory everything is so easy. It's the little dirty details that kill a man. Do me this favour: let your dreams stay where they belong; when an artist in temperament plays at being a businessman, it is bound to end in a court of law.'

'And if a businessman by temperament plays at being an artist?' Tom Henceforth asked.

'He is apt to make money. You are not a businessman.'

'You mentioned a man you called "Little Napoleon". Was his name Cseh, by any chance?'

'Gèza Cseh, yes. How do you know?'

'I met him in Manchester.'

'My Little Napoleon, eh? How is he?'

'He owes you some money, doesn't he?'

'How could you possibly know anything about that?'

'He swindled you, didn't he?'

'As it happened, he only thought he did. As Fate willed it, I owe my happiness to Gèza. Where is he now? I will write him a letter –'

'– Puzzle; find him.'

'Tell me more!'

'That's all,' said Tom Henceforth. 'Let me get dressed. I want to have a word or two with that shonk Bararon. Damn his eyes, he could have found me if he'd tried. Everybody else found me. And I had my share of hell in the meantime. I don't want to talk any more now . . .'

The green suit was the one Perp had dressed him in. He was never so light and comfortable as when he was wearing it.

'Let it be a bad book, only write it,' said Zobrany.

'Lend me half a quid for a cab fare and a haircut and shave, and leave me alone, will you?'

Zobrany gave him a pound. 'Or paint a picture. Let it be a bad picture, only paint it. Look: when an artistic person thinks of business he always makes a romance of it, and romance in business is always in fact something shady. Cardboard jockstraps, bulletproof shaving mirrors – no, really, I mean! Please stop thinking of such things.'

'Listen, I'm . . . obliged to you' – he couldn't quite say *grateful* – 'but let me be, will you?'

'Be, then, be! Go, go! Only I'm warning you: one day there may come a critical moment when you will laugh at yourself at the wrong end of your teeth. The end of Gèza may be horrible. Better be a sign-painter.'

'All right. Goodbye for the present.'

'Poor child,' said Zobrany; he was thinking also of Cseh.

NINETEEN

When Tom Henceforth came to Taryard, near Arundel, which was Sir Benoni Bararon's place in the country, he was received with an easy courtesy which put him out of countenance. 'There must be a hundred and one things I want to talk to you about,' Bararon said, delighted to see him. 'Why not let us have tea in the library? I've got all your papers there, and we may as well get them over and done with.'

Tom Henceforth was led into a great H-shaped place, fragrant with the perfume of thirty thousand books, and commanding, from six points of the compass, views of the sweetest bit of scenery in England, which somehow irritated him. He might have chuckled with Bararon in a closetful of directories, and fraternized with him over a mug of stewed tea out of a tin pot and a husky bun. But that little repast was something he could never forgive.

The peace of the library made his head ring like boxed ears, and what they had to eat and drink set his teeth on edge. It was nothing that might not be bought for sixpence at a café – little cakes, bread and butter, jam and an ordinary infusion of tea leaves – but the very simplicity of it was something for that embittered boy to take umbrage at. 'What a fine white flame those logs burn with,' he said, glancing at the mighty stone fireplace.

Bararon said, 'Elm. The boughs drop, and are good for nothing else. But yes, elm does burn clear.'

'They make coffins out of elm wood, don't they?' Tom Henceforth asked.

'Yes, it resists decay after it's seasoned. I don't much care for elms, do you? "Immemorial elms . . ." Hm . . . I like oak, or beech.'

'To burn?'

'As trees, as trees . . . Now let me get something off my mind, may I? I have some money for you, you know.'

'I heard so. How much?'

'I have the figures here. I don't know, if you're good at figures, but here they are. Perhaps you'd better check?'

'I'm not good at figures myself.'

'It doesn't matter much. You'll find they agree, I think. Firstly, there's a sum of seven hundred seventy-five pounds, plus twenty per cent interest. That makes nine hundred thirty pounds. Plus forty-eight pounds, eleven and sixpence.'

'What the hell's that for?' Tom Henceforth asked.

'Mr Zudd's memorandum itemizes it as "To Mr TH for out-of pocket expenditures". What a remarkable fellow he is!'

'Isn't he, though. Go on.'

'Yes, of course: twenty per cent interest on forty-eight pounds, eleven shillings and sixpence; nine pounds, fifteen shillings and tenpence. That makes fifty-eight pounds, seven shillings and fourpence. This brings your total to 988 pounds, seven and fourpence. With per annum bank interest, and something called "Marginal Incidentals", altogether 1088 pounds, seventeen shillings and some odd pennies. I think you'll find that accurate.'

'And you've been holding this money for how long, did you say?'

'Something over two years. I advertised for you in *The Times*, but you'd disappeared. Mrs Fell said she thought you must have joined the Army –'

'– Oh yes, with this gammy leg? Not that I would join the bloody British Army, even if I could, mind you.'

'I think you're right. This is not a workers' war –'

'– And if it were? You'd join the Army, being a worker yourself, I take it?'

'Allow me: identifying myself with the cause of the worker, yes. But tell me, where have you been keeping yourself all this time?'

'I prefer not to tell you.'

'I asked only . . .'

'It doesn't matter. This money – do you mean to say I can pick up a thousand-and-whatever-it-is pounds, and simply walk away with it, just like that?'

'Certainly. I can give you a cheque, my personal cheque, this very moment, if you like.'

'Two years, eh? I could have had it two years ago, could I?'

'If I'd been able to find you, certainly. Lady d'Ordinay also.'

'Oh, f-f-f-f –' he couldn't quite say it, in the presence of all those books '– *damn* Lady d'Ordinay! Who cares about *her*? . . . What happened to her, incidentally?'

'I don't know. I advertised for her, too. I heard she'd gone to Italy. She lost her father, you know?'

'Poor orphan. Cover her with leaves. Suffocate her in the Tower. To hell with Lady d'Ordinay. Let's have that money, if you don't mind, and I'll be off.'

'Why, yes, of course. I had hoped you'd stay and talk a little.'

'What about?'

'About yourself, for instance,' said Bararon. 'You interest me. You have an arresting personality. You impress me as being a person of great capacity.'

'Oh, do I? Capacity for what?'

'You have a predilection for the arts, I believe?'

'Have I? Who told you that?'

'I have seen some of your sketches on the margins of draft reports. They have a certain *searching* quality.'

'I'm not a painter, if that's what you mean.'

'Then Zudd mentioned that you were writing a novel.'

'Oh, *fa*-damn Zudd! And I dare say Mrs Fell showed you my private papers that I left behind?'

'My dear sir!'

'I'm sorry. Yes, I am writing a novel, but I haven't had much time lately. It's something I want a lot of raw material for. I haven't got my documents together, my human documents. If only I'd had this money a couple of years ago, I . . . Well, to cut a long story short, I had some upsetments, and I was hard up; and in two words, nothing's done yet, and there let the matter rest.'

'And now?'

'Now let me have that cheque and I'll say thank you and goodbye.'

'Wait, I have a suggestion, if it's agreeable to you. You're tired and impatient. Pause a little while, stay here.'

'What d'you mean?'

'Would you like the cottage in the dell? It's small, but quite comfortable. You may have it, and come and go as you please. One of the girls will clean for you. The library is yours to use, and you may take your meals here, or not, as you choose. Furnish yourself with pencils, pens, notebooks, sketching blocks, or what you will, and refresh your spirit a little down here. Why not do that?'

Tom Henceforth said, 'Sussex-by-the-Sea, eh? Me and Rudyard Kipling.'

'Surely anybody may enjoy the air of the downs without identifying himself with Kipling? You want fresh air and good food – you're so very pale and thin – and I can offer you these, at least, and peace and quiet, and privacy, and a good roof over your head; and you save your money, because it costs you nothing.'

'I promised myself, the first money I got I'd leave England.'

'To go where, in wartime?'

'Anywhere, anywhere, out of this God-forsaken country!'

'You'll find the cottage very pleasant, even in the winter. There's a good fireplace,' said Bararon, smiling at Tom Henceforth as he looked thoughtfully at the burning logs. 'You shall have as much elm as you want to burn. There is also modern plumbing. If you want books, here they are – you have only to walk a few hundred yards. Taryard is an unspoiled village, and the people there are pleasant.

There is an old inn, and a quaint old alehouse where they talk and tell stories in the evenings.'

'"Happy the man whose wish and care a few paternal acres bound," eh?'

'An outsider, listening to us, might think that I was an estate agent, trying to sell you the place,' said Bararon, laughing. 'I won't press you. Tell me about your novel.'

'No.'

'You're perfectly right. A sure way to make an idea miscarry is to talk about it . . . What do you think of the war?'

'England,' said Tom Henceforth with relish, 'England is taking a sound thrashing, a damned good hiding, a first-rate bashing on every front, and at sea, too. Ships can't beat submarines. By 1917 they'll be singing, "Deutschland Über Alles" instead of "God Save the King".'

'I hope not.'

Tom Henceforth jeered, 'Why, what's the difference? You're an Internationalist, and all that, aren't you?'

'Yes. But I'd rather sing "God Save the King" than "Deutschland Über Alles".'

Looking around him, Tom Henceforth said, '"Now we stand outcast and starving 'midst the wonders we have made", though, eh?'

'I have made nothing, Mr Henceforth,' said Bararon, unperturbed. 'I have no right to sing that song. And you have only half a right, until you have made some wonders, you know.'

'Less than half; you couldn't call me outcast and starving with a thousand pounds to my credit, could you? If that was what you were trying to rub in.'

'I think you know better than that. And don't forget that there are more ways of starving than going without bread, and more ways of being outcast than having nowhere to sleep.'

'– And stone walls do not a prison make, nor iron bars a cage; don't forget that one. Man cannot live by bread alone – if I may coin a phrase. Water, water, everywhere, nor any drop to drink. All that glisters is not gold. You can fool some of the people some of the time. Answer a fool according to his folly. Et cetera, et cetera. I don't sing any man's song but my own, for anybody but myself . . . Don't mind me: I've got quite a bit of outcasting and starving to sleep and eat away, and I'm a wee bit raw just now. I'll take that cottage, if the offer still holds.'

'Certainly, by all means!'

'But it'll be a little while before I'm fit to sing for my supper.'

'There are no conditions attached to my offer, do understand that. I'll drive you to the station, and you can get your things together and come back here. I'm delighted, delighted . . .'

He rang for the housekeeper, and said, 'Mrs Vidler, Mr Henceforth is going to stay with us at Dell Cottage, so please see to it that everything is in perfect order, warm and aired. Mr Henceforth will give you a list of whatever he happens to want, and you'll attend to it, if you please.' The old lady curtsied and withdrew.

'And how shall I make out your cheque?'

'To Bearer, please. Cash.'

'As you will, but it's a large sum to carry about, you know.'

With extraordinary vehemence, Tom Henceforth said, 'Never mind. I want no dealings with banks and cheque books and deposits – never again, as long as I live. I hate banks.'

'It's your money, of course. But if you draw cash, won't you let me keep it for you in my safe, at least?'

'Oh, I don't mind that.'

'Good.' Pointing apologetically to the chaste grey cheque he had filled out, Bararon said, 'It says *Bararon Brothers*, you'll notice. But I'm not actively interested in the business.'

'Aren't there Bararon Banks all over the place?'

'Yes, in Paris, Amsterdam, Geneva, New York, Milan, Lisbon, Buenos Aires, Rio de Janeiro, St Petersburg, Antwerp . . .'

'And Hamburg?'

'Yes, and Hamburg. Also Constantinople.'

'So it doesn't much matter how the war goes, does it? Whichever way the cat jumps, it's "fuck you, Jack, I'm all right". Eh?'

'It isn't quite as simple as all that. If we are dependent upon a monetary system we must accept some of its anomalies. But,' said Bararon, smiling, 'at all events, this cheque is perfectly good. Will you be back tomorrow? The day after? The cottage will be ready for you; you'll be expected whenever you arrive. If, by some chance, I'm not here, simply ask for whatever you happen to want, and Mrs Vidler or Harlow will attend to it at once. Harlow knows more about my cellar than I do; regard it as your own. I'd drive up to town, if it weren't for petrol. I'm a wretched driver, anyway, and the chauffeur's at the Front with the East Sussex . . . You don't know what a pleasure it'll be, to have you here . . .'

Admiring Bararon's overcoat, Tom Henceforth asked, 'Who makes your clothes?'

'Eh? My tailor? Scholte. If –'

'– No, no; I only asked out of curiosity. I liked to dress up, once upon a time' – he spoke as of a remote period, before living memory – 'but I've given all that up. Good clothes are something you miss, when you haven't got them. No more of that for me . . . No, no; no more of that!'

Late one afternoon several months later, when Tom Henceforth was looking out of his sitting-room window, letting his imagination float with the mists of the valley and thinking of nothing at all, a huge, draped figure came out from between two old apple trees and said, in a deep, thick voice, 'Hallo, kid.' And with this greeting came a powerful odour of pickled onions and gin.

'Perp,' said Tom Henceforth.

'That's right.' Perp came in, shrugging off a great black mackintosh. He might have gone to bed in his clothes the last time Tom Henceforth saw him, slept five years and just got up. Taking a pickle jar from one pocket and a square-faced bottle from another, he said, 'Sit down.'

Mastering a qualm of nameless terror, Henceforth said, 'I'll get some glasses.'

'That's right. Or cups'll do. I ain't particular. Draw the curtains and light the lamp.' He caught the boy by the sleeve and felt the cloth. 'Be buggered if it ain't the same suit o' clothes I loaned you! Never let it be said old Perp didn't know a good bit of material when he saw it. And not much the worse for wear, either.'

'How's Molly Irving?'

'Lovely, tell your mum, just lovely.' There was a click, and a seven-inch blade appeared in his great hand. 'I've got a bone to pick with you,' he said. Then he speared a pickled onion and offered it on the point of the knife. 'Have one. Have a bit o' gin. Go on.' The glasses being filled, he said, 'This is for old time's sake, just to make sure you haven't forgot me: no hard feeling –' and slapped Tom Henceforth's face.

'I told you once before there was no need to repeat that compliment,' the boy said. 'Wait a second, will you?' He went to the kitchen and came back with a shotgun. 'Keep your distance, you ugly bastard, or I'll blow your brains out.'

'Bad tactics,' said Perp. The thing to do was, shoot me first and call me names afterwards. Wipe off the bottle and spare glass, and tell the coppers "This ugly bastard came in with a knife in his fist, so . . ." and all that. Let's have that.' He took the gun away. Tom Henceforth's finger closed on empty air where the trigger had been. '. . . I could bend this round your neck, you know, only it'd be a pity to spoil a nice shotgun,' Perp said, turning the weapon over. 'One of a couple, too, and a hundred-pound note wouldn't buy the pair. Made by Greener, St James's. You lucky boy! Come on, let's have another bit o' gin and a chat. I've got a bone to pick with you.'

'If it's about those five dud sovereigns I passed for you –'

'– And kept the change, and ran away? No, I forgive you for that. It was a smart trick you pulled with The Schemer Merton, by the way – given *my* name to fiddle with, of course. You couldn't of got anywhere without *that*, not with The Schemer. Didn't he get your first and last five-pound note out o' you, and leave you with a silly old umbrella? That old brolly, eh? Oh Christ, that gamp!' Perp laughed. 'No, never mind that. A fiver's only money, after all.'

'Well then, what do you want? How did you know I was here, anyway?'

'Oh, as for that, somebody told me. I know all about *you*, kid. You lucky little bugger! Palling up with Benoni Bararon, and given the run o' the house; a place all to yourself, furnished with antiques, what's more. That chair you're sitting on's Queen Anne with the original French brocade, and this here glass is real Waterford: a hundred and twenty guineas wouldn't buy a dozen of 'em. Now I ask you, ain't that a way to live? To be able to give a pal a Waterford glass to drink out of, and threaten his life with a fifty-guinea shotgun – that's doing things like a gentleman, ain't it? Oh you lucky man, you lucky man . . .'

'What bone do you want to pick?' asked Tom Henceforth.

'First and foremost: you're not my enemy, you know. I'm your friend, and you know it, don't you?'

'What bone?'

'You went and made a berk of yourself, that's what I don't like.'

'What are you talking about?'

'Look. What I want to know, I know. If you was Douglas 'Aig's plan o' campaign, I could find you out if I liked. All right? All right. I'll tell you about yourself: you got mixed up with some high-class tart. I don't mind that – boys will be boys; let 'em get it out o' their cistern. But you went on the Cousin Sis – Christ, but you went on the piss! – and made a berk of yourself. You had a cheque book, and so you went and wrote yourself half a dozen cheques, signed with fancy signatures: false document, within the meaning of the Act – the 1913 Act, s. 7, I think – which is a felony. You uttered seven such documents, and you got caught. You lost your head and tried to make a break for it, and got knocked down by a lorry, and got your leg broke. In consideration whereof, et cetera, et cetera, you only got twelve months. Look at you, blushing red as fire! . . . What I've got against you is, that you went and spoilt yourself. If you were low, you ought to of come to me – you knew where to find me. Perp looks after his own.'

'I'm not your own.'

'Shut your jaw. As I was saying, you ought to of come to Perp. But no. Never mind, it might be all for the best. You've had a taster of what it's like inside, haven't you? Sometimes it improves a boy. I had a taster myself, six months for aggravated assault, when I was about the age you was then; and a burnt child dreads the fire. Does he, my arse! A burnt sensible child learns himself how to use the fire; like me.'

'What are you getting at?'

'I'll come to what I'm getting at, don't you worry.' Perp got up and slouched about the room, picking things up, appraising them and putting them down. '*How* the hell do you get pally with a man like Bararon?' he muttered. That's the point . . .'

'You don't get pally with Bararon – Bararon gets pally with you,' said Tom Henceforth.

'That's right. It's like you don't take a fancy to Perp – Perp takes a fancy to you. That makes sense . . . Well, as I was saying, you disappointed me a bit. But never mind,' Perp said, going back to his chair. 'Let bygones be bygones . . .'

'Yes. Go on.'

'Tell us now: where's the box?'

'What d'you mean?'

'That's right, be deaf and dumb and blind. Only not with me, get me? Listen: I've got a plan o' Taryard House. It's in the County Records – it was built donkey's years ago. Nobody messed about with the architecture; this I know. All I'm asking is, Where's Bararon keep his safe?'

'In the library.'

'Where's the lib'ry? Tell us, now: draw a North-South-East-West map, looking as from Taryard Village Cross. Take a pencil, and draw.'

'Go to hell.'

'Here's a pencil. Draw maps.'

'Go to the devil.'

'That's right. Squat. Sit you down. Give us a diagram. The lib'ry's where? On the first floor?'

'No.'

'When you keep a safe in a lib'ry it's generally behind dummy books covering a secret door, so called. What books? What side? Where?'

'There aren't any dummies.'

'A lot o' rare stuff, I'm told?'

'There's a printed catalogue of the Bararon Collection. Go and look it up in the British Museum.'

'Now don't be sulky – you've got such a beautiful smile, you know. Let's see you smile . . . Now I've got it on record' – Perp touched his forehead – 'about where Bararon's got a lot of oil paintings worth a mint o' money.'

'Perp,' said Tom Henceforth, 'don't be a fool. This kind of thing isn't in your class. Bararon's pictures are as well known as the dome of St Paul's. You wouldn't stand a chance in hell of getting away with any of them.'

'Look. If I made up my mind to get away with the dome of St Paul's, I'd have it down. Only I don't want the dome of St Paul's.'

'Look here,' said Tom Henceforth, 'it doesn't matter a damn to me if you screw Bararon's house – he's a multi-millionaire, and insured anyway. And I put him in the way of making a few thousands more, for God's sake!'

'– And didn't think o' Perp, did you, when there was a bit of bunce to be picked up? Perp, what clothed you when –'

'– You don't understand. I steered some suckers into an African trading deal because I was sure they'd lose on it.'

'Just out o' spite, eh? You don't want to be spiteful, you know. Where's the sense in it? Anyway, forget it. What is it you're raising objections about now, for instance?'

'I got into some trouble that time, with those cheques. If anything happens here, they'll question me . . .'

'You didn't tell this here Bararon about getting that stretch?'

'No.'

'You ought to of, you know; but never mind. You'll be out of the neighbourhood, with the family, you know.'

'What are you talking about?'

Perp's petrified smile widened. 'I've got an ear to every private telephone in Sussex, Kent, Middlesex, Surrey and Hampshire. There's no moon next Friday a week, so there won't be any air raids. Bararon rung up the Criterion and booked a box for *A Little Bit Of Fluff*. His son comes home from school then, and the family's going to have an evening in town. Bararon, the lady, the daughter and the boy makes four. There's room for six in a box. Pity to waste a seat. I'll lay thirteen to two they invite you. They like your company. There'll be nobody in the house except the housekeeper, the cook, the butler and two girl skivvies.'

'And a three-way burglar alarm, and what not.'

'Can't you try and remember that Perp never misses a trick?'

'The safe's behind an inlaid panel –'

'– Get hold of this here pencil, and draw.' Tom Henceforth obeyed. Perp went on, 'As for me, you know you only imagine you see me here. Actually, I'm over at Hastings. I'm having dinner with five respectable tradesmen right at this moment, so don't run away with the idea you see *me* . . . How did you like the skilly and cocoa in Brixton? They treat you gentle, there – Brixton's a first offender's clink. I wouldn't threaten a man like you with guns and things, because I know you, and you wouldn't scare. You'd enjoy it; or you think you would, never having had a Perp Special Dressing-Down. But if you tried any funny stuff with me, I tell you what I *would* do, if you like. I'd see to it that you got another dose o' jail – a nice steady five years of it, this time, and not in Brixton either, but in Reading, or maybe Portland; and hell on earth when you got there. I could fix you if you was as innocent as the Archbishop o'Canterbury, don't ever forget that.'

Tom Henceforth laughed. 'I've just remembered something – there's some money of my own in Bararon's safe.'

'All the better. If it's a little, I'll make it a lot; if it's a lot I'll double it. How much?'

'A thousand in banknotes.'

'You shall have it back, and another thousand on top of it. What's more, Bararon's responsible for it, so he'll give you another thousand all over again. You lucky boy! . . .'

Perp put the gin bottle and the pickle jar back in his pockets. He took his glass to the kitchen and washed it. Not forgetting that he had handled the shotgun, he polished that; poked a forefinger into one of its barrels and held it out at arm's length, saying, 'If you think that's easy, try it some time. I can do that with eight guns; one on each finger. Now I'll be off and see about my eggs and bacon.'

'Do you want something to eat?'

'A matter o' three hundred head o' swine and a couple o' thousand dozen eggs. By next year I'll have the price of a new-laid egg up to ninepence, retail . . .'

Then he was gone, leaving behind him nothing but a rancid odour and an atmosphere of incommunicable dread: something like the smell of a magistrate's court.

At first the countryside cried *Spies!* A barn full of straw went up in flames over by Harradene. A stable caught fire near Beeden. A truck crashed into a telegraph pole at Mincing, and the lines came down. Something went wrong with the main power cable, and all the electric lights in the area blinked out. Four men in khaki, wearing gas masks and led by somebody wearing the stars of a captain of infantry, demanded entrance to Taryard House, and said, 'Enemy gas attack – everybody into the cellar.' The servants locked up, they robbed the house at their leisure and departed in a lorry.

When the Bararons and Tom Henceforth returned from London at one o'clock in the morning they found a blown safe, a rifled library, and half a dozen empty frames – which had held a Raphael, two Rembrandts, a Tintoretto, an El Greco and a Velasquez. Of cash and securities, the thieves had got away with some ten thousand pounds – less than a tenth of the value of Lady Bararon's jewels, which were also missing. Cash, bonds and jewels together were as nothing in comparison with the books and pictures, the value of which was almost incalculable. A million pounds couldn't buy them, the papers said. This was evidently the work of a supremely efficient gang, superbly organized. Privately, the Commissioner said that he wished we had a couple of men with batons on their shoulders like the fellow who had planned and executed this job; the war would be over all the sooner. Bararon was assured that the works of art and the jewels, at least, would certainly be recovered: there was no place to sell them; they were too conspicuous; the thieves might as well try to sell the Albert Memorial.

A month later Bararon received a strange flat package, securely fastened. It contained – to his unspeakable horror – a square of painted canvas which he recognized as the right hand of Jesus cut from El Greco's *Gethsemane*. Also, one page neatly cut out of a Gutenberg Bible. A printed note said:

> WE HAVE NOT STOLEN YOUR PICTURES, ETC. WE HAVE KIDNAPPED THEM. IF IT HAD BEEN YOUR DAUGHTER WE WOULD HAVE SENT YOU AN EAR OR A FINGER TO PERSUADE YOU OF THE PRESSING NEED TO PART WITH RANSOM MONEY. MAKE NO REPORT OR COMPLAINT OF THIS IF YOU HOPE TO SEE YOUR BOOKS AND PICTURES AGAIN. DRAW TWO HUNDRED THOUSAND POUNDS IN GOLD AND UNMARKED BANKNOTES AND AWAIT FURTHER INSTRUCTIONS.

The mastermind had computed, with horrible precision, the potential anguish of the millionaire who loved books and pictures. How could a man like Bararon stand idle and watch the destruction of masterpieces?

'If they had only threatened my life,' he said to Tom Henceforth. 'I could have defied them.'

Bararon wrote Tom Henceforth another cheque. 'You look peaked,' he said. 'You look as if you hadn't been sleeping well. Perhaps you're overworking? Or has that wretched affair upset you? Don't let it. It upset me, at first – disproportionately, really. But then I told myself that it served me right for being inconsistent.'

'Inconsistent? How?'

'To own property really is to steal, in a way. One can't help having money, under a capitalist system. But to keep a thing of beauty all to oneself *is* immoral. I'm going to give my pictures to the National Gallery.'

'You could almost say, in that case, that whoever stole them was a public benefactor, in a way,' said Tom Henceforth, with a laugh.

'If he had stolen them with that end in view, assuming that I couldn't be induced to part with them by any other means.'

'Anyway, the public gets the pictures. That adds up to the greatest happiness of the greatest number, doesn't it?'

'Does the end justify the means?' Bararon asked. 'Does it always?'

'Well, doesn't it?'

'No, I don't see that. The pictures are only a little part of an end, when you consider the enormity of a character that will employ such monstrous means. All's well that ends well only if you can see where your "all" is going to end.'

'The road to hell is paved with good intentions. Nobody can see where anything is going to end,'

'I don't agree. I think that every means is an end in itself. Otherwise, a chain is stronger than its weakest link, which it can't be. There must be something utterly monstrous about a man who can cut a piece out of an El Greco.'

'But clever, don't forget that. The law can't do much to a man for messing up a work of art. The fellow who chucked a brick at the Portland Vase, for example, and smashed it to bits – they couldn't give him more than six months. But if he'd smashed the skull of the village idiot, they'd have hanged him.'

'A time will come when such creatures will cease to exist – they'll have no cause for existing,' said Bararon.

Tom Henceforth said, 'I doubt it. It's men like the one who stole your pictures that make revolutions and keep them going; not reformers.'

'Oh well. Do take care of your money, won't you? You really had better bank it.'

Tom Henceforth shook his head. 'I think I'll spend a few days in town and lark about a bit,' he said.

'That's a good idea. All work and no play never does. If you won't put your money in the bank, why not keep it in a safe-deposit box?'

'I might do that, now that you mention it.'

He had that morning received a letter – a blank sheet of paper to which was pinned a receipt for one handbag, left in the cloakroom at Waterloo Station. Suddenly he was weary of the placid undulations of the Sussex landscape.

Tom Henceforth was bored, and he was homesick for the proximity of crowds; and since the burglary, the presence of Bararon had become unbearable to him. So he packed his bag, and Bararon drove him to the station, saying, 'We'll miss you. We've all grown very fond of you. Don't forget that you're always welcome at Taryard.' And at last he was on the train, inhaling the sweet, nostalgic smells of hot iron and coal smoke from the engine, and hot people and tobacco smoke from the red plush seats.

Two hours later he was having tea at a restaurant near Charing Cross. The waitress, a motherly woman, smiled tenderly at him.

'Excuse me mentioning it,' she said, 'but you've been at the Front, haven't you?'

'Don't let's talk about it.'

'Is there anything more I can get you?'

'You could put your little finger in my tea to sweeten it,' he said. 'Saccharin makes me ill.'

'There's no nourishment in it. It passes right through the system, I'm told. But what can we do, with sugar rationed as it is . . . Were you at Ypres?'

He touched his stiff leg and said, 'Transport,' touched his scarred mouth with his teaspoon and said, 'Hand-to-hand . . . Ah well, if there's no sugar we must do without.'

'It's a shame,' she said. 'If anybody deserves it, you do.'

He replied bravely, '*C'est la guerrre*, my dear, *c'est la guerre.*'

'And you boys out there in the thick of it; and so young, too.'

'*Dulce et decorum est pro patria mori.* One does one's bit. Personally, I regret that I have only one life to give my country.'

'I don't like to give you a bill,' she said, when he was ready to go, 'but it's the rule. But' – she took a screw of paper from her pocket – 'it's my own ration. You need it more than me. I'm getting too fat anyway, and I want you to have it. It's only two lumps, but . . . I hear the profiteers are getting two shillings a pound for it, so . . .'

'No, no, I won't take it!'

'I shall be hurt if you don't. I *owe* it to you. God bless your brave heart!'

So he took the waitress's sugar, and went away thinking. First, he walked to Waterloo and presented the luggage slip. The attendant threw over the counter a worn leather valise with a broken lock, secured by a pair of straps. Back in his room at the Charing Cross Hotel he opened it and found a grey flannel suit, three flannel shirts, six handkerchiefs, three pairs of socks, an old-fashioned ink-stained morocco writing case, and three books – *Drawing For Beginners*, Southey's *Life Of Nelson*, and a rhyming dictionary. The writing case contained two neat bundles of assorted banknotes, each to the value of one thousand pounds.

Now, with Bararon's cheque, he had three thousand pounds; and he didn't know what to do with the money. Ten pounds was a lot of money, fifty pounds was a lot of money; but three thousand pounds wasn't money at all – it was beyond the scope of his imagination, as a spender. Invested at five per cent, it would bring him three pounds a week for life. Three pounds a week he understood: it was enough to live on, as the cost of living was in those days. But he needed more than enough to live on – he wanted spending money.

If I could turn this into twenty thousand pounds, and have twenty pounds a week for life . . . he thought . . .

That would be perfect. Wherever he was, in any part of the world, he would know that once a week, every week, forever, he would receive an envelope with twenty pounds in hard cash – twenty pounds, a hundred dollars, four hundred and eighty francs, God knows how many lire, escudos, pesetas, schillings, gulden or what not.

Then, playing a game of Slippery Sam with some Blue Button stockbrokers' clerks in a pub near Threadneedle Street, he met a traveller from a foreign land, who gave him a brief but vivid account of certain goings-on in Mexico.

'Carranza's the boy to watch,' he said. 'Carranza's the lad that played his chess and boxed clever. The Yanks "not recognizing government by assassination" is a lot of cock, all eyewash and political back-chat. Forget about Pershing and his cavalry – I know the territory, and you can't fight irregulars with Boy Scouts on horseback. Pancho Villa's cutting him to pieces. Besides, America's *got* to come into this scrap now, over here, and they can't fight on two fronts the way things are going. Carranza's been hand-in-glove with the big oil interests. I happen to know that for a fact, because I'm connected with oil myself, in the engineering way. But the market's wobbly just now, and if I were advising somebody who had a few hundred pounds to invest, I'd say, "Put your shirt on Paricutin Oil". Because, as I happen to be informed, the Yankee–Mexican affair is all part and parcel of a bearish market manipulation to buy out Paricutin, Mexican Eagle and the rest, for a dollar a share; and don't imagine for a moment that Pershing is in command of the US Army in Mexico. Wall Street's GOC there, as elsewhere. Overnight, there'll be a *rapprochement*; Wilson will recognize Carranza, and Mexican oil will boom!'

So Tom Henceforth got in touch with a reputable stockbroker and bought five thousand shares of Paricutin Petroleum for one thousand pounds. Paricutin fell two points. He bought fourteen hundred shares more. Paricutin steadied. Then it went up – 2¼—2½—3½—7¼—15 steady—18¼—22—25½—28¼.

The US withdrew from Mexico, and Carranza called a constitutional convention. The market vacillated. The stockbroker said, 'Sell now, Mr Henceforth, while you're in the money. Carranza isn't stable, and Zapata is still strong.'

Tom Henceforth said, 'Hold on a bit; I've got an instinct about it . . .'

Paricutin went up again. Carranza started to nationalize coal.

Paricutin went down again. Carranza gave land back to the peasants. Paricutin went up again. 'Sell?' the stockbroker suggested.

'Hold on just a little more,' said Tom Henceforth. Then President Carranza expropriated certain of the smaller foreign oil holdings, and Tom Henceforth cried in a voice of thunder, 'Sell now!'

The stockbroker replied, 'Sell what now? Paricutin was expropriated last night.'

'Sell for what my investment is worth, then.'

'It's value is only theoretical, at a nominal sixpence a share. As a matter of fact, you haven't got any investment . . .'

. . . Thus, Tom Henceforth's three thousand pounds was reduced to a miserably evocative six hundred twenty. *Never mind the odd twenty*, he thought; and remoulded the sum total nearer to his heart's desire, which was something that ended in two 0's – five hundred, as it happened, and not six hundred, which he had had in mind.

This round sum he let escape in round droplets until, in due course, having spent at the rate of two hundred pounds a year, he could count the eminently manoeuvrable figure of one hundred pounds, no shillings and no pence. With this amount in hand, he remembers, he went for a holiday to a seaport town – he can't recall exactly when – and there somebody, somehow, sold him a set of tattooer's needles complete with inks and transfer patterns, for a twenty-pound note.

Certain fanciful designs drawn in seven indelible colours are all that remain to prove he ever owned such an apparatus and practised with it on the hairless skin of his own left arm. They are there, and he can roll his sleeve to show them as corollary to certain tales he has told of his adventures between 1917 and 1919 – tales which might have been swapped by well-travelled salesmen in the less reputable commercial boarding houses on the outskirts of Gomorrah, the night before the fires came down. Whomever Tom Henceforth tattooed, it wasn't wartime soldiers or sailors, for by then the Versailles Treaty had been signed, and the terrible Peace of 1918–1939 was under way . . .

PART FOUR

TWENTY

'. . . And as for "Life Over Again",' said Zobrany, with a pleasant smile, making a corkscrew curl of half his moustache by turning it around a knife handle. 'Ah, as for that – were Howgego Zobrany, and Zobrany Howgego, there were a Zobrany that could have given you stories to fill a book of a thousand pages! A book to please readers of the literary supplements, of the gossip columns and of the sporting papers alike. I wish you could have known Howgego, my dear Ody. Of course, he would have kicked you out of the house. But not if I were there to say, "Howgego, this is a gentleman and a scholar, and my friend." Then he'd have said, "My dear Count, a friend of yours is a friend of mine, and we'll have up a tappit-hen of Old Tawny on that." You see, he hated newspapermen because, as he said, "They'd write anything for a plate of pickled pigs' feet and a pot of penny porter." And yet he liked George Augustus Sala for writing a cookery book for Kettner, saying, "I admire a man who'll turn his hand to anything to pay for what he eats and drinks." He hated the Irish, incidentally, but approved of Sala because he stood by Parnell – of whom he said, "I like a man who'll go to the devil for a lady." Yet he affected a profound contempt for women. He hated Jews, too, yet loved Disraeli "because he could twist the Queen round his little finger" – although he adored Victoria. By the bye, he was on Dreyfus's side at the time of the famous Case, and afterwards, because he thought Dreyfus was guilty. Anybody who was alleged to be for Germany against the French was certain of Howgego's approval. He was catholic in his hates, you know – liberal, impartial – but invariably made exceptions, and for the oddest reasons. He couldn't stand Americans at any price – yet he was on the friendliest terms with an American who was also a newspaperman: Ambrose Bierce, no less; not because he was a man of genius, but "because he never had a kind word for anybody".

'In politics, Howgego was, to put it mildly, an extremist. He said that all trades unionists and Socialists ought to be shot down like mad dogs – yet he spoke highly of the firebrand John Burns "because he had bottom" – meaning nerve. He even offered hospitality to the French-Jewish-Anarchist-Syndicalist journalist, Marcel Cahen, saying, "He's game, is handy with his dukes, and don't give a damn for anybody; and it's his misfortune, not his fault, that he was born on the wrong side of the water."

'Ah, it would take a better man than I to convey to you such a contradictory, yet consistent, character. He meant everything he said, and only seemed paradoxical because he meant so much more that he could not say. One had to learn to interpret him, like ideographs, like hieroglyphics.

'What I, in a roundabout and Howgegoish way, am trying to drive at, Ody, is that any man reliving a longish life is misled by hindsight, afterthought, wisdom after the event. And it is awfully easy to be led astray by being clever at the "ifs" of history. That is why the Youth Movements are invariably wrong. "The old men made a mess of the world" – it's easy to say that. But, my dear fellow, the old men were young men when they made a mess of the world: Ben Tillett, Arthur Henderson, John Burns, Ramsay Macdonald, Keir Hardie – pathetic old milk-and-watery moderates, now, to the young men of your generation – they were all blood and iron and youthful fire when they carried their cloth workmen's caps into the House of Commons and defied the gods. Yet from what I hear around the tables in this restaurant, they are "lackeys of the bourgeoisie", now; they "sold the Workers", and what not. Shall I ever forget the howls of execration that went up when the firebrand Macdonald put on evening dress? Or the groans, under this very roof, when HG Wells shyly intimated that there was a God? Even Bernard Shaw is a quaint relic, a kind of bric-à-brac; like (with all respect to genius) an old-fashioned water closet: he represented Progress, once.

'Time does not move, don't you see. It is a dimension. We move. Time keeps still. Our destinies are always in the hands of tomorrow's old men and yesterday's old men – never today's. And the young are always angry, my dear Ody, always . . .

'Y todas las cosas se pasan,
Las memorias se acaban,
Las lenguas se cansan –

'–Which is old Spanish for "Everything passes, memories die, tongues become silent". If I were to have a seal engraved, I believe I should be hackneyed enough – "corny" is the word, I believe, now – to have those lines engraved on it. One lives not according to what one remembers, but as how one is remembered. Similarly, if I were to leave instructions as to what was to be carved on my gravestone (which I won't) I should borrow my epitaph from the old German knight, and let it be said:

'That which Zobrany saved, he spent;
That which he gained, he lost;
That which he gave, he has.

'I'd have had that put on Howgego's stone, if I had imagined for a moment that his heirs would have stood for it. I suggested it. One of the comments, from a Youth-at-the-Helmer at that time was, "The old sod *would've* taken it with him if he could, I dare say. But it don't look respectful. Better have a Deeply Mourned, et cetera, et cetera." So I shut up. Confound you, my dear Ody, and your silly Symposium . . . I am living over again, don't you see?'

Ody asked, 'When, exactly, did he die?'

'I don't remember dates. It was at the time of Verdun.'

'I remember Verdun,' Ody said.

'Indeed? In what way?'

'I was old enough to read capital letters. My mother used to take *The Morning Post*. I read the headlines.'

'Ah. You were living where, if I may ask?'

'At Chobham, in Surrey.'

With something like irony, Zobrany said, 'Ah, then you have a kind of documentary evidence of the horrors of war. Given statistical tables, you are fit to lecture on it, no doubt.'

'There's no need to be sarcastic,' said Ody, with something like resentment. 'I don't recollect your telling me you were there either.'

'I stand corrected, my dear fellow. I wasn't there. I was here. Although I did enlist in the cavalry.'

Poppy, who could whistle like a schoolboy, sounded *Cookhouse*. Zobrany laughed, and said, 'Right, quite right.'

Ody asked, 'Steve, why didn't you take over the pub when Mr Howgego died? I'd like to see you in a good old pub.'

'My dear Ody, nothing would have given me greater pleasure! In fact, you know, I have sometimes thought that when I retire from this murderous café business with its eighteen hours a day, I shall take a quiet and pretty little inn somewhere in the country. Oak beams, log fires, prints, a canary-coloured waistcoat – good company, peace, plenitude – a vegetable and herb garden. I should put the Sordics to work in the garden. And Alma making embroidery in a bow window . . . However, to return to what you say: I would gladly have taken The Good Intent. But in the first place – at that time I was not yet a British subject, and of questionable antecedents: enemy alien by birth, and Italian by adoption; and this would have been troublesome with the licensing people. Again; Howgego's was a Free House (as if any house of his could have been otherwise!) unattached to any brewers' combine, and therefore very valuable.

'He sometimes spoke of the matter, vaguely suggesting that it might be a good idea if, one of these days . . . you know? For a man like Howgego, bless his heart, can't accept the idea of dying. He had, of course, his own mysterious system of reasoning. You or I would say, "I am nearly eighty; therefore it is time to think of the end." He argued, "I am nearly eighty; so what's the hurry?" But he did add a codicil to his will leaving me some of his best wine, and his watch and seals. The will itself was unbelievably complicated – he had drawn it up in 1886, and most of the legatees were dead or had disappeared. But as I say, the property was of high value. After his death there were six claimants, and one of those horrible legal battles was pending between the putative heirs, when a public-house broker persuaded them to sell the dear old Road To Hell to a firm of brewers, which they did, and for a very tidy figure. Hence, it ceased to be a Free House, and became "tied", as they say, to Basington's chain of pubs. A pity, but there it was.'

'The old gentleman didn't suffer much, I hope,' said Ody.

'No, not at all. Only, right to the end he couldn't bring himself to believe that we weren't fighting the French. "What news?" he asks me, on the twenty-first of February. I say, "Why, it seems that Portugal will be in on our side." "Oh ah, I knew it all along," says my dear Howgego, "they did us sterling service against the Froggies at Torres Vedras." There was no point in arguing. "It seems that Fort Douaumont has fallen," I said; and he said, "We'll have a glass of wine to that." An outsider would have thought that his mind had given way. It had not; only, all of a sudden his legs had become feeble, compared with what they had been only a few months before, and his face seemed a little fallen in, and relatively pale – I mean, it no longer matched the crimson plush of the upholstery, but had a violet tinge. I stake my word of honour that Howgego knew what was what; but he wasn't going to give way an inch! "Now we'll drink death to the French," says he. I say, with tears, "No, my dear Howgego – a Zobrany fought Napoleon at Eylau, but that toast I will not now drink." At this Howgego wheezes with laughter, and says, "Count" – it was his whim to call me that – "I honour you! We'll drink hob and nob to the British Grenadiers, then, or anybody you like."

'And just as we were drinking a glass of ruby port of '93, a man came into the saloon bar – a man I never forgot. He was of the shape and colour of a bale of wool, soft stuff compressed square; and if a bale of wool could walk it would walk as that man walked. It was not that he was enormous in actual bulk, although he appeared to occupy ever so much space, and looked strong in proportion. It was that he was somehow *strange* – alien; from the devil knows how far away, downwards and outwards! I saw him reflected in half a dozen of Howgego's bevelled mirrors, and he had no profile worth mentioning. A back, yes, with uneven sloping shoulders like a house falling down; a neck, of course, but wrapped in a scarf like a dirty bandage; no collar, no tie. A little colourless hair, and a vile old hat. A slack grey coat, slack trousers. So much for his back. No, I beg pardon – I could see the palms of his hands in his reflection from behind, for that is how he carried his arms; knuckle first, like a monkey. From this elevation, he might have been a tramp. Ah, but I wish you could have seen his face! . . . How am I to put it? . . .'

'Go on, Zobrany. His face?'

'Well, I wish *you* could have seen it, because you might be able to describe it. It was something like Portland stone after the soot has bitten into it, only . . . the features seemed to have been bruised away; and yet there remained a prevailing expression which was at once repulsive and fascinating. I have seen such an expression on the face of a criminal barrister turned judge. I have seen something like it in burglars, and also in very clever detectives. I have observed it in statesmen, hangmen, religious maniacs and admirals. It is Satanic – I don't mean Mephistophelian, with a triangular grin under a hooked nose – I mean that it pertains to somebody who has the key to the Underworld, whose *pied-à-terre* is Hell. And yet, somehow, there was a certain compassion behind it – even something like good nature! I know I was worried, and excited, and distressed by the war, and all that, so that my imagination was a little on end, so to speak. The appearance of this man, dressed like a scarecrow, smiling an awful smashed smile, looking everywhere and nowhere out of pale eyes, and carrying in his slack-shouldered slouch more authority than a Prussian colonel – it gave me an indescribable nervous spasm. I felt the hair rising on my neck. For no reason at all, I was afraid of him.

'Old Howgego said, pointing to the Public Bar for people in dirty clothes, "That side, my friend. Not this side – that side." The stranger said to the barman. "Let's have some of your pre-war Hollands" – he had a voice like the lowest string of a cello, loosened until it is scarcely audible, vibrating too slowly to be properly heard – "and get me some pickled onions."

'Howgego said, "You heard me, my good man. Go to the Public Bar and have your drink there. You're on the wrong side." "No, I'm not – I want to talk to you," the stranger said. "You, barman; fetch that drink and them onions over by the fire." The barman was a very old prizefighter named Joe Shelduck who had been punched in the face by nearly every pugilist in England, but by the side of the stranger he looked almost handsome. Shelduck looked doubtfully towards Howgego, who said, "All right, Joe . . . Well, what d'you want to say to me?" "What'll you gents drink?" Howgego chuckled, for here was a Character. "My friend and I will have a quart of Bull's Blood," he said, this being a mixture of champagne and old burgundy, and very expensive. But the stranger took out a sheaf of banknotes, threw one down and said to Shelduck, "Get it. Have a drink yourself." Old Shelduck said, "I can't change this 'ere, mister." Howgego said, "Change it, change it." "You change it, gov," said Shelduck, handing him the banknote. It was a Bank of England note for five hundred pounds!

'The stranger said, "Oh, sorry – I thought it was a fiver", and took the note back. "The smallest I've got on me is a fifty," he said, riffling his great wad of white paper money. "Half a mo. Here's chicken food" – he found two golden pounds in his waistcoat pocket, tossed them to Shelduck – "Keep the change." "What the hell's your game?" asked Howgego, hugely amused, for this kind of odd situation was pepper and salt to him. The man said, "This is a nice cosy little rub-a-dub, and a Free House, too. Name a price, cash money, for the lease." Howgego stared at him, and said, "Are you mad?" The man said, "Not a bit on it. You're eighty years of age – and I hope you live to a hundred. But there's fifty years of lease to go on these premises, and with all the luck in the world you couldn't last to a hundred and thirty – now could you?" When he had done laughing, Howgego said, "What I can't make out is, why you didn't send a lawyer or an agent, or somebody half respectable, with your damned impudent propositions, Mr –"

'The man said, "– Perp. Call me Perp.' He was cool as a cucumber. He said, "Because, if I read you right – and I don't often read a man wrong – you'd have nothing to say to a respectable-looking man of business, whereas I tickle your fancy. And the proof that I'm right is, here you are drinking with me and laughing fit to bust at me. If I was a lawyer or an agent, your boot would have been up my arse ten minutes ago . . ."

'Howgego asked him, "Who the devil *are* you, anyway?" "A kind of a sporting character," said the man who called himself Perp, "a sort of an informal speculator, and my reference is the Governor of the Bank of England" – he tapped the pocket where his money was – "so think it over, and I'll look in tomorrow . . ." And before he left, he said, "I wouldn't mind taking over all Masham Court – it ain't a thoroughfare or a right-of-way: a man could put up a gate at the arch and be real private" . . .

'After he'd gone, Howgego became strangely gloomy. "The man's right," he said. "None of us is immortal. One don't like to think of it, but it's as well to be reminded. I'll tell you what we'll do, my dear Count. Tomorrow, we'll go to my lawyer, and I'll make the lease over to you as from the date of my death, for a consideration – say, five shillings. It'll be a bill of sale executed in my lifetime, for God above knows what a swarm of locusts'll be let loose when I pop off. Although I regard myself as good for another ten years . . ." I said, "Damn that creepy creature for putting such thoughts into your mind, my dear friend!" He said, "No, no, I'm over the three-score-and-ten mark by half a dozen years, and it won't be long now. You'll be the man to take the house over. Though I can't help liking that fellow with his Hollands and pickled onions . . ." "Howgego," I said, "Bull's Blood on top of old port has pickled your judgement. He is of the lower depths."

'But the man Perp had the instincts of a vulture, for my friend Howgego died that very night . . .'

'. . . Shelduck told me that after he had locked up for the night, Howgego looked around him as usual, and then said, "Henry Pearce is hanging all awry." Henry Pearce was the name of a fighting cock – named after a famous pugilist who, in his turn, was known as The Game Chicken – that had died in battle after a long and victorious career. The stuffed body of this bird, mounted in an attitude of offence, was in a glass case in the saloon. Shelduck said, "He would do it, he wouldn't let me – climbed up on a stool to put the bird straight in the case, and then all of a sudden spun round and dropped. I was too slow to break his fall, or I'd ha' done it if it'd broke my back – and gladly . . . And there he lay," said the old prizefighter, who was so insensitive to pain that he would let anybody knock him down for half a crown, crying like a baby now, "there he lay, with old Hennery Pearce beside him busted, and the bran stuffing all around like snow . . . oh my God!"

'And that was my Verdun and my Fort Douaumont . . .

'The man Perp appeared, as he had said, next evening. I had closed the restaurant, in mourning. "It can't be helped," he said to me, "it was my fault, for once." I asked him, "What the devil do you mean, sir?" He said, "I mean, my fault for not having the idea of dealing for that pub a week sooner, for the old gentleman'd've done business with *me*." Oh, you should have heard that "*me*" – it had in it all the pride of hell! And in that moment I swore a great oath to myself that never, never, never would I have any dealings with that man!

'He said, almost to himself, "Still, I like this here Court, and I dare say I'll be back one of these days." Then he offered me his hand. I hesitated to take it. He smiled at me and said, "Go on, shake. I won't bite you," and took me by the hand.

'His handshake is something I have not forgotten, also: it was not that it was one of those vicelike grips such as weak-spirited fellows try and surprise one with, because they have read or heard that a firm handshake is a sign of a strong character. Such nonsense! It's like saying that children and dogs love good men, or that smoking a pipe is a sign of reliability! . . . No, this Perp's hand, which was as big as mine but much thicker, and coated with skin like shagreen, was impersonal and very dry; and it closed slowly but in a deadly kind of way – I thought of a raw oxhide shrinking in the sun – he could have crushed me if he had wanted to, but he didn't want to. It was I who did the hard squeezing, as, to my embarrassment, I discovered when I found myself hanging onto his paw as if for dear life, and not knowing quite how to let go of it.

'Then he said, "I know about you, you know. You ain't a bad sort. Go about your business – if I call you Pal, nobody'll bother you." I said, "I am not your pal." He asked, "Why not?" "I don't want your friendship," I said to him, "I am not afraid of you, I do not need your protection. Go about *your* business – whatever it is you do wrong for a living – for I do not like you." And he patted me on the shoulder, and smiled, and said, "That's right. Only you're a liar, you know. Bye-bye . . ." And he was right! I was lying – I *was* afraid of him. And do you know why? I sensed that this man was some kind of genius – a genius of crime, a criminal of power. And I was afraid of him because there was something about him that made me like him! All my instincts said, *Hate him.* But I did not hate him. For this reason, my dear fellow, I feared the man –'

Ody asked '– And what brings him so vividly back to mind after all these years? You didn't see a great deal of him after that, I imagine?'

'No, I have not seen him since. But I shall, I am sure . . . Eh, Poppy?'

Poppy said, 'Yesterday, he was here looking for Mr Zobrany while 'e was out seeing the Income Tax. I told 'm to come back some other time, and he said, "I might look in another day, like tomorrow or the day after" –'

'– How did he strike you?' asked Ody.

'Evil?' suggested Zobrany.

She said, 'I don't know. No, I can't say that, exactly – I didn't know what to make of him. He said, "What're you staring at, baby?" I said, "You." He said, "And what d'you think of me?" I told him, "There's only one thing I'd like worse than having a face like yours." He said, "Oh, and what's that?" and I said, "Being the bloke that gave it to you." He said, "Perp pays on the nail for a witty remark," and took out a handful of change and stuffed it down the front of my dress –'

'– Oh, he did?' said Ody.

'– He was too fast for me to stop him. I'm sure he didn't mean any harm; he didn't even look at me. Then he went out. I shook myself, and twenty-eight shillings came down my legs.'

Ody said, 'This Perp is well known. An astounding character. They call him the "GOC of Organized Crime." He's one of the most dangerous men in the world –'

'– You're wrong,' said a tremendously deep bass voice from the doorway. '*The* most.' The door closed quietly. There stood Perp.

His grey-green mackintosh – a thing of extraordinary antiquity and eccentric cut, with an Inverness cape and a staring tartan lining hung open over a suit of mud-coloured twill. Tilted to the back of his head he wore a shattered and fustigated hat, which had assumed the shape and tint of a rusty Spanish morion. A navvy's red bandanna handkerchief was twisted about his neck; he had threaded it through a gold ring set with an emerald surrounded with diamonds, and tucked the ends into a foul old blue corduroy waistcoat. He brought with him a night-cellar miasma of gin, stale tobacco smoke, half-digested onions, wet clothes steaming of coke fires, mildewed leather and rats.

Ody thought, *He fetches Hogarth into three dimensions*; sniffed, and added, *No, four!* And Zobrany, fascinated yet horrified, said to himself, *Surely he must have changed his shirt in the past twenty-one years? But where is the evidence?*

'*The* most, the most of the best ever, the one and only,' said Perp affably, seating himself. 'Count, how do? It's a long time since you've seen me, but I've heard a lot about you. You,' he said to Ody, 'I know you, son. You're a pal of a acquaintance o' mine.'

'I don't think so,' said Ody politely, since Perp was a prize packet valued above Zaharoff, Garbo and Mrs Simpson by discriminating newspapermen, 'nobody I know ever boasted of knowing you that I remember, sir.'

'That's right,' Perp laughed 'think again, son, and you'll remember.'

'What can I do for you?' asked Zobrany, drawing himself up to his full height.

'Where d'you buy your pickled onions?' Perp asked.

'Mainwaring's,' said Zobrany. He felt somewhat ridiculous. A man cannot stand like a grenadier on guard and talk of pickled onions.

'Not bad, but not good enough,' Perp took out a jar. 'I have these made up special. The shallots I have grown down in Lincolnshire, the vinegar I have brewed by Sarson, the bay leaves I import from Greece, the peppercorns I get in Mincing Lane, but the hot peppers and the cloves –'

'– What's your business with me?' demanded Zobrany.

'Since you're so impatient . . . let's see, where were we? Oh yes. One rainy evening in 1916, wasn't it? I forget the date, but I think it was on a Monday, around about 6.45, or thereabout. An idea I had kind of fell through. We shook hands – you didn't want to, but we shook hands – and said goodbye, and I told you I sort o' liked Masham Court. "I don't like you," you said. And I can see you still don't, or think you don't – though what I've done to hurt you, I don't know. I still sort o' like Masham Court –'

'– Well? And, as you say, I still do not like you. So?'

'And yet I bet you I'm an honester man than most you've come acrost,' said Perp, smiling, 'and better-hearted. Moral, too, I shouldn't be a bit surprised, if it comes to the final count. The Ten Commandments . . . well, well, you've got the name for being a broad-minded man yourself, you know, if it comes to *them*; and you fancy yourself as a likable kind o' bugger, don't you, now? As for the Seven Deadly Sins: I don't envy anybody, I hate nobody, I'm anything but lazy, I bear no malice, I ain't lustful or gluttonous or vain or a drunkard, and I never get angry. I never forget a good turn, what's more, and more often than not I forgive my enemies: they're not worth it. I sometimes make an example of somebody, but there's nothing personal in it. Cruelty ain't in me. All in all, I do unto others as I expect them to do unto me. I stand by 'em; I'd go to hell – or send somebody reliable there – to get a pal out. I'm The King Of The Scum Of The Earth, as you'd call 'em – but ask yourself how and why I am. Fear won't rule 'em, or crime'd've been abolished as soon as a man learnt how to knot a rope. What way do I do it, then? By kindness? No, that won't do, either. Well, how then? I'll tell you, by common savvy – reason. With me, they *know* they're well off and safe; they can trust me – I'm no bloody politician – I never made no treaties with an enemy, left-handed or right. My Yes is Yes, my No is No. How often has Scotland Yard said to me, "Perp, we know you done so-and-so. Open up, just one little crack – chuck us just a few o' your boys to make a case out of – let out only one little tiny squeak, and we'll not bother you!" And what have I said? "Gentlemen, if you want a confession, I'll give you one, or fifty – the more the merrier. But confession ain't evidence; the onus of proof is on you; I've studied every angle, and my job is airtight and waterproof. Catch me if you can, hang me if you do; but you've come to the wrong shop for a sell-out. Try Whitehall and Westminster if it's Judas you're after – you can't buy me and you can't scare me." I'm loyal, you see, and I'm generous, and I'm fair; and I live and let live. Now what is there to dislike about me, just answer me that?'

'Why are you talking to me like this?' Zobrany asked.

'To pass the time. Answer my question' – now, Perp looked Zobrany straight in the eyes.

'You devour, you terrorize, you corrupt,' said Zobrany, 'and I will have nothing to do with you.'

Perp laughed, and took out a beautifully enamelled hunting flask. 'This here was made for the Tsar of Russia,' he said, unscrewing the top, 'so don't go saying I haven't got a taste for pretty things . . . This here gin is Hollands, fifteen years in the cask. Have a bit.'

'I will not drink with you,' said Zobrany.

'That flask must have been made by Fabergé,' said Ody.

'That's right,' said Perp. 'You wouldn't believe it, but it holds a pint. The metal's thin as tissue paper, but you won't bend it because it's osmiridium; and them eyes in the eagle are what they call alexandrites – green in one light, red in another. Take a nip out of it, and have an onion, son.'

Ody did so, avoiding Zobrany's half-reproachful look. Perp went on, 'Devour, you say, do you? Who, me? Why, a fifth of what they pay a cabinet minister would cover twice what *I* eat and drink. *And* my wardrobe. As for Corrupt, I don't know what you mean. I find out what a man's price is, and pay him fair and square: if that's corrupting, then all right, I corrupt. But you can't buy somebody that don't want to be bought, you know. And I give a fairer and squarer deal than Jesus and Stalin and Hitler and Mohammed and all them, with their harps-and-wings and their social securities and their fat tits on green carpets, and all the rest of that pie in the sky in the sweet by-and-by – *I* pay on the nail. And as for terrorizing, I'm clean – *I* never threatened a man with liquidation or burning sulphur. If ever I picked a wrong 'un (which has been hardly ever) I blamed myself more than him – which is better than you give God credit for, you know . . .'

'What the devil do you want?' cried Zobrany.

Perp replied, 'Masham Court. I still kind o' like it.'

'I hope you may get it,' Zobrany said.

'I will, don't worry, I will. Never mind the pub. Basington's got that. Let it be. The rest, now the inside part – that's what I mean. You see,' Perp said, drawing a diagram with a fingernail on the tablecloth, 'it's shaped kind of like an old-fashioned coffin-shaped gin bottle, five-sided, with the archway where the neck is. You've got the lopsided bit where the angle breaks to the left at the bottom. Now the way I look at it: business is slack everywhere. You're just making your expenses, the way things are –'

'– That is my affair.'

'That's right. Well, name your price for the goodwill and lease, and we'll make a deal.'

'What are you talking about?'

'A deal,' said Perp. I'll pay you a good price, and what's more, find you premises anywhere else you like in the neighbourhood, within reason. What do you lose? Nothing, and you've everything to gain. You carry your business to a better place round the corner, hang your sign up there – I find you the place and install you free, and swap you leases –

and I pay you . . . how much? Name it, cash money! Into the bargain. What d'you say to three thousand?'

'No.'

'Four.'

'No.'

'Five.'

Ody caught his breath. Zobrany said, 'No.'

'Six,' said Perp. 'Be sensible.'

'I will not have any dealings with you,' said Zobrany.

'Doesn't your good lady have any say in this here matter?'

'Not now. I took over all that ten years ago. Mrs Zobrany has no concern with the sordid details of the property. In case you take it into your head to bother her, I tell you this categorically. Go away . . . I do not mean to be discourteous, you understand.'

'Sixty-five hundred,' said Perp, eating an onion. 'It's ridiculous, you know, but I've set my mind on it, and I don't care. See the difference between me and –'

'– No!' shouted Zobrany.

'Look: a new place, within shouting distance; all decorations and installations; good premises in a nice position, with upper part; a decent leasehold plus seven thousand pounds. You'd be a madman to say no.'

'Then I am a madman. I will not do business with you.'

'I've got all the other leases in the Court, don't you see; I could squeeze you out, you know.'

'You will take this place over my dead body.'

'Don't think I couldn't, but I won't. I don't want it that bad . . .'

'Look here. Money is nothing to me. I'll make it eight thousand, and chance it,' said Perp.

'Money *is* something to me. Therefore I say *No*!'

'Do you realize I'm talking hard cash?'

'Talk all the kingdoms of the earth, and I still say No.'

Perp slapped his knees, laughing. 'Ten thousand pounds!' he cried.

Zobrany spoke more soberly. 'No. Forgive me if I have been rude. No, sir, I don't want to sell.'

'You'd have your caffey, your goodwill, a better position *and* ten thousand in the bank, you know.'

Zobrany became tremendous. He put his hand on Perp's shoulder, and said, 'Sir. I have a feeling that if I sold to you for a hundred thousand pounds, not merely ten, I should wake up and find my pocket full of dead leaves. We are on opposite sides of something or other; don't ask me what. I cannot do business with you. You are an honest man; I am an honest man; but our honesties belong to different worlds. If you want my house you must fight me for it. Meanwhile, I am remiss. If you were the Devil himself, you are under my roof, and I have not offered you a cup of coffee.'

The smile deepened at the corners of Perp's mouth as he said, 'That's right. There now, you see? You don't not like me so much as all that, after all, do you?'

Zobrany replied, 'You are a force of Nature, sir. It is not a question of liking or disliking you. I must accept you, but still I am bound to resist you.' He felt almost sublime and was, in fact, beginning to enjoy himself.

'That's right,' said Perp. 'It's all right. Never mind. Don't give it another thought, for the present.'

He rose, pocketing his flask and his jar of onions. 'So long for now.'

'Excuse me,' said Ody. 'Who *is* it I know that's a friend of yours, Mr Perp?'

'I wish you'd just call me Perp . . . I told you to think again, and you'd remember. Did you?'

'Well, no, not exactly –'

'– Not exactly? What d'you mean, not exactly? It's exactly or nothing, don't you know that? All right, I took you by surprise – you wasn't expecting to see me, and I took up your interest. Right? Right. Well now, who's the boy that knows an inside personal private funny story about everybody who's anybody in the world? Who knows the answers to all the questions everybody asks before he's asked them, but hasn't got a single solitary tale to tell about Perp? Eh?'

'Not Tom Henceforth?' said Ody.

'That's right,' said Perp.

Zobrany cried, 'How do you mean, "That's right?" That's right it's not Tom Henceforth, or that's right it is?'

'That little toerag,' said Poppy.

Perp smiled, and said, 'That's right.'

'You mean that's right he's a toerag, or what?' Poppy asked.

'He *is* a friend of yours?' Zobrany asked.

Perp said, 'I don't say that, exactly. If he's a friend o' mine, why ain't he rich? Ask yourself the same question. On the other hand, you'd be surprised how few enemies I've got. *You're his* friend, though, that's about the size of it, ain't it?'

With this, Perp went out, with a friendly wave of the hand, leaving behind him – over and beyond a thieves' kitchen effluvium – a certain gap in the atmosphere. Noisome as he seemed, nobody would have said No to just a tiny bit more of his company. Zobrany lit a cigarette with a more than usually rakish flourish. He hoped he looked like a man who has just refused a fortune as a matter of principle.

Poppy winked at him. He thought: *Impudent girl! She is saying to herself, 'The poor old bugger is fed up with Masham Court, but he daren't leave for fear of upsetting Alma.'* And that is exactly what she was saying to herself; and she wasn't far wrong.

'I don't quite see where Tom Henceforth comes into it,' said Ody.

'Oh, my dear fellow, a blackguard like that would know everybody, while nobody would boast of knowing him – '

'– A blackguard like who? Tom Henceforth?' Poppy asked.

'Poppy, don't be a fool,' said Zobrany.

'Well, I still think that Henceforth's a sarcastic, selfish little bugger,' she said.

'That man, of course, may be lying,' said Zobrany.

Ody said, 'That's the hell of it – everybody lies, but the only man we've ever met who's above it is a wrong 'un so low that everybody knows hanging's too good for him!'

'Then his truth is a mockery. He doesn't tell the truth to shame the Devil, that fellow – he tells a fact to shame the truth. To him it is all a game, a fiendish game. There used to be a professional chess player who came here to make a few shillings at the board,' said Zobrany. 'He would say, when the pieces were set, "Move where you like – you'll lose." His opponents moved where they liked, and they lost. When he seemed to be exposing his intention, he was being doubly devious –'

'– Steve, haven't you ever thought of blaming the loser for wanting to win but lacking the skill?' asked Ody.

'Ody! Are you holding a brief for this man Perp?' Zobrany shouted.

Poppy said, 'If he was a ponce with 'is back broken or a pickpocket with arthritis, you'd be the first to help him. What way was he lying? How? What about? That toerag, Henceforth?'

'Poppy!' said Zobrany. 'The point is, it doesn't make sense – Tom Henceforth in that gallery!'

'And why not?' she asked. 'Ain't 'e got a story about everybody, right or wrong? Any kind of a story – anything for a laugh. And he's no more scared of getting a punch on the nose than a load of spew on the pavement's afraid of being trod in.'

Zobrany burst out laughing. 'God bless my soul – about who *hasn't* that boy a story?'

'Except Perp,' said Ody soberly. 'Why, I wonder. I know all of Henceforth's stories; I have 'em on record.'

'Oh, my dear fellow, I know,' said Zobrany, 'and I admire you for it. But to make a thing of Tom Henceforth, you would need to hold a mirror up to an age and imprison all the reflections. Scrape off the silver, so to speak. But look here: a man talks least of what he works hardest at. Could it be, perhaps, that our friend is writing his monumental novel about Perp? Eh?'

Poppy said, 'Yes, and he's painting you a monumental mural decoration.'

'Puzzle,' said Ody. 'Nobody knows what he's writing a book about or whether he's writing a book at all. Actually, Tom Henceforth is a sort of intellectual keyhole –'

'– Intellectual arsehole,' Poppy murmured.

'By keyhole, do you mean one that you open a door with, or listen at, or look through, or lock things out with?' asked Zobrany.

'All four,' said Ody.

'Ah, but from what side?' Poppy asked.

'This girl has more brains than the two of us put together,' said Zobrany. 'Next time he comes in, I must remember to ask Tom Henceforth all about that man.'

But a full year and more passed before Tom Henceforth paid his next visit to Masham Court.

TWENTY-ONE

In those days, only a handful of people, such as the Tamrodts who didn't matter, shared Poppy's opinion of Tom Henceforth. In general, he was recognized – and admired – as a monumental cynic and a tremendous egoist. Perhaps he was. But it does not follow that he had, therefore, any great conceit of himself. An egoist doesn't necessarily like his ego because he happens to be married to it. He may even feel sorry for himself, and pity is only distantly akin to love – it is more closely related to contempt, and may, in fact, be nothing but disgust in disguise.

The seething scorn in which Tom Henceforth cooked his contemporaries was nothing to the scalding contempt with which he scarified himself when he was alone with the festoons of dried cuttings, the bundles of desiccated leaves of paper and the pot-pourri of ideas that had lost their essential oils, which constituted the sum total of his life's work.

'The novel to end novels' remained unborn. He could make a joke of the fact, discussing the matter with a publisher who had advanced him fifty pounds to finish the book with and asked how it was coming along, saying: 'Look here, Humphrey, it isn't my fault, and I can't in decency blame my Muse – between us there is what the gynaecologists, or the haematologists, call "an R-H Factor". We've been at each other sporadically for twenty-five years, the Muse and I, so help me God at all kinds of odd hours! We've done it standing and kneeling, in bed and on chairs and tables, under trees in thunderstorms and in doorways in full view of the passers-by – anywhere and everywhere – but nothing seems to come of it. In the middle of a haircut, the bitch has whispered, "Come home, quick – I have a feeling we can bring it off now." She can't wait; she swarms all over me in the taxi, picks me up neck and crop and lays me on the stairs before the front door slams. It almost clicks, but not quite. Damn it all, she pursues me into public lavatories, insistently unbuttoning my poor chewed pencil and screaming for me to commit myself to toilet paper on the spot. The stuff she squeezes out is sterile, or else she isn't ovulating right; or else I am the victim of some perverse chemistry which changes the very genus of *Mungo* just at the critical moment, so that the egg of the book won't fertilize . . . Be patient. Rabbits like Wells can make three litters of books a year . . . I'm big game – I breed slowly . . .'

The publisher was inclined to reply, 'A gravid rabbit is better than an elephant full of wind, as far as production is concerned. If this were ten years ago, when one could break even on a two-shilling booklet, I'd accept for publication a collection of Henceforth's *Excuses For Not Writing A Novel* – only you'd make excuses for not making the excuses.'

But he didn't say it. Only a fool spits into the wind, and one never could tell what Tom Henceforth might construe as a personal affront. Touched on a sore spot, his retaliations were likely to be prolonged and damaging. His arms were a poisonously libellous pen and a defamatory tongue, which left wounds that took a year to heal; his armour was poverty; his psychological weapons, irresponsibility and unlimited spare time. He would drop anything to take up a quarrel, and work at it day and night: he had nothing better to do with his time; but you had, and he'd waste months of your life just for fun. Pretend to ignore Tom Henceforth and he would go from scurrility to outrageous scurrility until you were forced to put the matter in the hands of your solicitor – which cost you more time, and money, too, and got you nowhere, since he had nothing to lose. You, however, had something to lose; and if you tried to fight invective with counter-invective, Tom Henceforth could whistle up any number of small, hungry lawyers from the back alleys around Temple Bar, and make a nervous wreck of you with his writs and his suits and his interminable legal correspondence. Scotland Yard, appealed to by one of Tom Henceforth's victims, could only scratch its head and say, 'There isn't much we can do, unless he threatens you with bodily harm, or what not. Strictly unofficially, the best thing you can do is pay somebody a fiver to give him a bloody good hiding.' But Tom Henceforth never quarrelled with the sort of person who paid somebody a fiver for this kind of service, or who was apt to get up and do it himself.

So the publisher sighed, and shrugged, and said, 'Well, let's see some MS when it's ready.'

'Lend us another ten pounds,' said Tom Henceforth.

'I'm sorry, Tom, but I can't make any further advance. I would if I could, but I have partners.'

'Yah! Spenlow and Jorkens! Make it a personal loan, then.'

'I can't, Tom!'

'Make it a fiver, then.'

'You know you're only trying to aggravate me, because I hate to have to refuse.'

'Five shillings, then. You can't refuse to lend me five shillings, can you?'

The publisher not only could have refused – he certainly would have. But he thought it better not to, and handed over two half-crowns, which Henceforth took, saying, 'You can write yourself a chit saying you bought me lunch, and make ten shillings profit.' Then he walked to a florist's shop in the Strand and spent the five shillings on an exceptionally hideous potted cactus, which he had sent to the publisher with an affectionate note.

Which was as humorous, and whimsical, and impish as you like. *But where's the novel? Where* is *the accursed novel?* Tom Henceforth sometimes asks himself, sitting in his jealously guarded solitude at the back of the canal and admiring how deftly the candle flame balances a wisp of vapour on the tip of its nose in the draught.

Then there passes through his mind – through the fastidiously censorious inner sanctums of his mind, where Nausea minds its manners in pudding sleeves and Malice wears buckles and a small-sword – a shambling file of scabby bohemians, sturdy beggars and masterless men, ponces in rags with their whores in burlap; and to each his boast and his alibi for an empty canvas and an unpainted picture, or his snarl and his whimper for a blank page and an untold story. And it seems to Tom Henceforth that of all this bob-tailed rout of currish scavengers, he is the most despicable. They are nothing, but they have this grace: they would be something, if they could, and pretend to aspire to it. But he, having been something, has frittered himself away and made a nobody of himself, to the greater glory of Nothing. Jesuitry cannot condone, nor casuistry justify the wanton squandering of Henceforth by Henceforth! . . .

The candle flame completes its trick, bows and straightens itself. Upon the cue, a cigarette butt burning away in a saucer nods off a cap of ash and, falling back, spins a rope of smoke into slow spirals.

And in Tom Henceforth's head something glows red and bursts into a shower of blinding white sparks, like an indoor firework. It is an inspiration. He says to himself, *Since I (let's face it) am the most atrocious blackguard,* flâneur, *time-waster, parasite, pasticheur, braggart, liar, impostor, bully, coward, rake and rogue of them all why shouldn't I take upon myself the vices and follies of all mankind? Make of myself a Kapparah, a stupendous scapegoat, and whip myself out to die in the wilderness under the scourge of the most awful satire ever written – a satire against myself! I look into my heart and see Everyman; Everyman looks at me and sees himself as the offal that he is!*

This concept strikes him as something almost unthinkably huge – bigger than Dante, better than Milton – a hitherto undreamt-of osmotic marriage of Jesus and Satan, the Redeemer and the Accuser.

And that ever-nascent but never-born novel isn't to be a work of prose at all, but an epic poem.

This is the Moment of Truth. This is what I've been flirting my cape for. This is it! Henceforth thinks, gleefully.

Now he could be as proud of himself for having done no work, given encouragement, as another man might be who had achieved an improbable success against heavy odds.

Of course, there was no gainsaying that the money he had run through would have come in handy at this moment.

But now he has accused himself, and pleaded Guilty. The onus of proof is with the Prosecution, but he has an open-and-shut case. *I'll hang the whole world on one rope*, says he, going out for a late evening walk, unconscionably pleased with himself.

A week previous, Poppy had come to Zobrany and said, with a troubled look. 'I promised to ask you something, but I hope you say no.'

'What is it, my dear?'

'I promised to ask you if I could have next Sunday night off. If you say no, everything's all right.'

'Of course you may have the night off, child.'

'I was afraid you'd say that.'

'What is the mystery?'

'Well . . . Did you ever hear about the Jingle Club?'

'I have never been there, but I have heard that the Jingle is quite an exclusive theatrical club. Some two or three hundred members pay twenty guineas as an entrance fee, and ten pounds a year subscription, for the privilege of sitting on wooden benches at ten shillings a place, and consuming refreshments which would be dear at half the price while they watch impromptu performances by well-known artistes, somewhat in the style of the old music halls. But these performances, I have been informed, are worth twice whatever they cost you, because it is a sort of free-for-all theatrical catharsis. The audience participates . . . Why?'

'Mr Ody wants me to go.'

'Oh, go then, by all means! I wish I were going, too.'

'Do you? Because Mr Ody asked me to tell you he was getting you a ticket on the off-chance of you coming.'

'Utterly impossible, completely out of the question! Why should he invite me?'

'Because I asked him to.'

'What is this conspiracy? And why couldn't he ask me himself?'

'Because he knew you'd say no, and he didn't have time to argue with you.'

'And you have time to argue with me?'

'Yes. I can slip it in at odd moments. Besides, I've got to be in the show, and I want you to be there.'

'You are to be in the –'

'– *I* don't want to, but Ody made me.'

'*Made* you! Made *you*? This is something new.'

'Well, I don't mean forced me to. Only he *wanted* me to.'

'Oho. Aha. Look at me in the eyes.' She looked up at him, and he went on, 'Poppy, my dear, you know that I have a great tenderness for you?'

'I know that I've got one for you,' she said.

'No, I mean that I feel for you *in loco parentis*. That means, as it were, like a parent.'

'I never had any parents, and I don't miss 'em.'

'I should be a hypocrite if I said that I felt exactly as a father should feel towards a daughter, as far as you are concerned; but it had better be that way. Ody is, shall we say, sweet on you?' Poppy nodded. 'He is a good boy,' said Zobrany. 'Not like what I was at his age. You like Ody?'

'I'm not in love with Ody, if that's what you mean.'

Zobrany said, in his most masterful tone, '*Be* in love with Ody! Believe me, love is not all moonlight and roses . . . at least, so I have observed. I have never suffered disillusionment myself, but I am quite an old man, and I have seen a lot. "Not in love with Ody," for heaven's sake! Shall I tell you something? Liking lasts longer than loving. What is more, liking breeds love; love does not necessarily breed liking. I suppose you think you are in love with me, eh?'

'*I* think I am,' she said, in her candid way.

'Good. So marry Ody, and think kindly of me, no more. I am not in love with you, I am in love with my wife, and I am very happy – understand that. Twenty years from now you will still be of child-bearing age, and I shall be . . . elsewhere. Love Ody, and remember me: people live only as long as they are remembered. Do you hear?' She nodded again. 'Well now,' he said, 'what is this about being in the show?'

'Next Sunday they're doing a kind of funny "Maria Marten, or The Murder In The Red Barn". In between scenes I go round with a tray of beer and sandwiches and stuff, and sing some of those funny songs you tell me not to sing.'

'That is as a matter of form. I prefer your songs in the morning to the song of the skylark, as a matter of fact. It is a matter of taste. One man loves the Pope, another the Pope's wife. One man likes skylarks, I prefer "Jack the Ripper". But go on.'

'I'm dressed up as a Victorian waitress, in a bustle.'

'No, really! A bustle! No, I mean to say – a bustle!'

'Couldn't you come, just for a couple of hours?'

'Damn it all, I will! Ida is a good girl, and Sunday isn't a busy evening. Mrs Zobrany doesn't care much for the stage – only the screen – and so she won't feel deprived. At least I shall not feel that I am depriving her. Just for a couple of hours, if you and Ody really want me to come.'

'We do. *I* do. I told Ody I sing best for you.'

'But are there no rehearsals?'

'I went through a sort of act once, for Mr Lester, the manager. He's the Master of Ceremonies, too. He says I'm as natural as a sparrow. And it won't matter much if I make a mess of it, because there'll be somebody to help me out if I do, and it's only for a few minutes at a time, anyway.'

'And you aren't nervous?'

'What of? They can't kill me, can they?' she said. 'And anyway, it's all in fun – even the stars get the bird, just for fun, or so Ody tells me . . .'

Later, Ody told him, 'There'll be a fortune in talent on that little stage under Hungerford Bridge. You'll enjoy it.'

'But Poppy?'

'Poppy'll be all right, Steve.'

'Yes, yes . . . This is rather a delicate matter . . . Tell me truly – however old-fashioned I may sound – you have no dishonourable intentions towards Poppy?'

'I haven't any dishonourable intentions towards anybody, least of all Poppy. I'm very fond of Poppy – *very* fond of her.'

'Then why don't you marry her? She is a good and true girl. Beautiful, incidentally; that goes without saying.'

'I can't very well think of anything like that until I get back.'

'Back from where?'

'Assignments abroad. Foreign correspondent.'

'I am glad for your sake, my dear fellow, but you must be very careful. Europe is not a very nice place just now. What *if* . . .'

'Ah, *if*! Nobody likes to come right out and say it, but if a big do coalesces from all the little ones, then the *Special* will get me accredited. I'll be a battle correspondent.'

Zobrany sighed. 'In my day they were great heroes – the Special Correspondents. They rode with the cavalry and everything. Lucky boy! I envy you – I seem to have been born at the wrong place and at the wrong time. A ham-knife my sabre, an apron my sabretache, a napkin my dolman . . . Shall I wear evening dress to this affair?'

'It's optional. Why don't you, though? You'd look superb in tails.'

'If I tuck my stomach in. I will see if it still fits. I confess that I like to wear evening dress. I shall put on my fob seals and my studs, eh?'

'I'll send you an orchid for your buttonhole.'

'No, really! An orchid? No, I mean – an orchid!' said Zobrany, giggling.

'And Steve.'

'Yes?'

'You know something? You're a good man . . . however old-fashioned that may sound.'

'Nonsense, nonsense.'

. . . So for the first time in many years, Zobrany left Alma and a waitress to look after the café and, dressed to kill, went out to enjoy himself at six-thirty on a Sunday evening.

Glib, orotund and mellifluous, the Master of Ceremonies put down his gavel and said '. . . And now, ladies and gentlemen, for the first time on this or any other stage, the inimitable – the irresistible – the incomparable – the unquestionable –'

The audience shouted, in chorus, '– The one and only –'

'I – thank you, ladies and gentlemen; the only and only – irrepressible – unquenchable – irresponsible . . . *Poppy Oliver*!' There was applause.

Poppy came out dressed like a streetwalker of the '80s, in an extraordinary skirt with a bustle on springs, and a bonnet decorated with a daisy on a long stem. She curtsied, and a striped under-petticoat came down. She stepped out of it and curtsied again. A pair of crimson drawers fell about her feet. She kicked this garment into the orchestra, which struck up a melancholy refrain. Then she burst into her song:

'There lived a girl in London Town
Whose name was Marty Tabram,
And at the height of her renown
She charged as high as 'alf a crown.
Now she sleeps in the Bosom of Abram . . .'

And so, in her clear, sweet, piercing voice, she ran through the twenty verses of that moral ballad; so that at the end the audience stamped and bellowed for an encore.

But the Master of Ceremonies, hammering for silence, cried, 'Ladies and Gentlemen! The unrivalled – the unparalleled –'

'– The one and only! –'

'– I thank you, ladies and gents, one and all – the one and only Poppy will pass among you with refreshments as per your esteemed orders and express desires. Pray keep your seats, ladies and gents one and all, I beg and pray . . .'

Now Poppy appeared from behind the bar, balancing a great tray of drinks and sandwiches, and singing at the top of her voice:

''E drank twenty pints o' porter and a dozen double rums,
'E ate nineteen goes o' turkey and a pudden full o' plums,
'E ate 'alf a side of mutton with potatoes underneath,
'E ate sixteen pounds o' seedy-cake and licked up all
the crumbs;
Then they told 'im 'e was diggin' of 'is own grave with
'is teeth,
So 'e took 'em out and dug it with 'is gums!'

The Master of Ceremonies cried, '"The Awful Ballad Of Greedy Willie", ladies *and* gentlemen. All together – stand by, there, piano – all together, now!' Poppy led them through the first verse again, all the while dispensing mugs and glasses, and then, when the claque-leader bellowed, 'Second verse, there!' she went on:

''E ate forty pickled pigs' feet and a dozen bullocks hearts,
Thirteen dozen suet puddens and a gross o' raspberry tarts,
Fifteen stone o' pickled turnips and asparagus in sheaves,
And the onions 'e devoured was enough to fill three carts.
Cor! If Greedy Willie pongs the way 'e smells like when
'e breathes,
What on earth are we to do when Willie – Oops, excuse me –'

(Chorus of bassoon blasts, trombone tremolos and vulgar noises from the claque, in which the audience join with might and main.)

'What on earth are we to do when Willie – Oops, excuse me!
Oops, excuse me! Oops, excuse me! Oops, excuse me!
What are we to do when Willie –'

(Serpent and contrabassoon.)

As she came to Zobrany, she handed him a glass of cognac. People had thrown silver coins by the handful onto her tray, and stuffed money into her pockets as she passed.

'Ladies and gentlemen!' the Master of Ceremonies shouted. 'Pul-lease! – Ladies, gentlemen – the incorrigible – the reprehensible – the unconfusticatable Poppy –'

'– *The one and only!* –'

'– I thank you – shall have her turn again after the event of the evening. Poppy, come back! Come back, inimitable, or I won't be answerable! . . .'

'How was I?' she whispered to Ody.

He replied with a look of ecstasy and a heavenward flick of the fingers. And when 'Maria Marten' was played out to the last shriek, she went the rounds with her tray again, singing the gruesome ballad of 'The Catsmeat Seller Of The Isle of Dogs' and, called on for more, hitched up her skirt and stood with arms akimbo, shrieking a parody of 'Thanks For The Memory' –

'Of 'alf a dozen brats
In County Council flats,
And fish and chips
And greasy lips
And mother's cast-off 'ats . . .'

Zobrany said, rather sadly, 'She is a sensation.'

'A ball of fire,' said Ody. 'It's sheer personality.'

'Youth, vitality – consummate! . . . But I must go back now. Thank you, my dear Ody, for a delightful evening. You'll see that she gets home safely?'

'Won't you wait, Steve?'

'No, I had better go now. I'll congratulate her later.'

A knot of autograph hunters outside the Jingle Club started towards him. Zobrany smiled, pleasantly drunk, and squared his shoulders. A girl cried, 'Head 'em off – quick!'

'Calm, calm,' said Zobrany. But they brushed him aside, and made a cordon between the doorway and the kerb, at which a Rolls-Royce was waiting. A chauffeur all in black leapt out. Zobrany turned, and saw that the autograph hunters had made a pincer movement, converging upon a tall woman in a chinchilla stole and a little man with a big head.

'Chiquita!' they cried, 'Chiquita!' Zobrany gazed appreciatively at the tall woman, whom he recognized as a famous Brazilian actress, whose blazing flamboyance had recently set fire to the enthusiasm of moviegoers all over the world.

The little man looked about him with savage scorn; but then his eyes met Zobrany's, and widened. Zobrany started: there was no mistaking the cock of the insolent head, with its profile like the spiked back of a halberd as the face brandished itself.

'*Gèza!*' he bellowed. 'Gèza Cseh, by God!' And, parting the crowd like a pair of curtains, he threw his arms about the little man and clasped him to his bosom. 'In a silk dinner suit . . . *Aie!* – I have crushed your orchid –'

'– Put me down, you fool,' said the little man, between his teeth, 'you ox!'

The star Chiquita threw back her little head, opened a great wine-coloured mouth, and let out a leopard-scream of laughter, while she marked autograph books with her signature, which was like a conventionalized lightning flash. Ambidextrous as a jungle cat, she caught Zobrany by the moustache and gave him a swift kiss, as of smoke and flame, leaving a red-black smear on his chin. 'I adore you!' she said. 'Squash the friggin' mosquito! Squash him!'

'That's Gabriel Chess,' somebody said.

'*Loca brasilera! Borracha!*' hissed the little man, in pig-Spanish, '*Basura!* Is everybody mad? Is everybody drunk? . . . Chiquita, go back in the car. Go! . . . You – it *is* you? Zobrany?'

'My little *Gèza*!'

'Leave go of me, or have you gone crazy?'

Now a thin young man with light hair came running out of the club, looking left and right and wringing his hands. 'Oh, Mr Chess, Mr Chess –'

'– You, Ompteda, take Chiquita home. I will come later. Go! No, come back! Never mind, go go!'

'Yes, Mr Chess.'

'Wait a minute. No, it doesn't matter. Go! But, first of all –'

'– Yes, Mr Chess?'

'Nothing. Go.' He looked bitterly at the crowd about the windows of the car. The irrepressible Brazilian was pressing her nose against the glass and making faces at them, and they were crying, 'Chiquita! Chiquita!' He said to Zobrany, 'Come away, or they will tear buttons off my coat for souvenirs.'

'The lady –' Zobrany began.

'– Lady? What lady? Where lady? *Her?* I made her with these two hands! I could break her between these fingers! She used to dance naked with a tame anaconda on a table in a whorehouse in Rio de Janeiro. Lady! . . .'

'. . . But you,' said Chess, as they got into a taxi, 'look at you! What are you crying for?'

Zobrany, who was, in fact, shedding tears of pure joy, said, 'Pleasure. I am so full of all sorts of things, and I can think of nothing to say. My little Gèza!'

'Gaby. Not Gèza Cseh – Gabriel Chess.'

'Where to, guv?' the driver asked. When Zobrany said Masham Court, Chess cried, 'What? Do you mean to say you're still in that dump?'

'Yes, yes, I have been very lucky there, my dear Gaby.'

'My instinct was to be relied on, even then. It is infallible now. Did you notice that little girl tonight, who sang the gutter songs?'

'Poppy?'

'Poppy. Of that one I shall make a sensation.'

'No, really? Gaby, no, I mean . . . my Poppy?'

'*Your* Poppy?'

'She is my waitress. In a way she is like a daughter to me.'

'Then kiss her goodbye. She has *schwung*. Put her out of your mind. I have left instructions with my agent. So forget her.'

Hardly hearing him, Zobrany said, '*Aie*, my Little Napoleon! Do you still like champagne and sweet sponge cakes? Well then, I have a few bottles left of Vuilliam Père et Fils, Mareuil-sur-Ay, 1921! Give me two hours and Buol shall get out of bed and bake you ladyfingers! . . . Oh, but this will be a red-letter day in Alma's life!'

'Alma?'

'Yes. You don't remember Alma Nollekens? Little genius! Not only did you find me a restaurant, you also found me a beautiful wife . . . Look, here's Piccadilly Circus. Do you remember that map you drew? Oh, that map, that map!' cried Zobrany, with a shout of laughter. 'I have it still, framed, in my sitting room. Autographed – *Cseh Gèza fecit, 1911* if you please! Alma keeps a scrapbook of you. Oh, what a day this has been for me, what a day! What a night we shall make of it, what a night!' . . .

TWENTY-TWO

'Confess, you are happy to see your old friend,' said Zobrany.

Chess was silent. Looking at Zobrany, he felt somewhat as a famous author feels when a fond aunt produces from a drawer a composition that won him a prize when he was nine years old.

And Zobrany thought, with a trace of sadness, that this wasn't his Gèza, his wild little fireball of a Gèza Cseh. This was one Gabriel Chess. *Perhaps if I had something he thought worth borrowing or talking me out of, he might be my old Little Napoleon again*, he said to himself.

'Do you remember when you said that you were going to conquer England and bathe in a tubful of golden sovereigns?' he asked.

'So? Now I invade. And my barge is the *Queen Mary*. Well?' Chess snapped; and he was preoccupied and silent until they reached Masham Court. Then, when he saw Alma, he delighted the affectionate Zobrany by expanding his chest, making tremendous gestures with his manicured hands, and talking two hundred words a minute, every minute, until Zobrany, his eyes bright with tenderness and champagne, kissed him on both cheeks and said, 'Bless the boy! He has not changed. He will never change!' Then he giggled, 'Look, Alma – he's wearing a monocle! My Gèza in a monocle, a gold monocle!'

'Gabriel,' said Chess sourly.

'Gabriel. You little rascal, Alma said that you were the great producer, and I said . . . I forget what I said, but it is of no consequence at all . . . You see, Alma? I always had faith in him. Did I not, Gè— Gaby? That sounds like a girl's name. But he is no girl, are you, my dear fellow? Ah, what a devil he used to be among the waitresses! . . . And my Alma, is she not ten times more beautiful than ever? Answer me that' – and the little man nodded – 'Alma, the child Poppy has had an overwhelming success at the Jingle Club. The highest in the land fell prostrate at her feet. And better yet! This good fellow Gè— Gaby . . . But that can wait. And now, hurrah for the Sun of Austerlitz! Let us drink to Gabriel Chess, and old friendships.'

Gabriel Chess smiled sourly, and said, 'Pistö is very happy.'

'He has a happy disposition,' said Alma.

'He has good cause' – he looked hard at her – '*good* cause.'

'Yes, business has been nice and steady,' she replied.

'I was not thinking of business.'

'And you're going to make a film here?' she asked.

'Yes.'

'A big picture?'

'Quite big. For about a million pounds, a million and a quarter – what does it matter?'

Zobrany asked, 'Will you put Poppy in it? You see, Alma, Gaby discovered a new star this evening –'

'– Who? Poppy?' Alma blinked with astonishment. 'But she's so common and ordinary.'

'Yes,' said Gabriel Chess, taking his cue. 'Who knows if the girl will even survive a screen test? Pistö is talking off the top of his head – he's spitballing.'

'You mean, he lets his enthusiasm run away with him,' said Alma.

'It is a fault of mine,' said Zobrany. 'I always was a romantic – but enough of me. Gaby, you must tell us more about yourself and the cinema business. Alma's great interest in life is films, isn't it, my dear?'

'In that case, Pistö, if Alma is so interested, as you say, then I shall show her how these things are done. If there is any picture she wishes to see, for instance – if there were only one copy left on earth, I could get it and have it shown for her in my private theatre.'

'You see?' Zobrany cried. 'You see, Alma? What did I tell you, darling? He was always the one to give you the shirt off his back!' . . .

It was on this Sunday evening of all Sunday evenings that Tom Henceforth had been smitten with his great inspiration, so that all the scattered fragments of his life seemed to assemble themselves in a solid and thoughtful pattern. He couldn't possibly sit at home while his spirit was throbbing with the joy of his consummation, and so he put on his jacket and walked out into the warm, quiet streets. He walked briskly to Praed Street, cut right into the Edgware Road, almost bolted through the Marylebone Road, doubled into Marylebone High Street and, like a man throwing off pursuers, nipped up New Cavendish Street into Howland Street and ducked into Charlotte Street, reaching the Fitzroy Tavern half an hour before closing time.

A lot of people he knew were there, and among them was a girl named Tessie Oppoport, a fashion artist, whom he hated with a cold and raw hatred; not because she frankly detested him, nor even because she had publicly called him a phoney and a bore. Names could never hurt Tom Henceforth; on the whole, he rather liked them. It was because he knew that she saw through him, and she knew he knew. Her eyes, when she looked at him, were always heavy with understanding and distaste; not tolerance, but resigned acceptance of him as One Of Those Things. He ignored her and went to join a group of his admirers at the far end of the bar. 'How's everything going?' one of them asked.

He replied, 'Well, very well indeed. Well enough to call for a drink.' He put down a pound note and called to the barman, 'Let's have all these again, whatever they are, and make 'em doubles . . . A little celebration is in order, d'you see. When a man has been working on a problem for years, and all of a sudden that problem resolves itself, the years fall away from him. I feel as if I could piss out of the window over the moon!'

'Serge Essenin said that,' said a knowing voice, and there stood Tessie Oppoport, backed by a ginger man in ginger tweeds, with a moustache that might have been an oblong strip of stuff left over from his coat and pasted on to his lip.

'Oh, go away,' said Tom Henceforth.

She said, 'Do let me introduce Bill Rumney – he admires geniuses. Don't you, Bill? He's a writer himself. But unluckily, his stories get published, so he isn't in your class; are you, Bill?'

Tom Henceforth shook hands with the stranger and said, 'Let's see, Rumney. *Will* Rumney, isn't it?'

'That's right. William, actually, but Will's the name I write under.' He smiled shyly.

'Congratulations, Rumney. You're the sort of fellow who's somehow destined to get Discovered – it's a special kind of type. Not too high, not too low; not too clever, not too dumb; but always "sensitive". And "fresh" – always that. They go to Hugh Walpole for "encouragement and advice". If you're the type of fellow one can take to one's club, then one takes you to one's club for lunch – steak-and-kidney pie and a pint of bitter in a silver tankard at the Garrick. If you're not really *quite*, one takes you to the Café Royal and treats you to the three-and-sixpenny five-courser. Then one gives you a letter to Jonathan Cape, and you're off. If you click, Walpole or whoever-it-is gets the kudos. It used to be the Garnetts – before them it was Arnold Bennett, before Bennett it was Ford Madox Ford. I've read a few of your stories, Rumney. There was one particularly sensitive one about a man who wants to murder his wife, but is prevented by the sight of a mouse caught in a teeny-weeny trap. It was sensitive as all hell, and I cried for days. Do you get a living out of it, for Christ's sake?'

Rumney said apologetically, 'No, I'm afraid not. I have . . .' (he hated to say it) '. . . I have a regular job.'

'Selling cricket bats and motor bikes? You look as if you'd be just the man to sell cricket bats and motor bikes.'

'No, I'm in the Civil Service, I'm afraid; at the Central Office of Information.'

'Now stand back, Bill,' Tessie Oppoport said, 'and you'll hear what Genius has got to say about that.'

'I envy you,' said Tom Henceforth.

'Hold tight,' she said, 'Henceforth has been memorizing all the brilliant conversations in Aldous Huxley. Hold your horses, a Paraphrase is coming!'

'If I had a harp,' said Tom Henceforth, in high good humour, 'I'd improvise a bloody epic about it:

> *'The Ministry to which brave Rumney went*
> *Was like a privy in a tenement,*
> *Spattered with muck of twenty different hues,*
> *Stopped up with pages of forgotten news,*
> *Where men too dead of nose and eye to heed*
> *The stench and darkness, sit them down to read.*
> *Let frantic tenants kick the door and shout!*
> *They squat; stale news goes in, stale air comes out . . .*

'I could go on for hours.'

'No, he couldn't,' Tessie Oppoport said. 'It's probably taken him months to make those few lines up. Your name happens to have two syllables, so he fitted it in. Like the time he pretended to improvise a poem about Sylvine Tamrodt, the time Fritz hit him in the face. It's all right if you want to hit him, Bill.'

'No, no, not a bit,' said Rumney, 'I think it's very good.'

'It's a feeble imitation of Pope,' said she. 'But about Fritz Tamrodt. He's in the money – he's going to direct a picture for Gabriel Chess. How d'you like that, Henceforth? By the way, you pretend to know Gabriel Chess, don't you?'

'Is that something to pretend about?'

'Of course it is. You never met Chess in your life, and you know it.'

Tom Henceforth said, 'This girl is trying to rib me. She's trying to get the nail in under my back hair. Try it on your Great Portland Street rag merchants, Jaël; don't try it on me . . . I didn't know Chess was in England.'

'I saw him not half an hour ago at Steve Zobrany's,' Tessie Oppoport said. 'The pub's closing. Why don't we all go over there and have some coffee? You know Chess, my foot! Come on, then, and let's see the reunion of the Genius Who Arrived and the One That Missed The Bus. Or are you scared, Henceforth?'

He kept his temper and his tongue under control. (Never draw a weapon, at close quarters, on somebody who is competent to take it away from you.) She continued, 'Bill, the stories Henceforth tells about himself and Gabriel Chess would just about kill you. And Erabella Luna. In Manchester. Eh, Henceforth? Only apparently it wasn't in Manchester, and they were three different people of different names. And he didn't make it, he lost it.'

'Tessie,' said Tom Henceforth, very gently, 'if you keep on at me like this in public, everybody'll know, if they haven't already guessed it, that you're hot under the whiskers for me.'

'Much good it'd do me if I were,' she said.

'No good at all; you try hard, Tessie, but you don't attract me.'

'Much good it'd do you if I did, darling.'

He said, 'When these dames fail to make a man, they invariably imply that he must be either impotent or a homosexual.'

She replied, 'Even that poor crack he has to steal from Somerset Maugham! Come on, Bill; don't bother to argue with him. Can't you see that he's a Genius? Geniuses are always jealous of anybody who gets something published. He's jealous of you.'

'Not on account of the mistresses you pick up in the boozers around here, at all events,' Tom Henceforth said to Rumney.

'Look here,' said Rumney, 'aren't you going just a little bit too far?'

The barman shouted, 'Time, gentlemen, please!' A bell rang. 'Finish your drinks, gentlemen – time, gentlemen, *please*!'

Tom Henceforth grinned at Tessie Oppoport and said, 'You were saved by the bell that time' – then, to his friends, 'Come on, let's go to Zobrany's . . .'

As they left, Rumney asked Tessie, 'Ought I to have hit him?'

She said, 'No, of course not . . . Look, they're going to Zobrany's. Let's catch a taxi and get there first – we might see some fun.' They got there in ten minutes, and were sipping their coffee and eating Italian pastry when Tom Henceforth arrived with two men and two girls and took a table by the window. Zobrany, Alma and Gabriel Chess were in animated conversation at the Proprietor's Table near the counter.

'And is Marlene Dietrich really as beautiful as she's supposed to be?' Alma was asking.

Gabriel Chess said, 'Yes, she is, but you are more beautiful.'

'You're having fun with us,' said Alma. Zobrany had never seen her so keenly alive, so radiantly animated; he rubbed his hands with pleasure.

'Fun? I never have fun –'

'– And Greta Garbo?'

'To my mind, she is not beautiful. She has talent, yes, but emotionally she has no real *Schmelzpunkt* – no sexual melting point. Genius, yes. But you were talking of beauty . . . Pistö, Steve, do you know that your wife is *perfectly* beautiful?'

'*I* know,' said Zobrany. 'You hear, Alma? This one is an expert – he has seen them all, the most beautiful in the world. Eh, Gaby?'

'All. And I have scarcely ever seen one who did not need certain improvements. But I give you my sacred word of honour that to so much as touch you with a pencil would be a *Schlimmbesserung* – a redundant correction – the addition of a blemish to something finished.'

'You hear that, Alma? What have I always told you?' said Zobrany.

'And I will prove this to you,' said Gabriel Chess. 'I shall have Nullamanca make photographs of your head, and you shall see yourself as you actually are – because when you look at yourself in the mirror you see yourself turned left-to-right. Steve, you will allow me to make pictures of Alma?'

'Allow? But of course!'

'It shall be done. And in a week, two weeks, I shall show you how Chess works. Yes?'

'I must make time and get away, if only for a few hours,' said Zobrany. 'But Alma is free, whenever she wishes.'

Then Zobrany looked up and said, 'But here is a gentleman you should know, my dear Gaby. A man of great talent. I believe you met him once in Manchester.'

The word *Manchester* to Gabriel Chess was as the snapping of a twig to a hunted man on a dark night in a forest. He coiled himself tight, released his safety catch, and kept still.

'My dear Henceforth, where have you been hiding yourself? I have a surprise for you, a wonderful surprise – a dear old friend of mine,' Zobrany went on. 'Come, greet him.' A silence fell, as Tom Henceforth loomed over the little man.

'Well, well, well,' he said, feigning surprise, 'the Baron himself! How are you, Baron?'

Gabriel Chess said, 'I beg pardon?' and stared up at him with eyes of stone.

'Mr Henceforth,' said Zobrany.

'What Henceforth? Baron? What Baron?'

'We met in Manchester, if you remember,' said Tom Henceforth, with a sidelong smirk.

'I think not,' said Gabriel Chess coldly, 'I have never been in Manchester in my life.' His voice had the carrying power of a watchman's rattle. 'I do not know this gentleman. Who is this gentleman, Steve?'

'Come off it,' said Tom Henceforth. 'I introduced you to Era Moon, and you know it.'

'Era Moon,' said Gabriel Chess, 'was the maiden name of my wife.

It is not for the rabble who read the fan magazines to insult us by claiming acquaintance with her or with me. The hacks are free to write what they like, and it is the privilege of the Mob to read it. This person is not the first screen-struck maniac to make the ex-Mrs Chess, or myself, the subject of sick fantasy and filthy dreams. It is for this reason that a man in my position is compelled to remain unseen, Steve. But I took it into my head that the common people of this country were more restrained in their manners . . . Or it may be,' he added, more kindly, 'that you are under a misapprehension. Somebody impersonated me, and said to you, "I am So-and-so," and you were taken in. Excuse me. I do not know you. We have never met. This meeting is our first, and I trust our last. I have not yet had occasion to visit the city of Manchester –'

'– And Preston, you don't remember him? And the Grand Canal Hotel? And Samoon?'

'Samoon . . . Grand Canal . . . Preston? I'm sorry. You are in error. You link a name with a name, and you study my photographs in the illustrated magazines until you convince yourself that you know me personally. Thus' – Chess turned to Zobrany – 'thus virgins five thousand miles away get with child by Clark Gable. The man is infatuated, under a delusion.'

Tom Henceforth stared at him. Gabriel Chess stared back. A leopard escaped from a zoo may think itself dangerous – until it comes face to face with one fresh from the jungle.

'You bloody little scoundrel!' was all Tom Henceforth could say.

Zobrany said. 'No, really, Mr Henceforth – you must sit down, really you must. Please!'

Gabriel Chess looked pained. Henceforth cried, 'You unmitigated little liar! I'll get you for this! I'll –'

'– It is the influence of these Warner Brothers gangster films,' said Chess, 'only he is forgetting his lines. They should be said between the teeth: "I'll get you for this if it's the last thing I ever do." The fellow is demented. Next thing, he will write letters threatening to kidnap Shirley Temple. But they are not criminal types,' he said to Alma, 'only disturbed. One should not be angry, only sorry. It is not punishment they need, but therapy.'

'By Christ Jesus I'll murder the bloody little bastard!' Henceforth started forward, but Zobrany held him back with one hand, effortlessly, as he might have held back a swinging door.

'I am sorry to see you like this,' he said. 'You really had better go home now, my dear Henceforth. Now please do.' And Tom Henceforth might have gone, then, without further incident, if he had not happened to notice Tessie Oppoport biting her lip to suppress a laugh. Then, indignation turning to blind rage, he went berserk . . .

Tom Henceforth slapped Zobrany's hand aside and leapt at Chess's throat. Zobrany caught him by the collar and dragged him back, instinctively catching him by the slack of the trousers with the other hand; and having grasped Tom Henceforth like this, there was nothing to do with him except to run him out of doors.

Tessie Oppoport explained later that she burst into a peal of laughter, not at Henceforth's humiliation, but because of the expression on Zobrany's face – 'It was just as if he was an ambassador trying to pretend he hasn't noticed a king farting,' she said.

But that laugh lashed Tom Henceforth into frenzy. He yelled to his companions, 'Come on, smash him – you cowardly lot of dogs!'

'Better not,' said Zobrany, as they rose to follow him. Then he had Tom Henceforth out in the court. 'Go,' he said, 'go home,' and pushed him.

Staggering backwards, Henceforth trod on a beer bottle which somebody had dropped in the gutter. He spun wildly, like a man shot through the heart, and fell with a wild shriek. His friends were with him, now; they helped him to his feet and one of them picked up the bottle and handed it to him. He hurled it at Zobrany's head. The bottle flew high, and Zobrany heard the sharp crack of its impact on the wooden cherub over the door, before it rebounded, ringing and smashed on the cobblestones.

'Vandal!' Zobrany shouted; and, catching Tom Henceforth by the breast of his coat, slapped his head as one cuffs an obstreperous urchin.

But then the boldest of Henceforth's friends, a burly young man with a red beard, threw an arm about Zobrany's neck and drove a knee into the small of his back, while Henceforth, counter-attacking from the front, leapt upon him with the dry, crackling, bloodless, leggy frenzy of a praying mantis. Zobrany reached back over his shoulder, and his desperately groping hand found a beard, which he gripped with all his might. His elbow, coming up, took Tom Henceforth under the chin, and knocked him down.

The bearded man howled and disengaged his arm from Zobrany's throat to pummel him about the kidneys with both fists, while another man, attacking from the left flank, tried to gouge one of his eyes out with a persevering thumb. Henceforth, up again, hooked himself to Zobrany's lapels and went to work with his bony knees. But eyes and testicles are not as vulnerable as they are made out to be by the theoreticians of rough-and-tumble; and neither are solar plexuses, the buttons of jaws, Adam's apples, the nerves at the side of the neck, or the weak part at the base of the skull. Indeed, the more textbook science people put into unrehearsed rough-housing, the less damage they are likely to do, even when they are three against one.

The would-be gouger went flying out of the fight when one of Zobrany's ponderous, unscientific forearms came down like a flail upon his nose; and the kidney puncher, suffering acutely in his right foot, upon which one of Zobrany's heels had come down with two hundred and twenty pounds behind it, was clutching his intended victim to save himself from falling; Zobrany had caught Tom Henceforth by one ankle, and wouldn't let go, while he, his rage almost spent, ridiculously hopping on his free foot, sobbed to the third of his cronies, 'Paul, Paul, you yellow-gutted bastard, lend a hand here!'

But the man called Paul – one of those huge-boned, bull-shouldered, deadly looking fellows, who growl and glower like wild animals but wouldn't hurt a fly – stood, irresolute.

And it was Paul's hard luck that, at this moment, Poppy and Ody, returning in triumph from the Jingle Club, came into Masham Court.

It seemed to Poppy that this luckless giant, standing with his enormous hands raised in dismay, was poised to deliver some bone-cracking *coup de grâce*. Leaping, she struck like a wildcat, from midair, with all four limbs at once, and tore him down.

Ody, meanwhile, engaged the bearded man, who backed away saying, 'No, wait a minute, wait a minute – no, look here, wait a minute –'

Henceforth, his ankle suddenly released, sat heavily on the pavement.

Zobrany gasped, 'Poppy! Stop it at once! . . . Somebody hold her – she'll kill the man!' She was sitting on Paul's chest and hammering his forehead with the heel of one of her shoes – briskly, but without hurry, like a carpenter driving tenpenny nails.

'Are you all right?' she asked.

'Yes. Stop that at once,' said Zobrany.

'Why, Henceforth!' cried Ody. 'What the hell's all this?'

'Mind your own dirty stinking business,' said Henceforth, rising. His coat was torn and his lip was bleeding. The gouger's nose was bleeding. Paul's head was bleeding. The bearded man was limping heavily. Everybody seemed to be more or less damaged, except Zobrany.

He said, catching his breath, 'Really, once in a while this kind of thing is good for the glands.'

'I'll be back –' Tom Henceforth began.

'– You had better not,' said Zobrany. 'Go with your friends, and never come back.'

Tom Henceforth glanced towards the entrance to the court. The bearded man was following the other two out in to the street.

'I'll come back and pull your filthy coffee shop about your ears, you mongrel bastard son of a bitch.'

'What *is* this?' Ody asked.

'You'll find out, you dirty little pink-eyed eavesdropper!' said Tom Henceforth, walking away.

'Ain't 'e lovely, that toerag?' said Poppy. 'What's itching 'im, anyway? Did somebody mention Perp, or what?'

'No,' said Zobrany. 'He just met Gabriel Chess, and *pouf*.'

'Hello! Look at this,' said Ody, stooping. He picked up a bit of carved wood. The thrown bottle had snapped off that portion of the cherub's anatomy which had been its most conspicuously comical feature.

Carrying it back in the palm of his hand, Zobrany held it out and said, with tears in his voice, 'Alma, look what that ill-disposed fellow has done to me!'

'Never mind,' she said. 'You can have it mended.'

'It is a bad omen,' said Zobrany.

Glue and a rivet repaired the damage. But none of Tom Henceforth's acquaintances saw him again: that archway might have been a hole in the wall of the world, a disposal outlet. He disappeared. He was not destined to remain unheard-of for long, though . . .

TWENTY-THREE

Although they appeared to be motivated by irreconcilable ideals, the editors of the *Socialist Tactician* and the *Occidental* were so alike in practical fundamentals that Tom Henceforth found it relaxing to converse first with one and then with the other, both in the course of a couple of hours. He could go on putting out, or listening to, a similar ideological line in two different cadences, with little but a change of terminology to distract him.

Accepting his latest parable – a really mordant one, about a blind man accidentally locked up in a home for deaf-mutes – the editor of the *Tactician*, a jolly little fellow with a terrific laugh, advanced him three pounds and talked merrily of the European situation. 'Of course,' said he, 'Hitler'll move against Poland, and then the balloon goes up. Britain's *got* to put up a show, and she'll put up a damn good show. Then, when Uncle Joe has finished with Finland and tidied up, he'll tear up the Pact, and we save Western Europe.'

'The Japs can hold the Yanks in the Pacific for five years,' said Tom Henceforth. 'Their seaboard cities are vulnerable as all hell. And Germany has England licked before they start.'

'Britain can't fight Germany. With what? With how many planes, how many tanks? With what army? But she'll fight hard, damned hard. However, let the Yanks come in. Let 'em! They can't fight an efficient war on a Pacific *and* a European front. It's Our war, this time; it's Our war.'

'When d'you guess the whistle blows?' Tom Henceforth asked.

'When Hitler moves against Poland, he'll strike westward at the same time. By Spring 1940 is our guess.'

'Don't forget Musso: Italy's bound to come in.'

'Well, yes, of course; but not until Hitler has broken Britain's back by air attack. Italy's too vulnerable from the sea, and the Navy's strong here, remember; up to a point.'

'Chamberlain has to go, of course. Who's next?'

'Why, Churchill, of course! Churchill, for a gallant balls-up of a co-allied war effort, every time! They'll be all for him at first, of course. Come the fireworks, they'll remember the Dardanelles. Britain hasn't got an air force, and it's a known fact – we've proved it mathematically – that London can't stand up to a concentrated bombardment from the air. Five hundred tons of TNT well placed must paralyse the city. And the Jerries are certain to use gas – there's no chance of British retaliation, don't you see. It'll be short and sweet. But Britain'll put up a show, a damn good show, mind you . . .'

Tom Henceforth said, 'As long as somebody hangs Hitler, everybody'll be happy: it amounts to just about that.'

'Just about that.'

It was only a short walk from the *Tactician* office in Bedford Row to the office of the *Occidental* in High Holborn, and there the editor said to him '. . . Of course, you know and I know that the Hitler–Stalin Non-Aggression Pact is all my eye and Betty Martin. We aren't complete fools, I hope?'

He was a lean, sharp little man, with a clipped moustache of white sand and grey sand upon which you might have filed your nails, and horrified blue eyes. 'We can't fight Germany,' he went on, 'and we won't, and everybody knows it. War talk's a lot of Jew-Communist eyewash. If we'd meant war we'd be ready for war. That stands to reason. The real menace is Russia, and we know it. We stay neutral and let Germany mop up as far as the Polish border. Later, an Anglo-German Alliance, and two empires against Russia. The Yanks'll keep their noses out of it: they've got the Japs to watch; and in any case, the great mass of the American people are for us – fed up to the teeth with Jew Capitalism and the Yid Rosenfelt. So let's not worry for now.'

'What do we do if Germany invades Poland?'

'Same as we did when Germany walked into Czechoslovakia.'

'Or France?'

'No need for Germany to invade France. The Froggies are bought and sold, and the Maginot Line's wide open – this is a matter of fact. Occupy the industrial areas. Quiet capitulation. We might – we just *might* – be talked into putting up a show of resistance to another German move in Europe. A jolly good show, if at all, mind you; but a token show. Then Stalin's bound to tear up that Pact, and we'll have unity. Once the fun starts it'll be short and sweet, and very, very unsentimental, my boy! Just for once it'll be a People's War, a White Men's War – Our War. Our Peace, too . . . By the by, I've got good news for you.'

'What's that?'

'Want a holiday in the Black Forest?'

'The way I feel at the moment, I'd take a holiday in the Black Hole of Calcutta.'

'Forster's down with jaundice, and can't go to Stuttgart. How'd you like to cover the Greater German Art Festival? All your expenses, and fifty guineas.'

'When do I leave?'

'End of this week . . . I thought you'd be pleased. Do you speak any German?'

'A few phrases.'

'That's all you need. They'll give you the time of your life – eats, drinks, girls, everything. Incidentally; have you ever done any public speaking?'

'No. Why?'

'You have a wonderful voice for a microphone.'

Tom Henceforth laughed and said, 'I've heard it on a recording gadget. And girls have told me it's seductive – put me in a home for blind girls, and I'd leave no virgin unbroached.'

'I can imagine . . . Your passport all right?'

'Haven't got one. I'll have to get one.'

'If there's any trouble, we can expedite it through the Embassy, so long as you have a birth certificate.'

'I *was* born. At Gillingham, as a matter of fact. Registered in the usual way; name of Hardy. Thomas Hardy. Not wishing to be confused with the author of *The Dynasts* and *The Mayor of Casterbridge* . . . you know how people are. You say your name's Cooper: they ask, "Are you any relation to Gary Cooper?" That kind of thing.'

'That's all right, then. We'll give you some nice letters of introduction . . .'

And thus it came about that, early in August 1939, when he came back to London for reassignment, Ody received from Stuttgart a novelty postcard of a clown who rolled his eyes when shaken, with the message:

HAVING A WONDERFUL TIME

TH

And so Tom Henceforth was: here, from all over the English-speaking world, were literate men and women who had never heard his stories before. His scabrous anecdotes of English life and *mores* were received with uninhibited glee; and their laughter was infectious, even if there hadn't been something humorous in the very sound of his voice – let alone his facial contortions and his grotesquely graphic gestures – so that even those who could not understand a word he said joined in the laughter he provoked and enjoyed his company without knowing exactly why.

They treated him to fresh peaches in brandy globes of iced Rhine wine, cold golden beer in lidded pots as tall and ornate as Gothic spires, a dozen different kinds of schnapps, every glass of which had the twang and recoil of a crossbow. Within a few days, he was a central figure in The Schiller Café, The Albrecht Dürer Restaurant and The Neckar.

Women became infatuated with him, singly and in groups; among them a drawing teacher from Dusseldorf with the curiously un-German name of Margarete Tholefeud. Her father's family, she said, had fled Roxburghshire in 1775. She was twenty-eight years old, five feet eleven inches tall, and of a beauty indescribably compounded of the earthy and the spiritual.

There was nothing Era Moonish about this woman – none of your pearls-and-ether ectoplasm here, but something chryselephantine, pure gold and solid ivory. She had breasts like eight-inch shells (Tom Henceforth said) with nipples like contact detonators . . . When the time came for him to explore them, he compared other portions of her anatomy with nectarines, fresh-cut muskmelons, burst apricots, and everything he could think of that was at once animal, vegetable and mineral; befurred, succulent and gemlike. He avoided her at first, not liking a certain wild, lost look in her great grey eyes. Also, she talked too much.

'Making love to Margarete,' he said, before he had tried it, 'would be like being hungry and having soup fed to you with a teaspoon, while you were forced to make conversation at the same time.'

The morning after the third night he spent with her, Tom Henceforth awoke to a new sensation: there was no way to describe it except as a tumescence of the heart, a feeling of being young, an awareness of feeling happy.

He was in love.

She, opening her strange, wild eyes, told him that she worshipped him, would follow him to the ends of the earth, starve for him, beg in the streets for him and die for him. Even when she added that it was not so much his body as his 'consummate intellect' which she loved, his rapture persisted. He said, 'Let's go away somewhere quiet. Let's go into the Black Forest, and find a cabin, or a quiet inn, and stay there for a while. Then – if you want to – we can go back to England; get married, if that would please you. Actually, my sweet, if I put my mind to it I can make a perfectly good living –'

'– What do I care about living, perfectly good or perfectly bad? You shall write your beautiful poem, and I will work for you. This is love! The poets are right. Nothing else matters.'

'Not even the Führer?' he asked.

She sealed his lips with her hand and said, 'Hush!'

So they went away into the forest, where they found a pleasant inn on a hill overlooking a waterfall. And suddenly Tom Henceforth discovered that he could work. Several times in the course of every day, she would ask him if he was sure he was quite happy, doubting whether she was good enough for him. Occasionally she awoke him in the middle of the night to ask the same question.

He invariably replied, 'Perhaps I'm too happy. I'm not used to it. It shakes me. I'm beginning to forgive all my enemies. I'm even starting to feel kindly towards myself!'

'I, too, am afraid that this is too wonderful to last.'

'I'll have to go back soon. But it doesn't matter, so long as you're coming with.'

He had nothing to give her but a tiny netsuke, depicting a Japanese beggar with a little dog on his shoulder, which he had picked up one dawn in the Caledonian Market. She gave him an old signet ring, with the worn device of a fist gripping a dirk, and the half-obliterated words *Hac Lege*.

'It was my great-great-great-great-grandfather's,' she said. 'Wear it.'

'"By this law", eh?' he said, brandishing an imaginary dagger. 'Good! . . . Now let's go and look at the waterfall, and say all kinds of nice things to each other . . .'

Their idyll lasted twenty days. Then Great Britain declared war on Germany. Two men in plainclothes came to the inn, and one of them said to Tom Henceforth, 'You are under arrest. Come.' The other said to Margarete, 'You, too.'

'May I ask what for?' Tom Henceforth asked.

'No, you may not.'

'Shall I pack my bag?'

'No.'

'If I resist, I'll be shot, I suppose?'

'If you resist, you will be carried. Come.'

'Not shot?'

'No.'

'Pity . . .'

The officer into whose presence Tom Henceforth was at last conducted was an affable, almost apologetic gentleman, hard-soft in texture and opaquely colourless, who spoke nearly faultless English.

He invited Tom Henceforth to sit down, and offered him coffee, saying, 'Major Harbinger gives a good account of you, Mr Hardy.'

'I am flattered.'

'Your contributions to the *Occidental* were well received here. Dr Goebbels himself read them with approval.'

'I'm delighted.'

'And yet, you know, under the pseudonym of "Shchedrinson", you wrote some quite amusing pieces for the *Socialist Tactician*. I wonder why?'

'Do you? I don't. It makes no difference to me who pays me a few guineas for a thousand words.'

'You wrote exclusively for money, then?'

'And my own amusement.'

'It amused you, then, to be on both sides of the fence, Mr Hardy?'

'Yes.'

'Might this be described, perhaps, as a condition of spiritual desperation, Mr Hardy? Let us be civilized . . .'

'It might better be described as no condition at all, Mr – ?'

'– Colonel Grau. You are not a Communist, I believe?'

'No.'

'Nor a National Socialist, I think?'

'No.'

'Yet democracy you find pitiful?'

'I do.'

'The Will of the People means nothing to you?'

'The People have no will, and the Voice of the People is a babble. The Voice of God on a sofa.'

'You believe in God, then? Even a delirious God?'

'No. I was talking in metaphors.'

'Do you believe that Britain may win this war?'

'No.'

'Will Germany?'

'Yes.'

'Why?'

'Germany's stronger.'

'You believe, then, that the race is to the swift and the battle to the strong?'

'I believe that the conqueror's prize is dust and lost endeavour –'

'– You borrowed that from John Masefield. Mr Hardy, you are a terrible man! Do you not even believe in yourself? . . . Why do you hesitate?'

'I was about to say no.'

'But you did not say no. Why not? Could it be because you are in love, Mr Hardy?'

'I didn't answer your question.'

'Yet you are in love, Mr Hardy?'

'No.'

'Tell me frankly, do you say no because you believe that we might try to influence you by threatening to hurt Margarete Tholefeud?'

'Perhaps.'

'So that, in fact, you are in love with this young woman?'

'Yes.'

'You care what happens to her, but not what may happen to you, eh?'

'I never have cared what happened to me.'

'But you must, since the worst thing that could happen to the young woman would be for her to stand by helpless while something terrible happened to you,' said Colonel Grau, looking at a sheet of paper. 'Let us see. Your name is Thomas Hardy. You were born in Gillingham, Kent . . . and so on, and so forth. Father, Edmund Thomas Hardy, schoolteacher; mother, Winifred Gooch, a grocer's daughter. As a child you were precociously clever; won Junior County Scholarship at age eleven; at sixteen won the Davidson Prize for Art. Since which time, it would appear, you have simply gone to the dogs.'

'I felt so this morning when I came here, but I was too polite to say so.'

'You have courage to joke with me just now, Mr Hardy.'

'Perhaps.'

'I suggest that you are this kind of man, Mr Hardy: you hate whatever is, whenever it is, wherever you may chance to find yourself. Is this not so?'

Tom Henceforth said, 'If it makes you happy to generalize, go on and generalize.'

'I should advise you that my happiness is not your concern just now, Mr Hardy. Let us talk of you, rather. You are a funny fellow – you were endowed with mass, dimensions, life; and yet you have chosen to be blown about here and there like a dead leaf.'

'You borrowed that from Verlaine, Colonel Grau. I have chosen to be blown where I pleased. I have a penchant for the ridiculous side of things.'

'There are other sides. And the leaf does not choose the wind.'

'Suffering Jesus!' said Tom Henceforth, laughing. 'Have I been brought here to talk metaphysics? We could have done that more comfortably in a beer cellar.'

'No, not to talk metaphysics, Mr Hardy. Not metaphysics. Tell me, do you find Miss Tholefeud ridiculous, also, because she believes that you have a godlike soul?'

'Did she say that?'

'My dear Mr Hardy, we have a recording of your intimate conversations for the past three weeks' – the Colonel touched a folder – 'transcribed. I'm sorry, but . . .' He shrugged.

Tom Henceforth, feeling himself blushing, touched his glowing cheeks and said, 'This is physics – I can't help it any more than neon can help going red when the current is switched on . . . Yes, I *do* find Miss Tholefeud ridiculous because she believes I have a godlike soul. Well?'

'And yourself?'

'Myself? Ridiculous, because I like to hear her say it, and there is no God and no soul.'

'Mr Hardy, when I sit here and contemplate you, I feel a horror – I see a vortex, a nothingness.'

'That's very likely. I always did hold myself up as a kind of mirror for whatever company I happened to find myself in.'

'Good! I asked for that. Nevertheless, better men than you have swung for such witticisms, Mr Hardy.'

'I couldn't care less.'

'Yes, I know. Would you like some brandy?'

'If you like.'

The Colonel brought out a decanter, and called for fresh coffee. 'Why did you not continue your studies?' he asked.

'One man starts out to be a painter and ends up on one side of a desk,' he said. 'Another starts out to be a painter and ends on the other' – he pointed to the photograph of Hitler hanging on the wall at Colonel Grau's back. 'Why not come to the point? What is it you want of me?'

'Just to look and see – you know, Mr Hardy, when you are not laconic, as you are now, you have an easy wit and an excellent command of the English language. Also, we have analysed your voice. It is a persuasive voice: it soothes, it carries one with it, it pleases. If you will co-operate with us, we can employ you.'

'In what way?'

'Broadcasting in English on our senders.'

'And if I won't co-operate?'

'We will not have you shot, as you hope. Neither, as you hope, will you be tortured. You have nothing to tell us that we don't know already. If you will not co-operate, you shall be provided for: I can guarantee you about a litre of soup and a half kilo of bread – *pourvu que ça dure* – in a civilian internment camp. Co-operate, and you will be made comfortable and paid a salary – you may live, in fact, like a privileged official.'

'And the woman, Miss Tholefeud?'

'What do you mean?'

'As a matter of curiosity, what happens to her if I decide I don't want to co-operate? I suppose,' said Tom Henceforth, with his most offensive grin, 'I suppose you send her to a concentration camp?'

'No, not at all. She will merely have been guilty of indiscretion in her choice of company, in that she chose an enemy alien for a lover. Certainly, she would no longer be fit to teach art to our German youth. But she would be ever so far from being your immediate concern, in that case; or you hers . . . believe me, Mr Hardy, ever so far from it! . . . I should like to prolong this conversation indefinitely, but time is not mine to command.'

'You've been doing all the conversing, you know. If I say "It's a deal," what happens then?'

'Then you're committed. You're one of us. If the British catch you, they'll hang you up by the neck. But confess, now, Mr Hardy you've always hated the laws you had to abide by; even the law of self-preservation was intolerable to you; isn't that so? Now you graduate from the cafés – you live! Why do you look so grave? Are you a Kipling patriot at heart after all?'

'No. I was just thinking.'

'– That if, let us say, it chanced that we who have the pleasure of your company happened to be bright red Bolsheviks, or pink Social Democrats, or red-and-black Anarchist-Syndicalists or what not, your answer would still be the same?'

'Yes . . . only I want Margarete, remember.'

'That will be quite all right. Would you like some more brandy?'

'Thanks.'

So there came upon the air from the tremendous radio transmitters of Nazi Germany a voice which, announcing itself as 'The Voice Of Common Sense Calling From Between The Lines', held hundreds of thousands of listeners spellbound.

This voice, slow and full of good humour, beautifully rounded and reassuringly low-pitched, authoritative and soothing as the voice of a beast-tamer, had a wonderful variety of timbres and expressions, every one of which rang true. Men visualized the unseen speaker as a big-built, broad-faced, pipe-smoking fellow, handy with his fists but difficult to arouse to anger; easy to get along with but hell on wheels in a fight – a mediatory character of the 'Let's talk this over, over a pint, before we make an issue of it' type – a thoughtful handicapper of horses and dogs, a shrewd calculator (but never a big winner) in the football pools; a levelheaded moderate and an all-round decent sort. And yet there was a quality in his voice which made women think of Charles Boyer: 'It's not *what* he says, it's the *way* that he says it.' They agreed, with the men, that he deserved to be hanged as a dirty traitor; still, they listened to him. 'He always comes out with something interesting,' they said . . .

'. . . Now you know, and all the world knows, that the British people never wanted this war. Because, don't you see, if you'd wanted it, you'd have been prepared for it, wouldn't you? But you weren't, you know, and you aren't, and you won't have time to be prepared. In your heart of hearts you never dreamt of yourselves at war with Germany – not again! So you let your politicians catch you unawares, with scarcely a tank or an aeroplane to your name; and so all your generals have to boast of, to date, is a retreat from Dunkirk . . . I'm not telling you anything you don't know already, am I? This will be cleaning-parade time in the army camps, just about now. I hope you enjoyed your tea, boys. You'll find it harder to come by, I'm afraid, as Germany tightens the submarine blockade, and dear old Winnie learns – he's a Character, isn't he, though? – that all those fine grey battleships that look so heart-lifting as they smash through heavy seas in the newsreels, are vulnerable as cardboard boxes from the air and from under water. But where was I? Oh yes . . . Take a good look, will you, at the arms you're burnishing for tomorrow's parades. They're pretty rifles to drill with, the Short Lee-Enfields, Mark III – because they've been polished and burnished for twenty years. Look at the date stamped on the breech of your rifle, and if it's later than 1918, I'll eat my hat. I hate to have to say it, but those arms of yours, against modern German precision weapons, will prove to be – have already proved to be – as picturesque and as useless as old Brown Bess . . . So you must see that your leaders never meant to fight Germany, and don't seriously intend to fight Germany now – that what you are led to believe is total war against Germany is nothing but a show of war. And as per usual, the common man is the sucker, and he goes slogging along while his leaders in England are hoping and praying for allies to come along and help them out with arms and supplies that you, the taxpayer, will have to fork out for . . . Oh, and while you're about it, you might look to the dates stamped on your company commanders, too. If they are young, they know no more of soldiering than the rawest rookie in your barracks. If they're not young, they got – and have forgotten – what little experience they ever had, twenty years ago, in a war that bears as little relation to modern warfare as the Crimean War. They are either old men with old ideas, or young men with no ideas – for while Germany, struggling for life, studied warfare as an art and a science, your officers were either retired and playing golf and bridge, or at school and playing tennis . . . Oh, I beg pardon there *was* a certain amount of warlike exercise with guns, when your officers fired birdshot at pheasants and grouse. I forgot that . . . And now we are forced to bomb your cities . . .'

'The common touch,' said Ody bitterly, listening to Zobrany's radio. 'Golf, bridge and tennis: gentlemen's games. Not football and cricket. That makes it an upper-class sort of war, you see. The swine! And that part about the rifles, et cetera, is true – that's the hell of it.'

'I always did say, knowing the Germans,' said Zobrany, 'that it was foolish to give Von Seeckt the pick of Ludendorff's and Hoffmann's forces to make a hundred-thousand-man Germany Army of. It was like giving him a hundred thousand officers and drill sergeants. So every walking club and *Turnverein* became a military training unit, and every touring society became a training school for foreign service. And with cameras, too. No, really! . . . And that man really is Tom Henceforth?'

'Is there any mistaking the voice?'

'It's possible to be mistaken.'

'Anyway, my old newspaper will be giving it out. I gave them the break. You know I had recorded some of his witty talk on wire, God help me! I turned the spools over to the Monitors – it's Thomas Hardy *alias* Henceforth, all right . . . You know, I feel myself partly to blame, somehow; I gave him moral support and – I wouldn't mention it, except as something to kick myself for – I helped him out of more than one hole with money.'

'So did I,' said Zobrany, 'and a long time ago I picked him up out of the gutter when he was on the verge of killing himself. I would have done it for my enemy's dog, although it had bitten me. I couldn't help it. Must I reproach myself? What is a man to do? If people were made to calculate odds, all babies would be strangled at birth. The end isn't yet, Ody, not yet.'

'He's hellishly clever,' said Ody. 'I've never known him more so – that broadcast the other night, when he said that people are only human after all, and men away from home in the Army mustn't expect their wives to be faithful to them: that was a stinker! Most people listen and laugh. Then they read cases in the papers, and they brood. Men's morale suffers. I wish to God they wouldn't listen.'

Zobrany said, 'One must listen, because one *can* listen. One listens if only in order to say to oneself, "Here, at least, I have the right to listen" – which is good for the morale.'

'Get something else, Steve, will you?'

'Very well.'

'Morale. I could use a little of that, Steve.'

'Don't talk like that, my dear fellow. You are pining over Poppy – I am pining over Poppy. Everybody misses Poppy. Gaby Chess has torn the hair out of his head over Poppy. Much good that!'

'I wish that little rat had torn his bloody head off,' said Ody.

'Now why talk like that? Put yourself in Chess's position, my dear Ody.' Ody laughed hollowly. Zobrany went on, 'You are a great man, famous. Ten thousand beautiful women would gladly make carpets of themselves for you to walk on –'

'– Oh, pooey!'

'No, Ody, not pooey; sober truth. So. You have your pick of the beauty queens of the universe, but you say, "No, I will make a film star of this little waitress –'

'– Who happens to have more looks, vitality and talent than –'

'– Shush! All this is granted. But think of the talent walking the world unrecognized, and think of Poppy's luck. You – Gabriel Chess – say to her, "You shall be taught all you don't know and vetted for stardom, and for two years I will pay you fifty pounds a week while you learn how to make the most of yourself." "All right," says Poppy, and signs the document. She is taught to dress and all that. She benefits by all you have to offer her. And then, a few months later, when you are ready to put her to work, she says, "Ta-ta", and tears up her contract, and goes off to the wars.'

'Having incidentally torn *me* up with a "Sorry, Ody, let's call it off for now,"' said Ody.

'Whatever you do, my dear fellow, for God's sake don't be bitter!'

'Steve, you are the most God-fearing bloody atheist I ever came across in all my born days.'

'I am an atheist by God's grace, like I am an anarchist under democracy,' said Zobrany, laughing. 'If somebody offers to hit me because I say that I do not believe in Authority, I can always call a policeman. Be patient, is all I say. Let the child live a little. War is war – one goes to it, eh? Poppy will be back. And rest assured, she thinks of us all the time.'

'How do *you* know?'

'Because she didn't say goodbye. She spared us and herself the farewells, and just went. Tell me, did she make any promises of eternal fidelity? Did she weep tears and vow vows?'

'No.'

'Bless her for it, then! The child is wise. She knows that a war makes all kinds of new circumstances, and strange situations, and peculiar tensions. She made no protestations and she exacted none. She said, in effect, "Feel free."'

'In effect,' said Ody glumly.

'She didn't even say goodbye to me,' said Zobrany. 'It hurt me, but I honour her for it.'

'Yes, very likely.'

'But you must not take it out on Chess, you know.'

'Oh, all right, all right!' said Ody; and thought, *Where would be the sense in telling him? What purpose would it serve? . . .*

. . . Three months had passed since Poppy had gone under contract to Gabriel Chess. She and Ody were having tea in a pastry cook's shop in Bond Street, when he said, 'You've been pinching Alma Zobrany's perfume.'

'I haven't seen her in weeks,' said Poppy. 'Alma hasn't got any perfume like this.' She quoted a ribald limerick about a Young Girl Of Australia. '–"A penny a look was all very well, but a penny a smell was a failure" – this stuff is worth about five bob a sniff. It costs about a fiver a drop, or something. Very rare. Don't you like it?'

Ody said, 'Oh, you; you're a phenomenon. Stale bacon grease smells good on *you*. Where d'you get it, anyway?'

'Gaby gave me it. It's called "Hecate". You never smelt *this* stuff on anybody round Masham Court.'

'I smelt it only yesterday. Alma Zobrany was reeking of it.'

'Get out!'

'It's nothing so remarkable, actually. Chess takes Alma to private viewings, and so forth. He sends Steve Egyptian cigarettes. So I suppose he gave Alma a bottle of scent.'

'This one's supposed to be pretty rare,' said Poppy. 'Are you sure?'

'Dead certain. Does it matter?'

'Not specially . . .' She ate a chocolate éclair thoughtfully, and then said, 'Ode – I'm joining up with ENSA.'

'You're not!'

'Why not?'

'What about your contract with Chess?'

'What about it? There's a war on. And Ode – anything there is between you and me is off, for the duration. Any oaths, agreements, pledges, commitments, declarations –'

'– Don't laugh. You never made me any.'

'I'm not laughing. You made me plenty. I regard them as null and void. And Ode – don't let's have any of that let-us-live-for-tonight-since-who-knows-whether-we-shall-be-alive-to-love-tomorrow crap, eh?'

'But Poppy!'

'Say goodbye to Steve for me.'

'But –'

'– There aren't any buts, Ode.'

'Why didn't you tell me before?'

'What would have been the odds?'

So Poppy went away with the Entertainments National Service Association.

A week or so later Ody met an American newspaperman who had worked on a script with Gabriel Chess, and was full of amusing and instructive anecdotes of that memorable character. 'The only sensitive part of that otherwise insensitive son of a bitch is his nose,' he said. 'You get that sometimes in a man who was brought up sleeping six to a mattress, four families to a room. Gaby can't help it: as soon as a girl takes her clothes off his mind goes back to his mama and his old man, sweating and grunting, and his uncles and aunts and brothers and sisters likewise – and he's got to douse her with perfume. Not any old perfume, either – nothing but "Hecate" which costs about five times its weight in gold, if you can get it. You could always tell if a woman had been to bed with Gaby – she stank of "Hecate". He kept it exclusive to the girls he laid, if you could call that exclusive . . .'

Then Ody understood why Poppy had run away. Not having been to bed with Ody, she would feel no guilt at having played the fool elsewhere. But knowing that Alma was cuckolding Zobrany with Chess, she was ashamed for Zobrany's sake, and couldn't look him in the face.

Ody, the young man in love, bit his nails. Ody, the young man of letters, marvelled: if Dostoyevsky was such a true psychologist, why was one always so surprised to find something purely Dostoyevskian in real life? . . .

And all the time, impregnable in a force field of impenetrable faith, the ingenuous Zobrany sat affectionately smiling, immune.

There were times when Ody wanted to spit in his eye.

TWENTY-FOUR

While she was perfectly content with Zobrany, Alma had taken a fancy to Gabriel Chess: a fancy, that was the only word for it; a momentary flash of unpredictable appetite. In one way or another it happens to everybody. Somehow – it may be in the middle of the night – for no reason worth analysing, some concatenation of buried memories sparks an abrupt craving for something inconsequential like soused herrings, something sweet to drink, a crust of new bread, fried kippers; anything at all. Stirring in the long, sweet, mildly euphoric doze which was her life with her wholesome, easy husband, Alma fancied a sour pickle.

And so, with a voracity that had all the appearance of passion, she buried her teeth in the sharp pungency of Gabriel Chess; since he happened to be there at her elbow, as it were in an open jar. Like most other men, he found her desirable. He had had his fill of costly exotics. As he told Zobrany, 'Ah, when I was young I ran after women. Now they run after me. I have had thousands and thousands of women, and I am tired of them. I am sick to death of women.'

'Ah, Gabriel, the girls always did like you.'

'But who stood a chance when handsome Steve Zobrany was around, eh?'

'That was long ago,' said Zobrany, a trifle wistfully; twisting his moustache, however, and inflating his chest. 'The girls you must have loved since then!'

'Bah! At first I said to myself, "I shall run through the women of all the nations of the world, alphabetically, from Abyssinia to Zyriansk." But after a few hundred I became bored, and decided that I liked big blondes. And then? Nothing. In the dark everybody is a big blonde. In the light, too, what is the difference? You are the lucky one – you have the most beautiful woman of all, and she adores you; that is rarer than you think.'

Smiling with joy, Zobrany said, 'Yes, she is beautiful, and as good as she is beautiful. But you have been married, have you not? And to a famous beauty?'

'Ah,' said Chess, with a melancholy sigh. 'Erabella! I have forgot much, Erabella, gone with the wind – but I have been faithful to you, Erabella, in my fashion . . . You know that I never married again? Then enough said.'

'Forgive me, Gèz— Gabriel.'

'No, no, not at all. So you see how refreshing it is for me to give innocent pleasure to a good and beautiful woman with whom I am safe, because she accepts honest friendship and is true to her husband – never dreamt of being otherwise. I have films run for her, and her delight is that of a child. She asks to see again Douglas Fairbanks in *Robin Hood*. I tell them, "Run *Robin Hood*" – she claps her hands, so that it is a pleasure to see her. Does she want to see once more Greta Garbo and Nils Asther in *Wild Orchids*? So be it. Her naive enjoyment of my own efforts is charming – she has seen *Satan's Suite* three times, and I have replayed *Hotel Mammon* for her twice and she wants to see it again! This is more rewarding to me than all the money these productions have brought me, believe me. And to think that it was I who met her first! But who would have stood a chance with handsome Steve Zobrany around, eh?'

'My dear fellow,' Zobrany protested, 'in our case it wasn't a matter of looks, not looks alone, or mere attraction. It was love at first sight. It was . . .'

'Biochemistry?' Chess suggested, knowing all the jargon.

'No. If I make love to all women (which I used to do), that is biochemistry. If I am in love with one woman, that is something more that is . . . triochemistry.'

'I repeat, you are a lucky man. Here is a present for you.' He handed Zobrany a box.

'What!' shouted Zobrany, unwrapping it. 'Dimitrinos "Dragoons"! If it had been gold I couldn't have been more pleased. But Gabriel, where did you get these cigarettes? I have an oath to keep that I swore – I may touch nothing off the Black Market.'

'What Black Market, fool? These come in the diplomatic pouch. And this is for your sweet little lady' – it was a flask of the rare perfume 'Hecate' – 'you give it to her.'

'No, no, you must give it to her.'

'If I have your permission, then . . .'

'Here she is, bless her heart, all dressed up for you! But promise me that if there's an air raid, Alma, you will go to a shelter?'

Chess said, 'Steve, I give you my solemn word of honour that I will personally take her to as safe an air-raid shelter as any in London.'

'Bless you!' said Zobrany.

Having paid his share of hush money to blackmailers, contingency-basis lawyers, freelance cameramen, keyhole reporters, and other shake-down artists in Hollywood, Gabriel Chess had learnt that a man in his position cannot be too careful. So when he came to England, having installed himself in a suite at Claridge's, he established another very discreet private apartment which the newspapermen would undoubtedly have described as a Love Nest. Chess called it an air-raid shelter. He cleared a fireproof vault below the little private theatre on the ground floor of an office building which his company owned, and had it plastered, soundproofed, air-conditioned and tastefully decorated, thus converting it into an elegant bachelor flat.

Aerial photographs cunningly lighted, behind curtained panes of glass, conveyed to the lady visitor (he meant to invite no others) that she was in a penthouse a thousand feet above Manhattan, just after sunset of a summer evening. Other such panels in the bedroom created an illusion of Capri. In the lounge, a Buhl buffet had been pitilessly converted into a bar; but the little kitchen was severely functional, with its great refrigerator and its cabinets stocked with canned and potted foods in such profusion and of such diversity that, as Chess told Alma, two people could lunch and dine there for a month without once repeating the menu. The bedroom, though, was strictly Napoleonic. There was a gold-legged escritoire, at which the mighty Corsican himself had written dispatches, and one of Napoleon's own beds, a four-poster with the original canopy and hangings of faded rose velvet embroidered with wreathed eagles. An oval portrait of Napoleon hung over the false fireplace, in which flickered an artificial fire. Another frame protected a bit of paper marked with an undecipherable scrawl in faded ink: a card, just below in a little frame all to itself, explained that this was one of Napoleon's love letters to Josephine from Naples and offered a translation – the conqueror, whom the Pope himself was soon to crown, told the Creole widow that he 'kissed her dear body' in a manner which left nothing whatsoever to the imagination. Flanking this were the sword Napoleon had worn at Lodi and one of his little Mameluke sabres from Egypt.

The unastonishable Alma smiled her set smile at these treasures, but she gasped with surprise and pleasure when she first saw the bathroom. All the wonders of the world could not move her as that piece of plumbing did. Chess was annoyed.

He had planned her seduction with extraordinary care; shown her film stars who trembled at his frown, demonstrating his influence and his achievements; strutted like a bantam, boasted like a schoolboy, sighed like a Romeo, pranced like a Casanova, paraded like a satrap. She remained calm. While she sat, rapt, in the theatre, he gave her champagne cocktail after champagne cocktail. She might have been lined with porcelain. He touched her hand; she didn't notice. He touched her foot; she didn't feel it. He touched her thigh; she neither objected nor responded. He waited until an air-raid warning sounded at the end of a replay of *The Love Parade* – nothing would have budged her before the finale – and said, 'Let me show you my shelter.'

She nodded at the panels, and nodded at the Sheraton, and nodded at the priceless relics of the immortal Napoleon. Then she saw the bathroom and said, 'Oh!' There was a sunken tub in the shape of a huge rose-coloured scallop shell. The water spout was a silver dolphin. And there was a rose glass stall with not one, but five revolving shower heads; at the touch of a lever the bather might be sprayed with warm water from every conceivable angle.

'You like it?' he asked.

'Oh yes.'

He said, with an irritable little laugh, 'Go on, then – have a bath.'

She astonished him by saying, 'May I?'

'Have you no bathroom at home?'

'Oh yes, but not like this. May I really?'

'I should like to see you without your clothes.' She was half undressed when he rushed from the lounge into the bedroom and pounced on her like a bird-eating spider.

She said, 'You mustn't.'

'I'll give you anything in the world you want!'

'No, you mustn't.'

'Then I won't let you use my bathroom.'

'Oh . . . All right, then.' Their embrace was brief and spasmodic. At the end of it she uttered a strange cry, prolonged and forlorn, not unlike the lowing of a heifer and yet not dissimilar to the moan of a dove.

'What is the matter?' he asked.

'What happened then?'

'When?'

'Just now. I felt something happen. Do it again.'

'Do you mean that this had not happened to you before?'

'No, never like that.'

'Not even with that great kudu of a Zobrany?'

'No, never . . .' Afterwards, she said, 'I must come here often.'

'Steve must not know. But it is all right. He is an idiot. You come to see movies, that is enough. But you do not ask me if you have pleased me,' he said.

'Aren't you pleased? Steve always is.'

'Damn your God-damned Steve! I forbid you to have anything to do with him as long as I am your lover, do you hear?'

'I wonder why it never happens like that with Steve. You're such a *little* man compared.'

'– Shut up! Get out! Go home! I can't bear the sight of you! . . . And yet with me it is good, eh? Eh? With me it is good, eh? That is because I have electricity, magnetism, eh? Go back to your ox, you! Little, eh? Ha!' he gripped her by the shoulders and shook her – or rather, he shook himself, while holding her. She scarcely moved.

Releasing her, he went to the bathroom. She followed, to take another look at that beautiful tub. He was fumbling in a medicine cabinet. 'Aren't you well?' she asked.

He opened a little bottle and took a pill. 'It is nothing,' he said. 'Stupidity always upsets me. Go.'

'I'll have a bath next time, then.'

'There will be no next time.'

'Perhaps the day after tomorrow . . .' She looked into the open cabinet. 'What a lot of bottles,' she said, reading labels. 'Metatone. Benzedrine. Vitamin complex. Liver extract. Liver and iron. Methyl . . . methyltestos – testosterone. What are they for? Are you ailing?'

He slammed the door of the cabinet. 'I'll tell Barry to take you home in the car,' he said.

'I want to come here again.'

'Yes, yes,' he said, 'I should like you to come here again . . .' When she was gone he looked at himself in one of Napoleon's mirrors, and shouted, 'So what? Caligula was infatuated with a vile baker's wife! The great Monck, Duke of Albemarle, married a foul seamstress! The great Marlborough married a Sarah Jennings, a slut! King Charles loved an orange-selling costerwoman with smelly armpits and filthy feet! The great Napoleon himself was not above marrying the leavings of Barras, a bitch with rotten teeth who was a spittoon for half the Directoire, by God! . . . Then so what?'

He wrinkled his nostrils, and thought, *I must see to it that she gets a bottle of 'Hecate'*. Then he imitated the cry she had uttered: 'Moo-ooo, moo-ooo!' *So much for handsome Steve Zobrany!* he said to himself. *He never got such an orgasm out of her.* But, malice apart, thinking of Alma Zobrany, Gabriel Chess decided that he had never known a woman who gave him such unqualified satisfaction. Perhaps this was because she was the only woman who had ever completely convinced that suspicious little fellow that he had satisfied her.

'*Mi chiamono Moo-mooo . . .*' he sang, to the tune of an aria out of *La Bohème*. He was proud of himself: any hobbledehoy can seduce a virgin, any assistant director can debauch a startlet, but it takes a man of power to get an honest married women into his bed.

And what an honest married woman! Too incurious for intrigue, too phlegmatic for ambition, too lazy for lust, too simple to lie – a contented married woman. Only a Gabriel Chess could breathe life into such clay. He had directed any number of interesting performances by gifted actresses in bed, knowing always that the time would come, with dramatic inevitability, when the woman would talk business. It was as hackneyed as this: nobody had ever wanted Gabriel Chess for himself. The others had made him feel like a god; Alma Zobrany made him feel like a man. Therefore . . . 'Hell and damnation!' cried Chess. 'King Louis XIV was not above marrying Madame de Maintenon, the widow of a dirty, crippled poet. A touch of "Hecate", and . . . So what?'

An arid and fruitless summer was over, an uneasy autumn was in with its interminable twilights, and the decilitre flask of heady, insidious 'Hecate' was down to an ounce and a half. Gabriel Chess was in a grey mood. 'I am tired out,' he told Alma, 'I am *lasse*, pooped. I get no rest – I am nervous, irritable. Everything conspires to interfere with my plans; the war – everything.

'In the middle of *Hotel Sinister*, Lily Cacofuego gets herself a congestion of the lungs – of her disgusting lungs! Fritz Tamrodt gets big ideas. Christophe Spore, if you please – a *tapette*, a pederast whom I picked out of the *boîte* where he was a female impersonator, and hung a pair of balls on to, and made a performer of – he, if you don't mind, has broken his contract and run away to join the God-damned *Résistance*! Him! And Poppy is in ENSA, that *poule*! Here is half a million dollars down the drain, and nothing to show. Do you realize – are you listening?'

'Yes, of course I am.'

'Then what are you grinning at like a God-damned disgusting Cheshire cat?'

'Was I? I didn't know I was.'

'No. Pardon. It's your natural expression. Excuse me. I am overwrought, played out. I am frustrated. I wanted to make a super-spectacle based on the life of Napoleon. But that won't do now: the little people won't like it; it reminds them of Hitler. After the war I will make my *Napoleon*. Germany will have won – it'll be all right, then. At present I am fed up, I wish I had dropped dead before I came to England . . .

'Well, I take my precedent from that man' – he pointed to the oval portrait of Napoleon – 'I cut my losses, turn *Hotel Sinister* over to Vickerson, and get out, go home. It is not my fault if people I trust desert me. I shall sue them for the rest of their useless lives, the bastard sons of bitches! And the air raids distract everybody. Would you expect a watchmaker to make a watch on a merry-go-round? Would you expect Toscanini to conduct an orchestra in a boiler factory? Me, I am unmoved: I take my example from that man. Once, on the battlefield, when he was writing a letter, a cannonball fell at his feet, covering him and his aide-de-camp with dirt. The aide cringed, but Napoleon said, shaking the dirt off the paper, "This saves me the trouble of sanding my letter." I am like that. But the others – I can't get work out of them.'

'What did he want sand on his letter for?'

'To dry the ink.'

'Didn't it stick?'

'What the devil is she talking about, didn't it stick? What do I know? What is it to me? I pour out my heart, and all she can say is "Didn't it stick?"'

'Are you really going back to America?'

'Yes. There is nothing for me here, just now.' She had undressed, and was sitting naked on the edge of the bed. He lay languidly on a rose-velvet chaise-longue, still wearing his trousers and shirt.

'I'm sorry you're going,' she said.

'Yes, she is sorry, she is sorry! She will miss the velvet *fauteuil* in my theatre, nothing more. Oh yes: she will miss the bathtub. Bah!'

'Oh, I don't know . . .'

'Listen, Alma – for some reason which I cannot define, you are necessary to me. Come with me.'

'What about Steve?'

'To bloody hell with that kudu ox! Come with me. You shall have a theatre of your own, in your own house. A bathroom of carnelian, since you like pink; or if you prefer blue, lapis lazuli. Or both. You shall have two Korean maids to massage you with creams. Electric toothbrushes. You will not need to stir hand or foot for your pleasures. Come with me.'

She said, 'I've often thought how nice it would be not to have to walk, to get anywhere . . .'

'You shall have elevators and escalators instead of staircases' – he got up and sat beside her, passing his hands over her body.

'– I like that,' she said.

'How old are you, actually, for God's sake?'

'I must be nearly fifty.'

'Don't you *know*?'

'Steve brings me presents on my birthday; that's in May. But then he's always bringing me little things, flowers, chocolates, all wrapped up as if it was for a special occasion. I never bothered how old I was –'

'– You are a phenomenon, a phenomenon of beauty and dumbness. You are an animal. You look thirty, and feel less. Tell me: you have some affection for me, some real affection, have you not?'

'I wouldn't be here if I hadn't.'

'Is that an answer? Yes or no.'

'I suppose so.'

'She supposes so! Will you come with me?'

'It would break Steve's heart. He *has* been awfully good to me.'

'Alma, all life is a crushing, a devouring. A man like me must follow his destiny. If somebody is destined to get hurt when I move so much the worse. What I want I must have – I want you, I shall have you. There will be nothing for you to do; nothing but go for a walk and not come back. I will arrange everything when the moment comes, everything! Alma –' He leapt upon her in his pantherish way, with such desperate urgency that a dispassionate observer would have been reminded of some small frightened animal trying to dig a hole to hide in.

But Alma was thoughtful. 'Now! Now!' he yelled, again and again. At last, rolling over in exhaustion, he gasped, 'What's wrong today?'

'I was thinking. I can't do two things at once. I was thinking of what you said just now.'

'You will come with me to California.'

'I'll think about it.'

'Stop thinking. Try again.' There followed something like what the all-in wrestling announcers describe as 'one thirty-minute bout to a finish'. He hissed, grinding his teeth, 'Moo, damn you – *moo*!' And at last, having squeezed out of her that lost heifer's cry he so loved to hear, he collapsed, streaming with perspiration and breathing in short, shallow sighs.

'Are you all right?' she asked. 'Your lips are blue.' She took his hand. 'Your nails are blue, and you're cold.'

He said, 'Go to bathroom. In cupboard. Phenobarbital; small yellow bottle. It is nothing. But hurry.'

'Mr Nollekens's nails went blue.'

'God damn Mr Nollekens's disgusting claws! Don't excite me – do as I say.' She went to the bathroom. He heard her using the toilet in her voluptuous and uninhibited way. 'Stop that!' he yelled. The effort gave him a pain in the chest. 'Stop it and bring –' The toilet flushed. There came to his agonized ears the sibilant sound of the bidet. 'Cut it out, God damn it!' he screamed.

She was back, then, carrying twenty or thirty bottles and pill boxes. 'You'll have to pick it out for yourself,' she said. 'I nearly got into trouble with Mr Nollekens's medicine.'

'Damn your Nollekens! . . . Help me sit upright, then.' She propped him up with pillows.

'Shall I call a doctor?'

'Call Dr Jahn, at Cavendish 10903.'

'There's no sound at all' – she said, listening at the telephone – 'perhaps the line's down. There's an air raid on outside, by the sound of it. I thought I heard guns just now.'

'Then come and sit with me.'

Dressing with her customary deliberation, she turned her head and said, 'I can't.'

'What does she mean, she – I am in pain! Is that nothing to you?'

'I don't want the responsibility.' He half rose and threw a handful of pill bottles at her; then fell back with a groan.

'Bitch! . . . Oh, Alma!'

She placed the telephone close to his hand, and said, 'You ring. I've got to go, I can't stay. You'll be better soon. I'm no use to you, really. I nursed Mr Nollekens, once, and . . . Good night, Gaby. Get better and . . .' Through a mist, Gabriel Chess saw three Almas going out. He started after her, but fell forward, the upper part of his body hanging over the edge of the bed.

She saw, but left him lying that way. She didn't want to be involved. Then she walked out into the first great air-raid of that war. The Luftwaffe was out in force. All the guns in the world were thundering, and the sky was clamorous as a shaken sheet of iron. The great blitz of September 7 1940 was under way. Chess's Rolls-Royce was waiting. 'Yes, madam,' said the chauffeur, and the great car glided away. 'Enemy overhead, madam,' he said. Just then there was a roar too loud to hear.

A burning wind picked up the car, twirled it in the air and dropped it upside down on the pavement.

By midnight, Zobrany had telephoned Claridge's twelve times, at the rate of once every fifteen minutes. 'Mr Chess has not returned,' was all the operator told him, or 'Mr Chess does not reply.' The night operator at Chess's office said, 'I'm sorry, but Mr Gabriel Chess left long ago.'

He thought of calling all the hospitals and police stations in the Metropolitan Area, but decided not to in case the phone should ring while he was enquiring. It did ring at half-past one. A weary, exasperated voice said, 'Mr Zobrany?'

'Yes! Yes!'

'St George's Hospital. Your wife's here with Casualties.'

'Is she dead?'

'She wouldn't be with Casualties if she was.'

'Is she hurt?'

'She wouldn't be with Casualties if she wasn't. She asked us to ring. *Good*bye.'

He snatched up his hat and ran out. The town lay under the smoke of its burning – the foul and acrid smoke of a bombardment, in which floated the fine dust of pulverized buildings. Zobrany ran, hopelessly shouting. 'Taxi! Taxi!' and in Glasshouse Street he found a cruising cab. 'Take me to St George's Hospital,' he said, 'and I will pay you anything you ask.'

'All right, guv,' the driver said, 'take it easy, take it easy. You ain't hurt, are yer?'

'No, no, I wish I were – my wife is.'

'Then the thing to do is, take it easy. You ain't the only one.'

'True. I beg pardon.'

'It's gettin' real lively, ain't it?' Blast rocked the cab, and in the near distance a gush of flame went up. An incendiary bomb cracked and burst into intolerable white fire in the road ahead. Swerving to avoid it, the driver said, 'Sort o' fiendish kind o' style, ain't it, guv? The city's burnin' and the docks are alight. Peace in our time – three cheers for Neville Chamberlain.'

'You take it calmly, my friend.'

'So'd you better, guv.'

'Oh Alma, Alma!' Zobrany muttered.

''Ere y'are, then.'

Zobrany found himself walking through avenues of stretchers, on which lay women with burnt faces painted purple, some of whom moaned and wept while others lay silent, dazed.

'Alma Zobrany,' he kept asking, 'Alma Zobrany . . . please, will you tell me where to find Alma Zobrany? Is she burnt? Is she? Is she dead? Oh, will somebody please tell me where to find Alma Zobrany? –'

'– Ssh! She'll be all right – she has a sprained back. The man driving the car got his neck broken, though. The upholstery saved her. Here she is.'

'Alma!'

'Shut up, will you? We gave her a shot to keep her quiet. We'll shift her to a bed as soon as possible . . . Look, sleeping like a baby.' Zobrany thought that the sleeping Alma had never looked more beautiful. In his emotion he seized the man's hand and kissed it. He said, 'Look, you're in the way. She'll be examined tomorrow. Go home and have a rest. There's nothing you can do now. Take my word for it, she'll be all right. Now go away; I'm busy.'

Zobrany walked home. Over the way from the mouth of Masham Court, a house with a dancing academy on the ground floor lay in smoking rubble. To the left and the right of it, its neighbours seemed to totter, with blind, shattered faces. A policeman stopped him in the archway. 'Keep out,' he said, 'keep back.'

'But I live here,' said Zobrany.

'Oh, did you?' said the policeman. 'Oh yes, you're Mr Zobrany. Mind how you go.'

The blast of that bomb had not blown Masham Court up – it had sucked it down. The place had imploded, like an electric light bulb, and fallen inwards. The whole front wall of the café was heaped in the yard, under a fog of yellow brick-dust. The interior was revealed, naked in every detail, like an open dolls' house. There was the sitting room, with the mark of a brilliantined head (his own) on the wallpaper to the left of the fireplace. Zobrany heard himself saying, 'I had meant to have the room redecorated last spring . . . painted . . .'

'Stand back!' said a rescue worker, and the bedroom floor caved in. A chest of drawers came down with a crash, and as it fell the drawers flew out, spilling a shower of blue-green and Nile-green underclothes and nightdresses. The lavatory basin followed. But the bathtub remained, suspended on its pipes. Gazing up at it, Zobrany felt like an exhausted swimmer who, looking heavenward as he sinks for the last time, sees nothing but the belly of a great fish.

'Was there anybody in the house?' somebody asked him.

He said, 'Yes, two people; Mr and Mrs Sordic, in the basement.' They dug in the rubble for two hours, and at last forced a length of gas pipe into the space below.

'Can you hear me?' a rescue worker shouted.

A whisper came back, 'Yes.'

'We'll get you out. Put your mouth to the pipe; there's some hot soup coming down.' A pint of broth was poured into the pipe through a funnel.

Zobrany then bellowed down, 'Are you unhurt, Sordic?'

Venomous as ever, Sordic's voice hissed, 'Fut in the psoup a little more feffer – a pfinch of pfsalt fut in the psoup!'

'Bless their hearts,' said Zobrany, half laughing and half crying, 'they will live forever just to aggravate me!'

'Cheer up, it's only bricks and sticks,' said a little smoke-blackened fireman, half dead of fatigue. 'My sister was in *my* house when it went up.'

'How my wife loved that old house!' Zobrany sighed. Then, looking again at the ruins, 'I liked it for her sake,' he said. 'For my own part, I never cared much for it.'

Zobrany walked back to the hospital at dawn. A haggard Scots surgeon told him, 'It's nothing but a couple o' slipped discs. We've strapped her up, and ye can take her home tomorrow, for we need beds.'

'Thank God for that! But I have no home to take her to – my house was hit soon after I left to come here last night.'

'Then,' said the surgeon dryly, 'as ye'll no doubt say, it's an ill wind that blows nobody any good, for if ye'd both been at home and in your bed, or beds, ye'd both have got killed; whereas, the bomb that inflicted a trifling injury on your good wife saved the lives of the two of ye. A merciful dispensation o' Providence, hey?'

Caught off guard, Zobrany nodded; whereupon the surgeon snapped, 'Then I take my hat off to ye, for ye must be very, very important people, and Providence must set a very high value on ye; for the stick o' bombs that providentially saved your lives killed and maimed twenty-four women and children in a shelter down Belgravia way. Your Providence has a damned prodigal spendthrift way o' lookin' after his own, and ye may tell Him so when next ye meet Him.'

'I didn't mean –'

'– Tchah! Your vanity stinks to high heaven.' Abashed, Zobrany went upstairs.

In her ward, among the scorched and smashed victims of last night's raid, Alma was conspicuous as a lily in a slaughterhouse. She said, 'I hope you're not angry with me. I stayed late because Gaby wanted to talk.'

'Gaby was the dispensation of Providence, not the bomb. Who said anything about the bomb?' said Zobrany, thinking of the sardonic face of the surgeon.

'Take me home, Steve,' she said. 'I'm frightened of all these people.'

'My dear heart, you have no home,' said Zobrany, and told her of the destruction of their house. He had never seen her shed tears before. 'Don't fret,' was all he could say, 'it's only bricks and sticks. We have each other, and we are not poor.'

'But where are we to go?'

'Masham Court isn't the whole world, my love. I shall take you out of town for a little while, into the country. Only you must keep still for a week or so, darling, and then you will be perfectly all right. I shall wheel you in a chair, eh?'

'You're ever so good, Steve.'

'No, no. Only be patient for a little, no?'

'I think I'd like to be wheeled in a chair.'

'You are brave, brave! Thank God you were not at home, though. My Gaby – man of destiny indeed!'

'He didn't seem very well last night.'

'I will telephone him presently.'

A nurse said, 'Be off with you now – you've had your little visit.'

'Yes, yes, I'm going.' Zobrany telephoned Claridge's Hotel from a call box. One of Gabriel Chess's secretaries answered, saying, 'I'm sorry, Mr Zobrany, but Mr Chess passed away last night.'

'A bomb?'

'No, Mr Chess passed away of a heart attack.'

'Oh no,' said Zobrany, and stumbled blindly out of the booth.

But, walking back to Masham Court, he discovered that his mood was unaccountably placid. He said to a little Heavy Rescue man who stank of sweat and dried blood, 'Am I going out of my mind, or is it that I have a callous soul? My wife is hurt, my best friend is dead, my home lies in ruins, I have nowhere to go – and yet I feel light hearted! What's the matter with me?'

The little man grimaced in sympathy, and the brick dust of centuries, caked at the corners of his mouth, fell away in little flakes. 'Shock,' he said. 'Drink some hot sweet tea and then have a good cry, and you'll get over it.'

'The two old people in the basement?'

'They're okay. They're over at the Middlesex Hospital. Walking casualties; or staggering, rather. They had some brandy down there.' He yawned a half-laugh.

'Join me in a glass of beer, dear fellow?'

'All right. Thank God for small mercies – the boozer isn't much damaged,' said the rescue man, leading the way into the saloon bar of The Road To Hell.

Then something more ruinous than the rubble separated itself from a mass of shattered wood and broken bricks, and stood revealed as a man – one of those gnomes of the garbage pails, whom Zobrany had never forgotten, dragging by one foot the dusty carcass of a small boy. He dropped it at Zobrany's feet. It was the scarred and crippled remains of Zobrany's cherished sign. Having let it fall, the old man stepped back, and raised a graphite hand in a slow and awful salute.

Zobrany said, 'Oh dear me, there will be no more sandwiches left out for you here, my poor friend!' – and took out a handful of change.

The policeman – standing one calculated yard away, just beyond a flea's jumping distance – shouted, 'No looting! Push off!'

'Calm,' said Zobrany, 'this isn't looting, it's salvage. This is an old customer of mine' – and he pressed the money into the old man's palm.

Later, the landlord of The Road To Hell asked, 'Have you got any particular use for that old sign of yours, Mr Zobrany?'

'Well, I don't know,' Zobrany replied. 'I was disposed to hate it, lately, because of the man who made it. Why do you ask?'

'I'll have it if you don't want it, and nail it up as a sort of curio.'

'Now that the poor little thing is so cut about and excoriated, he has a species of dignity,' Zobrany said. 'I am going to the country. Perhaps I shall open a comfortable little inn. Then I may nail the boy up again . . . To hell with Associations! What is, is. As we go, we purify, we sublimate. And as my dear old friend Howgego would have said, let's have a bottle of wine on that . . .'

Fifteen years later, one autumn afternoon, a sedate little Maltese manservant came into the living room of a penthouse in Brighton, and said, 'Sare, the gentleman you are expecting is on his way up.'

At this, a huge old man turned from the window he had been looking out of, through which he seemed to have sucked all the sunset on the sea into the red, gold and green of his brocade smoking jacket – picking up, in the process, some of the muck at high-water mark; for his magnificence was marred by a jetsam of matchsticks, toothpicks and tobacco ash. He wore, pushed to the back of his tremendous head, a round black Egyptian fez embroidered with stars and crescents in seed pearls. The loose knot of a soiled satin scarf about his neck was secured with an ancient Italian brooch made of a Baroque pearl as big as a duck's egg and fragile as a bubble, surrounded by little golden children riding silver dolphins.

'All right, he said, 'let him in and bring some eats and drinks, will you?'

'Yes, Mr Perceval, sare . . . Sare, Mr Atherton!'

The visitor, a fresh-looking, clear-eyed, light-haired gentleman in his early forties, said, 'Mr Perceval, how d'you do? How kind –'

'– JO Atherton,' said the old man, looking at a card and then tossing it into an ashtray. 'The *O* stands for Ody, don't it? I told you once before not to stand on ceremony, didn't I? Call me Perp.'

'What a memory you have!' Ody said, offering his hand.

Perp took it, felt it as for quality and texture, and gave it back to him, saying, 'That's right. I'm seventy-six years old, and I can remember anything I like. Sit down. Have that chair with the blinkers, kind o' style, to keep out the draughts. It's a proper chair for a liter'y man, ain't it, Valletta?'

'Yes sare,' said the servant, wheeling in a trolley loaded with a profusion of bottles and trays of sandwiches.

'Who did it belong to? William the Conqueror, was it? Or William Shakespeare? Who was it, Valletta?'

'Alexander Pope, sare.'

'That's right. That'll be all for now, Valletta.' When the servant was gone, Perp said, 'You've changed, you know, young Ody.'

'Have I? You don't seem to have aged a day,' Ody replied.

'That's right. It's living healthy and not abusing myself that does it. Every hour, on the hour –' Perp took out a pickled onion and a wineglassful of Hollands gin. 'Yes, you've changed. You was a nice kid, in your way. But now, if you don't mind me saying so, I see a certain amount of shit in your eye.'

'In what way?'

'Well, you know it ain't your fault. I blame the bloody politicians for it. We used to call it narking, or peaching, or squeaking, or singing, or blabbing, or tale-bearing, or spying, or splitting, or informing, or ratting, and it was something only poor broken hearted, frightened little bastards went in for out of desperation. It was something between selling matches and chucking yourself in the river. But now the gentry go in for it. Men of education. They call it "Intelligence Work" now; not that I care, mind you.'

'I don't know what you're talking about,' said Ody. 'I'm a feature writer for Combined Newspapers – what they call a Reporter at Large.'

'That's right. And on the side you've got a serial number, 155/1493-zero, which dates you to about 1941 – and old enough to know better if you think you can put anything over on me, you know. God Almighty, son, if I wanted to get pinched I'd get myself locked up in your files and labelled Top Secret. Well?'

'I'd give a lot to know how you find out these things,' said Ody.

'That's right, so you would. Well, I'm not going to tell you. Go ahead and help yourself to something to eat and drink, son; there's no hard feeling. On the face of it you came here to ask some of the usual questions about Great Unsolved Crimes of the Past Forty Years, or something o' that sort – ain't that so?' Ody nodded. Perp went on, 'Then you was going to lead up to something else and put out a feeler; ain't that right?' Ody nodded again. 'Kind of pleading old acquaintance, sort o' style; am I wrong?'

'Not altogether,' said Ody.

'Well, out with it. What is it this time?'

Ody said, 'What did you do with Tom Henceforth?'

'Why,' said Perp, 'he's supposed to be dead, ain't he?'

'He was supposed to be dead in a Hamburg raid, but now he's supposed not to be.'

'Well, what d'you know about that! Tell me some more news. What happened to the Count, Zobrany?'

'You never did get to buy him out, did you?' said Ody.

'That's right,' said Perp. 'He sold his lease to Mandeville and Mandeville, the estate agents, and got fifteen thousand for it. What the eye don't see the heart don't grieve for. I'm Mandeville and Mandeville, among other things, you know . . . It was the boozer on the corner I never managed to get hold of. Still, Masham Court Chambers turns me over sixty thousand a year in rents. But they certainly bollixed up the jolly old Road To Hell; chromium, plastic and all; and a barman in a white coat that comes at you with a stirring rod as if he was going to shove it up your bum and take your temperature with it –'

'– Perp, I'm not fool enough to try and coax something important out of you. All I beg is some kind of hint –'

'– That's right. Just you keep on talking. You never know what I might let drop, if you get me in the right mood. What happened to that girl you was sweet on? She went on the stage, didn't she?'

'Poppy?'

'That's right.'

'She married an American whose father owns a chain of cafeterias, and went out to California. I haven't heard any news of her for ten years.'

'She had her head screwed on, that one. Now I'll bet a shilling she got married to an air force type o' character with whiskers.'

'An Eagle Squadron man. Yes, he did have a big moustache.'

'It stands to reason: she was soft on the Count, you know. You should've grown a Battle o' Britain stosh and opened a canteen, you silly bugger . . . If you was going in for Intelligence, why didn't you finish your doctor's exams and take up psychology, by the way? Think o' the snooping you could've put in that way! But like I was saying, son, it ain't your fault – that last bloody war turned everybody into a lousebag . . . well, practically everybody. Take me: an honest tea leaf. My spies cased a joint to screw it, nothing more, and turn a penny. Ah, but *I* played for keeps and fought to a finish, didn't I! But you make a romance and a penny gaff out of it all, though; don't you? I'll tell you about the size of it – you're shelter babies, you are; you're going underground. Why, believe me or believe me not,' said Perp, laughing low down in his chest, 'and strange as it may seem, there was a time, once upon a time, when it took nerve – I mean to say the nerve of a real rat, a bloody rogue cannibal rat – to come nibbling at *my* toes! But now you're mob-handed, and you've got Ideas. Is that the word? Theories? Whatever it is, take it from me the Count wouldn't've stood for it. Old Zobrany was a silly bugger, but straight as a die, and I tip my katy to him for it . . . You know I could've muscled him out o' Masham Court in no time flat, if I'd've had a mind to it, don't you? . . . Now, what was it you was saying happened to the Count, son?'

Patiently, Ody answered, 'He had it in mind to take a country inn, and be a landlord in a red waistcoat like his old friend Howgego. But the paper work and red tape were too much for him; he had an ailing wife to look after –'

'– Ah, that redhead.'

'She couldn't walk.'

'If she'd been mine, she'd 'a walked. She'd've done the hundred yards in just about ten seconds,' said Perp.

'Well, I thought that what was wrong with her was psychosomatic more than anything else.'

'That 'ere being another word for bone-bloody-lazy?'

'In a way, perhaps. Anyway, she never got out of the wheelchair, once she got settled in it. Steve *liked* to trundle her about. He took out a club licence, and opened a place near High Brooms, close to Tunbridge Wells, and he was in his glory –'

'– *Was*, eh?'

'He died last year,' said Ody.

'In pain?' Perp asked.

'No, peacefully, in his sleep.'

Perp raised a hand as large and grey as a steel gauntlet, and said, 'Don't tell me. See if I'm right. The ginger bitch got the use of her legs back!'

'Yes,' said Ody bitterly, 'she was sixty-odd, but looked like a well-kept forty, although she'd put on a little weight. She –'

'– Married the doctor, I bet a shilling,' said Perp.

'You lose, but only just. Steve kept a riding stable for members of the club – you know he always loved to pretend to be a cavalryman? She married the vet.'

Perp laughed, slapping his mighty thighs, and said, 'Pass me that jar of onions, like a good boy . . . Now what was it you was after? Tom Henceforth?'

'He was a protégé of yours, wasn't he?'

'I don't know exactly what you mean by that, you know. To tell you the honest truth, I made money out o' that boy, just listening to him. So could you've done, if you'd been a real thinking man like me. I was sorry to see Tom had no sticking power. Like all you talky bastards, he was a headless chicken in action. Still . . .'

'He was a traitor,' said Ody.

'Oh, was he? A traitor to what? A traitor to who? Who did that boy swear *his* oath to? I ask you, by word or deed, *who to* did he swear his oath?'

'Perp, you know as well as I do that Henceforth deserved to swing like Joyce or Amery.'

'Did *they*? I don't know. You don't want Tom Henceforth for no high treason, you know. You only want him because he's had a lot o' publicity, and he's no use to you alive. Why, what harm did he do? Confess: if he'd blowed up half the bloody country but still knew how to make a good V-2 bomb, they'd offer him a salary and a pension, they would – and so would the Russkys – and so would I, if I was them, or you, or whichever you are. Then what d'you want to waste my hard-earned money as a taxpayer, catching the kid, and trying him and hanging him for?'

'High treason, Perp. High treason. He plotted against us, in the pay of a foreign power, in time of war –'

'– And this is time o' peace, is it? And Moscow is home ground, is it? God strike me lucky, who gave a Sword of Honour to Joe Stalin –

and it's in black and white that he swore the vendetta against the King and the Queen and Capital and Democracy and Uncle Tom Cobleigh and all? And what's on your little mind, now? That I helped so-called War Criminals to escape?'

Ody said, 'Well, didn't you?'

'Yes, I did. You know very well I did. But never for any political considerations – strictly financial, you understand? Strictly business. I'm a Pacifist, I'm a sort of Quaker, I take the long view, son. Think how much enemy money I've put back in circulation. So a few fellers got away with their skins. They got away with precious little more, believe me! What d'you want? Blood for blood? And you a newspaper writer, and don't know that the general public'd swap you the necks of all the war criminals put together in a sack for one fart from Elizabeth Taylor. You kind of disgust me . . . But look here – you've put me in the mood, and I'll tell you where Tom Henceforth is, and how to get him. First take a bit more gin, and an onion, and have a cigar. Are you quite comfortable? Right? Right. Now first of all you want a few trained men . . .'

Perp paused. Ody asked, 'How many? How trained?'

'About half a million ought to be ample, if trained in jungle warfare and adequately armed. Get 'em to Africa. Start top left, round about Angola way, and work down to low right, near Dar-es-Salaam, mopping up the Consolidated Africa Party as you go, until you cop the Patriarch Mehmet Zudd.'

'Mehmet Zudd's dead,' said Ody.

'The original one is, but he left eleven sons, all of the same name, and numbered, Mehmet 1, Mehmet 2, Mehmet 3 and so forth. Of course, you can always start at any two or three sides of Africa and work towards the middle. I warn you: don't be surprised if you find the blacks armed with a few thousand Tokarev rifles, and some serviceable Mausers and Mannlichers and any amount of other stuff. Well, as I was saying, the probability is that when you cop Mehmet Zudd – whichever one's in succession – you're apt to find Tom Henceforth not very far away, together with a girl who still ought to be worth printing an early photo of.'

'Go on,' said Ody, with a laugh.

'That's about it, for the present,' said Perp. 'How d'you like that there historical chair you've been sitting in?'

'Very comfortable,' said Ody.

'That's right, draught-proof for all concerned – what you might call a screen in itself. You always was a one for recorders and other gadgets. Well, good luck to you, I say; only when you come to play back that teeny-weeny tape bug you've got on your person, and which I was too polite to have you frisked for, and you find that all you get out of it is a sort of high-pitched noise, you needn't mention that you were sitting in a high-power magnetic field. Say you pulled my hair and made me scream, and *I'll* bear you out.'

Ody rose. 'I know when I've bitten off more than I can chew,' he said.

'That's right. Good night, son. Mind the pig bucket.'

'Good night . . .'

Cragsmoor, New York, 1965

London Books

FLYING THE FLAG FOR
FREE-THINKING LITERATURE

www.london-books.co.uk

PLEASE VISIT OUR WEBSITE FOR

- Current and forthcoming books
- Author and title profiles
- A lively, interactive message board
- Events and news
- Secure on-line bookshop
- Recommendations and links
- An alternative view of London literature

ON SALE NOW

All titles hardback / £11.99

THE GILT KID – James Curtis
Introduction by Paul Willetts
ISBN 978-0-9551851-2-0

NIGHT AND THE CITY – Gerald Kersh
Introduction by John King
ISBN 978-0-9551851-3-7

A START IN LIFE – Alan Sillitoe
Introduction by DJ Taylor
ISBN 978-0-9551851-1-3

THEY DRIVE BY NIGHT – James Curtis
Introduction by Jonathan Meades
ISBN 978-0-9551851-4-4

WIDE BOYS NEVER WORK – Robert Westerby
Introduction by Iain Sinclair
ISBN 978-0-9551851-5-1

MAY DAY – John Sommerfield
Introduction by John King
ISBN 978-0-9551851-8-2

NIGHT AND THE CITY

GERALD KERSH

Harry Fabian is a cockney wide boy who will do anything for a pound note; a storyteller who craves recognition, his endless lies hiding a deeper, inner weakness. He is also a ponce, and one who is walking on the edge. It is only a matter of time before he topples over the side.

Set in 1930s London, against a fluorescent West End backdrop, *Night And The City* brings the Soho of legend to life, the streets a tangle of drinking dens and night-clubs, author Gerald Kersh's characters flamboyant creations who add a cosmopolitan edge to the book's journey into the darker shades of human nature.

Twice filmed, *Night And The City* remains a 'lowlife' classic, and comes with an introduction by John King, author of *The Football Factory* and *Human Punk*.

London Books
£11.99 hardback
ISBN 978-0-9551851-3-7
www.london-books.co.uk

London Classics

WIDE BOYS NEVER WORK

ROBERT WESTERBY

Young Jim Bankley yearns to leave behind the production line in a provincial town when he chances on a London razor-gang at a local dog track. Seduced by the opportunity to live life on the edge, he follows them back to London. He is thrown into a milieu of bruisers, brasses, car dealers and con-merchants. Drenched in sleaze and brutality, he begins to wonder if the simple life is so bad after all.

Robert Westerby's 1937 novel provoked a stir at the time, authentically lifting the lid on an underworld metropolis that many pretended did not exist. It has lost none of its punch in the ensuing 70 years – and slang historians generally credit Westerby with coining the term wide boy. The book was filmed in 1956 under the name *Soho Incident*.

This new edition boasts a penetrative introduction from leading London author and broadcaster Iain Sinclair, whose work includes *London Orbital* and *London, City of Disappearances*. He is a long-time champion of often overlooked vintage London writers such as Westerby, James Curtis and Gerald Kersh.